Jacques Futrelle's
"The Thinking Machine"

Jacques Futrelle's
"The Thinking Machine"

The Enigmatic Problems of
Prof. Augustus S. F. X. Van Dusen,
Ph. D., LL. D., F. R. S., M. D., M. D. S.

Edited and with an Introduction by
Harlan Ellison®

THE MODERN LIBRARY

NEW YORK

2003 Modern Library Paperback Edition

Compilation copyright © 2003 by Random House, Inc.
Introduction copyright © 2003 by The Kilimanjaro Corporation

LIBRARY OF CONGRESS CATALOGING-IN-PUBLICATION DATA
Futrelle, Jacques, 1875–1912.
Jacques Futrelle's "the thinking machine" / Jacques Futrelle; edited and
with an introduction by Harlan Ellison.
p. cm.
ISBN 0-8129-7014-4 (trade pbk.)
1. Van Dusen, Augustus S.F.X. (Fictitious character)—Fiction.   2. Detective
and mystery stories, American.   3. College teachers—Fiction.   4. Boston
(Mass.)—Fiction.   I. Ellison, Harlan.   II. Title.

PS3511.U97A6 2003
813'.52—dc22   2003060205

Modern Library website address: www.modernlibrary.com

Printed in the United States of America

2 4 6 8 9 7 5 3 1

Frontispiece: Portrait of Jacques Futrelle.

To the memory of

STANLEY ELLIN

Our generation's only candidate

to wear the mantle of Poe; one

of the greatest short story writers

of the twentieth, or any, century.

Contents

Enter: "The Thinking Machine"

It was absolutely impossible. Twenty-five chess masters from the world at large, foregathered for the annual championships, unanimously declared it impossible, and unanimity on any given point is an unusual mental condition for chess masters. Not one would concede for an instant that it was within the range of human achievement. Some grew red in the face as they argued it, others smiled loftily and were silent; still others dismissed the matter in a word as wholly absurd.

A casual remark by the distinguished scientist and logician, Professor Augustus S. F. X. Van Dusen, provoked the discussion. He had, in the past, aroused bitter disputes by some chance remark; in fact had been once a sort of controversial center of the sciences. It had been due to his modest announcement of a startling and unorthodox hypothesis that he had been invited to vacate the chair of Philosophy in a great university. Later that university had felt honored when he accepted its degree of LL. D.

For a score of years, educational and scientific institutions of the world had amused themselves by crowding degrees upon him. He had initials that stood for things he couldn't pronounce; degrees from

France, England, Russia, Germany, Italy, Sweden, and Spain. These were expressed recognition of the fact that his was the foremost brain in the sciences. The imprint of his crabbed personality lay heavily on half a dozen of its branches. Finally there came a time when argument was respectfully silent in the face of one of his conclusions.

The remark which had arrayed the chess masters of the world into so formidable and unanimous a dissent was made by Professor Van Dusen in the presence of three other gentlemen of note. One of these, Dr. Charles Elbert, happened to be a chess enthusiast.

"Chess is a shameless perversion of the functions of the brain," was Professor Van Dusen's declaration in his perpetually irritated voice. "It is a sheer waste of effort, greater because it is possibly the most difficult of all abstract problems. Of course logic will solve it. Logic will solve any problem—not *most* of them but *any* problem. A thorough understanding of its rules would enable anyone to defeat your greatest chess players. It would be inevitable, just as inevitable as that two and two make four, not *some*times but *all* the time. I don't know chess because I never do useless things, but I could take a few hours of competent instruction and defeat a man who has devoted his life to it. His mind is cramped; bound down to the logic of chess. Mine is not; mine employs logic in its widest scope."

Dr. Elbert shook his head vigorously.

"It is impossible," he asserted.

"Nothing is impossible," snapped the scientist. "The human mind can do anything. It is all we have to lift us above the brute creation. For Heaven's sake leave us that."

The aggressive tone, the uncompromising egotism brought a flush to Dr. Elbert's face. Professor Van Dusen affected many persons that way, particularly those fellow savants who, themselves men of distinction, had ideas of their own.

"Do you know the purposes of chess? Its countless combinations?" asked Dr. Elbert.

"No," was the crabbed reply. "I know nothing whatever of the game beyond the general purpose which, I understand to be, to move certain pieces in certain directions to stop an opponent from moving his King. Is that correct?"

"Yes," said Dr. Elbert slowly, "but I never heard it stated just that way before."

"Then, if that is correct, I maintain that the true logician can defeat the chess expert by the pure mechanical rules of logic. I'll take a few hours some time, acquaint myself with the moves of the pieces, and defeat you to convince you."

Professor Van Dusen glared savagely into the eyes of Dr. Elbert.

"Not me," said Dr. Elbert. "You say anyone—you for instance, might defeat the greatest chess player. Would you be willing to meet the greatest chess player after you 'acquaint' yourself with the game?"

"Certainly," said the scientist. "I have frequently found it necessary to make a fool of myself to convince people. I'll do it again."

This, then, was the acrimonious beginning of the discussion which aroused chess masters and brought open dissent from eminent men who had not dared for years to dispute any assertion by the distinguished Professor Van Dusen. It was arranged that at the conclusion of the championships Professor Van Dusen should meet the winner. This happened to be Tschaikowsky, the Russian, who had been champion for half a dozen years.

After this expected result of the tournament Hillsbury, a noted American master, spent a morning with Professor Van Dusen in the latter's modest apartments on Beacon Hill. He left there with a sadly puzzled face; that afternoon Professor Van Dusen met the Russian champion. The newspapers had said a great deal about the affair and hundreds were present to witness the game.

There was a little murmur of astonishment when Professor Van Dusen appeared. He was slight, almost child-like in body, and his thin shoulders seemed to droop beneath the weight of his enormous head. He wore a No. 8 hat. His brow rose straight and dome-like and a heavy shock of long, yellow hair gave him almost a grotesque appearance. The eyes were narrow slits of blue squinting eternally through thick spectacles; the face was small, clean shaven, drawn and white with the pallor of the student. His lips made a perfectly straight line. His hands were remarkable for their whiteness, their flexibility, and for the length of the slender fingers. One glance showed that physical development had never entered into the schedule of the scientist's fifty years of life.

The Russian smiled as he sat down at the chess table. He felt that he was humoring a crank. The other masters were grouped near by, curiously expectant. Professor Van Dusen began the game, opening with a Queen's gambit. At his fifth move, made without the slightest hesitation, the smile left the Russian's face. At the tenth, the masters grew tensely eager. The Russian champion was playing for honor now. Professor Van Dusen's fourteenth move was King's castle to Queen's four.

"Check," he announced.

After a long study of the board the Russian protected his King with a Knight. Professor Van Dusen noted the play, then leaned back in his chair with finger tips pressed together. His eyes left the board and dreamily studied the ceiling. For at least ten minutes there was no sound, no movement, then:

"Mate in fifteen moves," he said quietly.

There was a quick gasp of astonishment. It took the practiced eyes of the masters several minutes to verify the announcement. But the Russian champion saw and leaned back in his chair a little white and dazed. He was not astonished; he was helplessly floundering in a maze of incomprehensible things. Suddenly he arose and grasped the slender hand of his conqueror.

"You have never played chess before?" he asked.

"Never."

"*Mon Dieu!* You are not a man; you are a brain—a machine—a thinking machine."

"It's a child's game," said the scientist abruptly. There was no note of exultation in his voice; it was still the irritable, impersonal tone which was habitual.

This, then, was Professor Augustus S. F. X. Van Dusen, Ph. D., LL. D., F. R. S., M. D., etc., etc. This is how he came to be known to the world at large as The Thinking Machine. The Russian's phrase had been applied to the scientist as a title by a newspaper reporter, Hutchinson Hatch. It had stuck.

My First Experience
with the Great Logician

It was once my good fortune to meet in person Professor Augustus S. F. X. Van Dusen, Ph. D., LL. D., F. R. S., M. D., etc. The meeting came about through a singular happening, which was as mystifying as it was dangerous to me—he saved my life in fact; and in process of hauling me back from eternity—the edge of that appalling mist which separates life and death—I had full opportunity of witnessing the workings of that marvelously keen, cold brain which has made him the most distinguished scientist and logician of his day. It was sometime afterward, however, that Professor Van Dusen was identified in my mind with The Thinking Machine.

I had dined at the Hotel Teutonic, taken a cigar from my pocket, lighted it, and started for a stroll across Boston Common. It was after eight o'clock on one of those clear, nippy evenings of winter. I was near the center of the Common on one of the many little by paths which lead toward Beacon Hill when I became conscious of an acute pain in my chest, a sudden fluttering of my heart, and a constriction in my throat. The lights in the distance began to waver and grow dim, and perspiration broke out all over me from an inward, gnawing agony which grew more intense each moment. I felt myself reeling, my cigar dropped from my fingers, and I clutched at a seat to steady myself. There was no one near me. I tried to call, then everything grew dark, and I sank down on the ground. My last recollection was of a figure approaching me; the last words I heard were a petulant, irritable "Dear me!"; then I was lost to consciousness.

When I recovered consciousness I lay on a couch in a strange room. My eyes wandered weakly about and lingered with a certain childish interest on half a dozen spots which reflected glitteringly the light of an electric bulb set high up on one side. These bright spots, I came to realize after a moment, were metal parts of various instruments of a laboratory. For a time I lay helpless, listless, with trembling pulse and eardrums thumping, then I heard steps approaching, and someone bent over and peered into my face.

It was a man, but such a man as I had never seen before. A great shock of straw yellow hair tumbled about a broad, high forehead, a small, wrinkled, querulous face—the face of an aged child—a pair of watery blue eyes squinting aggressively through thick spectacles, and a thin lipped mouth as straight as the mark of a surgeon's knife, save for the drooping corners. My impression then was that it was some sort of hallucination, the distorted vagary of a disordered brain, but gradually my vision cleared and the grip of slender fingers on my pulse made me realize the actuality of the—the apparition.

"How do you feel?" The thin lips had opened just enough to let out the question, the tone was curt and belligerent, and the voice rasped unpleasantly. At the same time the squint eyes were focused on mine with a steady, piercing glare that made me uneasy. I tried to answer, but my tongue refused to move. The gaze continued for an instant, then the man—The Thinking Machine—turned away and prepared a particularly vile smelling concoction, which he poured into me. Then I was lost again.

After a time—it might have been minutes or hours—I felt again the hand on my pulse, and again The Thinking Machine favored me with a glare. An hour later I was sitting up on the couch, with unclouded brain, and a heartbeat which was nearly normal. It was then I learned why Professor Van Dusen, an eminent man of the sciences, had been dubbed The Thinking Machine; I understood firsthand how material muddles were so unfailingly dissipated by unadulterated, infallible logic.

Remember that I had gone into that room an inanimate thing, inert, unconscious, mentally and physically dead to all practical intents—

beyond the point where I might have babbled any elucidating fact. And remember, too, please, that I didn't know—had not the faintest idea—what had happened to me, beyond the fact that I had fallen unconscious. The Thinking Machine didn't ask questions, yet he supplied all the missing details, together with a host of personal, intimate things of which he could personally have had no knowledge. In other words, I was an abstruse problem, and he solved me. With head tilted back against the cushion of the chair—and such a head!—with eyes unwaveringly turned upward, and finger tips pressed idly together, he sat there, a strange, grotesque little figure in the midst of his laboratory apparatus. Not for a moment did he display the slightest interest in me, personally; it was all as if I had been written down on a slate, to be wiped off when I was solved.

"Did this ever happen to you before?" he asked abruptly.

"No," I replied. "What was it?"

"You were poisoned," he said. "The poison was a deadly one—corrosive sublimate, or bichlorid of mercury. The shock was very severe; but you will be all right in——"

"Poisoned!" I exclaimed, aghast. "Who poisoned me? Why?"

"You poisoned yourself," he replied testily. "It was your own carelessness. Nine out of ten persons handle poison as if it was candy, and you are like all the rest."

"But I couldn't have poisoned myself," I protested. "Why, I have had no occasion to handle poisons—not for—I don't know how long."

"I do know," he said. "It was nearly a year ago when you handled this; but corrosive sublimate is always dangerous."

The tone irritated me, the impassive arrogance of the little man inflamed my reeling brain, and I am not sure that I did not shake my finger in his face. "If I was poisoned," I declared with some heat, "it was not my fault. Somebody gave it to me; somebody tried to——"

"You poisoned yourself," said The Thinking Machine again impatiently. "You talk like a child."

"How do you know I poisoned myself? How do you know I ever handled a poison? And how do you know it was a year ago, if I did?"

The Thinking Machine regarded me coldly for an instant, and then those strange eyes of his wandered upward again. "I know those things," he said, "just as I know your name, address, and profession from cards I found in your pockets; just as I know you smoke, from half a dozen cigars on you; just as I know that you are wearing those clothes for the first time this winter; just as I know you lost your wife within a few months; that you kept house then; and that your house was infested with insects. I know just as I know everything else—by the rules of inevitable logic."

My head was whirling. I stared at him in blank astonishment. "But how do you know those things?" I insisted in bewilderment.

"The average person of today," replied the scientist, "knows nothing unless it is written down and thrust under his nose. I happen to be a physician. I saw you fall, and went to you, my first thought being of heart trouble. Your pulse showed it was not that, and it was obviously not apoplexy. Now, there was no visible reason why you should have collapsed like that. There had been no shot; there was no wound; therefore, poison. An examination confirmed this first hypothesis; your symptoms showed that the poison was bichlorid of mercury. I put you in a cab and brought you here. From the fact that you were not dead then I knew that your system had absorbed only a minute quantity of poison—a quantity so small that it demonstrated instantly that there had been no suicidal intent, and indicated, too, that no one else had administered it. If this was true, I knew—I didn't guess, I knew—that the poisoning was accidental. How accidental?

"My first surmise, naturally, was that the poison had been absorbed through the mouth. I searched your pockets. The only thing I found that you would put into your mouth were the cigars. Were they poisoned? A test showed they were, all of them. With intent to kill? No. Not enough poison was used. Was the poison a part of the gum used to bind the cigar? Possible, of course, but not probable. Then what?" He lowered his eyes and squinted at me suddenly, aggressively. I shook my head, and, as an afterthought, closed my gaping mouth.

"Perhaps you carried corrosive sublimate in your pocket. I didn't find any; but perhaps you once carried it. I tore out the coat pocket in which I found the cigars and subjected it to the test. At sometime there had been corrosive sublimate, in the form of powder or crystals, in the pocket, and in some manner, perhaps because of an imperfection in the package, a minute quantity was loose in your pocket.

"Here was an answer to every question, and more; here was how the cigars were poisoned, and, in combination with the tailor's tag inside your pocket, a short history of your life. Briefly it was like this: Once you had corrosive sublimate in your pocket. For what purpose? First thought—to rid your home of insects. Second thought—if you were boarding, married or unmarried, the task of getting rid of the insects would have been left to the servant; and this would possibly have been the case if you had been living at home. So I assumed for the instant that you were keeping house, and if keeping house, you were married—you bought the poison for use in your own house.

"Now, without an effort, naturally, I had you married, and keeping house. Then what? The tailor's tag, with your name, and the date your clothing was made—one year and three months ago. It is winter clothing. If you had worn it since the poison was loose in your pocket the thing that happened to you tonight would have happened to you before; but it never happened before, therefore I assume that you had the poison early last spring, when insects began to be troublesome, and immediately after that you laid away the suit until this winter. I know you are wearing the suit for the first time this winter, because, again, this thing has not happened before, and because, too, of the faint odor of moth balls. A band of crepe on your hat, the picture of a young woman in your watch, and the fact that you are now living at your club, as your bill for last month shows, establish beyond doubt that you are a widower."

"It's perfectly miraculous!" I exclaimed.

"Logic, logic, logic," snapped the irritable little scientist. "You are a lawyer, you ought to know the correlation of facts; you ought to know that two and two make four, not sometimes but all the time."

INTRODUCTION

Harlan Ellison®

And now that you've made his acquaintance—and trust me on this, after the celebrated "Problem of Cell 13" you will number this contact among the most unforgettable in your life—we'll return to the bewildering challenges to the ratiocinative intellect of The Thinking Machine in just a moment. But first, these words from our sponsors:

—

Friends, do you long for a respite from the anomie of modern detective fiction? Do you voicelessly cry out for deliverance from tea-cozy melodramas in which varicose-veined elderly matrons unravel nefarious plots among the forsythia? Do you weep, in the gentle, lonely, small hours for a world in which private eyes do not get sapped across the noggin by footpads and yeggs with lisle stockings stuffed with small change? Is your reading fare fairly fruitless? Do you feel hemmed in by homicides and henna-haired 'hoors who use the eff-word to the ultimate degree of shocklessness? If you tremble at my words, take heart: we offer you Escape! The sweet opportunity to fly thee hence, to go back to Edwardian times in genteel Boston, to an era of ominous gaslight and the clatter of Hansom cabs, to the recent invention of the 'phone and the introduction of the auto cab. A time of mystery and mayhem in which the Bertillon System was not yet wholly antiquated, while yet the Fingerprint Method was still in its adolescence. We offer you surcease from the hysteria and hype, the nonsense of nauseous semiliteracy of Modern Times.

We offer you Prof. Van Dusen.

———

He adored May. Though she was screaming and trying to claw an unbreakable hold on his life jacket, Futrelle managed to pry her loose and, crying, shoved her bodily into the lifeboat. He adored her, even to the final extreme of loss and heroism.

———

He never lived to see his little story become a thing Posterity could not ignore. A classic. To last more than a hundred years. One of the few "mystery" stories (indeed, one of the few pieces of fiction of *any* length or genre) to survive and to command ongoing popular appeal from the Edwardian Era. Futrelle died on the night of April 14–15, 1912 ... only seven years after his little story was published; he never lived to see even an edge of that glory.

Jacques Futrelle went down with the *Titanic.*

———

Only two matters of unarguably important scope happened in that earlier year. The first was the passage of The Pure Food & Drug Act of 1906. The other was the publication, in *The Boston American,* of a short story titled "The Problem of Cell 13" as penned by an American journalist (with a peculiarly French-sounding name): Jacques Futrelle.

There are those who annoyingly contend that the Russian Revolution, America's occupation of Cuba, an acquittal for Alfred Dreyfus in the infamous French trial, the San Francisco earthquake that killed more than a thousand people, Wasserman's development in Germany of a test to diagnose the scourge of syphilis, and Santos-Dumont's first powered flight in Europe were handily as significant as the publication of a mere "detective puzzle" (as it was called), but where were those smart alecks when we all fled the Dust Bowl? Where were they when full-service gas stations were squeezed out of existence by the invention of the DVD? Not to mention when "How Much Is That Doggie in the Window?" became number one on the Hit Parade and an entire nation was gulled and hoodwinked into believing Britney Spears actually could sing!

I ask you, where were those naysayers then?

—

With the firm resolve neither to regurgitate the lineage of detectives in fiction that has been iterated endlessly, nor to get too pedantic about all this, it is my desire to steal but a moment of your time to put Futrelle's great creation into lean, brief, minimal literary context. If I get too Pecksniffian, just feel free to give me a whack upside the melon.

Ahem.

As I've said elsewhere, there are only five native-born American art-forms. The banjo. The comic book. Jazz. Musical comedy in its contemporary form. And the mystery story, as "invented" by Edgar Allan Poe.

Monsieur C. Auguste Dupin, Poe's analytical investigator (nowhere is he actually referred to as a "detective"), made his debut in *Graham's Magazine,* April 1841. "The Murders in the Rue Morgue." The first modern detective story. Most everyone agrees on that; even the French. And you know how *they* are.

Then came Holmes. Than whom there is no greater, when the subject is "consulting detectives." (As an aside, the Conan Doyle canon also contains The Secret, as I have told college and high school students at hundreds of lectures. "The Secret," of course, is the one Willy Loman means when he asks the shade of his departed brother, *What's The Secret, Ben? The Secret of being successful, of helming your own life with satisfaction; what's the great Secret, Ben?* Dialogue to that effect. And I'd codify that Great Secret for you, but here is neither the time nor the place. You'll ask me sometime.)

Sherlock Holmes first appeared in print near the end of 1887, "A Study in Scarlet," a "little novel about 200 pages long" (his wife wrote to her sister-in-law, Lottie). It took him only a month to write it. And when it appeared in *Beeton's Christmas Annual,* well, it's been noted that one of the great doyens of classic mystery fiction, Dorothy L. Sayers, said that it was "flung like a bombshell into the field of detective fiction." (Another teeny aside, I'm fascinated by stuff like this: the first separate publication of the story appeared the following year, 1888. And that was the year Jack the Ripper was at work. Lovely coincidence.)

If you ask, "Why is he loitering with Sherlock Holmes when we've all paid our money to discuss The Thinking Machine?" it is because without the former, it is almost certain we would not have had the latter. Futrelle was, like every other writer worth his hire in those skinny times, utterly enthralled by Holmes and the metaphor of a lone, logical, observant savant with an unerring sense of Right vs. Wrong as representative of the most noble striving of the human race. This embodiment of a sort of, well, *homo superior,* achievable in *homo sapiens* if one uses deductive logic and strong ethical behavior, has been the dream of our species since prehistory.

And here it was, that dream of the rational man. Embodiment: Sherlock Holmes. So Futrelle was not (nor has been) the only conjurer of detective fiction to emulate the Doyle template. Whether Baynard Kendrick's blind sleuth Duncan McClain, or Rex Stout's memorable 1/7th of a ton 'tec named Nero Wolfe, or Baroness Orczy's Old Man in the Corner from 1909, or Ellery Queen, or even The Shadow and Batman, they are all children of the storytelling loins of Sir Arthur Conan Doyle, and his magnificent creation.

But The Thinking Machine was one of the first to manifest that Holmesian metaphor. Jacques Futrelle was so emboldened by the nascent possibilities of the detective story in this form that he even "borrowed" the plot-gimmick of "The Red-Headed League" for a short story originally published as "The Problem of the Deserted House" (which I have cavalierly retitled "The Anomaly of the Phone That Could Not Speak," appearing as the final yarn in this collection).

I'll explain, but not apologize for, the retitling madness that befell me when I set to work assembling this congeries. In a while. A bit later. Be patient.

———

I came to Prof. Van Dusen through the good offices of Fred Dannay and Manfred B. Lee, who wrote together as "Ellery Queen." In 1941, when I was a little kid, still listening to *The Shadow* on the Mutual Network, and starting to push colored pins into a war map of the South Pacific, somewhichway I got hold of a book edited by Ellery Queen, *101 Years' Entertainment: The Great Detective Stories, 1841–1941.* It was a sensational anthology, and I started reading it from front to back. It opened, naturally, with Poe's "The Purloined Letter," because 1841 was C. Auguste Dupin in full flight. But the sixth story, erroneously dated 1905, was "The Problem of Cell 13."

Oh, baby! What an epiphany. What a mortal lock sweetie of a story. I was knocked out by it. Blown away. A guy who could solve such unfathomable problems just using his wits and his intelligence. I don't know about you, but for a smart kid in a small Ohio town, it was a beacon. It was that illuminating moment when you understand the unarguable truth of Pasteur's admonition that "Chance favors the prepared mind."

It became the most evocative Burma-Shave sign on the road of my life. Sherlock Holmes and The Thinking Machine, their ratiocinative, deductive-logic m.o. has brought me to the state of success and near-godliness I now manifest. (The only thing that has ever held me back is my modesty.)

Fred and Manny called Van Dusen "this light-heartedly irritable little genius." Just so! Couldn't have capped-him-up better myself. Here's his mantra, repeated in almost every story:

"Two and two make four, not some times, but all the time. As the figure 'two,' wholly disconnected from any other, gives small indication of a result, so is an isolated fact of little consequence. Yet that fact added to another, and the resulting fact added to a third, and so on, will give a final result. That result, if every fact is considered, *must* be correct. Thus any problem may be solved by logic; logic is inevitable. . . . We prove a murder."

And what a pain in the *gotkes* (as we say in Yiddish) the Good Professor is! What he looks like, how he speaks to others, how he treats his confrere—the amiable but not-the-sharpest-knife-in-the-drawer journalist, Hutchinson Hatch—places him well up in the first percentile of literary curmudgeons. This is how Futrelle capped-him-up in "The Haunted Bell":

This man of the large head and small body was the Court of Last Appeal in contemporaneous science. His was the sanest, coldest, clearest brain in scientific achievement. His word was the final one. Once upon a time a newspaper man, Hutchinson Hatch, had dubbed him The Thinking Machine, and so it came about that the world at large had heard of, and knew him, by that title. . . . The scientist spoke in a tone of perpetual annoyance; but a long acquaintance had taught the reporter that it was what the man said and not the manner in which he said it, that was to be heeded.

As compelling as "The Problem of Cell 13" was in 1941, it never occurred to my adolescent mind that there might be *other* Futrelle stories about this exemplary gentleman. I had no difficulty extrapolating additional adventures of Porthos, Athos and Aramis, because Dumas took up half a shelf in the Painesville, Ohio, library. Holmes, yes, of course, because there they were, right alongside the Prof. Challenger books. Eugène Sue, Sir Walter Scott, volume after volume of Mark Twain and H. Rider Haggard; not to mention all those Hardy Boys mysteries and Clarence Budington Kelland's charming potboilers about Mark Tidd. Sequels, lots of them. But of Jacques Futrelle and Prof. Van Dusen I heard no more . . . not for thirty long years.

Let me pause for a moment to dwell on the cruelties of Posterity.

No matter what it is a writer may say is his or her "reason" for writing (Heinrich von Kleist said, "I write only because I cannot stop"), I suggest it is pure codswallop, whether self-delusional or purposely obfuscatory, unless that writer cops to hungering for permanence. The nod of Posterity. Let me be read and remembered, if only a little, O Beloved, ten, twenty-five, a hundred years after I have gone back to the essential salts and minerals that made me from the stones and rains of Ninevah and Atlantis. Let some reader decades from now smile at the sound of my name, and quote a line from my best story.

This life, like a guttering candle, claws for just one more moment of light. I mention Clarence Budington Kelland, who was, for more than thirty years, the most popular writer in America, and you look at me without recognition. Who? Kelland, I say; not a *great* writer, by any means; but so overwhelmingly present and popular that hardly was an issue of *The Saturday Evening Post* or *Collier's* released that Kelland was not featured on the cover. (*Collier's*, you repeat, without comprehension; *Saturday Evening Post?*) Let me pause for a moment and speak of Posterity.

If Kelland cannot survive, what chance have the rest of us poor minstrels at challenging Chaucer and Ovid and Will and Aesop for a place in the pantheon? No matter what it is a writer says ("All writers are liars. How else can we caress the truth?" Gwyn Thomas, Welsh novelist, playwright, scholar), as the toe scuffs the dirt and aw-shucks accompanies the self-effacing bullshit. We miss those nights with our spouse, the movie we're dying to see, the dinners with friends, the trip to Glacier National Park because . . . because . . . well, I have a T-shirt I sometimes wear. My wife knows it well. It is black, and in white on its front is the following legend:

NOT TONIGHT, DEAR, I HAVE A DEADLINE.

Even Futrelle, an enormous and immediate success with "The Problem of Cell 13," even Futrelle hungered to belly-up to that free lunch, Posterity. And it was denied him not only because his life was cut short, but because he was (my publisher will not care for this) rather a one-trick pony.

I'll get to that in a moment. Your continued patience is much appreciated by the management.

———

Thirty years later, the estimable bibliophile and editor Everett F. Bleiler went prowling through the dusty back shelves of mystery arcana, and unearthed the two collections of Thinking Machine stories that had appeared in hardcover in 1906 and 1907. He picked and chose, and edited most brilliantly two trade paperback selections for Dover Publications (1973 & 1976) that brought back into the light a double-dozen+1 Van Dusen adventures.

Thereafter, another deadly silence, with Thinking Machine aficionados, such as myself, thrusting copies of the stories into friends' hands. A year or so ago, in an anthology edited by Lawrence Block, I picked "The Problem of Cell 13" as my all-time favorite mystery, and from that carom connection to Futrelle, well, here I sit trying to inveigle you.

(And I urge you to ferret out those two Dover collections edited by Ev Bleiler. *His* introductions are so good that, were I to quote more from them it would no longer be "research," it would be blind theft.)

So, apart from using Bleiler as my reference for the following paragraph, the observations and opinions are mine. We submerge all packages received at my office in a vat of sure-fire bomb quencher, Vernor's Ginger Ale and llama urine.

"Jacques Futrelle was born in Georgia in 1875, of French Huguenot stock. He did newspaper work in Richmond, Virginia; acted as a theatrical manager for a short time; and then settled in the Boston area. At the time that he created The Thinking Machine he was a member of the editorial staff of the *Boston American*, the local Hearst newspaper."

On the night of April 14–15, 1912, on his way back to New York with May, the maiden voyage of the *Titanic*, Jacques Futrelle died, as Hemingway might have codified it, demonstrating not only heroism, but "grace under pressure."

Like Kelland, like all of the great and small dreamers whose visions and philosophies went up in smoke when they burned the

Great Library of Alexandria, like every brilliant novelist and every cheap hack, Jacques Futrelle went through that last doorway, and—like all but a few of us—his work went with him.

Six decades went by before he appeared again, a quick blip on the screen, then gone again for almost thirty more—and now, o frabjous day calloo callay, Futrelle is in the Modern Library. May would be ever so proud.

———

There is only one reason to read these stories.

Joy.

Unbridled, unalloyed, unfettered pleasure. Joy. They are fables from another time, written simply and directly. And entertainment is their one desire. To pleasure you. They were written in form, and appeared in mediums, intended for fast consumption. This is not Proust, folks, in case you got into the wrong queue. They are pleasant reading experiences that demand a bit of ratiocination, a bit of trying to outguess the author (which oughtn't to be too hard; remember, they were written almost a century ago, when science and technology were arcane and awe-inspiring to a nation just in its sophomore years of the Industrial Revolution).

Let me give you an example. In "The Superfluous Finger" (written in 1906), a woman comes to a doctor and requests he cut off one of her fingers. He refuses, she goes away, shows up next afternoon with the finger lopped off. The doctor tends to her, but calls Van Dusen to hurry over. When The Thinking Machine is apprised of the situation, one of the first things he does . . . well, here's how it reads:

> "What do you make of it?" demanded the surgeon.
>
> The Thinking Machine didn't say. At the moment he was leaning over the unconscious woman, squinting at her forehead. With his disengaged hand he stroked the delicately pencilled eye-brows several times the wrong way, and again at close range squinted at them. Dr. Prescott saw and seeing, understood.

Yeah, well *I* didn't understood. Not even when, near the denouement of the story, when The Thinking Machine is explaining how he solved the riddle of why the woman wanted her finger off, he says, "Naturally the first supposition was insanity. We pass that as absurd on its face. Then disease—a taint of leprosy perhaps which had been visible on the left forefinger. I tested for that, and that was eliminated." What...? *When* the hell did he test for leprosy? I had to reread the story, and the only thing I couldn't figure out was that brushing of the eye-brows. So I did my homework, and in one of my old *Britannicas* (I have four sets) I found this:

> LEPROSY   Etiology/epidemiology
> *Clinical Manifestations:* Early leprosy blah blah blah; tuberculoid blah blah blah; lepromatous blah blah *loss of lateral eyebrows* blah blah further.

Now, in 1906 that would've been an even *more* enigmatic and startling bit of deduction for the average reader. Futrelle was fascinated by the burgeoning sciences of his day, and the headlong plummet of new technologies adapted for everyday life.

Okay, wait, here's another one. And this isn't intended to be a spoiler when you read the story, but for those of you whose memories only go back as far as a week ago (I heard a contestant on *Who Wants to Be a Millionaire?* confess she didn't know the answer to a question about some product that had been introduced to the market in 1967, because she hadn't been born till 1975) this may help you understand the payoff to the mystery.

When you read "The Silver Box" and therein reference is made to a telephone, don't think cell phone, don't think a pink Princess, don't think a push-button board with a HOLD button. What you should think is this:

Because that's what a telephone *looked* like in June of 1907 when "The Silver Box" was published. Similarly—and I've misplaced the damned note I made, so you'll just have to remember I mentioned this when you come across it in one of the stories—at one point Futrelle writes that the driver of a cab "bends down" to talk to the passenger. Now, if you picture a Yellow Cab, you'll never get it. You'll think the passenger is on the floor in front, and won't *you* be confused! This was a *Hansom cab*, horse-drawn, with the hackney riding on an elevated seat in front, leaning down to speak through the aperture into the cab. I am a full-service prefacer; I also do windows and floors.

———

Which brings me to that "one-trick pony" remark a while ago.

Friends, I will not diddle you. This is not great literature. It is not even the greatest mystery writing, such as that purveyed by Donald Westlake or Hammett or the late Stanley Ellin. It is good, solid, competent writing. The best story in this book is "The Problem of Cell 13." The rest are good, some better than good, a few just adequate. I will not lie to you. Futrelle was a one-hit wonder.

Though The Thinking Machine stories were enormously popular in their time, though they still amuse and entertain, they creak more than a little. I have chosen to arrange these pieces somewhat unorthodoxly, because I wanted you to meet him, get a taste of him, read his first case, and *then* come to these sober remarks. Because in a moment (unless you're wise beyond your years and bypass this yammer and go straight to "Cell 13") you will read one of the most remarkable bravura efforts you'll ever encounter.

One-hit wonders are rare. Malcolm Lowry wrote *Under the Volcano* and that was it. Thereafter, zip. The artist Richard Dadd gave us the breathtaking canvas "The Fairy Feller's Master Stroke" and then they clapped the guy away in a madhouse. Ross Lockridge wrote the hugely successful *Raintree County* and then offed himself. Same with Thomas Heggen and *Mister Roberts.* Margaret Mitchell, *Gone With the Wind* and then sudden death. Harper Lee: *To Kill a Mockingbird.* There is no Dumas-long Harper Lee shelf in the library. Baron Corvo, Walter M. Miller, Jr., J. D. Salinger, Tom Godwin and "The Cold Equations," Baudelaire, Rimbaud, the *New Yorker*'s "Inflexible Logic" by Russell Maloney. Once, and out.

(Yes, I know some of these people did a bit more writing, some good, most forgettable, but they never hit the peak of the mountain again. Not even Salinger. So don't come all punctillious with me. The point I'm making is pretty much okay.)

"The Problem of Cell 13" is a once-in-a-career jackpot of a story. Futrelle kept at work, did novels and more stories and lots of journalism before and after; even a collaboration with May; but never did he achieve the wonder that came to him in "Cell 13."

I tell you this so you do not think either I, or the Modern Library, are fools or näifs. Nor bait-and-switch crooks.

We offer you a big, nice, pleasant book of stories that mean you no harm, that gather here to amuse you, that serve to fill out all the other pages to pay for "The Problem of Cell 13." Consider this an effort at open covenants, openly entered into. I leave the final judgment to Posterity.

——

Oh, one more thing before I release you. I *hate* the titles on these stories. To one who has worked in magazines and newspapers for most of his life, I can smell a dull title that has been thrust onto a piece of writing by a blurb-writer, copy editor, headline-hack, or office ribbon clerk with the imagination of an O-Cel-O sponge mop.

So I retitled most of them. I *loved* retitling them. But the Modern Library is a noble gray eminence that says to me, Ellison, guttersnipe, pain in the *gotkes,* we cannot trifle with Literary History. (They use CAPS like that a lot.) So I beefed, and dragged my tail, and tried to hide out, but they had their way. Nonetheless, I present to you here, on a page all by itself in the middle of my very own words, where they are compelled to include it BY THEIR OWN RULES, ha! take *that,* you *eminence grise,* my own delicious yet nonetheless humbly offered retitlings of the stories, in the same order you'll find them under their pallid, plebian names on the contents page.

I wish to thank the following for shepherding me through this. In no particular, and certainly not alphabetical, order:

Ms. MJ Devaney, who picked me out of the dustheaps to do this job, then had the unlimited good sense to dash off and have a baby, turning me over to Ms. Judy Sternlight, my editor, and easily the sweetest person I have ever dealt with in more than fifty years as a scrivener. This is a paragon, folks, and trust me when I tell you that this job has been a *kodiak!* Not once did she raise her voice, and only threatened to throw me off the project twice. Mr. Richard Curtis, who is not only my long-time friend and agent but a miracle worker who got me hired back both times Sternlight kicked my ass outta here. My wife. Susan. What a doll. You cannot know, you simply cannot know. When I get bogged down in a gig like this, my usual easygoing, humble self turns into Godhelpuszilla, and Susan keeps her head down, pushes me forward, and drives me to do the job. The one who drove me to the hospital was Sharon Buck, my assistant. There was Judy's colleague, Dominique Troiano, there was John Gregory Betancourt, there was Otto Penzler and an article by Jeffrey Marks in *Mystery Scene;* and there were Fred and Manny, "Ellery Queen," who got me into this in the first place.

You've been gracious from the outset, and I reward your patience with the timeless and glorious legacy of Jacques Futrelle, "The Problem of Cell 13."

Jacques Futrelle's

"The Thinking Machine"

Dressing Room "A"

That strange, seemingly inexplicable chain of circumstances which had to do with the mysterious disappearance of the famous actress, Irene Wallack, from her dressing room in a Springfield theater during a performance, while the echo of tumultuous appreciation still rang in her ears, was one of the most fascinating problems which was not purely scientific that The Thinking Machine was ever asked to solve. The scientist's aid was enlisted in this singular mystery by Hutchinson Hatch, reporter.

"There is something far beyond the ordinary in this affair," Hatch explained to the scientist. "A woman has disappeared, evaporated into thin air in the hearing, almost in sight, of her friends. The police can make nothing of it. It is a problem for a greater mind than theirs."

Professor Van Dusen waved the newspaperman to a seat and himself sank back into a great cushioned chair in which his diminutive figure seemed even more child-like than it really was.

"Tell me the story," he commanded petulantly. "All of it."

The enormous yellow head rested against the chair back, the blue eyes squinted steadily upward, the slender fingers were pressed tip to tip. The Thinking Machine was in a receptive mood.

"Miss Wallack is thirty years old and beautiful," the reporter began. "As an actress she has won recognition not only in this country but in England. You may have read something of her in the daily papers, and if——"

"I never read the papers unless I am compelled to," the other interrupted curtly. "Go on."

"She is unmarried, and so far as anyone knows, had no immediate intention of changing her condition," Hatch resumed, staring curiously at the thin face of the scientist. "I presume she had admirers— all beautiful women of the stage have—but she is one whose life has been perfectly clean, whose record is an open book. I tell you this because it might have a bearing on your conclusion as to a possible reason for her disappearance.

"Now the actual circumstances of that disappearance. Miss Wallack has been playing a Shakespearean repertoire. Last week she was in Springfield. On Saturday night, which concluded her engagement there, she appeared as Rosalind in 'As You Like It.' The house was crowded. She played the first two acts amid great enthusiasm, and this despite the fact that she was suffering intensely from a headache to which she was subject at times. After the second act she returned to her dressing room and just before the curtain went up for the third the stage manager called her. She replied that she would be out immediately. There seems no possible shadow of a doubt but that it was her voice.

"Rosalind does not appear in the third act until the curtain has been up for six minutes. When Miss Wallack's cue came she did not answer it. The stage manager rushed to her door and again called her. There was no answer. Then, fearing that she might have fainted, he went in. She was not there. A hurried search was made without result, and the stage manager, finally, was compelled to announce to the audience that the sudden illness of the star would cause a slight delay; that he hoped within ten or fifteen minutes she would be able to resume her part.

"The curtain was lowered and the search resumed. Every nook and corner back of the footlights was gone over. The stage doorkeeper, William Meegan, had seen no one go out. He and a policeman had been standing at the stage door talking for at least twenty minutes. It is, therefore, conclusive that Miss Wallack did not leave the theater by the stage door. The only other way it was possible to leave the stage was over the footlights. Of course she didn't go that way. Yet no trace of her has been found. Where is she?"

"The windows?" asked The Thinking Machine.

"The stage is below the street level," Hatch explained. "The window of her dressing room, Room A, is small and barred with iron. It opens into an air shaft that goes straight up for ten feet, and that is covered with an iron grating. The other windows on the stage are not only inaccessible but are also barred with iron. She could not have approached either of these windows without being seen by other members of the company or the stage hands."

"Under the stage?" suggested the scientist.

"Nothing," the reporter went on. "It is a large cemented basement which was vacant. It was searched because there was, of course, a chance that Miss Wallack might have become temporarily unbalanced and wandered down there. There was even a search made of the 'flies'—that is, the galleries over the stage where the men who work the drop-curtains are stationed."

There was silence for a long time. The Thinking Machine twiddled his fingers and continued to stare upward. He had not looked at the reporter. He broke the silence after a time.

"How was Miss Wallack dressed at the time of her disappearance?"

"In doublet and hose—that is, tights," the newspaperman responded. "She wears that costume from the second act until practically the end of the play."

"Was all her street clothing in her room?"

"Yes, everything, spread across an unopened trunk of costumes. It was all as if she had left the room to answer her cue—all in order—even to an open box of candy on her table."

"No sign of a struggle?"

"No."

"Or trace of blood?"

"Nothing."

"Her maid? Did she have one?"

"Oh, yes. I neglected to tell you that the maid, Gertrude Manning, had gone home immediately after the first act. She grew suddenly ill and was excused."

The Thinking Machine turned his squint eyes on the reporter for the first time.

"Ill?" he repeated. "What was the matter?"

"That I can't say," replied the reporter.

"Where is she now?"

"I don't know. Everyone forgot all about her in the excitement about Miss Wallack."

"What kind of candy was it?"

"I'm afraid I don't know that, either."

"Where was it bought?"

The reporter shrugged his shoulders; that was something else he didn't know. The Thinking Machine shot out the questions aggressively, staring meanwhile steadily at Hatch who squirmed uncomfortably.

"Where is the candy now?" demanded the scientist.

Again Hatch shrugged his shoulders.

"How much did Miss Wallack weigh?"

The reporter was willing to guess at this. He had seen her half a dozen times.

"Between a hundred and thirty and a hundred and forty pounds," he ventured.

"Does there happen to be a hypnotist connected with the company?"

"I don't know," Hatch replied.

The Thinking Machine waved his slender hands impatiently; he was annoyed.

"It is perfectly absurd, Mr. Hatch," he expostulated, "to come to me with only a few facts and ask advice. If you had all the facts I might be able to do something, but this——"

The newspaperman was nettled. In his own profession he was accredited a man of discernment and acumen. He resented the tone, the manner, even the seemingly trivial questions which the other asked.

"I don't see," he began, "that the candy, even if it had been poisoned as I imagine you think possible, or a hypnotist could have had anything to do with Miss Wallack's disappearance. Certainly neither poison nor hypnotism would have made her invisible."

"Of course you don't see," blazed The Thinking Machine. "If you did you wouldn't have come to me. When did this thing happen?"

"Saturday night, as I said," the reporter informed him a little more humbly. "It closed the engagement in Springfield. Miss Wallack was to have appeared here tonight."

"When did she disappear—what time by the clock, I mean?"

"The stage manager's time slip shows that the curtain for the third act went up at 9:41—he spoke to her, say, one minute before, or at 9:40. The action of the play before she appears in the third act takes six minutes, therefore——"

"In precisely seven minutes a woman, weighing more than 130 pounds, certainly not dressed for the street, disappeared from her dressing room. It is now 5:18 Monday afternoon. I think we may solve this crime within a few hours."

"Crime?" Hatch repeated eagerly. "Do you imagine there is a crime then?"

Professor Van Dusen didn't heed the question. Instead, he arose and paced back and forth across the reception room half a dozen times, his hands behind his back and his eyes cast down. At last he stopped and faced the reporter who had also arisen.

"Miss Wallack's company, I presume, with the baggage, is now here," he said. "See every male member of the company, talk to them and particularly *study their eyes.* Don't overlook anyone, however humble. Also find out what became of the box of candy, and if possible how many pieces are out of it. Then report here to me. Miss Wallack's safety may depend upon your speed and accuracy."

Hatch was frankly startled.

"How——?" he began.

"Don't stop to talk—hurry," commanded The Thinking Machine. "I will have a cab waiting when you come back. We must get to Springfield."

FITTING A HYPOTHESIS

The newspaperman rushed away to obey orders.

He didn't understand them at all—studying men's eyes was not in his line, but he obeyed nevertheless. An hour and a half later he returned to be thrust unceremoniously into a waiting cab by The Thinking Machine. The cab rattled away toward South Station where the two men caught a train, just about to move out, for Springfield. Once settled in their seats the scientist turned to Hatch who was nearly suffocating with suppressed information.

"Well?" he asked.

"I found out several things," the reporter burst out. "First, Miss Wallack's leading man, Langdon Mason, who has been in love with her for three years, bought the candy at Schuyler's in Springfield early Saturday evening before he went to the theater. He told me so himself, rather reluctantly, but I—I made him say it."

"Ah!" exclaimed The Thinking Machine. It was a most unequivocal ejaculation. "How many pieces of candy are out of the box?"

"Only three," explained Hatch. "Miss Wallack's things were packed into the open trunk in her dressing room, the candy with them. I induced the manager——"

"Yes, yes, yes," interrupted The Thinking Machine impatiently. "What sort of eyes has Mason? What color?"

"Blue, frank in expression, nothing unusual about them," said the reporter.

"And the others?"

"I didn't quite know what you meant by studying their eyes, so I got a set of photographs. I thought perhaps they might help."

"Excellent! Excellent!" commented The Thinking Machine. He shuffled the pictures through his fingers, stopping now and then to study one, and to read the names printed below. "Is that the leading man?" he asked at last, and handed one to Hatch.

"Yes."

Professor Van Dusen did not speak again. The train pulled into Springfield at 9:20. Hatch followed him out of the station and, without a word, climbed into a cab.

"Schuyler's candy store," commanded The Thinking Machine. "Hurry."

The cab rushed off through the night. Ten minutes later it stopped before a brilliantly lighted confectionery shop. The Thinking Machine led the way inside and approached the girl behind the chocolate counter.

"Will you please tell me if you remember this man's face?" he asked as he produced Mason's photograph.

"Oh, yes, I remember him," the girl replied. "He's an actor."

"Did he buy a small box of chocolates of you Saturday evening early?" was the next question.

"Yes. I recall it because he seemed to be in a hurry—in fact, said he was anxious to get to the theater to pack."

"And do you recall that *this* man ever bought candy here?" asked the scientist. He produced another photograph and handed it to the girl. She studied it a moment while Hatch craned his neck, vainly, to see.

"I don't recall that he ever did," the girl answered finally.

The Thinking Machine turned away abruptly and disappeared into a telephone booth. He remained there for five minutes, then rushed out to the cab again, with Hatch following closely.

"City Hospital," he commanded.

Again the cab dashed away. Hatch was dumb; there seemed to be nothing to say. The Thinking Machine was plainly pursuing some definite line of inquiry yet the reporter didn't know what. The case was getting kaleidoscopic. This impression was strengthened when he found himself standing beside The Thinking Machine in City Hospital conversing with the house surgeon, Dr. Carlton.

"Is there a Miss Gertrude Manning here?" was the scientist's first question.

"Yes," replied the surgeon. "She was brought here Saturday night suffering from——"

"Strychnine poisoning, yes I know," interrupted the other. "Picked up in the street, probably. I am a physician. If she is well enough I should like to ask her a couple of questions."

Dr. Carlton agreed and Professor Van Dusen, still followed faithfully by Hatch, was ushered into the ward where Miss Wallack's maid lay, pallid and weak. The Thinking Machine picked up her hand and his slender finger rested for a minute on her pulse. He nodded as if satisfied.

"Miss Manning, can you understand me?" he asked.

"Yes," she replied weakly.

"How many pieces of the candy did you eat?"

"Two," said the girl. She stared into the face above her with dull eyes.

"Did Miss Wallack eat any of it up to the time you left the theater?"

"No."

If The Thinking Machine had been in a hurry previously he was racing now. Hatch trailed on dutifully behind, down the stairs and into a cab, whence Professor Van Dusen shouted a word of thanks to Dr. Carlton. This time their destination was the stage door of the theater from which Miss Wallack had disappeared.

The reporter was muddled. He didn't know anything very clearly except that three pieces of candy were missing from the box. Of these the maid had eaten only two. She had been poisoned. Therefore it seemed reasonable to suppose that if Miss Wallack had eaten the third piece she also would be poisoned. But poison would not make her invisible. The reporter shook his head hopelessly.

William Meegan, the stage door-keeper, was easily found.

"Can you inform me, please," began The Thinking Machine, "if Mr. Mason left a box of candy with you last Saturday night for Miss Wallack?"

"Yes," Meegan replied good-naturedly. He was amused at the little man. "Miss Wallack hadn't arrived. Mason brought a box of candy for her nearly every night and usually left it here. I put the one Saturday night on the shelf here."

"Did Mr. Mason come to the theater before or after the others on Saturday night?"

"Before," replied Meegan. "He was unusually early, presumably to pack."

"And the other members of the company coming in stop here, I imagine, to get their mail?" and the scientist squinted up at the mail box above the shelf.

"Sure, always."

The Thinking Machine drew a long breath. Up to this time there had been little perplexed wrinkles in his brow. Now they disappeared.

"Now, please," he went on, "was any package or box of any kind taken from the stage on Saturday night between nine and eleven o'clock?"

"No," said Meegan positively. "Nothing at all until the company's baggage was removed at midnight."

"Miss Wallack had two trunks in her dressing room?"

"Yes. Two whacking big ones, too."

"How do you know?"

"Because I helped put 'em in, and helped take 'em out," replied Meegan.

Suddenly The Thinking Machine turned and rushed out to the cab, with Hatch, his shadow, close behind.

"Drive, drive as fast as you know how to the nearest long distance telephone," the scientist instructed the cabby. "A woman's life is at stake."

Half an hour later Professor Van Dusen and Hutchinson Hatch were on a train rushing back to the city. The Thinking Machine had been in the telephone booth for fifteen minutes. When he came out Hatch had asked several questions to which the scientist vouchsafed no answer. They were perhaps thirty minutes out of Springfield before the scientist showed any disposition to talk. Then he began without preliminary much as if he were resuming a former conversation.

"Of course if Miss Wallack didn't leave the stage of the theater, she was there," he said. "We will admit that she did not become invisible. The problem, therefore, was to find her on the stage. The fact that no violence was used against her was conclusively proven by half a dozen instances. No one heard her scream, there was no struggle, no trace of blood. Ergo, we assume in the beginning that she must have consented to the first steps which led to her disappearance.

"Now let's shape a hypothesis which will fit all the circumstances. Miss Wallack had a severe headache. Hypnotic influence will cure headaches. Was there a hypnotist to whom Miss Wallack would have submitted herself? Assume there was. Then would that hypnotist take advantage of his control to place her in a cataleptic condition? Assume a motive and he would. Then, how would he dispose of her?

"From this point questions radiate in all directions. We will confine ourselves to the probable, granting for the moment that the hypothesis—the only one that fits all the circumstances—is correct. Obviously, a hypnotist would not have attempted to get her out of the dressing room. What remains? One of the two trunks in her room."

Hatch gasped.

"You mean you think it possible that she was hypnotized and placed in that second trunk, the one that was strapped and locked?" he asked.

"It's the only thing that *could* have happened," said The Thinking Machine emphatically, "therefore that is just what *did* happen."

"Why it's horrible!" exclaimed Hatch. "A live woman in a trunk for forty-eight hours? Even if she were alive then, she must be dead now."

The reporter shuddered a little and gazed curiously at the inscrutable face of his companion. He saw no pity, no horror there; there was merely the reflection of the working of a brain.

"It does not necessarily follow that she is dead," explained The Thinking Machine. "If she ate that third piece of candy *before* she was hypnotized she may be dead. If it were placed in her mouth after she was in a cataleptic condition the chances are that she is not dead. The candy would not melt and her system could not absorb the poison."

"But she would be suffocated—her bones would be broken by the rough handling of the trunk—there are a hundred possibilities," the reporter suggested.

"A person in a cataleptic condition is singularly impervious to injury," replied the scientist. "There is, of course, a chance of suffocation, but a great deal of air may enter a trunk."

"And the candy?" Hatch asked.

"Yes, the candy. We know that two pieces of it nearly killed the maid. Yet Mr. Mason admitted having bought it. This admission indicated that this poisoned candy is not the candy he bought. Is Mr. Mason a hypnotist? He hasn't the eyes. His picture tells me that. We know that Mr. Mason did buy candy for Miss Wallack on several occasions. We know that sometimes he left it with the stage doorkeeper. We know that members of the company stopped there for mail. We instantly see that it is possible for one to take away that box and substitute poisoned candy. All the boxes are alike.

"Madness and the cunning of madness lie back of all this. It was a deliberate attempt to murder Miss Wallack, long pondered and due, perhaps, to unrequited or hopeless infatuation. It began with the poisoned candy, and that failing, went to a point immediately following the moment when the stage manager last spoke to the actress. The hypnotist was probably in her room then. You must remember that it would have been possible for him to ease the headache, and at the same time leave Miss Wallack free to play. She might have known this from previous experience."

Hatch was silent for a long time as he mentally reviewed the case. He couldn't yet quite believe. It seemed inconceivable that human ingenuity could devise such a crime; and it was equally inconceivable that the brain of a man wholly disassociated with it could fathom it by pure logic.

"Is Miss Wallack still in the trunk?" he asked at last.

"No," replied The Thinking Machine. "She is out now, dead or alive—I am inclined to believe alive."

"And the man?"

"I will turn him over to the police in half an hour after we reach the city."

From South Station the scientist and Hatch were driven immediately to police headquarters. Detective Mallory received them.

"We got your 'phone from Springfield――――" he began.

"Was she dead?" interrupted the scientist.

"No," Mallory replied. "She's unconscious but no bones are broken, although she is badly bruised. The doctor says she's hypnotized."

"Was the piece of candy taken from her mouth?"

"Sure, a chocolate cream. It hadn't melted."

"I'll come back here in a few minutes and awake her," said The Thinking Machine. "Come along with us now, and get the man."

Wonderingly the detective entered the cab and the three were driven to a big hotel a dozen blocks away. Before they entered the lobby The Thinking Machine handed a photograph to Mallory, who studied it under an electric light.

"That man is upstairs with several others," explained the scientist. "Pick him out and get behind him when we enter the room. He may attempt to shoot. Don't touch him until I say so."

In a large room on the fifth floor Manager Stanfeld of the Irene Wallack Company had assembled the men who played in her support. This was done at the request by 'phone of The Thinking Machine. There were no preliminaries when Professor Van Dusen entered. He squinted comprehensively about him, then went straight to Langdon Mason, and stared into his eyes for a moment.

"Were you on the stage in the third act of your play before Miss Wallack was to appear—I mean the play last Saturday night?" he asked.

"I was," Mason replied, "for at least three minutes."

"Mr. Stanfeld, is that correct?"

"Yes," replied the manager.

There was a long tense silence broken only by the heavy footsteps of Mallory as he walked toward a distant corner of the room. A faint flush crept into Mason's face as he realized that the questions had been almost an accusation. He started to speak, but the steady, impassive voice of The Thinking Machine stopped him.

"Mr. Mallory, take your prisoner!"

Instantly there was a fierce, frantic struggle and those present turned to see the detective with his great arms locked about Stanley Wightman, the melancholy Jaques of "As You Like It." The actor's face was distorted, madness blazed in the eyes, and he snarled like a beast at bay. By a sudden movement Mallory threw Wightman and manacled the hands, then looked up to find The Thinking Machine peering over his shoulder into the eyes of the prostrate man.

"Yes, he's a hypnotist," the scientist remarked in self-satisfied conclusion. "It always tells in the pupils of the eyes."

An hour later Miss Wallack was aroused, told a story almost identical with that of The Thinking Machine, and three months later resumed her tour. And meanwhile Stanley Wightman, whose brooding over a hopeless love for her made a maniac of him, raves and shrieks the lines of Jaques in the seclusion of a padded cell. Alienists pronounce him incurable.

THE PROBLEM OF CELL 13

I

Practically all those letters remaining in the alphabet after Augustus S. F. X. Van Dusen was named were afterward acquired by that gentleman in the course of a brilliant scientific career, and, being honorably acquired, were tacked on to the other end. His name, therefore, taken with all that belonged to it, was a wonderfully imposing structure. He was a Ph. D., an LL. D., and F. R. S., and M. D., and an M. D. S. He was also some other things—just what he himself couldn't say—through recognition of his ability by various foreign educational and scientific institutions.

In appearance he was no less striking than in nomenclature. He was slender with the droop of the student in his thin shoulders and the pallor of a close, sedentary life on his clean-shaven face. His eyes wore a perpetual, forbidding squint—the squint of a man who studies little things—and when they could be seen at all through his thick spectacles, were mere slits of watery blue. But above his eyes was his most striking feature. This was a tall, broad brow, almost abnormal in height and width, crowned by a heavy shock of bushy, yellow hair.

All these things conspired to give him a peculiar, almost grotesque, personality.

Professor Van Dusen was remotely German. For generations his ancestors had been noted in the sciences; he was the logical result, the master mind. First and above all he was a logician. At least thirty-five years of the half-century or so of his existence had been devoted exclusively to proving that two and two always equal four, except in unusual cases, where they equal three or five, as the case may be. He stood broadly on the general proposition that all things that start must go somewhere, and was able to bring the concentrated mental force of his forefathers to bear on a given problem. Incidentally it may be remarked that Professor Van Dusen wore a No. 8 hat.

The world at large had heard vaguely of Professor Van Dusen as The Thinking Machine. It was a newspaper catch-phrase applied to him at the time of a remarkable exhibition at chess; he had demonstrated then that a stranger to the game might, by the force of inevitable logic, defeat a champion who had devoted a lifetime to its study. The Thinking Machine! Perhaps that more nearly described him than all his honorary initials, for he spent week after week, month after month, in the seclusion of his small laboratory from which had gone forth thoughts that staggered scientific associates and deeply stirred the world at large.

It was only occasionally that The Thinking Machine had visitors, and these were usually men who, themselves high in the sciences, dropped in to argue a point and perhaps convince themselves. Two of these men, Dr. Charles Ransome and Alfred Fielding, called one evening to discuss some theory which is not of consequence here.

"Such a thing is impossible," declared Dr. Ransome emphatically, in the course of the conversation.

"Nothing is impossible," declared The Thinking Machine with equal emphasis. He always spoke petulantly. "The mind is master of all things. When science fully recognizes that fact a great advance will have been made."

"How about the airship?" asked Dr. Ransome.

"That's not impossible at all," asserted The Thinking Machine. "It will be invented some time. I'd do it myself, but I'm busy."

Dr. Ransome laughed tolerantly.

"I've heard you say such things before," he said. "But they mean nothing. Mind may be master of matter, but it hasn't yet found a way to apply itself. There are some things that can't be *thought* out of existence, or rather which would not yield to any amount of thinking."

"What, for instance?" demanded The Thinking Machine.

Dr. Ransome was thoughtful for a moment as he smoked.

"Well, say prison walls," he replied. "No man can *think* himself out of a cell. If he could, there would be no prisoners."

"A man can so apply his brain and ingenuity that he can leave a cell, which is the same thing," snapped The Thinking Machine.

Dr. Ransome was slightly amused.

"Let's suppose a case," he said, after a moment. "Take a cell where prisoners under sentence of death are confined—men who are desperate and, maddened by fear, would take any chance to escape—suppose you were locked in such a cell. Could you escape?"

"Certainly," declared The Thinking Machine.

"Of course," said Mr. Fielding, who entered the conversation for the first time, "you might wreck the cell with an explosive—but inside, a prisoner, you couldn't have that."

"There would be nothing of that kind," said The Thinking Machine. "You might treat me precisely as you treated prisoners under sentence of death, and I would leave the cell."

"Not unless you entered it with tools prepared to get out," said Dr. Ransome.

The Thinking Machine was visibly annoyed and his blue eyes snapped.

"Lock me in any cell in any prison anywhere at any time, wearing only what is necessary, and I'll escape in a week," he declared, sharply.

Dr. Ransome sat up straight in the chair, interested. Mr. Fielding lighted a new cigar.

"You mean you could actually *think* yourself out?" asked Dr. Ransome.

"I would get out," was the response.

"Are you serious?"

"Certainly I am serious."

Dr. Ransome and Mr. Fielding were silent for a long time.

"Would you be willing to try it?" asked Mr. Fielding, finally.

"Certainly," said Professor Van Dusen, and there was a trace of irony in his voice. "I have done more asinine things than that to convince other men of less important truths."

The tone was offensive and there was an undercurrent strongly resembling anger on both sides. Of course it was an absurd thing, but Professor Van Dusen reiterated his willingness to undertake the escape and it was decided upon.

"To begin now," added Dr. Ransome.

"I'd prefer that it begin tomorrow," said The Thinking Machine, "because——"

"No, now," said Mr. Fielding, flatly. "You are arrested, figuratively, of course, without any warning locked in a cell with no chance to communicate with friends, and left there with identically the same care and attention that would be given to a man under sentence of death. Are you willing?"

"All right, now, then," said The Thinking Machine, and he arose.

"Say, the death-cell in Chisholm Prison."

"The death-cell in Chisholm Prison."

"And what will you wear?"

"As little as possible," said The Thinking Machine. "Shoes, stockings, trousers and a shirt."

"You will permit yourself to be searched, of course?"

"I am to be treated precisely as all prisoners are treated," said The Thinking Machine. "No more attention and no less."

There were some preliminaries to be arranged in the matter of obtaining permission for the test, but all three were influential men and everything was done satisfactorily by telephone, albeit the prison commissioners, to whom the experiment was explained on purely scientific grounds, were sadly bewildered. Professor Van Dusen would be the most distinguished prisoner they had ever entertained.

When The Thinking Machine had donned those things which he was to wear during his incarceration he called the little old woman who was his housekeeper, cook, and maid servant all in one.

"Martha," he said, "it is now twenty-seven minutes past nine o'clock. I am going away. One week from tonight, at half-past nine, these gentlemen and one, possibly two, others will take supper with me here. Remember Dr. Ransome is very fond of artichokes."

The three men were driven to Chisholm Prison, where the Warden was awaiting them, having been informed of the matter by telephone. He understood merely that the eminent Professor Van Dusen was to be his prisoner, if he could keep him, for one week; that he had committed no crime, but that he was to be treated as all other prisoners were treated.

"Search him," instructed Dr. Ransome.

The Thinking Machine was searched. Nothing was found on him; the pockets of the trousers were empty; the white, stiff-bosomed shirt had no pocket. The shoes and stockings were removed, examined, then replaced. As he watched all these preliminaries—the rigid search and noted the pitiful, child-like physical weakness of the man, the colorless face, and the thin, white hands—Dr. Ransome almost regretted his part in the affair.

"Are you sure you want to do this?" he asked.

"Would you be convinced if I did not?" inquired The Thinking Machine in turn.

"No."

"All right. I'll do it."

What sympathy Dr. Ransome had was dissipated by the tone. It nettled him, and he resolved to see the experiment to the end; it would be a stinging reproof to egotism.

"It will be impossible for him to communicate with anyone outside?" he asked.

"Absolutely impossible," replied the warden. "He will not be permitted writing materials of any sort."

"And your jailers, would they deliver a message from him?"

"Not one word, directly or indirectly," said the warden. "You may rest assured of that. They will report anything he might say or turn over to me anything he might give them."

"That seems entirely satisfactory," said Mr. Fielding, who was frankly interested in the problem.

"Of course, in the event he fails," said Dr. Ransome, "and asks for his liberty, you understand you are to set him free?"

"I understand," replied the warden.

The Thinking Machine stood listening, but had nothing to say until this was all ended, then:

"I should like to make three small requests. You may grant them or not, as you wish."

"No special favors, now," warned Mr. Fielding.

"I am asking none," was the stiff response. "I would like to have some tooth powder—buy it yourself to see that it is tooth powder—and I should like to have one five-dollar and two ten-dollar bills."

Dr. Ransome, Mr. Fielding and the warden exchanged astonished glances. They were not surprised at the request for tooth powder, but were at the request for money.

"Is there any man with whom our friend would come in contact that he could bribe with twenty-five dollars?" asked Dr. Ransome of the warden.

"Not for twenty-five hundred dollars," was the positive reply.

"Well, let him have them," said Mr. Fielding. "I think they are harmless enough."

"And what is the third request?" asked Dr. Ransome.

"I should like to have my shoes polished."

Again the astonished glances were exchanged. This last request was the height of absurdity, so they agreed to it. These things all being attended to, The Thinking Machine was led back into the prison from which he had undertaken to escape.

"Here is Cell 13," said the warden, stopping three doors down the steel corridor. "This is where we keep condemned murderers. No one can leave it without my permission; and no one in it can communicate with the outside. I'll stake my reputation on that. It's only three doors back of my office and I can readily hear any unusual noise."

"Will this cell do, gentlemen?" asked The Thinking Machine. There was a touch of irony in his voice.

"Admirably," was the reply.

The heavy steel door was thrown open, there was a great scurrying and scampering of tiny feet, and The Thinking Machine passed into the gloom of the cell. Then the door was closed and double locked by the warden.

"What is that noise in there?" asked Dr. Ransome, through the bars.

"Rats—dozens of them," replied The Thinking Machine, tersely.

The three men, with final good-nights, were turning away when The Thinking Machine called:

"What time is it exactly, warden?"

"Eleven seventeen," replied the warden.

"Thanks. I will join you gentlemen in your office at half-past eight o'clock one week from tonight," said The Thinking Machine.

"And if you do not?"

"There is no 'if' about it."

II

Chisholm Prison was a great, spreading structure of granite, four stories in all, which stood in the center of acres of open space. It was surrounded by a wall of solid masonry eighteen feet high, and so smoothly finished inside and out as to offer no foothold to a climber, no matter how expert. Atop of this fence, as a further precaution, was a five-foot fence of steel rods, each terminating in a keen point. This fence in itself marked an absolute deadline between freedom and imprisonment, for, even if a man escaped from his cell, it would seem impossible for him to pass the wall.

The yard, which on all sides of the prison building was twenty-five feet wide, that being the distance from the building to the wall, was by day an exercise ground for those prisoners to whom was granted the boon of occasional semi-liberty. But that was not for those in Cell 13. At all times of the day there were armed guards in the yard, four of them, one patrolling each side of the prison building.

By night the yard was almost as brilliantly lighted as by day. On each of the four sides was a great arc light which rose above the prison wall and gave to the guards a clear sight. The lights, too, brightly illuminated the spiked top of the wall. The wires which fed the arc lights ran up the side of the prison building on insulators and from the top story led out to the poles supporting the arc lights.

All these things were seen and comprehended by The Thinking Machine, who was only enabled to see out his closely barred cell window by standing on his bed. This was on the morning following his incarceration. He gathered, too, that the river lay over there beyond the wall somewhere, because he heard faintly the pulsation of a motor boat and high up in the air saw a river bird. From that same direction came the shouts of boys at play and the occasional crack of a batted ball. He knew then that between the prison wall and the river was an open space, a playground.

Chisholm Prison was regarded as absolutely safe. No man had ever escaped from it. The Thinking Machine, from his perch on the bed, seeing what he saw, could readily understand why. The walls of the cell, though built he judged twenty years before, were perfectly solid, and the window bars of new iron had not a shadow of rust on them. The window itself, even with the bars out, would be a difficult mode of egress because it was small.

Yet, seeing these things, The Thinking Machine was not discouraged. Instead, he thoughtfully squinted at the great arc light—there was bright sunlight now—and traced with his eyes the wire which led from it to the building. That electric wire, he reasoned, must come down the side of the building not a great distance from his cell. That might be worth knowing.

Cell 13 was on the same floor with the offices of the prison—that is, not in the basement, nor yet upstairs. There were only four steps up to the office floor, therefore the level of the floor must be only three or four feet above the ground. He couldn't see the ground directly beneath his window, but he could see it further out toward the wall. It would be an easy drop from the window. Well and good.

Then The Thinking Machine fell to remembering how he had come to the cell. First, there was the outside guard's booth, a part of the wall. There were two heavily barred gates there, both of steel. At this gate was one man always on guard. He admitted persons to the prison after much clanking of keys and locks, and let them out when ordered to do so. The warden's office was in the prison building, and in order to reach that official from the prison yard one had to pass a gate of solid steel with only a peep-hole in it. Then coming from that inner office to Cell 13, where he was now, one must pass a heavy wooden door and two steel doors into the corridors of the prison; and always there was the double-locked door of Cell 13 to reckon with.

There were then, The Thinking Machine recalled, seven doors to be overcome before one could pass from Cell 13 into the outer world, a free man. But against this was the fact that he was rarely interrupted. A jailer appeared at his cell door at six in the morning with a breakfast of prison fare; he would come again at noon, and again at six in the afternoon. At nine o'clock at night would come the inspection tour. That would be all.

"It's admirably arranged, this prison system," was the mental tribute paid by The Thinking Machine. "I'll have to study it a little when I get out. I had no idea there was such great care exercised in the prisons."

There was nothing, positively nothing, in his cell, except his iron bed, so firmly put together that no man could tear it to pieces save with sledges or a file. He had neither of these. There was not even a chair, or a small table, or a bit of tin or crockery. Nothing! The jailer stood by when he ate, then took away the wooden spoon and bowl which he had used.

One by one these things sank into the brain of The Thinking Machine. When the last possibility had been considered he began an examination of his cell. From the roof, down the walls on all sides, he examined the stones and the cement between them. He stamped over the floor carefully time after time, but it was cement, perfectly solid. After the examination he sat on the edge of the iron bed and was lost in thought for a long time. For Professor Augustus S. F. X. Van Dusen, The Thinking Machine, had something to think about.

He was disturbed by a rat, which ran across his foot, then scampered away into a dark corner of the cell, frightened at its own daring. After a while The Thinking Machine, squinting steadily into the darkness of the corner where the rat had gone, was able to make out in the gloom many little beady eyes staring at him. He counted six pair, and there were perhaps others; he didn't see very well.

Then The Thinking Machine, from his seat on the bed, noticed for the first time the bottom of his cell door. There was an opening there of two inches between the steel bar and the floor. Still looking steadily at this opening, The Thinking Machine backed suddenly into the corner where he had seen the beady eyes. There was a great scampering of tiny feet, several squeaks of frightened rodents, and then silence.

None of the rats had gone out the door, yet there were none in the cell. Therefore there must be another way out of the cell, however small. The Thinking Machine, on hands and knees, started a search for this spot, feeling in the darkness with his long, slender fingers.

At last his search was rewarded. He came upon a small opening in the floor, level with the cement. It was perfectly round and somewhat larger than a silver dollar. This was the way the rats had gone. He put his fingers deep into the opening; it seemed to be a disused drainage pipe and was dry and dusty.

Having satisfied himself on this point, he sat on the bed again for an hour, then made another inspection of his surroundings through the small cell window. One of the outside guards stood directly opposite, beside the wall, and happened to be looking at the window of Cell 13 when the head of The Thinking Machine appeared. But the scientist didn't notice the guard.

Noon came and the jailer appeared with the prison dinner of repulsively plain food. At home The Thinking Machine merely ate to live; here he took what was offered without comment. Occasionally he spoke to the jailer who stood outside the door watching him.

"Any improvements made here in the last few years?" he asked.

"Nothing particularly," replied the jailer. "New wall was built four years ago."

"Anything done to the prison proper?"

"Painted the woodwork outside, and I believe about seven years ago a new system of plumbing was put in."

"Ah!" said the prisoner. "How far is the river over there?"

"About three hundred feet. The boys have a baseball ground between the wall and the river."

The Thinking Machine had nothing further to say just then, but when the jailer was ready to go he asked for some water.

"I get very thirsty here," he explained. "Would it be possible for you to leave a little water in a bowl for me?"

"I'll ask the warden," replied the jailer, and he went away.

Half an hour later he returned with water in a small earthen bowl.

"The warden says you may keep this bowl," he informed the prisoner. "But you must show it to me when I ask for it. If it is broken, it will be the last."

"Thank you," said The Thinking Machine. "I shan't break it."

The jailer went on about his duties. For just the fraction of a second it seemed that The Thinking Machine wanted to ask a question, but he didn't.

Two hours later this same jailer, in passing the door of Cell No. 13, heard a noise inside and stopped. The Thinking Machine was down on his hands and knees in a corner of the cell, and from that same corner came several frightened squeaks. The jailer looked on interestedly.

"Ah, I've got you," he heard the prisoner say.

"Got what?" he asked, sharply.

"One of these rats," was the reply. "See?" And between the scientist's long fingers the jailer saw a small gray rat struggling. The prisoner brought it over to the light and looked at it closely. "It's a water rat," he said.

"Ain't you got anything better to do than to catch rats?" asked the jailer.

"It's disgraceful that they should be here at all," was the irritated reply. "Take this one away and kill it. There are dozens more where it came from."

The jailer took the wriggling, squirmy rodent and flung it down on the floor violently. It gave one squeak and lay still. Later he reported the incident to the warden, who only smiled.

Still later that afternoon the outside armed guard on Cell 13 side of the prison looked up again at the window and saw the prisoner looking out. He saw a hand raised to the barred window and then something white fluttered to the ground, directly under the window of Cell 13. It was a little roll of linen, evidently of white shirting material, and tied around it was a five-dollar bill. The guard looked up at the window again, but the face had disappeared.

With a grim smile he took the little linen roll and the five-dollar bill to the warden's office. There together they deciphered something which was written on it with a queer sort of ink, frequently blurred. On the outside was this:

"Finder of this please deliver to Dr. Charles Ransome."

"Ah," said the warden, with a chuckle. "Plan of escape number one has gone wrong." Then, as an afterthought: "But why did he address it to Dr. Ransome?"

"And where did he get the pen and ink to write with?" asked the guard.

The warden looked at the guard and the guard looked at the warden. There was no apparent solution of that mystery. The warden studied the writing carefully, then shook his head.

"Well, let's see what he was going to say to Dr. Ransome," he said at length, still puzzled, and he unrolled the inner piece of linen.

"Well, if that—what—what do you think of that?" he asked, dazed.

The guard took the bit of linen and read this:

"Epa cseot d'net niiy awe htto n'si sih.   T."

III

The warden spent an hour wondering what sort of a cipher it was, and half an hour wondering why his prisoner should attempt to communicate with Dr. Ransome, who was the cause of him being there. After this the warden devoted some thought to the question of where the prisoner got writing materials, and what sort of writing materials he had. With the idea of illuminating this point, he examined the linen again. It was a torn part of a white shirt and had ragged edges.

Now it was possible to account for the linen, but what the prisoner had used to write with was another matter. The warden knew it would have been impossible for him to have either pen or pencil, and, besides, neither pen nor pencil had been used in this writing. What, then? The warden decided to personally investigate. The Thinking Machine was his prisoner; he had orders to hold his prisoners; if this one sought to escape by sending cipher messages to persons outside, he would stop it, as he would have stopped it in the case of any other prisoner.

The warden went back to Cell 13 and found The Thinking Machine on his hands and knees on the floor, engaged in nothing more alarming than catching rats. The prisoner heard the warden's step and turned to him quickly.

"It's disgraceful," he snapped, "these rats. There are scores of them."

"Other men have been able to stand them," said the warden. "Here is another shirt for you—let me have the one you have on."

"Why?" demanded The Thinking Machine, quickly. His tone was hardly natural, his manner suggested actual perturbation.

"You have attempted to communicate with Dr. Ransome," said the warden severely. "As my prisoner, it is my duty to put a stop to it."

The Thinking Machine was silent for a moment.

"All right," he said, finally. "Do your duty."

The warden smiled grimly. The prisoner arose from the floor and removed the white shirt, putting on instead a striped convict shirt the warden had brought. The warden took the white shirt eagerly, and then and there compared the pieces of linen on which was written the cipher with certain torn places in the shirt. The Thinking Machine looked on curiously.

"The guard brought *you* those, then?" he asked.

"He certainly did," replied the warden triumphantly. "And that ends your first attempt to escape."

The Thinking Machine watched the warden as he, by comparison, established to his own satisfaction that only two pieces of linen had been torn from the white shirt.

"What did you write this with?" demanded the warden.

"I should think it a part of your duty to find out," said The Thinking Machine, irritably.

The warden started to say some harsh things, then restrained himself and made a minute search of the cell and of the prisoner instead. He found absolutely nothing; not even a match or toothpick which might have been used for a pen. The same mystery surrounded the fluid with which the cipher had been written. Although the warden left Cell 13 visibly annoyed, he took the torn shirt in triumph.

"Well, writing notes on a shirt won't get him out, that's certain," he told himself with some complacency. He put the linen scraps into his desk to await developments. "If that man escapes from that cell I'll—hang it—I'll resign."

On the third day of his incarceration The Thinking Machine openly attempted to bribe his way out. The jailer had brought his dinner and was leaning against the barred door, waiting, when The Thinking Machine began the conversation.

"The drainage pipes of the prison lead to the river, don't they?" he asked.

"Yes," said the jailer.

"I suppose they are very small?"

"Too small to crawl through, if that's what you're thinking about," was the grinning response.

There was silence until The Thinking Machine finished his meal. Then:

"You know I'm not a criminal, don't you?"

"Yes."

"And that I've a perfect right to be freed if I demand it?"

"Yes."

"Well, I came here believing that I could make my escape," said the prisoner, and his squint eyes studied the face of the jailer. "Would you consider a financial reward for aiding me to escape?"

The jailer, who happened to be an honest man, looked at the slender, weak figure of the prisoner, at the large head with its mass of yellow hair, and was almost sorry.

"I guess prisons like these were not built for the likes of you to get out of," he said, at last.

"But would you consider a proposition to help me get out?" the prisoner insisted, almost beseechingly.

"No," said the jailer, shortly.

"Five hundred dollars," urged The Thinking Machine. "I am not a criminal."

"No," said the jailer.

"A thousand?"

"No," again said the jailer, and he started away hurriedly to escape further temptation. Then he turned back. "If you should give me ten thousand dollars I couldn't get you out. You'd have to pass through seven doors, and I only have the keys to two."

Then he told the warden all about it.

"Plan number two fails," said the warden, smiling grimly. "First a cipher, then bribery."

When the jailer was on his way to Cell 13 at six o'clock, again bearing food to The Thinking Machine, he paused, startled by the unmistakable scrape, scrape of steel against steel. It stopped at the sound of his steps, then craftily the jailer, who was beyond the prisoner's range of vision, resumed his tramping, the sound being apparently that of a man going away from Cell 13. As a matter of fact he was in the same spot.

After a moment there came again the steady scrape, scrape, and the jailer crept cautiously on tiptoes to the door and peered between the bars. The Thinking Machine was standing on the iron bed working at the bars of the little window. He was using a file, judging from the backward and forward swing of his arms.

Cautiously the jailer crept back to the office, summoned the warden in person, and they returned to Cell 13 on tiptoes. The steady scrape was still audible. The warden listened to satisfy himself and then suddenly appeared at the door.

"Well?" he demanded, and there was a smile on his face.

The Thinking Machine glanced back from his perch on the bed and leaped suddenly to the floor, making frantic efforts to hide something. The warden went in, with hand extended.

"Give it up," he said.

"No," said the prisoner, sharply.

"Come, give it up," urged the warden. "I don't want to have to search you again."

"No," repeated the prisoner.

"What was it, a file?" asked the warden.

The Thinking Machine was silent and stood squinting at the warden with something very nearly approaching disappointment on his face—nearly, but not quite. The warden was almost sympathetic.

"Plan number three fails, eh?" he asked, good-naturedly. "Too bad, isn't it?"

The prisoner didn't say.

"Search him," instructed the warden.

The jailer searched the prisoner carefully. At last, artfully concealed in the waist band of the trousers, he found a piece of steel about two inches long, with one side curved like a half moon.

"Ah," said the warden, as he received it from the jailer. "From your shoe heel," and he smiled pleasantly.

The jailer continued his search and on the other side of the trousers waist band found another piece of steel identical with the first. The edges showed where they had been worn against the bars of the window.

"You couldn't saw a way through those bars with these," said the warden.

"I could have," said The Thinking Machine firmly.

"In six months, perhaps," said the warden, good-naturedly.

The warden shook his head slowly as he gazed into the slightly flushed face of his prisoner.

"Ready to give it up?" he asked.

"I haven't started yet," was the prompt reply.

Then came another exhaustive search of the cell. Carefully the two men went over it, finally turning out the bed and searching that. Nothing. The warden in person climbed upon the bed and examined the bars of the window where the prisoner had been sawing. When he looked he was amused.

"Just made it a little bright by hard rubbing," he said to the prisoner, who stood looking on with a somewhat crestfallen air. The warden grasped the iron bars in his strong hands and tried to shake them. They were immovable, set firmly in the solid granite. He examined each in turn and found them all satisfactory. Finally he climbed down from the bed.

"Give it up, professor," he advised.

The Thinking Machine shook his head and the warden and jailer passed on again. As they disappeared down the corridor The Thinking Machine sat on the edge of the bed with his head in his hands.

"He's crazy to try to get out of that cell," commented the jailer.

"Of course he can't get out," said the warden. "But he's clever. I would like to know what he wrote that cipher with."

———

It was four o'clock next morning when an awful, heart-racking shriek of terror resounded through the great prison. It came from a cell, somewhere about the center, and its tone told a tale of horror, agony, terrible fear. The warden heard and with three of his men rushed into the long corridor leading to Cell 13.

IV

As they ran there came again that awful cry. It died away in a sort of wail. The white faces of prisoners appeared at cell doors upstairs and down, staring out wonderingly, frightened.

"It's that fool in Cell 13," grumbled the warden.

He stopped and stared in as one of the jailers flashed a lantern. "That fool in Cell 13" lay comfortably on his cot, flat on his back with his mouth open, snoring. Even as they looked there came again the piercing cry, from somewhere above. The warden's face blanched a little as he started up the stairs. There on the top floor he found a man in Cell 43, directly above Cell 13, but two floors higher, cowering in a corner of his cell.

"What's the matter?" demanded the warden.

"Thank God you've come," exclaimed the prisoner, and he cast himself against the bars of his cell.

"What is it?" demanded the warden again.

He threw open the door and went in. The prisoner dropped on his knees and clasped the warden about the body. His face was white with terror, his eyes were widely distended, and he was shuddering. His hands, icy cold, clutched at the warden's.

"Take me out of this cell, please take me out," he pleaded.

"What's the matter with you, anyhow?" insisted the warden, impatiently.

"I heard something—something," said the prisoner, and his eyes roved nervously around the cell.

"What did you hear?"

"I—I can't tell you," stammered the prisoner. Then, in a sudden burst of terror: "Take me out of this cell—put me anywhere—but take me out of here."

The warden and the three jailers exchanged glances.

"Who is this fellow? What's he accused of?" asked the warden.

"Joseph Ballard," said one of the jailers. "He's accused of throwing acid in a woman's face. She died from it."

"But they can't prove it," gasped the prisoner. "They can't prove it. Please put me in some other cell."

He was still clinging to the warden, and that official threw his arms off roughly. Then for a time he stood looking at the cowering wretch, who seemed possessed of all the wild, unreasoning terror of a child.

"Look here, Ballard," said the warden, finally, "if you heard anything, I want to know what it was. Now tell me."

"I can't, I can't," was the reply. He was sobbing.

"Where did it come from?"

"I don't know. Everywhere—nowhere. I just heard it."

"What was it—a voice?"

"Please don't make me answer," pleaded the prisoner.

"You must answer," said the warden, sharply.

"It was a voice—but—but it wasn't human," was the sobbing reply.

"Voice, but not human?" repeated the warden, puzzled.

"It sounded muffled and—and far away—and ghostly," explained the man.

"Did it come from inside or outside the prison?"

"It didn't seem to come from anywhere—it was just here, here, everywhere. I heard it. I heard it."

For an hour the warden tried to get the story, but Ballard had become suddenly obstinate and would say nothing—only pleaded to be placed in another cell, or to have one of the jailers remain near him until daylight. These requests were gruffly refused.

"And see here," said the warden, in conclusion, "if there's any more of this screaming I'll put you in the padded cell."

Then the warden went his way, a sadly puzzled man. Ballard sat at his cell door until daylight, his face, drawn and white with terror, pressed against the bars, and looked out into the prison with wide, staring eyes.

That day, the fourth since the incarceration of The Thinking Machine, was enlivened considerably by the volunteer prisoner, who spent most of his time at the little window of his cell. He began proceedings by throwing another piece of linen down to the guard, who picked it up dutifully and took it to the warden. On it was written:

"Only three days more."

The warden was in no way surprised at what he read; he understood that The Thinking Machine meant only three days more of his imprisonment, and he regarded the note as a boast. But how was the thing written? Where had The Thinking Machine found this new piece of linen? Where? How? He carefully examined the linen. It was white, of fine texture, shirting material. He took the shirt which he had taken and carefully fitted the two original pieces of the linen to the torn places. This third piece was entirely superfluous; it didn't fit anywhere, and yet it was unmistakably the same goods.

"And where—where does he get anything to write with?" demanded the warden of the world at large.

Still later on the fourth day The Thinking Machine, through the window of his cell, spoke to the armed guard outside.

"What day of the month is it?" he asked.

"The fifteenth," was the answer.

The Thinking Machine made a mental astronomical calculation and satisfied himself that the moon would not rise until after nine o'clock that night. Then he asked another question:

"Who attends to those arc lights?"

"Man from the company."

"You have no electricians in the building?"

"No."

"I should think you could save money if you had your own man."

"None of my business," replied the guard.

The guard noticed The Thinking Machine at the cell window frequently during that day, but always the face seemed listless and there was a certain wistfulness in the squint eyes behind the glasses. After a while he accepted the presence of the leonine head as a matter of course. He had seen other prisoners do the same thing; it was the longing for the outside world.

That afternoon, just before the day guard was relieved, the head appeared at the window again, and The Thinking Machine's hand held something out between the bars. It fluttered to the ground and the guard picked it up. It was a five-dollar bill.

"That's for you," called the prisoner.

As usual, the guard took it to the warden. That gentleman looked at it suspiciously; he looked at everything that came from Cell 13 with suspicion.

"He said it was for me," explained the guard.

"It's a sort of a tip, I suppose," said the warden. "I see no particular reason why you shouldn't accept——"

Suddenly he stopped. He had remembered that The Thinking Machine had gone into Cell 13 with one five-dollar bill and two ten-dollar bills; twenty-five dollars in all. Now a five-dollar bill had been tied around the first pieces of linen that came from the cell. The warden still had it, and to convince himself he took it out and looked at it. It was five dollars; yet here was another five dollars, and The Thinking Machine had only had ten-dollar bills.

"Perhaps somebody changed one of the bills for him," he thought at last, with a sigh of relief.

But then and there he made up his mind. He would search Cell 13 as a cell was never before searched in this world. When a man could write at will, and change money, and do other wholly inexplicable things, there was something radically wrong with his prison. He planned to enter the cell at night—three o'clock would be an excellent time. The Thinking Machine must do all the weird things he did sometime. Night seemed the most reasonable.

Thus it happened that the warden stealthily descended upon Cell 13 that night at three o'clock. He paused at the door and listened. There was no sound save the steady, regular breathing of the prisoner. The keys unfastened the double locks with scarcely a clank, and the warden entered, locking the door behind him. Suddenly he flashed his dark-lantern in the face of the recumbent figure.

If the warden had planned to startle The Thinking Machine he was mistaken, for that individual merely opened his eyes quietly, reached for his glasses and inquired, in a most matter-of-fact tone:

"Who is it?"

It would be useless to describe the search that the warden made. It was minute. Not one inch of the cell or the bed was overlooked. He found the round hole in the floor, and with a flash of inspiration thrust his thick fingers into it. After a moment of fumbling there he drew up something and looked at it in the light of his lantern.

"Ugh!" he exclaimed.

The thing he had taken out was a rat—a dead rat. His inspiration fled as a mist before the sun. But he continued the search. The Thinking Machine, without a word, arose and kicked the rat out of the cell into the corridor.

The warden climbed on the bed and tried the steel bars in the tiny window. They were perfectly rigid; every bar of the door was the same.

Then the warden searched the prisoner's clothing, beginning at the shoes. Nothing hidden in them! Then the trousers waist band. Still nothing! Then the pockets of the trousers. From one side he drew out some paper money and examined it.

"Five one-dollar bills," he gasped.

"That's right," said the prisoner.

"But the—you had two tens and a five—what the—how do you do it?"

"That's my business," said The Thinking Machine.

"Did any of my men change this money for you—on your word of honor?"

The Thinking Machine paused just a fraction of a second.

"No," he said.

"Well, do you make it?" asked the warden. He was prepared to believe anything.

"That's my business," again said the prisoner.

The warden glared at the eminent scientist fiercely. He felt—he knew—that this man was making a fool of him, yet he didn't know how. If he were a real prisoner he would get the truth—but, then, perhaps, those inexplicable things which had happened would not have been brought before him so sharply. Neither of the men spoke for a long time, then suddenly the warden turned fiercely and left the cell, slamming the door behind him. He didn't dare to speak, then.

He glanced at the clock. It was ten minutes to four. He had hardly settled himself in bed when again came that heart-breaking shriek through the prison. With a few muttered words, which, while not elegant, were highly expressive, he relighted his lantern and rushed through the prison again to the cell on the upper floor.

Again Ballard was crushing himself against the steel door, shrieking, shrieking at the top of his voice. He stopped only when the warden flashed his lamp in the cell.

"Take me out, take me out," he screamed. "I did it, I did it, I killed her. Take it away."

"Take what away?" asked the warden.

"I threw the acid in her face—I did it—I confess. Take me out of here."

Ballard's condition was pitiable; it was only an act of mercy to let him out into the corridor. There he crouched in a corner, like an animal at bay, and clasped his hands to his ears. It took half an hour to calm him sufficiently for him to speak. Then he told incoherently what had happened. On the night before at four o'clock he had heard a voice—a sepulchral voice, muffled and wailing in tone.

"What did it say?" asked the warden, curiously.

"Acid—acid—acid!" gasped the prisoner. "It accused me. Acid! I threw the acid, and the woman died. Oh!" It was a long, shuddering wail of terror.

"Acid?" echoed the warden, puzzled. The case was beyond him.

"Acid. That's all I heard—that one word, repeated several times. There were other things, too, but I didn't hear them."

"That was last night, eh?" asked the warden. "What happened tonight—what frightened you just now?"

"It was the same thing," gasped the prisoner. "Acid—acid—acid!" He covered his face with his hands and sat shivering. "It was acid I used on her, but I didn't mean to kill her. I just heard the words. It was something accusing me—accusing me." He mumbled, and was silent.

"Did you hear anything else?"

"Yes—but I couldn't understand—only a little bit—just a word or two."

"Well, what was it?"

"I heard 'acid' three times, then I heard a long, moaning sound, then—then—I heard 'No. 8 hat.' I heard that twice."

"No. 8 hat," repeated the warden. "What the devil—No. 8 hat? Accusing voices of conscience have never talked about No. 8 hats, so far as I ever heard."

"He's insane," said one of the jailers, with an air of finality.

"I believe you," said the warden. "He must be. He probably heard something and got frightened. He's trembling now. No. 8 hat! What the——"

V

When the fifth day of The Thinking Machine's imprisonment rolled around, the warden was wearing a hunted look. He was anxious for the end of the thing. He could not help but feel that his distinguished prisoner had been amusing himself. And if this were so, The Thinking Machine had lost none of his sense of humor. For on this fifth day he flung down another linen note to the outside guard, bearing the words: "Only two days more." Also he flung down half a dollar.

Now the warden knew—he *knew*—that the man in Cell 13 didn't have any half dollars—he *couldn't* have any half dollars, no more than he could have pen and ink and linen, and yet he did have them. It was a condition, not a theory; that is one reason why the warden was wearing a hunted look.

That ghastly, uncanny thing, too, about "acid" and "No. 8 hat" clung to him tenaciously. They didn't mean anything, of course, merely the ravings of an insane murderer who had been driven by fear to confess his crime, still there were so many things that "didn't mean anything" happening in the prison now since The Thinking Machine was there.

On the sixth day the warden received a postal stating that Dr. Ransome and Mr. Fielding would be at Chisholm Prison on the following evening, Thursday, and in the event Professor Van Dusen had not yet escaped—and they presumed he had not because they had not heard from him—they would meet him there.

"In the event he had not yet escaped!" The warden smiled grimly. Escaped!

The Thinking Machine enlivened this day for the warden with three notes. They were on the usual linen and bore generally on the appointment at half-past eight o'clock Thursday night, which appointment the scientist had made at the time of his imprisonment.

On the afternoon of the seventh day the warden passed Cell 13 and glanced in. The Thinking Machine was lying on the iron bed, apparently sleeping lightly. The cell appeared precisely as it always did from a casual glance. The warden would swear that no man was going to leave it between that hour—it was then four o'clock—and half-past eight o'clock that evening.

On his way back past the cell the warden heard the steady breathing again, and coming close to the door looked in. He wouldn't have done so if The Thinking Machine had been looking, but now—well, it was different.

A ray of light came through the high window and fell on the face of the sleeping man. It occurred to the warden for the first time that his prisoner appeared haggard and weary. Just then The Thinking Machine stirred slightly and the warden hurried on up the corridor guiltily. That evening after six o'clock he saw the jailer.

"Everything all right in Cell 13?" he asked.

"Yes, sir," replied the jailer. "He didn't eat much, though."

It was with a feeling of having done his duty that the warden received Dr. Ransome and Mr. Fielding shortly after seven o'clock. He intended to show them the linen notes and lay before them the full story of his woes, which was a long one. But before this came to pass the guard from the river side of the prison yard entered the office.

"The arc light in my side of the yard won't light," he informed the warden.

"Confound it, that man's a hoodoo," thundered the official. "Everything has happened since he's been here."

The guard went back to his post in the darkness, and the warden 'phoned to the electric light company.

"This is Chisholm Prison," he said through the 'phone. "Send three or four men down here quick, to fix an arc light."

The reply was evidently satisfactory, for the warden hung up the receiver and passed out into the yard. While Dr. Ransome and Mr. Fielding sat waiting the guard at the outer gate came in with a special delivery letter. Dr. Ransome happened to notice the address, and, when the guard went out, looked at the letter more closely.

"By George!" he exclaimed.

"What is it?" asked Mr. Fielding.

Silently the doctor offered the letter. Mr. Fielding examined it closely.

"Coincidence," he said. "It must be."

It was nearly eight o'clock when the warden returned to his office. The electricians had arrived in a wagon, and were now at work. The warden pressed the buzz-button communicating with the man at the outer gate in the wall.

"How many electricians came in?" he asked, over the short 'phone. "Four? Three workmen in jumpers and overalls and the manager?

Frock coat and silk hat? All right. Be certain that only four go out. That's all."

He turned to Dr. Ransome and Mr. Fielding. "We have to be careful here—particularly," and there was broad sarcasm in his tone, "since we have scientists locked up."

The warden picked up the special delivery letter carelessly, and then began to open it.

"When I read this I want to tell you gentlemen something about how—— Great Caesar!" he ended, suddenly, as he glanced at the letter. He sat with mouth open, motionless, from astonishment.

"What is it?" asked Mr. Fielding.

"A special delivery letter from Cell 13," gasped the warden. "An invitation to supper."

"What?" and the two others arose, unanimously.

The warden sat dazed, staring at the letter for a moment, then called sharply to a guard outside in the corridor.

"Run down to Cell 13 and see if that man's in there."

The guard went as directed, while Dr. Ransome and Mr. Fielding examined the letter.

"It's Van Dusen's handwriting; there's no question of that," said Dr. Ransome. "I've seen too much of it."

Just then the buzz on the telephone from the outer gate sounded, and the warden, in a semi-trance, picked up the receiver.

"Hello! Two reporters, eh? Let 'em come in." He turned suddenly to the doctor and Mr. Fielding. "Why, the man *can't* be out. He must be in his cell."

Just at that moment the guard returned.

"He's still in his cell, sir," he reported. "I saw him. He's lying down."

"There, I told you so," said the warden, and he breathed freely again. "But how did he mail that letter?"

There was a rap on the steel door which led from the jail yard into the warden's office.

"It's the reporters," said the warden. "Let them in," he instructed the guard; then to the two other gentlemen: "Don't say anything about this before them, because I'd never hear the last of it."

The door opened, and the two men from the front gate entered.

"Good-evening, gentlemen," said one. That was Hutchinson Hatch; the warden knew him well.

"Well?" demanded the other, irritably. "I'm here."

That was The Thinking Machine.

He squinted belligerently at the warden, who sat with mouth agape. For the moment that official had nothing to say. Dr. Ransome and Mr. Fielding were amazed, but they didn't know what the warden knew. They were only amazed; he was paralyzed. Hutchinson Hatch, the reporter, took in the scene with greedy eyes.

"How—how—how did you do it?" gasped the warden, finally.

"Come back to the cell," said The Thinking Machine, in the irritated voice which his scientific associates knew so well.

The warden, still in a condition bordering on trance, led the way.

"Flash your light in there," directed The Thinking Machine.

The warden did so. There was nothing unusual in the appearance of the cell, and there—there on the bed lay the figure of The Thinking Machine. Certainly! There was the yellow hair! Again the warden looked at the man beside him and wondered at the strangeness of his own dreams.

With trembling hands he unlocked the cell door and The Thinking Machine passed inside.

"See here," he said.

He kicked at the steel bars in the bottom of the cell door and three of them were pushed out of place. A fourth broke off and rolled away in the corridor.

"And here, too," directed the erstwhile prisoner as he stood on the bed to reach the small window. He swept his hand across the opening and every bar came out.

"What's this in the bed?" demanded the warden, who was slowly recovering.

"A wig," was the reply. "Turn down the cover."

The warden did so. Beneath it lay a large coil of strong rope, thirty feet or more, a dagger, three files, ten feet of electric wire, a thin, powerful pair of steel pliers, a small tack hammer with its handle, and—and a Derringer pistol.

"How did you do it?" demanded the warden.

"You gentlemen have an engagement to supper with me at half-past nine o'clock," said The Thinking Machine. "Come on, or we shall be late."

"But how did you do it?" insisted the warden.

"Don't ever think you can hold any man who can use his brain," said The Thinking Machine. "Come on; we shall be late."

VI

It was an impatient supper party in the rooms of Professor Van Dusen and a somewhat silent one. The guests were Dr. Ransome, Albert Fielding, the warden, and Hutchinson Hatch, reporter. The meal was served to the minute, in accordance with Professor Van Dusen's instructions of one week before; Dr. Ransome found the artichokes delicious. At last the supper was finished and The Thinking Machine turned full on Dr. Ransome and squinted at him fiercely.

"Do you believe it now?" he demanded.

"I do," replied Dr. Ransome.

"Do you admit that it was a fair test?"

"I do."

With the others, particularly the warden, he was waiting anxiously for the explanation.

"Suppose you tell us how——" began Mr. Fielding.

"Yes, tell us how," said the warden.

The Thinking Machine readjusted his glasses, took a couple of preparatory squints at his audience, and began the story. He told it from the beginning logically; and no man ever talked to more interested listeners.

"My agreement was," he began, "to go into a cell, carrying nothing except what was necessary to wear, and to leave that cell within a week. I had never seen Chisholm Prison. When I went into the cell I asked for tooth powder, two ten- and one five-dollar bills, and also to have my shoes blacked. Even if these requests had been refused it would not have mattered seriously. But you agreed to them.

"I knew there would be nothing in the cell which you thought I might use to advantage. So when the warden locked the door on me I was apparently helpless, unless I could turn three seemingly innocent things to use. They were things which would have been permitted any prisoner under sentence of death, were they not, warden?"

"Tooth powder and polished shoes, yes, but not money," replied the warden.

"Anything is dangerous in the hands of a man who knows how to use it," went on The Thinking Machine. "I did nothing that first night but sleep and chase rats." He glared at the warden. "When the matter was broached I knew I could do nothing that night, so suggested next day. You gentlemen thought I wanted time to arrange an escape with outside assistance, but this was not true. I knew I could communicate with whom I pleased, when I pleased."

The warden stared at him a moment, then went on smoking solemnly.

"I was aroused next morning at six o'clock by the jailer with my breakfast," continued the scientist. "He told me dinner was at twelve and supper at six. Between these times, I gathered, I would be pretty much to myself. So immediately after breakfast I examined my outside surroundings from my cell window. One look told me it would be useless to try to scale the wall, even should I decide to leave my cell by the window, for my purpose was to leave not only the cell, but the prison. Of course, I could have gone over the wall, but it would have taken me longer to lay my plans that way. Therefore, for the moment, I dismissed all idea of that.

"From this first observation I knew the river was on that side of the prison, and that there was also a playground there. Subsequently these surmises were verified by a keeper. I knew then one important thing—that anyone might approach the prison wall from that side if necessary without attracting any particular attention. That was well to remember. I remembered it.

"But the outside thing which most attracted my attention was the feed wire to the arc light which ran within a few feet—probably three or four—of my cell window. I knew that would be valuable in the event I found it necessary to cut off that arc light."

"Oh, you shut it off tonight, then?" asked the warden.

"Having learned all I could from that window," resumed The Thinking Machine, without heeding the interruption, "I considered the idea of escaping through the prison proper. I recalled just how I had come into the cell, which I knew would be the only way. Seven doors lay between me and the outside. So, also for the time being, I gave up the idea of escaping that way. And I couldn't go through the solid granite walls of the cell."

The Thinking Machine paused for a moment and Dr. Ransome lighted a new cigar. For several minutes there was silence, then the scientific jail-breaker went on:

"While I was thinking about these things a rat ran across my foot. It suggested a new line of thought. There were at least half a dozen rats in the cell—I could see their beady eyes. Yet I had noticed none come under the cell door. I frightened them purposely and watched the cell door to see if they went out that way. They did not, but they were gone. Obviously they went another way. Another way meant another opening.

"I searched for this opening and found it. It was an old drain pipe, long unused and partly choked with dirt and dust. But this was the way the rats had come. They came from somewhere. Where? Drain pipes usually lead outside prison grounds. This one probably led to the river, or near it. The rats must therefore come from that direction. If they came a part of the way, I reasoned that they came all the way, because it was extremely unlikely that a solid iron or lead pipe would have any hole in it except at the exit.

"When the jailer came with my luncheon he told me two important things, although he didn't know it. One was that a new system of plumbing had been put in the prison seven years before; another that the river was only three hundred feet away. Then I knew positively that the pipe was a part of an old system; I knew, too, that it slanted generally toward the river. But did the pipe end in the water or on land?

"This was the next question to be decided. I decided it by catching several of the rats in the cell. My jailer was surprised to see me engaged in this work. I examined at least a dozen of them. They were perfectly dry; they had come through the pipe, and, most important of all, they were *not house rats, but field rats.* The other end of the pipe was on land, then, outside the prison walls. So far, so good.

"Then, I knew that if I worked freely from this point I must attract the warden's attention in another direction. You see, by telling the warden that I had come there to escape you made the test more severe, because I had to trick him by false scents."

The warden looked up with a sad expression in his eyes.

"The first thing was to make him think I was trying to communicate with you, Dr. Ransome. So I wrote a note on a piece of linen I tore from my shirt, addressed it to Dr. Ransome, tied a five-dollar bill around it and threw it out the window. I knew the guard would take it to the warden, but I rather hoped the warden would send it as addressed. Have you that first linen note, warden?"

The warden produced the cipher.

"What the deuce does it mean, anyhow?" he asked.

"Read it backward, beginning with the 'T' signature and disregard the division into words," instructed The Thinking Machine.

The warden did so.

"T-h-i-s, this," he spelled, studied it a moment, then read it off, grinning:

"This is not the way I intend to escape."

"Well, now what do you think o' that?" he demanded, still grinning.

"I knew that would attract your attention, just as it did," said The Thinking Machine, "and if you really found out what it was it would be a sort of gentle rebuke."

"What did you write it with?" asked Dr. Ransome, after he had examined the linen and passed it to Mr. Fielding.

"This," said the erstwhile prisoner, and he extended his foot. On it was the shoe he had worn in prison, though the polish was gone— scraped off clean. "The shoe blacking, moistened with water, was my ink; the metal tip of the shoe lace made a fairly good pen."

The warden looked up and suddenly burst into a laugh, half of relief, half of amusement.

"You're a wonder," he said, admiringly. "Go on."

"That precipitated a search of my cell by the warden, as I had intended," continued The Thinking Machine. "I was anxious to get the warden into the habit of searching my cell, so that finally, constantly finding nothing, he would get disgusted and quit. This at last happened, practically."

The warden blushed.

"He then took my white shirt away and gave me a prison shirt. He was satisfied that those two pieces of the shirt were all that was missing. But while he was searching my cell I had another piece of that same shirt, about nine inches square, rolled into a small ball in my mouth."

"Nine inches of that shirt?" demanded the warden. "Where did it come from?"

"The bosoms of all stiff white shirts are of triple thickness," was the explanation. "I tore out the inside thickness, leaving the bosom only two thicknesses. I knew you wouldn't see it. So much for that."

There was a little pause, and the warden looked from one to another of the men with a sheepish grin.

"Having disposed of the warden for the time being by giving him something else to think about, I took my first serious step toward freedom," said Professor Van Dusen. "I knew, within reason, that the pipe led somewhere to the playground outside; I knew a great many boys played there; I knew that rats came into my cell from out there. Could I communicate with someone outside with these things at hand?

"First was necessary, I saw, a long and fairly reliable thread, so—but here," he pulled up his trousers legs and showed that the tops of both stockings, of fine, strong lisle, were gone. "I unraveled those—after I got them started it wasn't difficult—and I had easily a quarter of a mile of thread that I could depend on.

"Then on half of my remaining linen I wrote, laboriously enough I assure you, a letter explaining my situation to this gentleman here," and he indicated Hutchinson Hatch. "I knew he would assist me—for the value of the newspaper story. I tied firmly to this linen letter a ten-dollar bill—there is no surer way of attracting the eye of anyone—and wrote on the linen: 'Finder of this deliver to Hutchinson Hatch, *Daily American,* who will give another ten dollars for the information.'

"The next thing was to get this note outside on that playground where a boy might find it. There were two ways, but I chose the best. I took one of the rats—I became adept in catching them—tied the linen and money firmly to one leg, fastened my lisle thread to another, and turned him loose in the drain pipe. I reasoned that the natural fright of the rodent would make him run until he was outside the pipe and then out on earth he would probably stop to gnaw off the linen and money.

"From the moment the rat disappeared into that dusty pipe I became anxious. I was taking so many chances. The rat might gnaw the string, of which I held one end; other rats might gnaw it; the rat might run out of the pipe and leave the linen and money where they would never be found; a thousand other things might have happened. So began some nervous hours, but the fact that the rat ran on until only a few feet of the string remained in my cell made me think he was outside the pipe. I had carefully instructed Mr. Hatch what to do in case the note reached him. The question was: Would it reach him?

"This done, I could only wait and make other plans in case this one failed. I openly attempted to bribe my jailer, and learned from him that he held the keys to only two of seven doors between me and freedom. Then I did something else to make the warden nervous. I took the steel supports out of the heels of my shoes and made a pretense of sawing the bars of my cell window. The warden raised a pretty row about that. He developed, too, the habit of shaking the bars of my cell window to see if they were solid. They were—then."

Again the warden grinned. He had ceased being astonished.

"With this one plan I had done all I could and could only wait to see what happened," the scientist went on. "I couldn't know whether my note had been delivered or even found, or whether the mouse had gnawed it up. And I didn't dare to draw back through the pipe that one slender thread which connected me with the outside.

"When I went to bed that night I didn't sleep, for fear there would come the slight signal twitch at the thread which was to tell me that Mr. Hatch had received the note. At half-past three o'clock, I judge, I felt this twitch, and no prisoner actually under sentence of death ever welcomed a thing more heartily."

The Thinking Machine stopped and turned to the reporter.

"You'd better explain just what you did," he said.

"The linen note was brought to me by a small boy who had been playing baseball," said Mr. Hatch. "I immediately saw a big story in it, so I gave the boy another ten dollars, and got several spools of silk, some twine, and a roll of light, pliable wire. The professor's note suggested that I have the finder of the note show me just where it was picked up, and told me to make my search from there, beginning at two o'clock in the morning. If I found the other end of the thread I was to twitch it gently three times, then a fourth.

"I began the search with a small bulb electric light. It was an hour and twenty minutes before I found the end of the drain pipe, half hidden in weeds. The pipe was very large there, say twelve inches across. Then I found the end of the lisle thread, twitched it as directed and immediately I got an answering twitch.

"Then I fastened the silk to this and Professor Van Dusen began to pull it into his cell. I nearly had heart disease for fear the string would break. To the end of the silk I fastened the twine, and when that had been pulled in I tied on the wire. Then that was drawn into the pipe and we had a substantial line, which rats couldn't gnaw, from the mouth of the drain into the cell."

The Thinking Machine raised his hand and Hatch stopped.

"All this was done in absolute silence," said the scientist. "But when the wire reached my hand I could have shouted. Then we tried another experiment, which Mr. Hatch was prepared for. I tested the pipe as a speaking tube. Neither of us could hear very clearly, but I dared not speak loud for fear of attracting attention in the prison. At last I made him understand what I wanted immediately. He seemed to have great difficulty in understanding when I asked for nitric acid, and I repeated the word 'acid' several times.

"Then I heard a shriek from a cell above me. I knew instantly that someone had overheard, and when I heard you coming, Mr. Warden, I feigned sleep. If you had entered my cell at that moment that whole plan of escape would have ended there. But you passed on. That was the nearest I ever came to being caught.

"Having established this improvised trolley it is easy to see how I got things in the cell and made them disappear at will. I merely dropped them back into the pipe. You, Mr. Warden, could not have reached the connecting wire with your fingers; they are too large. My fingers, you see, are longer and more slender. In addition I guarded the top of that pipe with a rat—you remember how."

"I remember," said the warden, with a grimace.

"I thought that if anyone were tempted to investigate that hole the rat would dampen his ardor. Mr. Hatch could not send me anything useful through the pipe until next night, although he did send me change for ten dollars as a test, so I proceeded with other parts of my plan. Then I evolved the method of escape, which I finally employed.

"In order to carry this out successfully it was necessary for the guard in the yard to get accustomed to seeing me at the cell window. I arranged this by dropping linen notes to him, boastful in tone, to make the warden believe, if possible, one of his assistants was communicating with the outside for me. I would stand at my window for hours gazing out, so the guard could see, and occasionally I spoke to him. In that way I learned that the prison had no electricians of its own, but was dependent upon the lighting company if anything should go wrong.

"That cleared the way to freedom perfectly. Early in the evening of the last day of my imprisonment, when it was dark, I planned to cut the feed wire which was only a few feet from my window, reaching it with an acid-tipped wire I had. That would make that side of the prison perfectly dark while the electricians were searching for the break. That would also bring Mr. Hatch into the prison yard.

"There was only one more thing to do before I actually began the work of setting myself free. This was to arrange final details with Mr. Hatch through our speaking tube. I did this within half an hour after the warden left my cell on the fourth night of my imprisonment. Mr. Hatch again had serious difficulty in understanding me, and I repeated the word 'acid' to him several times, and later the words: 'No. 8 hat'—that's my size—and these were the things which made a prisoner upstairs confess to murder, so one of the jailers told me next day. This prisoner heard our voices, confused of course, through the pipe, which also went to his cell. The cell directly over me was not occupied, hence no one else heard.

"Of course the actual work of cutting the steel bars out of the window and door was comparatively easy with nitric acid, which I got through the pipe in thin bottles, but it took time. Hour after hour on the fifth and sixth and seven days the guard below was looking at me as I worked on the bars of the window with the acid on a piece of wire. I used the tooth powder to prevent the acid spreading. I looked away abstractedly as I worked and each minute the acid cut deeper into the metal. I noticed that the jailers always tried the door by shaking the upper part, never the lower bars, therefore I cut the lower bars, leaving them hanging in place by thin strips of metal. But that was a bit of dare-deviltry. I could not have gone that way so easily."

The Thinking Machine sat silent for several minutes.

"I think that makes everything clear," he went on. "Whatever points I have not explained were merely to confuse the warden and jailers. These things in my bed I brought in to please Mr. Hatch, who wanted to improve the story. Of course, the wig was necessary in my plan. The special delivery letter I wrote and directed in my cell with Mr. Hatch's fountain pen, then sent it out to him and he mailed it. That's all, I think."

"But your actually leaving the prison grounds and then coming in through the outer gate to my office?" asked the warden.

"Perfectly simple," said the scientist. "I cut the electric light wire with acid, as I said, when the current was off. Therefore when the current was turned on the arc didn't light. I knew it would take some time to find out what was the matter and make repairs. When the guard went to report to you the yard was dark. I crept out the window—it was a tight fit, too—replaced the bars by standing on a narrow ledge and remained in a shadow until the force of electricians arrived. Mr. Hatch was one of them.

"When I saw him I spoke and he handed me a cap, a jumper, and overalls, which I put on within ten feet of you, Mr. Warden, while you were in the yard. Later Mr. Hatch called me, presumably as a workman, and together we went out the gate to get something out of the wagon. The gate guard let us pass out readily as two workmen who had just passed in. We changed our clothing and reappeared, asking to see you. We saw you. That's all."

There was silence for several minutes. Dr. Ransome was first to speak.

"Wonderful!" he exclaimed. "Perfectly amazing."

"How did Mr. Hatch happen to come with the electricians?" asked Mr. Fielding.

"His father is manager of the company," replied The Thinking Machine.

"But what if there had been no Mr. Hatch outside to help?"

"Every prisoner has one friend outside who would help him escape if he could."

"Suppose—just suppose—there had been no old plumbing system there?" asked the warden, curiously.

"There were two other ways out," said The Thinking Machine, enigmatically.

Ten minutes later the telephone bell rang. It was a request for the warden.

"Light all right, eh?" the warden asked, through the 'phone. "Good. Wire cut beside Cell 13? Yes, I know. One electrician too many? What's that? Two came out?"

The warden turned to the others with a puzzled expression.

"He only let in four electricians, he has let out two and says there are three left."

"I was the odd one," said The Thinking Machine.

"Oh," said the warden. "I see." Then through the 'phone: "Let the fifth man go. He's all right."

The Phantom Motor

Two dazzling white eyes bulged through the night as an automobile swept suddenly around a curve in the wide road and laid a smooth, glaring pathway ahead. Even at the distance the rhythmical crackling-chug informed Special Constable Baker that it was a gasoline car, and the headlong swoop of the unblinking lights toward him made him instantly aware of the fact that the speed ordinance of Yarborough County was being a little more than broken—it was being obliterated.

Now the County of Yarborough was a wide expanse of summer estates and superbly kept roads, level as a floor and offered distracting temptations to the dangerous pastime of speeding. But against this was the fact that the county was particular about its speed laws, so particular in fact that it had stationed half a hundred men upon its highways to abate the nuisance. Incidentally it had found that keeping record of the infractions of the law was an excellent source of income.

"Forty miles an hour if an inch," remarked Baker to himself.

He arose from a camp stool where he was wont to make himself comfortable from six o'clock until midnight on watch, picked up his lantern, turned up the light and stepped down to the edge of the road.

He always remained on watch at the same place—at one end of a long stretch which autoists had unanimously dubbed The Trap. The Trap was singularly tempting—a perfectly macadamized road bed lying between two tall stone walls with only enough of a sinuous twist in it to make each end invisible from the other. Another man, Special Constable Bowman, was stationed at the other end of The Trap and there was telephonic communication between the points, enabling the men to check each other and incidentally, if one failed to stop a car or get its number, the other would. That at least was the theory.

So now, with the utmost confidence, Baker waited beside the road. The approaching lights were only a couple of hundred yards away. At the proper instant he would raise his lantern, the car would stop, its occupants would protest and then the county would add a mite to its general fund for making the roads even better and tempting autoists still more. Or sometimes the cars didn't stop. In that event it was part of the special constables' duties to get the number as it flew past, and reference to the monthly automobile register would give the name of the owner. An extra fine was always imposed in such cases.

Without the slightest diminution of speed the car came hurtling on toward him and swung wide so as to take the straight path of The Trap at full speed. At the psychological instant Baker stepped out into the road and waved his lantern.

"Stop!" he commanded.

The crackling-chug came on, heedless of the cry. The auto was almost upon him before he leaped out of the road—a feat at which he was particularly expert—then it flashed by and plunged into The Trap. Baker was, at the instant, so busily engaged in getting out of the way that he couldn't read the number, but he was not disconcerted because he knew there was no escape from The Trap. On the one side a solid stone wall eight feet high marked the eastern boundary of the John Phelps Stocker country estate, and on the other side a stone fence nine feet high marked the western boundary of the Thomas Q. Rogers country estate. There was no turnout, no place, no possible way for an auto to get out of The Trap except at one of the two ends guarded by the special constables. So Baker, perfectly confident of results, seized the 'phone.

"Car coming through sixty miles an hour," he bawled. "It won't stop. I missed the number. Look out."

"All right," answered Special Constable Bowman.

For ten, fifteen, twenty minutes Baker waited expecting a call from Bowman at the other end. It didn't come and finally he picked up the 'phone again. No answer. He rang several times, battered the box and did some tricks with the receiver. Still no answer. Finally he began to feel worried. He remembered that at that same post one special constable had been badly hurt by a reckless chauffeur who refused to stop or turn his car when the officer stepped out into the road. In his mind's eye he saw Bowman now lying helpless, perhaps badly injured. If the car held the pace at which it passed him it would be certain death to whoever might be unlucky enough to get in its path.

With these thoughts running through his head and with genuine solicitude for Bowman, Baker at last walked on along the road of The Trap toward the other end. The feeble rays of the lantern showed the unbroken line of the cold, stone walls on each side. There was no shrubbery of any sort, only a narrow strip of grass close to the wall. The more Baker considered the matter the more anxious he became and he increased his pace a little. As he turned a gentle curve he saw a lantern in the distance coming slowly toward him. It was evidently being carried by some one who was looking carefully along each side of the road.

"Hello!" called Baker, when the lantern came within distance. "That you, Bowman?"

"Yes," came the hallooed response.

The lanterns moved on and met. Baker's solicitude for the other constable was quickly changed to curiosity.

"What're you looking for?" he asked.

"That auto," replied Bowman. "It didn't come through my end and I thought perhaps there had been an accident so I walked along looking for it. Haven't seen anything."

"Didn't come through your end?" repeated Baker in amazement. "Why it must have. It didn't come back my way and I haven't passed it so it must have gone through."

"Well, it didn't," declared Bowman conclusively. "I was on the lookout for it, too, standing beside the road. There hasn't been a car through my end in an hour."

Special Constable Baker raised his lantern until the rays fell full upon the face of Special Constable Bowman and for an instant they stared each at the other. Suspicion glowed from the keen, avaricious eyes of Baker.

"How much did they give you to let 'em by?" he asked.

"Give me?" exclaimed Bowman, in righteous indignation. "Give me nothing. I haven't seen a car."

A slight sneer curled the lips of Special Constable Baker.

"Of course that's all right to report at headquarters," he said, "but I happened to know that the auto came in here, that it didn't go back my way, that it couldn't get out except at the ends, therefore it went your way." He was silent for a moment. "And whatever you got, Jim, seems to me I ought to get half."

Then the worm—i.e., Bowman—turned. A polite curl appeared about his lips and was permitted to show through the grizzled mustache.

"I guess," he said deliberately, "you think because you do that, everybody else does. I haven't seen any autos."

"Don't I always give you half, Jim?" Baker demanded, almost pleadingly.

"Well I haven't seen any car and that's all there is to it. If it didn't go back your way there wasn't any car." There was a pause; Bowman was framing up something particularly unpleasant. "You're seeing things, that's what's the matter."

So was sown discord between two officers of the County of Yarborough. After a while they separated with mutual sneers and open derision and went back to their respective posts. Each was thoughtful in his own way. At five minutes of midnight when they went off duty Baker called Bowman on the 'phone again.

"I've been thinking this thing over, Jim, and I guess it would be just as well if we didn't report it or say anything about it when we go in," said Baker slowly. "It seems foolish and if we did say anything about it it would give the boys the laugh on us."

"Just as you say," responded Bowman.

Relations between Special Constable Baker and Special Constable Bowman were strained on the morrow. But they walked along side by side to their respective posts. Baker stopped at his end of The Trap; Bowman didn't even look around.

"You'd better keep your eyes open tonight, Jim," Baker called as a last word.

"I had 'em open last night," was the disgusted retort.

Seven, eight, nine o'clock passed. Two or three cars had gone through The Trap at moderate speed and one had been warned by

Baker. At a few minutes past nine he was staring down the road which led into The Trap when he saw something that brought him quickly to his feet. It was a pair of dazzling white eyes, far away. He recognized them—the mysterious car of the night before.

"I'll get it this time," he muttered grimly, between closed teeth.

Then when the onrushing car was a full two hundred yards away Baker planted himself in the middle of the road and began to swing the lantern. The auto seemed, if anything, to be traveling even faster than on the previous night. At a hundred yards Baker began to shout. Still the car didn't lessen speed, merely rushed on. Again at the psychological instant Baker jumped. The auto whisked by as the chauffeur gave it a dextrous twist to prevent running down the special constable.

Safely out of its way Baker turned and stared after it, trying to read the number. He could see there was a number because a white board swung from the tail axle, but he could not make out the figures. Dust and a swaying car conspired to defeat him. But he did see that there were four persons in the car dimly silhouetted against the light reflected from the road. It was useless, of course, to conjecture as to sex for even as he looked, the fast receding car swerved around the turn and was lost to sight.

Again he rushed to the telephone; Bowman responded promptly.

"That car's gone in again," Baker called. "Ninety miles an hour. Look out!"

"I'm looking," responded Bowman.

"Let me know what happens," Baker shouted.

With the receiver to his ear he stood for ten or fifteen minutes, then Bowman hallooed from the other end.

"Well?" Baker responded. "Get 'em?"

"No car passed through and there's none in sight," said Bowman.

"But it went in," insisted Baker.

"Well it didn't come out here," declared Bowman. "Walk along the road till I meet you and look out for it."

Then was repeated the search of the night before. When the two men met in the middle of The Trap their faces were blank—blank as the high stone walls which stared at them from each side.

"Nothing!" said Bowman.

"Nothing!" echoed Baker.

Special Constable Bowman perched his head on one side and scratched his grizzly chin.

"You're not trying to put up a job on me?" he inquired coldly. "You did see a car?"

"I certainly did," declared Baker, and a belligerent tone underlay his manner. "I certainly saw it, Jim, and if it didn't come out your end, why—why——"

He paused and glanced quickly behind him. The action inspired a sudden similar caution on Bowman's part.

"Maybe—maybe——" said Bowman after a minute, "maybe it's a—a spook auto?"

"Well it must be," mused Baker. "You know as well as I do that no car can get out of this trap except at the ends. That car came in here, it isn't here now, and it didn't go out your end. Now where is it?"

Bowman stared at him a minute, picked up his lantern, shook his head solemnly and wandered along the road back to his post. On his way he glanced around quickly, apprehensively three times—Baker did the same thing four times.

On the third night the phantom car appeared and disappeared precisely as it had done previously. Again Baker and Bowman met half way between posts and talked it over.

"I'll tell you what, Baker," said Bowman in conclusion, "maybe you're just imagining that you see a car. Maybe if I was at your end I couldn't see it."

Special Constable Baker was distinctly hurt at the insinuation.

"All right, Jim," he said at last, "if you think that way about it we'll swap posts tomorrow night. We won't have to say anything about it when we report."

"Now that's the talk," exclaimed Bowman with an air approaching enthusiasm. "I'll bet I don't see it."

On the following night Special Constable Bowman made himself comfortable on Special Constable Baker's camp-stool. And *he* saw the phantom auto. It came upon him with a rush and a crackling-chug of engine and then sped on leaving him nerveless. He called Baker over the wire and Baker watched half an hour for the phantom. It didn't appear.

Ultimately all things reach the newspapers. So with the story of the phantom auto. Hutchinson Hatch, reporter, smiled incredulously when his city editor laid aside an inevitable cigar and tersely stated the known facts. The known facts in this instance were meager almost to the disappearing point. They consisted merely of a corroborated statement that an automobile, solid and tangible enough to all appearances, rushed into The Trap each night and totally disappeared.

But there was enough of the bizarre about it to pique the curiosity, to make one wonder, so Hatch journeyed down to Yarborough County, an hour's ride from the city, met and talked to Baker and Bowman and then, in broad daylight strolled along The Trap twice. It was a leisurely, thorough investigation with the end in view of finding out how an automobile once inside might get out again without going out either end.

On the first trip through Hatch paid particular attention to the Thomas Q. Rogers side of the road. The wall, nine feet high, was an unbroken line of stone with not the slightest indication of a secret wagon-way through it anywhere. Secret wagon-way! Hatch smiled at the phrase. But when he reached the other end—Bowman's end—of The Trap he was perfectly convinced of one thing—that no automobile had left the hard, macadamized road to go over, under or through the Thomas Q. Rogers wall. Returning, still leisurely, he paid strict attention to the John Phelps Stocker side, and when he reached the other end—Baker's end—he was convinced of another thing—that no automobile had left the road to go over, under or through the John Phelps Stocker wall. The only opening of any sort was a narrow footpath, not more than sixteen inches wide.

Hatch saw no shrubbery along the road, nothing but a strip of scrupulously cared for grass, therefore the phantom auto could not be hidden any time, night or day. Hatch failed, too, to find any holes in the road so the automobile didn't go down through the earth. At this point he involuntarily glanced up at the blue sky above. Perhaps, he thought whimsically, the automobile was a strange sort of bird, or—or—and he stopped suddenly.

"By George!" he exclaimed. "I wonder if——"

And the remainder of the afternoon he spent systematically making inquiries. He went from house to house, the Stocker house, the Rogers house, both of which were at the time unoccupied, then to cottage, cabin, and hut in turn. But he didn't seem overladen with information when he joined Special Constable Baker at his end of The Trap that evening about seven o'clock.

Together they rehearsed the strange points of the mystery as the shadows grew about them until finally the darkness was so dense that

Baker's lantern was the only bright spot in sight. As the chill of the evening closed in a certain awed tone crept into their voices. Occasionally an auto bowled along and each time as it hove in sight Hatch glanced at Baker questioningly. And each time Baker shook his head. And each time, too, he called Bowman, in this manner accounting for every car that went into The Trap.

"It'll come all right," said Baker after a long silence, "and I'll know it the minute it rounds the curve coming toward us. I'd know its two lights in a thousand."

They sat still and smoked. After a while two dazzling white lights burst into view far down the road and Baker, in excitement, dropped his pipe.

"That's her," he declared. "Look at her coming!"

And Hatch did look at her coming. The speed of the mysterious car was such as to make one look. Like the eyes of a giant the two lights came on toward them, and Baker perfunctorily went through the motions of attempting to stop it. The car fairly whizzed past them and the rush of air which tugged at their coats was convincing enough proof of its solidity. Hatch strained his eyes to read the number as the auto flashed past. But it was hopeless. The tail of the car was lost in an eddying whirl of dust.

"She certainly does travel," commented Baker, softly.

"She does," Hatch assented.

Then, for the benefit of the newspaperman, Baker called Bowman on the wire.

"Car's coming again," he shouted. "Look out and let me know!"

Bowman, at his end, waited twenty minutes, then made the usual report—the car had not passed. Hutchinson Hatch was a calm, cold, dispassionate young man but now a queer, creepy sensation stole along his spinal column. He lighted a cigarette and pulled himself together with a jerk.

"There's one way to find out where it goes," he declared at last, emphatically, "and that's to place a man in the middle just beyond the bend of The Trap and let him wait and see. If the car goes up, down, or evaporates he'll see and can tell us."

Baker looked at him curiously.

"I'd hate to be the man in the middle," he declared. There was something of uneasiness in his manner.

"I rather think I would, too," responded Hatch.

On the following evening, consequent upon the appearance of the story of the phantom auto in Hatch's paper, there were twelve other reporters on hand. Most of them were openly, flagrantly skeptical; they even insinuated that no one had seen an auto. Hatch smiled wisely.

"Wait!" he advised with deep conviction.

So when the darkness fell that evening the newspapermen of a great city had entered into a conspiracy to capture the phantom auto. Thirteen of them, making a total of fifteen men with Baker and Bowman, were on hand and they agreed to a suggestion for all to take positions along the road of The Trap from Baker's post to Bowman's, watch for the auto, see what happened to it, and compare notes afterwards. So they scattered themselves along a few hundred feet apart and waited. That night the phantom auto didn't appear at all and twelve reporters jeered at Hutchinson Hatch and told him to light his pipe with the story. And next night when Hatch and Baker and Bowman alone were watching the phantom auto reappeared.

THE GAP IN THE TRAIL

Like a child with a troublesome problem, Hatch took the entire matter and laid it before Professor Augustus S. F. X. Van Dusen, the master brain. The Thinking Machine, with squint eyes turned steadily upward and long, slender fingers pressed tip to tip, listened to the end.

"Now I know of course that automobiles don't fly," Hatch burst out savagely in conclusion, "and if this one doesn't fly, there is no earthly way for it to get out of The Trap, as they call it. I went over the thing carefully—I even went so far as to examine the ground and the tops of the walls to see if a runway had been let down for the auto to go over."

The Thinking Machine squinted at him inquiringly.

"Are you sure you saw an automobile?" he demanded irritably.

"Certainly I saw it," blurted the reporter. "I not only saw it—I smelled it. Just to convince myself that it was real I tossed my cane in front of the thing and it smashed it to tooth-picks."

"Perhaps, then, if everything is as you say, the auto actually *does* fly," remarked the scientist.

The reporter stared into the calm, inscrutable face of The Thinking Machine, fearing first that he had not heard aright. Then he concluded that he had.

"You mean," he inquired eagerly, "that the phantom may be an auto-aeroplane affair, and that it actually does fly?"

"It's not at all impossible," commented the scientist.

"I had an idea something like that myself," Hatch explained, "and questioned every soul within a mile or so but I didn't get anything."

"The perfect stretch of road there might be the very place for some daring experimenter to get up sufficient speed to soar a short distance in a light machine," continued the scientist.

"Light machine?" Hatch repeated. "Did I tell you that this car had four people in it?"

"Four people!" exclaimed the scientist. "Dear me! Dear me! That makes it very different. Of course four people would be too great a lift for an——"

For ten minutes he sat silent, and tiny, cobwebby lines appeared in his dome-like brow. Then he arose and passed into the adjoining room. After a moment Hatch heard the telephone bell jingle. Five minutes later The Thinking Machine appeared, and scowled upon him unpleasantly.

"I suppose what you really want to learn is if the car is a—a material one, and to whom it belongs?" he queried.

"That's it," agreed the reporter, "and of course, why it does what it does, and how it gets out of The Trap."

"Do you happen to know a fast, long-distance bicycle rider?" demanded the scientist abruptly.

"A dozen of them," replied the reporter promptly. "I think I see the idea, but—"

"You haven't the faintest inkling of the idea," declared The Thinking Machine positively. "If you can arrange with a fast rider who can go a distance—it might be thirty, forty, fifty miles—we may end this little affair without difficulty."

Under these circumstances Professor Augustus S. F. X. Van Dusen, Ph. D., LL. D., F. R. S., M. D., etc., etc., scientist and logician, met the famous Jimmie Thalhauer, the world's champion long-distance bicyclist. He held every record from five miles up to and including six hours, had twice won the six-day race and was, altogether, a master in his field. He came in chewing a tooth-pick. There were introductions.

"You ride the bicycle?" inquired the crusty little scientist.

"Well, *some,*" confessed the champion modestly with a wink at Hatch.

"Can you keep up with an automobile for a distance of, say, thirty or forty miles?"

"I can keep up with anything that ain't got wings," was the response.

"Well, to tell you the truth," volunteered The Thinking Machine, "there is a growing belief that this particular automobile has wings. However, if you can keep up with it——"

"Ah, quit your kiddin'," said the champion, easily. "I can ride rings around anything on wheels. I'll start behind it and beat it where it's going."

The Thinking Machine examined the champion, Jimmie Thalhauer, as a curiosity. In the seclusion of his laboratory he had never had an opportunity of meeting just such another worldly young person.

"How fast *can* you ride, Mr. Thalhauer?" he asked at last.

"I'm ashamed to tell you," confided the champion in a hushed voice. "I can ride so fast that I scare myself." He paused a moment. "But it seems to me," he said, "if there's thirty or forty miles to do I ought to do it on a motor-cycle."

"Now that's just the point," explained The Thinking Machine. "A motor-cycle makes noise and if it could have been used we would have hired a fast automobile. This proposition briefly is: I want you to ride without lights behind an automobile which may also run without lights and find out where it goes. No occupant of the car must suspect that it is followed."

"Without lights?" repeated the champion. "Gee! Rubber shoe, eh?"

The Thinking Machine looked his bewilderment.

"Yes, that's it," Hatch answered for him.

"I guess it's good for a four-column head? Hunh?" inquired the champion. "Special pictures posed by the champion? Hunh?"

"Yes," Hatch replied.

" 'Tracked on a Bicycle' sounds good to me. Hunh?"

Hatch nodded.

So arrangements were concluded and then and there The Thinking Machine gave definite and conclusive instructions to the champion. While these apparently bore broadly on the problem in hand they conveyed absolutely no inkling of his plan to the reporter. At the end the champion arose to go.

"You're a most extraordinary young man, Mr. Thalhauer," commented The Thinking Machine, not without admiration for the sturdy, powerful figure.

And as Hatch accompanied the champion out the door and down the steps Jimmie smiled with easy grace.

"Nutty old guy, ain't he? Hunh?"

———

Night! Utter blackness, relieved only by a white, ribbon-like road which winds away mistily under a starless sky. Shadowy hedges line either side and occasionally a tree thrusts itself upward out of the sombreness. The murmur of human voices in the shadows, then the crackling-chug of an engine and an automobile moves slowly, without lights, into the road. There is the sudden clatter of an engine at high speed and the car rushes away.

From the hedge comes the faint rustle of leaves as of wind stirring, then a figure moves impalpably. A moment and it becomes a separate entity; a quick movement and the creak of a leather bicycle saddle. Silently the single figure, bent low over the handle bars, moves after the car with ever increasing momentum.

Then a long, desperate race. For mile after mile, mile after mile, the auto goes on. The silent cyclist has crept up almost to the rear axle and hangs there doggedly as a racer to his pace. On and on they rush together through the darkness, the chauffeur moving with a perfect knowledge of his road, the single rider behind clinging on grimly with set teeth. The powerful, piston-like legs move up and down to the beat of the engine.

At last, with dust-dry throat and stinging, aching eyes the cyclist feels the pace slacken and instantly he drops back out of sight. It is only by sound that he follows now. The car stops; the cyclist is lost in the shadows.

For two or three hours the auto stands deserted and silent. At last the voices are heard again, the car stirs, moves away and the cyclist drops in behind. Another race which leads off in another direction. Finally, from a knoll, the lights of a city are seen. Ten minutes elapse, the auto stops, the head lights flare up and more leisurely it proceeds on its way.

———

On the following evening The Thinking Machine and Hutchinson Hatch called upon Fielding Stanwood, president of the Fordyce National Bank. Mr. Stanwood looked at them with interrogative eyes.

"We called to inform you, Mr. Stanwood," explained The Thinking Machine, "that a box of securities, probably United States bonds, is missing from your bank."

"What?" exclaimed Mr. Stanwood, and his face paled. "Robbery?"

"I only know the bonds were taken out of the vault tonight by Joseph Marsh, your assistant cashier," said the scientist, "and that he, together with three other men, left the bank with the box and are now at—a place I can name."

Mr. Stanwood was staring at him in amazement.

"You know where they are?" he demanded.

"I said I did," replied the scientist, shortly.

"Then we must inform the police at once, and——"

"I don't know that there has been an actual crime," interrupted the scientist. "I do know that every night for a week these bonds have been taken out through the connivance of your watchman and in each instance have been returned, intact, before morning. They will be returned tonight. Therefore I would advise, if you act, not to do so until the four men return with the bonds."

It was a singular party which met in the private office of President Stanwood at the bank just after midnight. Marsh and three companions, formally under arrest, were present as were President Stanwood, The Thinking Machine and Hatch, besides detectives. Marsh had the bonds under his arms when he was taken. He talked freely when questioned.

"I will admit," he said without hesitating, "that I have acted beyond my rights in removing the bonds from the vault here, but there is no ground for prosecution. I am a responsible officer of this bank and have violated no trust. Nothing is missing, nothing is stolen. Every bond that went out of the bank is here."

"But why—why did you take the bonds?" demanded Mr. Stanwood.

Marsh shrugged his shoulders.

"It's what has been called a get-rich-quick scheme," said The Thinking Machine. "Mr. Hatch and I made some investigations today. Mr. Marsh and these other three are interested in a business venture which is ethically dishonest but which is within the law. They have sought backing for the scheme amounting to about a million dollars. Those four or five men of means with whom they have discussed the matter have called each night for a week at Marsh's country place. It was necessary to make them believe that there was already a million or so in the scheme, so these bonds were borrowed and represented to be owned by themselves. They were taken to and fro between the bank and his home in a kind of an automobile. This is really what happened, based on knowledge which Mr. Hatch has gathered and what I myself developed by the use of a little logic."

And his statement of the affair proved to be correct. Marsh and the others admitted the statement to be true. It was while The Thinking Machine was homeward bound that he explained the phantom auto affair to Hatch.

"The phantom auto as you call it," he said, "is the vehicle in which the bonds were moved about. The phantom idea came merely by chance. On the night the vehicle was first noticed it was rushing along—we'll say to reach Marsh's house in time for an appointment. A road map will show you that the most direct line from the bank to Marsh's was through The Trap. If an automobile should go half way through there, then out across the Stocker estate to the other road, the distance would be lessened by a good five miles. This saving at first was of course valuable, so the car in which they rushed into The Trap was merely taken across the Stocker estate to the road in front."

"But how?" demanded Hatch. "There's no road there."

"I learned by 'phone from Mr. Stocker that there is a narrow walk from a very narrow foot-gate in Stocker's wall on The Trap leading through the grounds to the other road. The phantom auto wasn't really an auto at all—it was merely two motor-cycles arranged with seats and a steering apparatus. The French Army has been experimenting with them. The motor-cycles are, of course, separate machines and as such it was easy to trundle them through a narrow gate and across to the other road. The seats are light; they can be carried under the arm."

"Oh!" exclaimed Hatch suddenly, then after a minute: "But what did Jimmie Thalhauer do for you?"

"He waited in the road at the other end of the foot-path from The Trap," the scientist explained. "When the auto was brought through and put together he followed it to Marsh's home and from there to the bank. The rest of it you and I worked out today. It's merely logic, Mr. Hatch, logic."

There was a pause.

"That Mr. Thalhauer is really a marvelous young man, Mr. Hatch, don't you think?"

The Mystery of the Grip of Death

I

Deep silence, then a long shuddering wail of terror, a stifled, strangling cry for help, the sound of a body falling, and again deep silence. A pause, and after a while the tramp, tramp of heavy shoes through a lower hall. A door slammed and a man staggered out into a deserted street, haggard, trembling and with lips hard set. He reeled down the street and turned the first corner, waving his trembling hands fantastically.

Another pause, and spears of light flashed through the black night from the second floor of a great six-story tenement in South Boston, then came the sound of stockinged feet hurrying along the hall. Half a dozen horror-stricken men and women gathered at the door of the room whence had come the cry, helplessly gazing into one another's eyes, waiting, waiting, listening.

Finally, from inside the room, they heard a faint whispering sound as of wind rustling through dead leaves, or the silken swish of skirts, or the gasp of a dying man. They listened with strained attention until the noise stopped.

At last one of the men rapped on the door lightly. There was no answer, no sound. Again he rapped, this time louder; then he beat his fists on the door and called out. Still a silence that was terrifying. Mute inquiry lay in the eyes of all.

"Break in the door," said someone at length, in an awed whisper.

"Send for the police," said another.

The police came. They smashed in the door, old and rotting from age, and two of them entered the dark room. One of them used his lantern and those who crowded the door heard an exclamation.

"He's dead!"

Peering curiously around the corner of the door the white-faced watchers in the hall saw a man, dressed for bed, lying still on the floor. Two chairs had been overturned; the bed clothing was disarranged. One of the policemen was bending over the body, making a hurried examination. He finally arose.

"Strangled to death with a rope—but no rope here," he explained to the other. "This is a case for a medical examiner and detectives."

"What's his name?" asked one of the policemen of a man who stood looking in curiously.

"Fred Boyd," was the reply.

"Have a roommate?"

"No."

The other policeman was fumbling about the table with his light. At last he turned and held up something in his hand.

"Look here," he said.

It was a new wedding ring. The bright gold glittered in the lantern light.

———

An hour later a man turned from a side street into the avenue where stood the big tenement house, and swung along in that direction. It was the man who had left the lower door soon after the cries were heard on the second floor. Then his face had been haggard, distorted; now it was calm. One might even trace a line of melancholy and regret there.

Around the street door of the tenement was gathered a crowd of half a hundred curious ones, half-clad and shivering in the chill of the night, all craning their necks to see into the hall over the broad shoulders of a policeman who barred the door.

From a score of windows the heads of other curious ones were thrust out; there was the hum of subdued conversation.

The stranger paused on the outskirts of the little knot and peered curiously into the hall, as others were doing. He saw nothing, and turned to a bystander.

"What is it?" he asked.

"Man murdered inside," was the short response.

"Murdered?" exclaimed the stranger. "Who was it?"

"Fellow named Fred Boyd."

A flash of horror passed over the stranger's face and he made an involuntary motion with his hand toward his heart. Then he steadied himself with an effort.

"How was he—he murdered?" he asked.

"Choked to death," said the other. "Somebody heard him yell for help a little while ago, and when a policeman came he smashed in the door and found him dead. The body was still warm."

The stranger's face was white as death now and his lips moved nervously. His hands, thrust deep into his pockets, were clenched until the nails cut the flesh.

"What time did it happen?" he said.

"The cop says about fifteen minutes to eleven," was the reply. "One of the tenants who lived on the second floor, where Boyd had a room, looked at his clock when he got up after he heard Boyd shout, so they know just when it was."

Uncontrollable terror glittered in the stranger's eyes, but none noted it. All were intently looking into the hall waiting for something.

"Medical Examiner Barry and Detective Mallory are up there now," volunteered the bystander. "The body will be coming out in a minute."

Then an awed whisper went around: "It's coming."

The stranger stood peering on as the others did.

"Do they know who did it?" he asked. His voice was tense, and he fiercely repressed a quaver in it.

"No," said his informant. "I heard, though, that a fellow had been up in Boyd's room tonight, and the man who had the next room heard them talking very loud. They had been playing cards."

"Did the man go out?" asked the stranger.

"Nobody saw him if he did," was the reply. "I guess, though, the police know who he was, and they're probably looking for him by this time. If they don't know, Mallory'll find him out all right."

"Great God!" exclaimed the stranger between his tightly compressed lips.

The other man turned and looked at him curiously.

"What's the matter?" he asked.

"Nothing, nothing," said the stranger, hurriedly. "Look, there it comes—that's all. It's awful, awful, awful."

The big policeman in the door stepped to one side, and men came out bearing a litter, on which lay a grim, grisly something that had been a man. It was covered with a sheet. Beside it were Detective Mallory and Medical Examiner Barry. The little knot of onlookers was silent in the presence of death.

The stranger looked, looked as if fascinated by the horrid thing which lay there, watched them put the litter into the police ambulance, heard the medical examiner give some instructions and then Detective Mallory re-entered the house. The wagon drove away.

Turning suddenly, the stranger strode quickly down the avenue to the first corner. There he turned away and was swallowed up in the darkness. After a moment, from a distance, came the sound of a man's footsteps, running.

II

Several newspapermen, among them Hutchinson Hatch, went over the scene of the crime with Detective Mallory. It was a square, corner room on the second floor. The furniture consisted only of a bed, a table, a wash stand, chairs; there was no carpet to cover the gaping cracks in the floor, no curtains on the two windows.

The building was old and poorly constructed. Here a part of the cornice was sagging and broken, there the walls were mouldy; the ceiling was blotched with smoke; over by the steam radiator rats had gnawed a hole big enough to put one's fist in; the single-stemmed gas jet was grimy with dirt.

Of the two windows one was in the back wall and one in the side. Hutchinson Hatch trailed around the room with Detective Mallory. He saw that the two windows were securely fastened down with a sliding catch over the middle of the lower sash; there were no broken panes so that one leaving by the window might have reached in and fastened it after him.

Mr. Mallory explored the closet, but found only the things that belong to a poor man: clothing, an old hat, a battered trunk. There was no opening, the walls were solid. Then Mr. Mallory went to the door that had been smashed in. It was the only door except that of the closet. There was no transom.

Mr. Mallory and the reporter looked at this door a long time. It had been fastened when the police came—barred with an iron rod from one side to the other—held in round, iron sockets, set in the door facing. Neither of the sockets was open at the top; the bar had to be pushed through one straight on across the door into the other.

Thus early in the investigation Hutchinson Hatch saw this problem. If the windows were fastened inside and the murderer could not have passed out that way; if the door was fastened inside with an iron bar in both sockets and the murderer could not have gone that way—What then?

Hatch thought instinctively of a certain scientist and logician of note. Professor Augustus S. F. X. Van Dusen, Ph. D., M. D., LL. D., etc., so-called The Thinking Machine, whom he had occasion to know well because of certain previous adventures in which the scientist had accomplished seemingly impossible things.

"And I think this would stump even him," Hatch said to himself with a grim smile.

Then he listened as Detective Mallory questioned the various tenants of the house. Briefly the detective brought out these facts:

A man, whose description the detective carefully noted, had called to see Boyd that evening about half-past eight o'clock. He had been there many times before. Four persons had seen him this evening in Boyd's room, but no one of these knew his name. Someone passing had seen Boyd playing cards with him.

Shortly after ten o'clock, when practically everyone in the house had gone to bed, a man and woman in the next room heard Boyd's voice and that of his caller raised suddenly as if in argument. This continued for five minutes or so, then it quieted down. Such things were common in the tenement and the man and woman dropped off to sleep, thinking nothing of it.

Some time later, evidently only a few minutes, they were awakened by that pitiful, terror-stricken cry which made them shudder. With others in the house who had been aroused they dressed hurriedly. It was then they heard heavy footsteps in the hall below and the street door opened with a bang.

Both were of the opinion not five minutes could have elapsed from the time they heard the cry until they stood outside the door where the man lay. They would have heard, they thought, anyone leave Boyd's room after they were awakened by the cry, yet there was no sound from there when they stood in the hall. Then they heard—what?

"It was a peculiar sound," the man explained. "It struck me first that it was the swish of a silk skirt. Then, of course, as no woman was in the room, it must have been the dying man breathing."

"Silk skirt! Woman! Woman! Wedding ring!" Hatch thought. Whose was it? How could a woman have escaped from the room when it seemed that it would have been impossible for a man to escape? The questionings concluded, Detective Mallory turned graciously to the representatives of the press who were waiting impatiently. It was after midnight, dangerously near the first edition time, and the reporters were anxious for the detective's comment.

He was about to begin when another reporter, one of Hatch's fellow workers, entered, called Hatch to one side and said something quickly. Hatch nodded his head and idly fingered a pack of playing cards he had taken from the table.

"Good," he said. "Go back to the office and write the story. I'll 'phone Mallory's statement and tell him that other thing. I want to do a little more work, but I'll be at the office by half-past two o'clock."

The reporter went out hurriedly.

"I suppose you boys want to know something about how all this happened?" the detective was saying. He lighted a cigar and spread his feet wide apart. "I'll tell you all I can—not all I know, mind you, because that wouldn't be wise, but how the murder happened, and you can put in the thrill and all that to suit yourself.

"About half-past eight o'clock tonight a man called here to see Boyd. He knew Boyd very well—was probably a friend of several years' standing—and had called here frequently. We have an accurate description of him. He was seen by several persons who knew him by sight, therefore we will be able to absolutely identify him when we arrest him.

"Now, those two men were together in this room for possibly two hours. They were playing cards. More than half the murders on record are committed in the heat of passion. These men quarreled over their game, probably 'pitch' or 'casino'———"

"It's a pinochle pack," said Hatch.

"Then the crime was committed," the detective went on, not heeding the interruption, "the unknown man was sitting here," and Mallory indicated an overturned chair to his right.

"He leaped like this," and the detective, with a full eye for dramatic effect, illustrated, "seized Boyd by the throat, there was a struggle, notice the other overturned chair—and the unknown man bore Boyd down gripping his throat. He choked him to death."

"I thought the dead man was undressed when he was found?" asked Hatch. "The bed, too," and he indicated its disordered condition.

"He was, but—but it must have happened as I said," said the detective. He didn't like reporters who asked embarrassing questions. "His victim dead, the murderer went out by that door," and he pointed dramatically.

"Through the keyhole, I suppose?" said Hatch, quietly. "That door was fastened inside as no mere mortal could fasten it after he left the room."

"It's an old burglar's trick to fasten a door after you leave the room," said the detective, loftily.

"How about the wedding ring?"

"Ah!" and the detective looked wise. "There's nothing to be said of that now." He saw suddenly that he had made one mistake and he felt his prestige slipping away. The reporters turned a flood of questions upon him: "How did it happen Boyd was undressed?" "Who put out the gas?" "How would a burglar replace an iron bar like that?" "Do you suspect a burglar?"

Mr. Mallory raised his hand. "I will say absolutely nothing else about the case."

"Let's see if we understand you," said Hatch, and there was a mocking smile on his lips. "The police theory briefly is this: A man came here, there was a quarrel, a struggle; Boyd was killed, choked; then the murderer left this room by that door, possibly through the keyhole or a convenient crack. Then, being dead, Boyd got up, took off his clothes, turned out the gas, lay down on the floor, screamed for help, and died again. Is that right?"

"Bah!" thundered Mr. Mallory, on the verge of apoplexy. "Perhaps," he added scornfully, "you know more about it than I do."

"Well, yes, I'll confess that," said Hatch. "I know at least the name of the man who was here tonight, and these other reporters will know it when their outside men come in."

"You do, eh," demanded Mr. Mallory. "Who is it?"

"His name is Frank Cunningham, a watchmaker of No. 213 —— Street."

"Then he is Boyd's murderer," Mr. Mallory declared. "We'll have him under arrest in an hour."

"He has disappeared," said Hatch, and he left the room.

III

From the South Boston tenement house Hutchinson Hatch went to the undertaking establishment where the body of Fred Boyd lay, made a careful examination of the mark which showed that he had been throttled, and then went in a cab to the home of Professor Van Dusen, The Thinking Machine. As he drove up he noticed a bright light in the professor's laboratory. It was just fifteen minutes past one o'clock when he ascended the steps.

The Thinking Machine in person answered the door bell, the leonine head with its shock of yellow hair, the clean-shaven face, and the perpetually squinted eyes behind thick glasses standing out boldly and grotesquely in the light from a nearby arc.

"Who is it?" asked The Thinking Machine.

"Hutchinson Hatch," said the reporter. "I saw your light and I was particularly anxious for a little advice, so I thought——"

"Come in," said the scientist, and he extended his long, slender fingers cordially.

Hatch followed the thin, bowed figure of the scientist, which seemed that of a child, into the laboratory where he was motioned to a seat. Then Hatch told the story of the crime, so far as it was known, while the professor sat squinting steadily at him, his long, tapered fingers pressed together.

"Did you see the man?" asked The Thinking Machine.

"Yes."

"What kind of marks, exactly, were those on his neck?"

"They seemed to be such marks as would be made by a large rope drawn about the throat."

"Was the skin broken?"

"No, but whoever strangled him must have had tremendous

strength," said the reporter. "The pressure seemed to have been all around."

The Thinking Machine sat silent for several minutes.

"Door fastened inside with iron bar," he mused, "and no transom, so the bar was not placed back in position. Both windows fastened inside."

"It would have been absolutely impossible for any person to leave that room after Boyd was dead," said the reporter, emphatically.

"Nothing is impossible, Mr. Hatch," said The Thinking Machine, testily. "I thought I had demonstrated that clearly, once. The worst anything can be is extremely difficult—not impossible."

Hatch bowed gravely. He had walked over one of The Thinking Machine's pet hobbies.

"Man was undressed," went on The Thinking Machine. "Bed disordered, chairs overturned, gas out." He paused a moment, then asked: "You reason that the man must have gone to bed after putting out the light, and that his murderer came upon him unawares?"

"That seems to be the only possible thing to imagine," said Hatch.

"And in that case the other man—Cunningham—would not have been there?"

"Precisely."

"What sort of a wedding ring was it?"

"Perfectly new. It didn't seem to have ever been worn."

The Thinking Machine arose from his seat and took down a heavy volume, one of hundreds which lined his walls.

"You don't believe it probable that Cunningham left the room while angry and returned after Boyd was asleep and killed him?" asked The Thinking Machine as he fingered the leaves.

"He couldn't have come back if that door was fastened," said Hatch, doggedly.

"He *could* have, of course," said The Thinking Machine, "but it is hardly probable. Do you think it reasonable to suppose then that someone hidden in the closet waited until Cunningham was gone and then killed Boyd?"

"That sounds more plausible," said Hatch, after a moment's consideration. "But he couldn't have gone out of that room and fastened the door or window behind him."

"Of course he could have," said The Thinking Machine, irritably. "Don't keep saying he couldn't have done anything. It annoys me exceedingly."

Properly rebuked Hatch sat silent while The Thinking Machine sought something in the book.

"In the event, of course, that somebody was hidden in the room it would make it a premeditated murder, wouldn't it?" asked the scientist.

"Yes, unquestionably," replied the reporter.

"Here is something," said The Thinking Machine, as he squinted into the volume he held. "It is logic reduced to figures. Criminologists agree, practically, that thirty and one-third per cent of all premeditated crimes are committed because of money, directly or indirectly; that two per cent are committed because of insanity; and that the others, sixty-seven and two-thirds per cent, are committed because of women."

Hatch nodded.

"We'll shut out for the time being the matter of insanity—it is only a remote chance; money would hardly enter into the case because of the fact that both men were poor. Therefore, there remains a woman. The wedding ring found in the room also indicates a woman, though in what connection is not clear.

"Now, Mr. Hatch," he continued, glaring at the reporter almost fiercely, "find out all you can about the private life of this man Boyd—it will probably be like every other man of his class—and particularly his love affairs; find out also all you can about Cunningham and his love affairs. If the name of any woman appears in the case at all, find out all about her—and her love affairs. You understand?"

"Yes," was the reply.

"Don't delude yourself with the thought that it was impossible for anyone to leave that room after Boyd was dead," went on the scientist, with the stubborn persistence of a child. "Suppose this—I don't offer it as a solution—suppose that Boyd had been engaged to be married, that someone else loved the girl he was to marry, that that someone else had hidden in his room until Cunningham went away, then—you see?"

"By George!" exclaimed the reporter. "I never thought of that. But how did he get out?" he added helplessly.

"If a man did do such a thing he would have made every arrangement to leave that room in a manner calculated to puzzle anyone who came after. Mind, I don't say this is what happened at all—I merely suggest it as a possibility until I find more to work on."

Hatch arose, stretched his long legs and thanked The Thinking Machine as he pulled on his gloves.

"I'm sorry I could not have been of any more direct assistance," said the scientist. "When you do these things I ask come back to see me—I may be able to help you then. You see I'm at a tremendous disadvantage in not having seen the place where Boyd was killed. There is one thing, though, which I particularly would like for you to find out for me now—tonight."

"What is it?" asked Hatch.

"This tenement is an old building, I understand. I should like to know if the occupants have ever been annoyed by rats and mice, and if they are so annoyed now?"

"I don't quite see——" began the reporter in surprise.

"Of course not," said The Thinking Machine petulantly. "But I should like to know just the same."

"I'll find out for you."

Hutchinson Hatch had still nearly an hour, and he drove to the tenement in South Boston, to wake up its occupants and ask them— of all the silly questions in the world—"Are you annoyed by mice?" He set his teeth grimly and smiled.

When he reached the tenement he went straight on to the second floor. The steps ended within a few feet of the door where the crime had been committed. Hatch looked at the door curiously; the police had gone, the room was silent again, hiding its own mystery.

As he stood there he heard something which startled him. It came from the room where Boyd had been found dead. There was no question of that. It was a faint whispering sound as of wind rustling through dead leaves, or the silken swish of skirts, or the gasp of a dying man.

With blood tingling, Hatch rushed to the door and threw it open. He stepped inside, lighting a match as he did so. The room was empty save for the poor furniture. No sign of a living thing!

IV

Straining his ears to catch every sound, Hatch stood still, peering this way and that until the match burned his fingers. Then he lighted another and still another, but there was no repetition of the noise. At last the ghostly quiet of the room, its gloom and thoughts of the mystery which its walls had witnessed began to press on his nerves. He laughed shortly.

"A very pronounced case of enlargement of the imagination," he said to himself, and he passed out. "This thing is getting on my nerves."

Then, feeling very foolish, he aroused several persons and inquired solicitously as to whether or not they had ever been troubled with mice or rats, and when this annoyance had stopped, if it had stopped.

The consensus of opinion was that it was a silly thing to ask, but that up to a fortnight ago the rodents had been very bad. Since then no one had noticed particularly. These things, insofar as they related to rodents of any kind, were telephoned to The Thinking Machine.

"Uh, huh," he said over the 'phone. "Thanks. Good night."

From that point on every effort of the police and the press was directed to finding Frank Cunningham, who was openly charged with the murder of Fred Boyd. His disappearance had been complete. If there had been any doubt whatsoever of his guilt, this was convincing—to the police.

It was Hatch's personal efforts that uncovered the fact that Cunningham had had a bank account of $287 in a small institution, that on the morning following the mysterious crime in the South Boston tenement a check to "cash" had been presented for the full sum, and that check had been honored. This began to look conclusive.

It was also due to Hatch's personal efforts that the police learned Cunningham was to have been married a week after his disappearance to Caroline Pierce, a working girl of the West End. Then Hatch discovered that Caroline Pierce had also disappeared; that she went away presumably to work on the morning after the murder of Boyd. Where had she gone? No one knew, not even Miss Jerrod, the girl who, with her, occupied a suite of three rooms in the West End. Why had she gone? No one knew that. When had she gone? Still no one knew. When would she return? Again the same answer.

To the reporter there seemed only one plausible explanation. This was that Cunningham had drawn his money from the bank—which he had saved to make a little home for the girl he loved—and they had gone away together. In the natural course of his duty Hatch printed this, and it came to the eyes of the police. Detective Mallory smiled.

But the wedding ring in Boyd's room?

There was no explanation of that. Boyd had had no love affair so far as anyone knew. He had been a hard-working, steady-going man in his trade—electrician employed by a telephone company—and he and Cunningham had been friends since boyhood.

All these things, while interesting in themselves, still threw no light on the actual crime. Who killed Boyd, and why? How did the murderer get away? Hatch had put the question to himself time and again. There was no answer. Thus the intangible pall of mystery which lay over the happenings in the South Boston tenement was still impenetrable.

On the second day after the crime Hatch again consulted The Thinking Machine. The scientist listened patiently and carefully, but without any enthusiastic interest to the reporter's recital of what he had discovered.

"Have you a man watching the place where the girl lives?" he asked.

"No," Hatch replied. "I think she's gone for good."

"I don't think so," said The Thinking Machine. "I should send a man there to see if she returns."

"If you think best," said Hatch. "But don't you think now this man Cunningham must have been the criminal?"

The scientist squinted at the reporter a long time, seemingly having heard nothing of the question.

"It looks that way to me," Hatch went on, hesitatingly. "But frankly, I can't imagine a way that he might have left that room after Boyd was dead."

Still the scientist was silent, and the reporter nervously fingered his hat.

"That information you gave me about the rats was very interesting," said The Thinking Machine at last, irrelevantly.

"Perhaps, but I don't see how it applies."

"Looking out the windows of the room where Boyd was found, what did you see?" the scientist interrupted.

Hatch did not recall that he had ever looked out either of the windows; he had merely satisfied himself that neither had been used as a means of exit. Now he blushed guiltily.

"I'm afraid you haven't looked," said The Thinking Machine, testily.

"I thought probably you wouldn't have. Suppose we go to South Boston this afternoon and see that room."

"If you only would," said Hatch, delightedly. Here was better luck than he dreamed of. "If you only would," he repeated.

"We'll go now," said The Thinking Machine. He left the room and returned a moment later dressed for the street. The slender, bent figure and the great head seemed more grotesque than ever.

"Before we go," he instructed, "telephone to your office and have a reliable man sent to watch the girl's house. Tell him under no circumstances to try to enter or speak with anyone there until he hears from us."

The Thinking Machine stood waiting impatiently while Hatch did this. Then they took a cab to the tenement in South Boston.

"Dear me, what an old, ramshackle affair it is!" commented the scientist as they climbed the stairs.

The door of Boyd's room was not locked. The furniture and the personal effects of the man had been moved out—taken in charge by the medical examiner for possible use at an inquest.

"Just how was this room fastened when Boyd was found?" asked the scientist.

Hatch showed him, at the door and windows. The Thinking Machine was interested for a moment and then looked out the side window. Straight down fifteen feet was a wilderness of ash barrels and boxes and papers—a typical refuse heap of a cheap tenement. Then The Thinking Machine squinted out the back window. There he saw an open space, a rough baseball diamond, intersected at two places by the trampled down rings of a circus.

Perfunctorily he peered into the closet, after which his eyes swept the room in one comprehensive squint. He noted the begrimed condition of the place; the drooping cornice, the smoky ceiling, the gaping cracks in the floor, the rat holes beside the radiator, the dirty gas pipe leading down to a single jet. He leaned against a wall and wrote for several minutes on a sheet of paper torn from his notebook.

"Have you an envelope?" he asked.

Hatch produced one. The Thinking Machine put what he had written into the envelope, sealed it and handed it back.

"There's something that may interest you some time," he said, "but don't open it until I give you permission to do so."

"Certainly not," said the reporter, puzzled but without question. "But may I ask——"

"What it is?" snapped the scientist. "No, I will tell you when to open it."

They descended the stairs together.

"Somewhere to a public telephone," were The Thinking Machine's instructions to the cabby. At a nearby drugstore, he disappeared into a telephone booth and remained for five minutes. When he came out he asked for the envelope he had given Hatch and in a little crabbed hand wrote on it:

"November 9–10."

"Keep it," he commanded, as he returned it to the reporter. "Now we'll drive to the girl's place."

When the cab reached the West End address it was a little later than dusk. Caroline Pierce and her girl chum occupied a front apartment on the ground floor. As The Thinking Machine and Hatch were about to enter the building, Tom Manning, another reporter on Hatch's paper, approached them.

"The girl hasn't returned," he reported. "The other girl—Miss Jerrod—came back home from work just a few minutes ago."

"We'll see her," said The Thinking Machine. Then to Manning: "At the end of two minutes, by your watch, after I enter this apartment, ring the bell several times. Don't be afraid. Ring it! If any person runs out, man or woman, hold him. Mr. Hatch, you go to the back entrance of this apartment. Stop any person, man or woman, coming from this suite."

"You believe then——" Hatch began.

"I'll give you two minutes to get to the back door," snapped The Thinking Machine.

Hatch disappeared hurriedly, and for just two minutes, not a second more, The Thinking Machine waited. Then he rang the bell of the apartment. Miss Jerrod appeared at the door. He followed her into the suite.

Manning at the front door waited, watch in hand. When the two minutes were up he rang the bell time after time, long, insistent rings. He could hear it tinkling furiously. Then he heard something else. It was the slamming of a door, a rush of feet and a struggle. Then The Thinking Machine appeared before him.

"Come in," he said, modestly. "We have Cunningham inside."

V

A little drama of human emotion was being enacted in the tiny front suite. Frank Cunningham, wanted for the murder of Fred Boyd, sat wearily resigned in the corner furthest from the door under the watchful eye of Hutchinson Hatch. The man was unshaven, haggard, and there lay in his eyes the restless, feverish look of one who lives his life in terror of the law. Caroline Pierce, who was to have been his wife, had flung herself on a couch, weeping hysterically.

Towering above the slender, shrinking figure of The Thinking Machine, Miss Jerrod was bitterly denouncing him for a trick which had given Cunningham into his hands. The scientist listened patiently, albeit unhappily. He couldn't help himself.

"You told me," stormed Miss Jerrod, "that you believed him innocent, and now this—this."

"Well?" said The Thinking Machine meekly.

Miss Jerrod was about to say something else when Cunningham stopped her with a gesture.

"I'm rather glad of it," he said, "or rather I would be if it were not for her," and he indicated Caroline Pierce. "I have never spent such hours of mortal fear as those since the murder of Fred Boyd. Now, somehow, it's a relief to know it must all come out."

"You know you were a fool to try to hide, anyway," said The Thinking Machine, frankly.

"I know I made a mistake—now," replied Cunningham. "But we were afraid—Caroline and I—and I couldn't help it."

"Well, go on with your story," commanded the scientist testily.

Manning, the other reporter, crossed the room and sat beside Hatch, while Cunningham moved over, took a seat beside the couch where the girl lay weeping and gently stroked her hair.

"I'll tell what story I can," he said at last. "I don't know what you'll think of it, but——"

"Pardon me just a moment," said The Thinking Machine. He went to Cunningham and ran his long, slender fingers over the prisoner's head several times. Suddenly he leaned forward and squinted at Cunningham's head.

"What is this?" he asked.

"That is where a silver plate was put in," Cunningham replied. "I was badly injured by a fall when I was about fourteen years old."

"Yes, yes," said the scientist. "Go on with your story."

"I have known Boyd since we were boys together up in Vermont," Cunningham began, "and there, too, I knew Caroline. All three of us came from the same little town—Caroline only two years ago. Boyd and I had been in Boston for seven years when she came. Boyd lived for five years in that—that room in South Boston, where———"

"Never mind," said The Thinking Machine. "Go on."

"Well, Caroline came here two years ago as I said and I believe that Boyd loved her as well as I do," said Cunningham. "But she promised to be my wife and we were to be married next Wednesday———"

"But the night Boyd was killed," interrupted The Thinking Machine impatiently. "Come down to that."

"I went to Boyd's room that night at a few minutes after eight o'clock. We sat for an hour or more and talked of our work, our plans and various things as we played cards—pinochle it was. Neither of us was particularly interested in the game.

"Boyd didn't know of my coming marriage to Caroline and finally I happened to mention her name. I also showed him the wedding ring I had bought that day for her. He looked at it, and asked me what I intended to do with it. I then told him that Caroline and I were to be married.

"He was surprised. I think any man in his position would have been surprised, because I think it was his intention to ask her to marry him. Well, at any rate, he grew angry about it, and I tried to placate him.

"I guess he was pretty hard hit—worse than I thought—for several times between the deals he picked up the ring and looked at it, then he'd put it down each time on his side of the table.

"After a while he threw down his hand with the remark that he didn't care to play. 'Now look here, Fred,' I said, 'I didn't think of the thing hitting you so hard.' He replied something about it not being fair to him, though just what he meant I didn't know.

"Then word led to word, until finally I was in a fury at a careless reference he made to Caroline—a thing he would never have thought of doing in his proper senses—and I demanded an apology. He grew ugly and said still more, and then, somehow, I don't know quite what happened. I know that I had an insane desire to take hold of him—but—"

Cunningham paused and gently stroked the hand of the girl.

"And then?" asked The Thinking Machine.

"You know this hurt on my head was more serious than you may imagine," said Cunningham. "There are times, in moments of anger particularly, when things are not clear to me. I lose myself, I don't know what to do. A surgeon once explained to me why it was but I don't remember."

"I understand," said The Thinking Machine. "Go on."

"Well, from the moment the quarrel became really serious I would not swear to anything that happened," Cunningham resumed. "I know at last I found myself in the lower hall after what seemed a long time, and I remember leaving there, slamming the door behind me.

"I went down the avenue and was almost home when it occurred to me that the ring was in Boyd's room. By that time, too, I was seeing things more clearly. I wanted to go back and talk to Boyd more calmly and see if both of us hadn't said things we should not have said. It was with this double purpose of seeing him and getting the ring that I started back to the tenement.

"Outside, I found a crowd. I wondered why, and asked. One man told me Boyd had been murdered—choked to death; that the police knew who did it and were searching for him. I was terror-stricken, and after the body was taken out I walked away. The terror was on me, and after I turned into a side street I broke into a run. I knew myself, you see, and my own irresponsibility.

"Then, although it was midnight, I came straight here, aroused Caroline and Miss Jerrod and told them both what had happened so far as I knew. There seemed to be nothing else to do but hide; I did it. I remained here, as I thought safely enough. Two or three reporters came and asked questions, and once a detective was here, but Miss Jerrod answered their inquiries satisfactorily and that seemed to be all—until now. Tomorrow Caroline and I were going back to Vermont."

There was a long pause. Caroline pressed the hand of the man she loved to her cheek with a gesture of infinite confidence. The Thinking Machine sat silent with the tips of his long, slender fingers together.

"Mr. Cunningham," he said at last, "you have not told us the one vital thing. Did you or did you not kill Fred Boyd?"

"I don't know," was the reply. "If I only could know!"

"Uh," grunted The Thinking Machine. "I was afraid you wouldn't know."

VI

Hutchinson Hatch and Manning, the other reporter, gazed at Cunningham thunderstruck, and from him to The Thinking Machine.

"Don't know whether or not you killed a man?" asked Hatch incredulously.

"It's perfectly possible, Mr. Hatch," said The Thinking Machine, curtly. "I understand, Mr. Cunningham," he explained. "I suppose you would be perfectly willing to go with me now?"

"No, no, no," exclaimed Caroline Pierce suddenly, in evident terror.

"Not to the police, Miss Pierce," said The Thinking Machine. He paused a moment and looked at the girl curiously. Of women he knew nothing, and knew he knew nothing. "Perhaps it would assure you, Miss Pierce, if I told you I know that Mr. Cunningham did not kill Boyd."

"You believe he didn't, then?" she asked eagerly.

"I *know* he didn't," said The Thinking Machine tersely. "Two and two make four not sometimes, but all the time," he went on enigmatically. "If Mr. Cunningham will come with me now we will establish beyond all doubt the cause of Boyd's death. Do you believe me?"

"Yes," said the girl slowly, and she looked steadily into the squint eyes of the scientist. "I—I have faith in you."

The Thinking Machine coughed, slightly embarrassed, and turned to Hatch with a faint color in his cheeks.

"Well, who did kill Boyd?" asked Hatch, amazed.

"That's what we will now demonstrate," was the reply. "Come on."

After Cunningham had himself assured the girl of his safety the four men passed out into the night—it was nearly ten o'clock—entered a cab and were driven to the tenement in South Boston. There they passed up the one flight of stairs into the room where Boyd had been found, and after lighting the gas the scientist made one quick survey of the room.

"These walls are awfully thin," he commented petulantly. "If I should fire a pistol in here I might kill someone in another room. Yes, a knife would do better. Have any of you gentlemen a knife—one with a blade that won't break easily?"

"Will this do?" asked Cunningham, and he produced one.

The Thinking Machine examined it and nodded his satisfaction.

"Now a revolver," he said.

Manning went out to get one. While he was gone The Thinking Machine gave some formal instructions to Cunningham and Hatch.

"I'm going to put out this light and remain in this room alone," he said. "I may be here fifteen minutes or I may be here till daylight. I don't know. But I want you three to remain quietly outside the door and listen. When I need you I shall need you quickly. My life may be in danger, and I am not a strong man."

"What is it anyway?" asked Hatch curiously.

"After a while you will hear something inside, I have no doubt," went on the scientist, paying no attention to the question. "But don't enter the room under any circumstances until I call out or you hear a struggle."

"But what is it?" asked Hatch again. "I don't understand at all."

"I'm going to find the murderer of Fred Boyd," said the scientist. "Please do not ask so many absurd questions. They annoy me exceedingly. I may have to kill him," he added reflectively.

"Kill him?" gasped Hatch. "Who, the murderer?" He couldn't help it.

"Yes, the murderer," was the tart reply.

Manning returned with the revolver, which The Thinking Machine examined and handed to Hatch.

"You will know what to do with it when you enter the room," he instructed. "You, Manning, come in with these other two and light this gas. Keep your matches in your hand."

Then the two reporters and Cunningham passed out of the room, closing the door, but not fastening it. Pressed close against the panels outside, listening, Hatch started to explain to Manning in a whisper when they heard the irritated voice of the scientist.

"Keep silent," was the sharp command.

Five minutes, ten minutes, half an hour of utter silence, save for a distant sound of some sort in the big tenement. But no one came up the stairs. The dim gaslight fluttered weirdly down the hall.

A full hour passed, still nothing. Hatch could hear his heartbeat, also he thought the regular breathing of The Thinking Machine. At last there came a slight sound, and Hatch started. The other men heard, too.

It was a faint whispering sound, as of the wind rustling through dead leaves, or the silken swish of skirts or the gasp of a dying man.

Hatch clutched the revolver more firmly and set his teeth hard together. He was going to face something—a deadly, terrible some-thing—and had not the faintest idea of what it might be. Manning held a match ready for instant use.

Then, as they listened, there was another sound, still faint, as of something sliding over the floor. Suddenly there was a heavy thump, a half-strangled cry from The Thinking Machine and the sounds of a fearful struggle. Hatch rushed into the room with revolver raised; Manning was just behind him. A match flared up and they saw a strug-gling heap on the floor. The arm of the scientist rose and fell thrice, burying the knife each time in flesh.

In the light of the gas, which hissed into a brilliant light under the match, the reporter placed the revolver flat against the head of a writhing, twisting body and fired. For the second time he fired, and the struggling bodies lay still.

Then for the first time Hatch realized what had happened. A giant boa constrictor held The Thinking Machine in its coils and was, in its death struggle, almost crushing the life out of him. It required the combined efforts of the three men to release the scientist from the deadly coils. He lay still for a moment, but finally the life came back into his frail body with a rush. He raised up from Hatch's arms and looked curiously at the snake.

"Dear me, dear me," he commented. "What a brain would have been lost to scientific inquiry if that snake had killed me."

———

Occupants of the house, aroused by the two pistol shots, rushed again terror-stricken to the room, and after a while the police came and rescued the four men from the besieging mob of questioners. All went to the police station, and there The Thinking Machine, with several caustic comments on the police in general, told his story. The body of the giant reptile lay full length on the floor.

"Mr. Hatch here asked for my advice in the matter," he explained to the police captain, "and I did what I could to assist him. When he explained the condition of the body and the room when it was broken open—the fact the door and both windows were fastened securely inside—it instantly occurred to me that, with suicide removed as a possibility, the thing which had killed Boyd was still in the room or else had escaped only after the body was found.

"It was not unreasonable to suppose that any animal, a snake for instance, would have attempted to leave the room while a crowd of people blocked the door; in fact it was not unreasonable to suppose that such a snake, snugly fixed in a large, tumble-down building, with the infinite possibility of feeding on rats and mice, would attempt to leave the building at all. It could get water easily from a dozen places.

"Therefore I presumed it was a snake, and I asked Mr. Hatch to ascertain for me first if the people in the house had ever been greatly annoyed by rodents; if they were now, and if not, when they had noticed that they were not. He reported to me that they had been annoyed up to a fortnight preceding the crime, but since, they had not noticed. Of course a boa constrictor can live on rodents, therefore they would leave the building or be eaten out of it gradually.

"A fortnight since they missed the rodents? That meant that the snake must have been in the building at least that long. All these conclusions I reached before I personally went over the scene. If it were a snake, as I thought possible, it must have come from somewhere. Where, then?"

The Thinking Machine paused and looked from one to another of his hearers. Each in turn shook his head, Hatch being the last to do so.

"And yet your own paper published a full solution of the mystery before it ever occurred," said the scientist sharply. "Looking from the back window of the room there, perfectly visible, were three banked rings, plainly where a circus had been. Possibly the snake escaped from that circus and crept into the house.

"I called up your office on the 'phone, Mr. Hatch, and ascertained that there had been a circus on that place two weeks before, November 9 and 10, and further I found that a boa constrictor had escaped from that circus. You printed a column of it on the first page."

"Lord, and we really thought that was a press agent's yarn," remarked Hatch sadly.

"Tonight when we went to the room it was my intention to allow the snake to creep out of that large hole near the radiator—I suppose you noticed there was one there?—then to pass between the snake and the hole and call for Mr. Hatch and these other gentlemen who were waiting outside the door. If the snake attacked me I had a knife and Mr. Hatch had a revolver.

"But I'm afraid I didn't give the snake credit for quickness and such enormous strength," he went on ruefully. "I heard the snake come out of the hole, and then instantly almost I felt its folds crushing me. Then these gentlemen rushed in. I can readily understand how it choked Boyd, he having no way to defend himself, and then crawled away when those people knocked on the door. It nearly crushed the life out of me."

That seemed to be all, and The Thinking Machine stopped.

"But Frank Cunningham?" asked the police captain. "Why did he run away, and where is he now?"

"Cunningham?" repeated the scientist, puzzled.

"Yes," said the captain. "Where is he?"

"Why here he is," and The Thinking Machine indicated the accused man. "Mr. Cunningham, permit me to introduce you to Captain—er—er. I don't know his name."

The captain was not surprised; he was nonplussed. It had never occurred to him to ask the name of the fourth member of the party; he knew the two newspapermen.

"How—where—when did you——" he began.

"Not knowing whether or not he had killed his friend Boyd," explained the scientist, "he' was hiding in the suite of Miss Caroline Pierce, his fiancé. His lack of knowledge was due entirely to a queer mental condition. He was badly hurt at one time and wears a silver plate in his head. That accounts for many things."

"How did you get him?" asked the captain, amazed.

"I walked into Miss Pierce's suite after I had put a man at the back and front to stop anyone who ran out, and told Miss Pierce's friend, Miss Jerrod, that I believed—in fact knew—that Cunningham was innocent, and that I had come merely to warn him," said The Thinking Machine.

"I told her then that three policemen were at the front door, and then Mr. Manning here rang the bell violently, as I had instructed him, and Cunningham dashed out of a rear room and started out the back way. Mr. Hatch got him there. It was perfectly simple—that part of it. Of course, there was a chance that he wasn't there at all—but he was."

The Thinking Machine arose.

"Is that all?" he asked.

"Why did you examine Cunningham's head before he told us his story?" asked Hatch.

"I have some idea of the cranial formation of criminals and I merely wanted to satisfy myself," said the scientist. "It was then that I discovered the silver plate in his head."

"And this?" asked Hatch. He took from his pocket the sealed envelope which The Thinking Machine had given him in the tenement room immediately after he had inspected the room. On this envelope was written "November 9–10," this being the date the circus was in South Boston.

"Oh, that?" said Professor Van Dusen a little impatiently, "that is merely a solution to the mystery."

Hatch opened the envelope and looked at it. There were only a few words:

"Snake. Came through hole near radiator. Lived in walls. Escaped from circus. Cunningham innocent."

"That all?" again asked The Thinking Machine.

There was no answer, and the scientist and the two newspapermen left the police station, followed by Cunningham.

The Problem of the Hidden Million

The gray hand of death had already left its ashen mark on the wrinkled, venomous face of the old man who lay huddled up in bed. Save for the feverishly brilliant eyes—cunning, vindictive, hateful—there seemed to be no spark of life in the aged form. The withered lips were mute, and the thin, yellow, claw-like hands lay helplessly outstretched on the white sheets. All physical power was gone; only the brain remained doggedly alive. Two men and two women stood beside the death bed. Upon each in turn the glittering eyes rested with the merciless, unreasoning hatred of age. Crouched on the floor was a huge St. Bernard dog, and on a perch across the room was a parrot which screeched abominably.

The gloom of the wretched little room was suddenly relieved by a ruddy sunbeam, which shot athwart the bed and lighted the scene fantastically. The old man noted it, and his lips curled into a hideous smile.

"That's the last sun I'll ever see," he piped feebly. "I'm dying—dying! Do you hear? And you're all glad of it, every one of you. Yes, you are! You are glad of it because you want my money. You came here to make me believe you were paying a last tribute of respect to your old grandfather. But that isn't it. It's the money you want—the money! But I've got a surprise for you. You'll never get the money. It's hidden safely—you'll never get it. You all hate me, you have hated me for years, and after that sun dies, you'll all hate me worse. But not more than I hated you. You'll all hate me worse then, because I'll be gone and you'll never know where the money is hidden. It will lie there safely where I put it, rotting and crumbling away; but you shall never warm your fingers with it! It's hidden—hidden—hidden!"

There was rasping in the shrunken throat, a deeply drawn breath, then the figure stiffened, and a distorted soul passed out upon the Eternal Way.

———

Martha held a card within the blinding light of the reflector, and Professor Augustus S. F. X. Van Dusen, with his hands immersed to the elbows in some chemical mess, squinted at it.

"Dr. Walter Ballard," he read. "Show him in."

After a moment Dr. Ballard entered. The scientist was still absorbed in his labors, but paused long enough to jerk his head toward a chair. Dr. Ballard accepted this as an invitation, and sat down, staring curiously at the singular, child-like figure of this eminent man of science, at the mop of tangled, straw-yellow hair, the enormous brow, and the peering blue eyes.

"Well?" demanded the scientist abruptly.

"I beg your pardon," began Dr. Ballard with a little start. "Your name was mentioned to me some time ago by a newspaper reporter, Hutchinson Hatch, whom I chanced to meet in his professional capacity. He suggested then that I come and see you, but I thought it useless. Now the affair in which we were both interested at that time seems hopelessly beyond solution, so I come to you for aid.

"We want to find one million dollars in gold and United States bonds, which were hidden by my grandfather, John Walter Ballard, some time before his death just a month ago. The circumstances are altogether out of the ordinary."

The Thinking Machine abandoned his labors, and dried his hands carefully, after which he took a seat facing Dr. Ballard. "Tell me about it," he commanded.

"Well," began Dr. Ballard reminiscently, as he settled back in his chair, "the old man—my grandfather—died, as I said, a month ago. He was nearly eighty-six, and the last five or six years of his life he spent as a recluse in a little house twenty-five miles from the city, a place some distance from any other house. He had a spot of ground there, half an acre or so, and lived like a pauper, despite the fact that he was worth at least a million dollars. Previous to the time he went there to live, there had been an estrangement with my family, his sole heirs. My family consists of myself, wife, son, and daughter.

"My grandfather lived in the house with me for ten years before he went out to this hut, and why he left us then is not clear to any member of my family, unless," and he shrugged his shoulders, "he was mentally unbalanced. Anyway, he went. He would neither come to see us, nor would he permit us to go to see him. As far as we know, he owned no real property of any sort, except this miserable little place, worth altogether—furnishing and all—not more than a thousand or twelve hundred dollars.

"Well, about a month ago, some one stopped at the house for something, and found he was ill. I was notified, and with my wife, son, and daughter, went to see what we could do. He took occasion on his death bed to heap vituperation upon us, and incidentally to state that something like a million dollars was left behind, but hidden.

"For the sake of my son and daughter, I undertook to recover this money. I consulted attorneys, private detectives, and in fact exhausted every possibility. I ascertained beyond question that the money was not in a bank anywhere, and hardly think he would have left it there, because, of course, if he had, even with a will disinheriting us, the law would have turned it over to us. He had no safe deposit vault as far as one month of close searching could reveal, and the money was not hidden in the house or grounds. He stated on his death bed that it was in bonds and gold, and that we should never find it. He was just vindictive enough not to destroy it, but to leave it somewhere, believing we should never find it. Where did he hide it?"

The Thinking Machine sat silently for several minutes, with his enormous yellow head tilted back, and slender fingers pressed together. "The house and grounds were searched?" he asked.

"The house was searched from cellar to garret," was the reply. "Workmen, under my direction, practically wrecked the building. Floors, ceilings, walls, chimney, stairs, everything—little cubby holes in the roof, the foundation of the chimney, the pillars, even the flagstones leading from the gate to the door, everything was examined. The posts were sounded to see if they were solid, and a dozen of them were cut through. The posts on the veranda were cut to pieces, and every stick of furniture was dissected—mattresses, beds, chairs, tables, bureaus—all of it. Outside in the grounds the search was just as thorough. Not one square inch but what was overturned. We dug it all up to a depth of ten feet. Still nothing."

"Of course," said the scientist, at last, "the search of the house and grounds was useless. The old man was shrewd enough to know that they would be searched. Also it would appear that the search of banks and safety deposit vaults was equally useless. He was shrewd enough to foresee that, too. We shall for the present assume that he did not destroy the money or give it away; so it is hidden. If the brain of man is clever enough to conceal a thing, the brain of man is clever enough to find it. It's a little problem in subtraction, Dr. Ballard." He was silent for a moment. "Who was your grandfather's attending physician?"

"I was. I was present at his death. Nothing could be done. It was merely the collapse consequent upon old age. I issued the burial certificate."

"Were any special directions left as to the place or manner of burial?"

"No."

"Have all his papers been examined for a clue as to the possible hiding place?"

"Everything. There were no papers to amount to anything."

"Have you those papers now?"

Dr. Ballard silently produced a packet and handed it to the scientist."

"I shall examine these at my leisure," said The Thinking Machine. "It may be a day or so before I communicate with you."

Dr. Ballard went his way. For a dozen hours The Thinking Machine sat with the papers spread out before him, and the keen, squinting, blue eyes dissected them, every paragraph, every sentence, every word. At the end he rose and bundled up the papers impatiently.

"Dear me! Dear me!" he exclaimed irritably. "There's no cipher—that's certain. Then what?"

———

Devastating hands had wrought the wreck of the little house where the old man died. Standing in the midst of its litter, The Thinking Machine regarded it closely and dispassionately for a long time. The work of destruction had been well done.

"Can you suggest anything?" asked Dr. Ballard impatiently.

"One mind may read another mind," said The Thinking Machine, "when there is some external thing upon which one can concentrate as a unit. In other words, when we have a given number, the logical brain can construct either backward or forward. There are so many thousands of ways in which your grandfather could have disposed of this money that the task becomes tremendous in view of the fact that we have no starting point. It is a case for patience, rather than any other quality; therefore, for greater speed, we must proceed psychologically. The question then becomes, not one of where the money is hidden, but one of where that sort of man would hide it.

"Now what sort of man was your grandfather?" the scientist continued. "He was crabbed, eccentric, and possibly not mentally sound. The cunning of a diseased mind is greater than the cunning of a normal one. He boasted to you that the money was in existence, and his last words were intended to arouse your curiosity; to hang over you all the rest of your life, and torment you. You can imagine the vindictive, petty brain like that putting a thing safely beyond your reach—but just beyond it—near enough to tantalize, and yet far enough to remain undiscovered. This seems to me to be the mental attitude in this case. Your grandfather knew that you would do just what you have done here; that is, search the house and lot. He knew, too, that you would search banks and safety deposit vaults, and with a million at stake he knew it would be done thoroughly. Knowing this, naturally he would not put the money in any of those places.

"Then what? He doesn't own any other property, as far as we know, and we shall assume that he did not buy property in the name of some other person; therefore, what have we left? Obviously, if the money is still in existence, it is hidden on somebody else's property. And the minute we say that, we have the whole wide world to search. But again, doesn't the deviltry and maliciousness of the old man narrow that down? Wouldn't he have liked to remember as a dying thought that the money was always just within your reach, and yet safely beyond it? Wouldn't it have been a keener revenge to have you dig over the whole place, while the money was hidden just six feet outside in a spot where you would never dig? It might be sixty or six hundred or six thousand. But there we have the law of probability to narrow these limits; so——"

Professor Van Dusen turned suddenly and strolled across the uneven ground to the property line. Walking slowly and scrutinizing the ground as he went, he circled the lot, returning to the starting point. Dr. Ballard had followed along behind him.

"Are all your grandfather's belongings still in the house?" asked the scientist.

"Yes, everything just as he left it, that is, except his dog and a parrot. They are temporarily in charge of a widow down the road here."

The scientist looked at Dr. Ballard quickly. "What sort of dog is it?" he inquired.

"A St. Bernard, I think," replied Dr. Ballard wonderingly.

"Do you happen to have a glove or something that you know your grandfather wore?"

"I have a glove, yes."

From the debris which littered the floor of the house, a well-worn glove was recovered.

"Now the dog, please," commanded the scientist.

A short walk along the country road brought them to a house, and here they stopped. The St. Bernard, a shaggy, handsome, boisterous old chap with wise eyes, was led out in leash. The Thinking Machine thrust the glove forward, and the dog sniffed at it. After a moment he sank down on his haunches, and with head thrust forward and upward, whined softly. It was the call to its master.

The Thinking Machine patted the heavy-coated head, and with the glove still in his hand made as if to go away. Again came the whine, but the dog sank down on the floor, with his head between his forepaws, regarding him intently. For ten minutes the scientist sought to coax the animal to follow him, but he lay motionless.

"I don't mind keepin' that dog here, but that parrot is powerful noisy," said the woman after a moment. She had been standing by, watching the scientist curiously. "There ain't no peace in the house."

"Noisy—how?" asked Dr. Ballard.

"He swears, and sings and whistles, and does 'rithmetic all day long," the woman explained. "It nearly drives me distracted."

"Does arithmetic?" inquired The Thinking Machine.

"Yes," replied the woman, "and he swears just terrible. It's almost like havin' a man about the house. There he goes now."

From another room came a sudden, squawking burst of profanity, followed instantly by a whistle, which caused the dog on the floor to prick up his ears.

"Does the parrot talk well?" asked the scientist.

"Just like a human bein'," replied the woman, "an' just about as sensible as some I've seen. I don't mind his whistling, if only he wouldn't swear so, and do all his figgering out loud."

For a minute or more the scientist stood, staring down at the dog in deep thought. Gradually there came some subtle change in his expression. Dr. Ballard was watching him closely.

"I think perhaps it would be a good idea for me to keep the parrot for a few days," suggested the scientist finally. He turned to the woman. "Just what sort of arithmetic does the bird do?"

"All kinds," she answered promptly. "He does all the multiplication table. But he ain't very good in subtraction."

"I shouldn't be surprised," commented The Thinking Machine. "I'll take the bird for a few days, doctor, if you don't mind."

And so it came to pass that when The Thinking Machine returned to his apartment he was accompanied by as noisy and vociferous a companion as anyone would care to have.

Martha, the aged servant, viewed him with horror as he entered. "The professor must be getting old," she muttered. "I suppose there'll be a cat next."

Two days later Dr. Ballard was called to the telephone. The Thinking Machine was at the other end of the wire.

"Take two men whom you can trust and go down to your grandfather's place," instructed the scientist curtly. "Take picks, shovels, a compass, and a long tape line. Stand on the front steps facing east. To your right will be an apple tree some distance off that lot on the adjoining property. Go to that apple tree. A boulder is at its foot. Measure from the edge of that stone twenty-six feet due north by the compass, and from that point fourteen feet due west. You will find your money there. Then please have someone come and take this bird away. If you don't, I'll wring its neck. It's the most obnoxious creature I've ever heard. Good by."

———

Dr. Ballard slipped the catch on the suitcase and turned it upside down on the laboratory table. It was packed—literally packed—with United States bonds. The Thinking Machine fingered them idly.

"And there is this, too," said Dr. Ballard.

He lifted a stout sack from the floor, cut the string, and spilled out its contents beside the bonds. It was gold, thousands and thousands of dollars. Dr. Ballard was frankly excited about it. The Thinking Machine accepted it as he accepted all material things.

"How much is there of it?" he asked quietly.

"I don't know," replied Dr. Ballard.

"And how did you find it?"

"As you directed—twenty-six feet north from the boulder, and fourteen feet west from that point."

"I knew that, of course," snapped The Thinking Machine. "But how was it hidden?"

"It's rather peculiar," explained Dr. Ballard. "Fourteen feet brought the man who had measured it to the edge of an old dried-up well, twelve or fifteen feet deep, not expecting any such thing, he tumbled into it. In his efforts to get out, he stepped upon a stone which protruded from one side. That fell out and revealed the wooden box, which contained all this."

"In other words," said the scientist, "the money was hidden in such a manner that it would in time have come to be buried twelve or fifteen feet below the surface, because the well, being dry, would ultimately, of course, have been filled in."

Dr. Ballard had been listening only hazily. His hands had been playing in and out of the heap of gold. The Thinking Machine regarded him with something like contempt about his thin-lipped mouth.

"How—how did you ever do it?" asked Dr. Ballard.

"I am surprised that you want to know," remarked The Thinking Machine cuttingly. "You know how I reached the conclusion that the money was not hidden either in the house or lot. The plain logic of the thing told me that, even before the search you made demonstrated it. You saw how logic narrowed down the search, and you saw my experiment with the dog. That was purely an experiment. I wanted to see the instinct of the animal. Would it lead him anywhere?—perhaps the spot where the money had been hidden? It did not.

"But the parrot? That was another matter. It just happens that once before I had an interesting experience with a bird—a cockatoo which figured in a sleepwalking case—and naturally was interested in this bird. Now, what were the circumstances in this case? Here was a bird that talked exceptionally well, yet that bird had been living for five years alone with an old man. It is a fact that no matter how well a parrot may talk, it will forget in the course of time, unless there is someone around who talks. This old man was the only person near this bird. Therefore from the fact that the bird talks, we know that the old man talked; from the fact that the bird repeated the multiplication table, we know that the old man repeated it. From the fact that the bird whistles, we know that the old man whistled, perhaps to the dog. And in the course of five years of these circumstances, a bird would have come to that point where it would repeat only those words or sounds that the old man used.

"All this shows, too, that the old man talked to himself. Most people who live alone a great deal do that. Then came a question as to whether at any time the old man had ever repeated the secret of the hiding place within the hearing of the bird—not once, but many times, because it takes a parrot a long time to learn phrases. When we know the vindictiveness which lay behind the old man's actions in hiding the money, when we know how the thing preyed on his mind, coupled with the fact that he talked to himself, and was not wholly sound mentally, we can imagine him doddering about the place alone, repeating the very thing of which he had made so great a secret. Thus, the bird learned it, but learned it disjointedly, not connectedly, so when I brought the parrot here, my idea was to know by personal observation what the bird said that didn't connect—that is, that had no obvious meaning. I hoped to get a clue which would result, just as the clue I did get, did result.

"The bird's trick of repeating the multiplication table means nothing except it shows the strange workings of an unbalanced mind. And yet, there is one exception to this. In a disjointed way, the bird knows all the multiplication tables to ten, except one. For instance—listen."

The Thinking Machine crept stealthily to a door and opened it softly a few inches. From somewhere out there came the screeching of the parrot. For several minutes they listened in silence. There was a flood of profanity, a shrill whistle or two, then the squawking voice ran off into a monotone.

"Six times one are six, six times two are twelve, six times three are eighteen, six times four are twenty-four—and add two——"

"That's it," explained the scientist, as he closed the door. "Six times four are twenty-four—add two. That's the one table the bird does not know. The thing is incoherent, except as applied to a peculiar method of remembering a number. That number is twenty-six. On one occasion I heard the bird repeat a dozen times, 'Twenty-six feet to the polar star.' That could mean nothing except the direction of the twenty-six feet—due north. One of the first things I noticed the bird saying was something about fourteen feet to the setting sun—or due west. When set down with twenty-six, I could readily see that I had something to go on.

"But where was the starting point? Again, logic. There was no tree or stone inside the lot, except the apple tree which your workmen cut down, and that was more than twenty-six feet from the boundary of the lot in all directions. There was one tree in the adjoining lot, an apple tree with a boulder at its foot. I knew that by observation. And there was no other tree, I knew also, within several hundred feet; therefore, that tree or boulder, rather, was a starting point—not the tree so much as the boulder, because the tree might be cut down, or would in time decay. The chances are the stone would have been allowed to remain there indefinitely. Naturally your grandfather would measure from a prominent point—the boulder. That is all. I gave you the figures. You know the rest."

For a minute or more, Dr. Ballard stared at him blankly. "How was it you knew," he asked, "that the directions should have been first twenty-six feet north, then fourteen feet west, instead of first fourteen west, and then twenty-six feet north."

The Thinking Machine looked at him with scorn. "What difference would it have made?" he said peevishly. "Try it on a piece of paper, if you cannot do it mentally."

Half an hour later Dr. Ballard went away carrying the money and the parrot in its cage. The bird cursed The Thinking Machine roundly, as Dr. Ballard went down the steps.

THE RALSTON BANK BURGLARY

I

With expert fingers Phillip Dunston, receiving teller, verified the last package of one-hundred-dollar bills he had made up—ten thousand dollars in all—and tossed it over on the pile beside him, while he checked off a memorandum. It was correct; there were eighteen packages of bills, containing $107,231. Then he took the bundles, one by one, and on each placed his initials, "P. D." This was a system of checking in the Ralston National Bank.

It was care in such trivial details, perhaps, that had a great deal to do with the fact that the Ralston National had advanced from a small beginning to the first rank of those banks which were financial powers. President Quinton Fraser had inaugurated the system under which the Ralston National had so prospered, and now, despite his seventy-four years, he was still its active head. For fifty years he had been in its employ; for thirty-five years of that time he had been its president.

Publicly the aged banker was credited with the possession of a vast fortune, this public estimate being based on large sums he had given to charity. But as a matter of fact the private fortune of the old man, who had no one to share it save his wife, was not large; it was merely a comfortable living sum for an aged couple of simple tastes.

Dunston gathered up the packages of money and took them into the cashier's private office, where he dumped them on the great flat-top desk at which that official, Randolph West, sat figuring. The cashier thrust the sheet of paper on which he had been working into his pocket and took the memorandum which Dunston offered.

"All right?" he asked.

"It tallies perfectly," Dunston replied.

"Thanks. You may go now."

It was an hour after closing time. Dunston was just pulling on his coat when he saw West come out of his private office with the money to put it away in the big steel safe which stood between depositors and thieves. The cashier paused a moment to allow the janitor, Harris, to sweep the space in front of the safe. It was the late afternoon scrubbing and sweeping.

"Hurry up," the cashier complained, impatiently.

Harris hurried, and West placed the money in the safe. There were eighteen packages.

"All right, sir?" Dunston inquired.

"Yes."

West was disposing of the last bundle when Miss Clarke—Louise Clarke—private secretary to President Fraser, came out of his office with a long envelope in her hand. Dunston glanced at her and she smiled at him.

"Please, Mr. West," she said to the cashier, "Mr. Fraser told me before he went to put these papers in the safe. I had almost forgotten."

She glanced into the open safe and her pretty blue eyes opened wide. Mr. West took the envelope, stowed it away with the money without a word, the girl looking on interestedly, and then swung the heavy door closed. She turned away with a quick, reassuring smile at Dunston, and disappeared inside the private office.

West had shot the bolts of the safe into place and had taken hold of the combination dial to throw it on, when the street door opened and President Fraser entered hurriedly.

"Just a moment, West," he called. "Did Miss Clarke give you an envelope to go in there?"

"Yes. I just put it in."

"One moment," and the aged president came through a gate which Dunston held open and went to the safe. The cashier pulled the steel door open, unlocked the money compartment where the envelope had been placed, and the president took it out.

West turned and spoke to Dunston, leaving the president looking over the contents of the envelope. When the cashier turned back to the safe the president was just taking his hand away from his inside coat pocket.

"It's all right, West," he instructed. "Lock it up."

Again the heavy door closed, the bolts were shot and the combination dial turned. President Fraser stood looking on curiously; it just happened that he had never witnessed this operation before.

"How much have you got in there tonight?" he asked.

"One hundred and twenty-nine thousand," replied the cashier. "And all the securities, of course."

"Hum," mused the president. "That would be a good haul for someone—if they could get it, eh, West?" and he chuckled dryly.

"Excellent," returned West, smilingly. "But they can't."

Miss Clarke, dressed for the street, her handsome face almost concealed by a veil which was intended to protect her pink cheeks from boisterous winds, was standing in the door of the president's office.

"Oh, Miss Clarke, before you go, would you write just a short note for me?" asked the president.

"Certainly," she responded, and she returned to the private office. Mr. Fraser followed her.

West and Dunston stood outside the bank railing, Dunston waiting for Miss Clarke. Every evening he walked over to the subway with her. His opinion of her was an open secret. West was waiting for the janitor to finish sweeping.

"Hurry up, Harris," he said again.

"Yes, sir," came the reply, and the janitor applied the broom more vigorously. "Just a little bit more. I've finished inside."

Dunston glanced through the railing. The floor was spick and span and the hardwood glistened cleanly. Various bits of paper came down the corridor before Harris's broom. The janitor swept it all up into a dustpan just as Miss Clarke came out of the president's room. With Dunston she walked up the street. As they were going they saw Cashier

West come out the front door, with his handkerchief in his hand, and then walk away rapidly.

"Mr. Fraser is doing some figuring," Miss Clarke explained to Dunston. "He said he might be there for another hour."

"You are beautiful," replied Dunston, irrelevantly.

———

These, then, were the happenings in detail in the Ralston National Bank from 4:15 o'clock on the afternoon of November 11. That night the bank was robbed. The great steel safe which was considered impregnable was blown and $129,000 was missing.

The night watchman of the bank, William Haney, was found senseless, bound and gagged, inside the bank. His revolver lay beside him with all the cartridges out. He had been beaten into insensibility; at the hospital it was stated that there was only a bare chance of his recovery.

The locks, hinges, and bolts of the steel safe had been smashed by some powerful explosive, possibly nitroglycerine. The tiny dial of the time-lock showed that the explosion came at 2:39; the remainder of the lock was blown to pieces.

Thus was fixed definitely the moment at which the robbery occurred. It was shown that the policeman on the beat had been four blocks away. It was perfectly possible that no one heard the explosion, because the bank was situated in a part of the city wholly given over to business and deserted at night.

The burglars had entered the building through a window of the cashier's private office, in the full glare of an electric light. The window sash here had been found unfastened and the protecting steel bars, outside from top to bottom, seemed to have been dragged from their sockets in the solid granite. The granite crumbled away, as if it had been chalk.

Only one possible clew was found. This was a white linen handkerchief, picked up in front of the blown safe. It must have been dropped there at the time of the burglary, because Dunston distinctly recalled it was not there before he left the bank. He would have noticed it while the janitor was sweeping.

This handkerchief was the property of Cashier West. The cashier did not deny it, but could offer no explanation of how it came there. Miss Clarke and Dunston both said that they had seen him leave the bank with a handkerchief in his hand.

II

President Fraser reached the bank at ten o'clock and was informed of the robbery. He retired to his office, and there he sat, apparently stunned into inactivity by the blow, his head bowed on his arms. Miss Clarke, at her typewriter, frequently glanced at the aged figure with an expression of pity on her face. Her eyes seemed weary, too. Outside, through the closed door, they could hear the detectives.

From time to time employees of the bank and detectives entered the office to ask questions. The banker answered as if dazed; then the board of directors met and voted to personally make good the loss sustained. There was no uneasiness among depositors, because they knew the resources of the bank were practically unlimited.

Cashier West was not arrested. The directors wouldn't listen to such a thing; he had been cashier for eighteen years, and they trusted him implicitly. Yet he could offer no possible explanation of how his handkerchief had come there. He asserted stoutly that he had not been in the bank from the moment Miss Clarke and Dunston saw him leave it.

After investigation the police placed the burglary to the credit of certain expert cracksmen, identity unknown. A general alarm, which meant a rounding up of all suspicious persons, was sent out, and this dragnet was expected to bring important facts to light. Detective Mallory said so, and the bank officials placed great reliance on his word.

Thus the situation at the luncheon hour. Then Miss Clarke, who, wholly unnoticed, had been waiting all morning at her typewriter, arose and went over to Fraser.

"If you don't need me now," she said, "I'll run out to luncheon."

"Certainly, certainly," he responded, with a slight start. He had apparently forgotten her existence.

She stood silently looking at him for a moment.

"I'm awfully sorry," she said, at last, and her lips trembled slightly.

"Thanks," said the banker, and he smiled faintly. "It's a shock, the worst I ever had."

Miss Clarke passed out with quiet tread, pausing for a moment in the outer office to stare curiously at the shattered steel safe. The banker arose with sudden determination and called to West, who entered immediately.

"I know a man who can throw some light on this thing," said Fraser, positively. "I think I'll ask him to come over and take a look. It might aid the police, anyway. You may know him? Professor Van Dusen."

"Never heard of him," said West, tersely, "but I'll welcome anybody who can solve it. My position is uncomfortable."

President Fraser called Professor Van Dusen—The Thinking Machine—and talked for a moment through the 'phone. Then he turned back to West.

"He'll come," he said, with an air of relief. "I was able to do him a favor once by putting an invention on the market."

Within an hour The Thinking Machine, accompanied by Hutchinson Hatch, reporter, appeared. President Fraser knew the scientist well, but on West the strange figure made a startling, almost uncanny, impression. Every known fact was placed before The Thinking Machine. He listened without comment, then arose and wandered aimlessly about the offices. The employees were amused by his manner; Hatch was a silent looker-on.

"Where was the handkerchief found?" demanded The Thinking Machine, at last.

"Here," replied West, and he indicated the exact spot.

"Any draught through the office—ever?"

"None. We have a patent ventilating system which prevents that."

The Thinking Machine squinted for several minutes at the window which had been unfastened—the window in the cashier's private room—with the steel bars guarding it, now torn out of their sockets, and at the chalklike softness of the granite about the sockets. After a while he turned to the president and cashier.

"Where is the handkerchief?"

"In my desk," Fraser replied. The police thought it of no consequence, save, perhaps—perhaps——," and he looked at West.

"Except that it might implicate me," said West, hotly.

"Tut, tut, tut," said Fraser, reprovingly. "No one thinks for a——"

"Well, well, the handkerchief?" interrupted The Thinking Machine, in annoyance.

"Come into my office," suggested the president.

The Thinking Machine started in, saw a woman—Miss Clarke, who had returned from luncheon—and stopped. There was one thing on earth he was afraid of—a woman.

"Bring it out here," he requested.

President Fraser brought it and placed it in the slender hands of the scientist, who examined it closely by a window, turning it over and over. At last he sniffed at it. There was the faint, clinging odor of violet perfume. Then abruptly, irrelevantly, he turned to Fraser.

"How many women employed in the bank?" he asked.

"Three," was the reply; "Miss Clarke, who is my secretary, and two general stenographers in the outer office."

"How many men?"

"Fourteen, including myself."

If the president and Cashier West had been surprised at the actions of The Thinking Machine up to this point, now they were amazed. He thrust the handkerchief at Hatch, took his own handkerchief, briskly scrubbed his hands with it, and also passed that to Hatch.

"Keep those," he commanded.

He sniffed at his hands, then walked into the outer office, straight toward the desk of one of the young women stenographers. He leaned over her, and asked one question:

"What system of shorthand do you write?"

"Pitman," was the astonished reply.

The scientist sniffed. Yes, it was unmistakably a sniff. He left her suddenly and went to the other stenographer. Precisely the same thing happened; standing close to her he asked one question, and at her answer sniffed. Miss Clarke passed through the outer office to mail a letter. She, too, had to answer the question as the scientist squinted into her eyes, and sniffed.

"Ah," he said, at her answer.

Then from one to another of the employees of the bank he went, asking each a few questions. By this time a murmur of amusement was running through the office. Finally The Thinking Machine approached the cage in which sat Dunston, the receiving teller. The young man was bent over his work, absorbed.

"How long have you been employed here?" asked the scientist, suddenly.

Dunston started and glanced around quickly.

"Five years," he responded.

"It must be hot work," said The Thinking Machine. "You're perspiring."

"Am I?" inquired the young man, smilingly.

He drew a crumpled handkerchief from his hip pocket, shook it out, and wiped his forehead.

"Ah!" exclaimed The Thinking Machine, suddenly.

He had caught the faint, subtle perfume of violets—an odor identical with that on the handkerchief found in front of the safe.

III

The Thinking Machine led the way back to the private office of the cashier, with President Fraser, Cashier West, and Hatch following.

"Is it possible for anyone to overhear us here?" he asked.

"No," replied the president. "The directors meet here."

"Could anyone outside hear that, for instance?" and with a sudden sweep of his hand he upset a heavy chair.

"I don't know," was the astonished reply. "Why?"

The Thinking Machine went quickly to the door, opened it softly and peered out. Then he closed the door again.

"I suppose I may speak with absolute frankness?" he inquired.

"Certainly," responded the old banker, almost startled. "Certainly."

"You have presented an abstract problem," The Thinking Machine went on, "and I presume you want a solution of it, no matter where it hits?"

"Certainly," the president again assured him, but his tone expressed a grave, haunting fear.

"In that case," and The Thinking Machine turned to the reporter, "Mr. Hatch, I want you to ascertain several things for me. First, I want to know if Miss Clarke uses or has ever used violet perfume—if so, when she ceased using it."

"Yes," said the reporter. The bank officials exchanged wondering looks.

"Also, Mr. Hatch," and the scientist squinted with his strange eyes straight into the face of the cashier, "go to the home of Mr. West, here, see for yourself his laundry mark, and ascertain beyond any question if he has ever, or any member of his family has ever, used violet perfume."

The cashier flushed suddenly.

"I can answer that," he said, hotly. "No."

"I knew you would say that," said The Thinking Machine, curtly. "Please don't interrupt. Do as I say, Mr. Hatch."

Accustomed as he was to the peculiar methods of this man, Hatch saw faintly the purpose of the inquiries.

"And the receiving teller?" he asked.

"I know about him," was the reply.

Hatch left the room, closing the door behind him. He heard the bolt shot in the lock as he started away.

"I think it only fair to say here, Professor Van Dusen," explained the president, "that we understand thoroughly that it would have been impossible for Mr. West to have had anything to do with or know——"

"Nothing is impossible," interrupted The Thinking Machine.

"But I won't——" began West, angrily.

"Just a moment, please," said The Thinking Machine. "No one has accused you of anything. What I am doing may explain to your satisfaction just how your handkerchief came here and bring about the very thing I suppose you want—exoneration."

The cashier sank back into a chair; President Fraser looked from one to the other. Where there had been worry on his face there was now only wonderment.

"Your handkerchief was found in this office, apparently having been dropped by the persons who blew the safe," and the long, slender fingers of The Thinking Machine were placed tip to tip as he talked. "It was not there the night before. The janitor who swept says so; Dunston, who happened to look, says so; Miss Clarke and Dunston both say they saw you with a handkerchief as you left the bank. Therefore, that handkerchief reached that spot after you left and before the robbery was discovered."

The cashier nodded.

"You say you don't use perfume; that no one in your family uses it. If Mr. Hatch verifies this, it will help to exonerate you. But some person who handled that handkerchief after it left your possession and before it appeared here did use perfume. Now who was that person? Who would have had an opportunity?

"We may safely dismiss the possibility that you lost the handkerchief, that it fell into the hands of burglars, that those burglars used perfume, that they brought it to your bank—your own bank, mind you!—and left it. The series of coincidences necessary to bring that about would not have occurred once in a million times."

The Thinking Machine sat silent for several minutes, squinting steadily at the ceiling.

"If it had been lost anywhere, in the laundry, say, the same rule of coincidence I have just applied would almost eliminate it. Therefore, because of an opportunity to get that handkerchief, we will assume—there is—there must be—someone employed in this bank who had some connection with or actually participated in the burglary."

The Thinking Machine spoke with perfect quiet, but the effect was electrical. The aged president staggered to his feet and stood staring at him dully; again the flush of crimson came into the face of the cashier.

"Someone," The Thinking Machine went on, evenly, "who either found the handkerchief and unwittingly lost it at the time of the burglary, or else stole it and deliberately left it. As I said, Mr. West seems eliminated. Had he been one of the robbers, he would not wittingly have left his handkerchief; we will still assume that he does not use perfume, therefore personally did not drop the handkerchief where it was found."

"Impossible! I can't believe it, and of my employees———" began Mr. Fraser.

"Please don't keep saying things are impossible," snapped The Thinking Machine. "It irritates me exceedingly. It all comes to the one vital question: Who in the bank uses perfume?"

"I don't know," said the two officials.

"I do," said The Thinking Machine. "There are two—only two, Dunston, your receiving teller, and Miss Clarke."

"But they———"

"Dunston uses a violet perfume not *like* that on the handkerchief, but *identical* with it," The Thinking Machine went on. "Miss Clarke uses a strong rose perfume."

"But those two persons, above all others in the bank, I trust implicitly," said Mr. Fraser, earnestly. "And, besides, they wouldn't know how to blow a safe. The police tell me this was the work of experts."

"Have you, Mr. Fraser, attempted to raise, or have you raised lately, any large sum of money?" asked the scientist, suddenly.

"Well, yes," said the banker, "I have. For a week past I have tried to raise ninety thousand dollars on my personal account."

"And you, Mr. West?"

The face of the cashier flushed slightly—it might have been at the tone of the question—and there was the least pause.

"No," he answered finally.

"Very well," and the scientist arose, rubbing his hands; "now we'll search your employees."

"What?" exclaimed both men. Then Mr. Fraser added: "That would be the height of absurdity; it would never do. Besides, any person who robbed the bank would not carry proofs of the robbery, or even any of the money about with them—to the bank, above all places."

"The bank would be the safest place for it," retorted The Thinking Machine. "It is perfectly possible that a thief in your employ would carry some of the money; indeed, it is doubtful if he would dare do anything else with it. He could see you would have no possible reason for suspecting anyone here—unless it is Mr. West."

There was a pause. "I'll do the searching, except the three ladies, of course," he added, blushingly. "With them each combination of two can search the other one."

Mr. Fraser and Mr. West conversed in low tones for several minutes.

"If the employees will consent I am willing," Mr. Fraser explained, at last; "although I see no use of it."

"They will agree," said The Thinking Machine. "Please call them all into this office."

Among some confusion and wonderment the three women and fourteen men of the bank were gathered in the cashier's office, the outer doors being locked. The Thinking Machine addressed them with characteristic terseness.

"In the investigation of the burglary of last night," he explained, "it has been deemed necessary to search all employees of this bank." A murmur of surprise ran around the room. "Those who are innocent will agree readily, of course; will all agree?"

There were whispered consultations on all sides. Dunston flushed angrily; Miss Clarke, standing near Mr. Fraser, paled slightly. Dunston looked at her and then spoke.

"And the ladies?" he asked.

"They, too," explained the scientist. "They may search one another—in the other room, of course."

"I for one will not submit to such a proceeding," Dunston declared, bluntly, "not because I fear it, but because it is an insult."

Simultaneously it impressed itself on the bank officials and The Thinking Machine that the one person in the bank who used a perfume identical with that on the handkerchief was the first to object to a search. The cashier and president exchanged startled glances.

"Nor will I," came in the voice of a woman.

The Thinking Machine turned and glanced at her. It was Miss Willis, one of the outside stenographers; Miss Clarke and the other woman were pale, but neither had spoken.

"And the others?" asked The Thinking Machine.

Generally there was acquiescence, and as the men came forward the scientist searched them, perfunctorily, it seemed. Nothing! At last there remained three men, Dunston, West, and Fraser. Dunston came forward, compelled to do so by the attitude of his fellows. The three women stood together. The Thinking Machine spoke to them as he searched Dunston.

"If the ladies will retire to the next room they may proceed with their search," he suggested. "If any money is found, bring it to me— nothing else."

"I will not, I will not, I will not," screamed Miss Willis, suddenly. "It's an outrage."

Miss Clarke, deathly white and half fainting, threw up her hands and sank without a sound into the arms of President Fraser. There she burst into tears.

"It is an outrage," she sobbed. She clung to President Fraser, her arms flung upward and her face buried on his bosom. He was soothing her with fatherly words, and stroked her hair awkwardly. The Thinking Machine finished the search of Dunston. Nothing! Then Miss Clarke roused herself and dried her eyes.

"Of course I will have to agree," she said, with a flash of anger in her eyes.

Miss Willis was weeping, but, like Dunston, she was compelled to yield, and the three women went into an adjoining room. There was a tense silence until they reappeared. Each shook her head. The Thinking Machine nearly looked disappointed.

"Dear me!" he exclaimed. "Now, Mr. Fraser." He started toward the president, then paused to pick up a scarf pin.

"This is yours," he said. "I saw it fall," and he made as if to search the aged man.

"Well, do you really think it necessary in my case?" asked the president, in consternation, as he drew back, nervously. "I—I am the president, you know."

"The others were searched in your presence, I will search you in their presence," said The Thinking Machine, tartly.

"But—but——" the president stammered.

"Are you afraid?" the scientist demanded.

"Why, of course not," was the hurried answer; "but it seems so—so unusual."

"I think it best," said The Thinking Machine, and before the banker could draw away, his slender fingers were in the inside breast pocket, whence they instantly drew out a bundle of money—one hundred $100 bills—ten thousand dollars—with the initials of the receiving teller, "P. D."—"o. k.—R. W."

"Great God!" exclaimed Mr. Fraser, ashen white.

"Dear me, dear me!" said The Thinking Machine again. He sniffed curiously at the bundle of bank notes, as a hound might sniff at a trail.

IV

President Fraser was removed to his home in a dangerous condition. His advanced age did not withstand the shock. Now alternately he raved and muttered incoherently, and the old eyes were wide, staring fearfully always. There was a consultation between The Thinking Machine and West after the removal of President Fraser, and the result was another hurried meeting of the board of directors. At that meeting West was placed, temporarily, in command. The police, of course, had been informed of the matter, but no arrest was probable.

Immediately after The Thinking Machine left the bank Hatch appeared and inquired for him. From the bank he went to the home of the scientist. There Professor Van Dusen was bending over a retort, busy with some problem.

"Well?" he demanded, as he glanced up.

"West told the truth," began Hatch. "Neither he nor any member of his family uses perfume; he has few outside acquaintances, is regular in his habits, but is a man of considerable wealth, it appears."

"What is his salary at the bank?" asked The Thinking Machine.

"Fifteen thousand a year," said the reporter. "But he must have a large fortune. He lives like a millionaire."

"He couldn't do that on fifteen thousand dollars a year," mused the scientist. "Did he inherit any money?"

"No," was the reply. "He started as a clerk in the bank and has made himself what he is."

"That means speculation," said The Thinking Machine. "You can't save a fortune from a salary, even fifteen thousand dollars a year. Now, Mr. Hatch, find out for me all about his business connections. His source of income particularly I would like to know. Also whether or not he has recently sought to borrow or has received a large sum of money; if he got it and what he did with it. He says he has not sought such a sum. Perhaps he told the truth."

"Yes, and about Miss Clarke——"

"Yes; what about her?" asked The Thinking Machine.

"She occupies a little room in a boarding-house for women in an excellent district," the reporter explained. "She has no friends who call there, at any rate. Occasionally, however, she goes out at night and remains late."

"The perfume?" asked the scientist.

"She uses a perfume, the housekeeper tells me, but she doesn't re-call just what kind it is—so many of the young women in the house use it. So I went to her room and looked. There was no perfume there. Her room was considerably disarranged, which seemed to as-tonish the housekeeper, who declared that she had carefully arranged it about nine o'clock. It was two when I was there."

"How was it disarranged?" asked the scientist.

"The couch cover was jerked awry and the pillows tumbled down, for one thing," said the reporter. "I didn't notice any further."

The Thinking Machine relapsed into silence.

"What happened at the bank?" inquired Hatch.

Briefly the scientist related the facts leading up to the search, the search itself and its startling result. The reporter whistled.

"Do you think Fraser had anything to do with it?"

"Run out and find out those other things about West," said The Thinking Machine, evasively. "Come back here tonight. It doesn't matter what time."

"But who do you think committed the crime?" insisted the news-paperman.

"I may be able to tell you when you return."

For the time being The Thinking Machine seemed to forget the bank robbery, being busy in his tiny laboratory. He was aroused from his labors by the ringing of the telephone bell.

"Hello," he called. "Yes, Van Dusen. No, I can't come down to the bank now. What is it? Oh, it has disappeared? When? Too bad! How's Mr. Fraser? Still unconscious? Too bad! I'll see you tomorrow."

The scientist was still engrossed in some delicate chemical work just after eight o'clock that evening when Martha, his housekeeper and maid of all work, entered.

"Professor," she said, "there's a lady to see you."

"Name?" he asked, without turning.

"She didn't give it, sir."

"There in a moment."

He finished the test he had under way, then left the little laboratory and went into the hall leading to the sitting room, where unprivileged callers awaited his pleasure. He sniffed a little as he stepped into the hall. At the door of the sitting room he paused and peered inside. A woman arose and came toward him. It was Miss Clarke.

"Good evening," he said. "I knew you'd come."

Miss Clarke looked a little surprised, but made no comment.

"I came to give you some information," she said, and her voice was subdued. "I am heart-broken at the awful things which have come out concerning—concerning Mr. Fraser. I have been closely associated with him for several months, and I won't believe that he could have had anything to do with this affair, although I know positively that he was in need of a large sum of money—ninety thousand dollars—because his personal fortune was in danger. Some error in titles to an estate, he told me."

"Yes, yes," said The Thinking Machine.

"Whether he was able to raise this money I don't know," she went on. "I only hope he did without having to—to do that—to have any——"

"To rob his bank," said the scientist, tartly. "Miss Clarke, is young Dunston in love with you?"

The girl's face changed color at the sudden question.

"I don't see——" she began.

"You may not see," said The Thinking Machine, "but I can have him arrested for robbery and convict him."

The girl gazed at him with wide, terror-stricken eyes, and gasped.

"No, no, no," she said, hurriedly. "He could have had nothing to do with that at all."

"Is he in love with you?" again came the question.

There was a pause.

"I've had reason to believe so," she said, finally, "though——"

"And you?"

The girl's face was flaming now, and, squinting into her eyes, the scientist read the answer.

"I understand," he commented, tersely. "Are you going to be married?"

"I could—could never marry him," she gasped suddenly. "No, no," emphatically. "We are not, ever."

She slowly recovered from her confusion, while the scientist continued to squint at her curiously.

"I believe you said you had some information for me?" he asked.

"Y—yes," she faltered. Then more calmly: "Yes. I came to tell you that the package of ten thousand dollars which you took from Mr. Fraser's pocket has again disappeared."

"Yes," said the other, without astonishment.

"It was presumed at the bank that he had taken it home with him, having regained possession of it in some way, but a careful search has failed to reveal it."

"Yes, and what else?"

The girl took a long breath and gazed steadily into the eyes of the scientist, with determination in her own.

"I have come, too, to tell you," she said, "the name of the man who robbed the bank."

V

If Miss Clarke had expected that The Thinking Machine would show either astonishment or enthusiasm, she must have been disappointed, for he neither altered his position nor looked at her. Instead, he was gazing thoughtfully away with lackluster eyes.

"Well?" he asked. "I suppose it's a story. Begin at the beginning."

With a certain well-bred air of timidity, the girl began the story; and occasionally as she talked there was a little tremor of the lips.

"I have been a stenographer and typewriter for seven years," she said, "and in that time I have held only four positions. The first was in a law office in New York, where I was left an orphan to earn my own living; the second was with a manufacturing concern, also in New York. I left there three years ago to accept the position of private secretary to William T. Rankin, president of the —— National Bank, at Hartford, Connecticut. I came from there to Boston and later went to work at the Ralston Bank, as private secretary to Mr. Fraser. I left the bank in Hartford because of the failure of that concern, following a bank robbery."

The Thinking Machine glanced at her suddenly.

"You may remember from the newspapers——" she began again.

"I never read the newspapers," he said.

"Well, anyway," and there was a shade of impatience at the interruption, "there was a bank burglary there similar to this. Only seventy thousand dollars was stolen, but it was a small institution and the theft precipitated a run which caused a collapse after I had been in that position for only six months."

"How long have you been with the Ralston National?"

"Nine months," was the reply.

"Had you saved any money while working in your other positions?"

"Well, the salary was small—I couldn't have saved much."

"How did you live those two years from the time you left the Hartford Bank until you accepted this position?"

The girl stammered a little.

"I received assistance from friends," she said, finally.

"Go on."

"That bank in Hartford," she continued, with a little gleam of resentment in her eyes, "had a safe similar to the one at the Ralston National, though not so large. It was blown in identically the same way as this one was blown."

"Oh, I see," said the scientist. "Someone was arrested for this, and you want to give me the name of that man?"

"Yes," said the girl. "A professional burglar, William Dineen, was arrested for that robbery and confessed. Later he escaped. After his arrest he boasted of his ability to blow any style of safe. He used an invention of his own for the borings to place the charges. I noticed that safe and I noticed this one. There is a striking similarity in the two."

The Thinking Machine stared at her.

"Why do you tell me?" he asked.

"Because I understood you were making the investigation for the bank," she responded, unhesitatingly, "and I dreaded the notoriety of telling the police."

"If this William Dineen is at large you believe he did this?"

"I am almost positive."

"Thank you," said The Thinking Machine.

Miss Clarke went away, and late that night Hatch appeared. He looked weary and sank into a chair gratefully, but there was satisfaction in his eye. For an hour or more he talked. At last The Thinking Machine was satisfied, nearly.

"One thing more," he said, in conclusion. "Notify the police to look out for William Dineen, professional bank burglar, and his pals, whose names you can get from the newspapers in connection with a bank robbery in Hartford. They are wanted in connection with this case."

The reporter nodded.

"When Mr. Fraser recovers I intend to hold a little party here," the scientist continued. "It will be a surprise party."

It was two days later, and the police were apparently seeking some tangible point from which they could proceed, when The Thinking Machine received word that there had been a change for the better in Mr. Fraser's condition. Immediately he sent for Detective Mallory, with whom he held a long conversation. The detective went away tugging at his heavy mustache and smiling. With three other men he disappeared from police haunts that afternoon on a special mission.

That night the little "party" was held in the apartments of The Thinking Machine. President Fraser was first to arrive. He was pale and weak, but there was a fever of impatience in his manner. Then came West, Dunston, Miss Clarke, Miss Willis, and Charles Burton, a clerk whose engagement to the pretty Miss Willis had been recently announced.

The party gathered, each staring at the others curiously, with questions in their eyes, until The Thinking Machine entered, rubbing his fingers together briskly. Behind him came Hatch, bearing a shabby gripsack. The reporter's face showed excitement despite his rigid efforts to repress it. There were some preliminaries, and then the scientist began.

"To come to the matter quickly," he said, in preface, "we will take it for granted that no employee of the Ralston Bank is a professional burglar. But the person who was responsible for that burglary, who shared the money stolen, who planned it and actually assisted in its execution is in this room—now."

Instantly there was consternation, but it found no expression in words, only in the faces of those present.

"Further, I may inform you," went on the scientist, "that no one will be permitted to leave this room until I finish."

"Permitted?" demanded Dunston. "We are not prisoners."

"You will be if I give the word," was the response, and Dunston sat back, dazed. He glanced uneasily at the faces of the others; they glanced uneasily at him.

"The actual facts in the robbery you know," went on The Thinking Machine. "You know that the safe was blown, that a large sum of money was stolen, that Mr. West's handkerchief was found near the safe. Now, I'll tell you what I have learned. We will begin with President Fraser.

"Against Mr. Fraser is more direct evidence than against anyone else, because in his pocket was found one of the stolen bundles of money, containing ten thousand dollars. Mr. Fraser needed ninety thousand dollars previous to the robbery."

"But——" began the old man, with death-like face.

"Never mind," said the scientist. "Next, Miss Willis." Curious eyes were turned on her, and she, too, grew suddenly white. "Against her is less direct evidence than against anyone else. Miss Willis positively declined to permit a search of her person until she was compelled to do so by the fact that the other two permitted it. The fact that nothing was found has no bearing on the subject. She did refuse.

"Then Charles Burton," the inexorable voice went on, calmly, as if in mere discussion of a problem of mathematics. "Burton is engaged to Miss Willis. He is ambitious. He recently lost twenty thousand dollars in stock speculation—all he had. He needed more money in order to give this girl, who refused to be searched, a comfortable home.

"Next Miss Clarke, secretary to Mr. Fraser. Originally she came under consideration through the fact that she used perfume, and that Mr. West's handkerchief carried a faint odor of perfume. Now it is a fact that for years Miss Clarke used violet perfume, then on the day following the robbery suddenly began to use strong rose perfume, which smothers a violet odor. Miss Clarke, you will remember, fainted at the time of the search. I may add that a short while ago she was employed in a bank which was robbed in the identical manner of this one."

Miss Clarke sat apparently calm, and even faintly smiling, but her face was white. The Thinking Machine squinted at her a moment, then turned suddenly to Cashier West.

"Here is the man," he said, "whose handkerchief was found, but he does not use perfume, has never used it. He is the man who would have had best opportunity to leave unfastened the window in his private office by which the thieves entered the bank; he is the man who would have had the best opportunity to apply a certain chemical solution to the granite sockets of the steel bars, weakening the granite so they could be pulled out; he is the man who misrepresented facts to me. He told me he did not have and had not tried to raise any especially large sum of money. Yet on the day following the robbery he deposited $125,000 in cash in a bank in Chicago. The stolen sum was $129,000. That man, there."

All eyes were now turned on the cashier. He seemed choking, started to speak, then dropped back into his chair.

"And last, Dunston," resumed The Thinking Machine, and he pointed dramatically at the receiving teller. "He had equal opportunity with Mr. West to know of the amount of money in the bank; he refused first to be searched, and you witnessed his act a moment ago. To this man now there clings the identical odor of violet perfume which was on the handkerchief—not a perfume like it, but the identical odor."

There was silence, dumfounded silence, for a long time. No one dared to look at his neighbor now; the reporter felt the tension. At last The Thinking Machine spoke again.

"As I have said, the person who planned and participated in the burglary is now in this room. If that person will stand forth and confess it will mean a vast difference in the length of the term in prison."

Again silence. At last there came a knock at the door, and Martha thrust her head in.

"Two gentlemen and four cops are here," she announced.

"There are the accomplices of the guilty person, the men who actually blew that safe," declared the scientist, dramatically. "Again, will the guilty person confess?"

No one stirred.

VI

There was tense silence for a moment. Dunston was the first to speak.

"This is all a bluff," he said. "I think, Mr. Fraser, there are some explanations and apologies due to all of us, particularly to Miss Clarke and Miss Willis," he added, as an afterthought. "It is humiliating, and no good has been done. I had intended asking Miss Clarke to be my wife, and now I assert my right to speak for her. I demand an apology."

Carried away by his own anger and by the pleading face of Miss Clarke and the pain there, the young man turned fiercely on The Thinking Machine. Bewilderment was on the faces of the two banking officials.

"You feel that an explanation is due?" asked The Thinking Machine, meekly.

"Yes," thundered the young man.

"You shall have it," was the quiet answer, and the stooped figure of the scientist moved across the room to the door. He said something to someone outside and returned.

"Again I'll give you a chance for a confession," he said. "It will shorten your prison term." He was speaking to no one in particular; yet to them all. "The two men who blew the safe are now about to enter this room. After they appear it will be too late."

Startled glances were exchanged, but no one stirred. Then came a knock at the door. Silently The Thinking Machine looked about with a question in his eyes. Still silence, and he threw open the door. Three policemen in uniform and Detective Mallory entered, bringing two prisoners.

"These are the men who blew the safe," The Thinking Machine explained, indicating the prisoners. "Does anyone here recognize them?"

Apparently no one did, for none spoke.

"Do you recognize any person in this room?" he asked of the prisoners.

One of them laughed shortly and said something aside to the other, who smiled. The Thinking Machine was nettled and when he spoke again there was a touch of sarcasm in his voice.

"It may enlighten at least one of you in this room," he said, "to tell you that these two men are Frank Seranno and Gustave Meyer, Mr. Meyer being a pupil and former associate of the notorious bank burglar, William Dineen. You may lock them up now," he said to Detective Mallory. "They will confess later."

"Confess!" exclaimed one of them. Both laughed.

The prisoners were led out and Detective Mallory returned to lave in the font of analytical wisdom, although he would not have expressed it in those words. Then The Thinking Machine began at the beginning and told his story.

"I undertook to throw some light on this affair a few hours after its occurrence, at the request of President Fraser, who had once been able to do me a very great favor," he explained. "I went to the bank—you all saw me there—looked over the premises, saw how the thieves had entered the building, looked at the safe and at the spot where the handkerchief was found. To my mind it was demonstrated clearly that the handkerchief appeared there at the time of the burglary. I inquired if there was any draught through the office, seeking in that way to find if the handkerchief might have been lost at some other place in the bank, overlooked by the sweeper and blown to the spot where it was found. There was no draught.

"Next I asked for the handkerchief. Mr. Fraser asked me into his office to look at it. I saw a woman—Miss Clarke it was—in there and declined to go. Instead, I examined the handkerchief outside. I don't know that my purpose there can be made clear to you. It was a possibility that there would be perfume on the handkerchief, and the woman in the office might use perfume. I didn't want to confuse the odors. Miss Clarke was not in the bank when I arrived; she had gone to luncheon.

"Instantly I got the handkerchief I noticed the odor of perfume—violet perfume. Perfume is used by a great many women, by very few men. I asked how many women were employed in the bank. There were three. I handed the scented handkerchief to Mr. Hatch, removed all odor of the clinging perfume from my hands with my own handkerchief and also handed that to Mr. Hatch, so as to completely rid myself of the odor.

"Then I started through the bank and spoke to every person in it, standing close to them so that I might catch the odor if they used it. Miss Clarke was the first person who I found used it—but the perfume she used was a strong rose odor. Then I went on until I came to Mr. Dunston. The identical odor of the handkerchief he revealed to me by drawing out his own handkerchief while I talked to him."

Dunston looked a little startled, but said nothing; instead he glanced at Miss Clarke, who sat listening, interestedly. He could not read the expression on her face.

"This much done," continued The Thinking Machine, "we retired to Cashier West's office. There I knew the burglars had entered; there I saw a powerful chemical solution had been applied to the granite around the sockets of the protecting steel bars to soften the stone. Its direct effect is to make it of chalk-like consistency. I was also curious to know if any noise made in that room would attract attention in the outer office, so I upset a heavy chair, then looked outside. No one moved or looked back; therefore no one heard.

"Here I explained to President Fraser and to Mr. West why I connected some one in the bank with the burglary. It was because of the scent on the handkerchief. It would be tedious to repeat the detailed explanation I had to give them. I sent Mr. Hatch to find out, first, if Miss Clarke here had ever used violet perfume instead of rose; also to find out if any members of Mr. West's family used any perfume, particularly violet. I knew that Mr. Dunston used it.

"Then I asked Mr. Fraser if he had sought to raise any large sum of money. He told me the truth. But Mr. West did not tell me the truth in answer to a question along the same lines. Now I know why. It was because as cashier of the bank he was not supposed to operate in stocks, yet he has made a fortune at it. He didn't want Fraser to know this, and willfully misrepresented the facts.

"Then came the search. I expected to find just what was found, money, but considerably more of it. Miss Willis objected, Mr. Dunston objected and Miss Clarke fainted in the arms of Mr. Fraser. I read the motives of each aright. Dunston objected because he is an egotistical young man and, being young, is foolish. He considered it an insult. Miss Willis objected also through a feeling of pride."

The Thinking Machine paused for a moment, locked his fingers behind his head and leaned far back in his chair.

"Shall I tell what happened next?" he asked, "or will you tell it?"

Everyone in the room knew it was a question to the guilty person. Which? Whom? There came no answer, and after a moment The Thinking Machine resumed, quietly, very quietly.

"Miss Clarke fainted in Mr. Fraser's arms. While leaning against him, and while he stroked her hair and tried to soothe her, she took from the bosom of her loose shirtwaist a bundle of money, ten thousand dollars, and slipped it into the inside pocket of Mr. Fraser's coat."

There was death-like silence.

"It's a lie!" screamed the girl, and she rose to her feet with anger-distorted face. "It's a lie!"

Dunston arose suddenly and went to her. With his arm about her he turned defiantly to The Thinking Machine, who had not moved or altered his position in the slightest. Dunston said nothing, because there seemed to be nothing to say.

"Into the inside pocket of Mr. Fraser's coat," The Thinking Machine repeated. "When she removed her arms his scarf pin clung to the lace on one of her sleeves. That I saw. That pin could not have caught on her sleeve where it did if her hand had not been to the coat pocket. Having passed this sum of money—her pitiful share of the theft—she agreed to the search."

"It's a lie!" shrieked the girl again. And her every tone and every gesture said it was the truth. Dunston gazed into her eyes with horror in his own and his arm fell limply. Still he said nothing.

"Of course nothing was found," the quiet voice went on. "When I discovered the bank notes in Mr. Fraser's pocket I smelled them—seeking the odor, this time not of violet perfume, but of rose perfume. I found it."

Suddenly the girl whose face had shown only anger and defiance leaned over with her head in her hands and wept bitterly. It was a confession. Dunston stood beside her, helplessly; finally his hand was slowly extended and he stroked her hair.

"Go on, please," he said to Professor Van Dusen, meekly. His suffering was no less than hers.

"These facts were important, but not conclusive," said The Thinking Machine, "so next, with Mr. Hatch's aid here, I ascertained other things about Miss Clarke. I found out that when she went out to luncheon that day she purchased some powerful rose perfume; that, contrary to custom, she went home; that she used it liberally in her room; and that she destroyed a large bottle of violet perfume which you, Mr. Dunston, had given her. I ascertained also that her room was disarranged, particularly the couch. I assume from this that when she went to the office in the morning she did not have the money about her; that she left it hidden in the couch; that through fear of its discovery she rushed back home to get it; that she put it inside her shirtwaist, and there she had it when the search was made. Am I right, Miss Clarke?"

The girl nodded her head and looked up with piteous, tear-stained face.

"That night Miss Clarke called on me. She came ostensibly to tell me that the package of money, ten thousand dollars, had disappeared again. I knew that previously by telephone, and I knew, too, that she had that money then about her. She has it now. Will you give it up?"

Without a word the girl drew out the bundle of money, ten thousand dollars. Detective Mallory took it, held it, amazed for an instant, then passed it to The Thinking Machine, who sniffed at it.

"An odor of strong rose perfume," he said. Then: "Miss Clarke also told me that she had worked in a bank which had been robbed under circumstances identical with this by one William Dineen, and expressed the belief that he had something to do with this. Mr. Hatch ascertained that two of Dineen's pals were living in Cambridge. He found their rooms and searched them, later giving the address to the police.

"Now, why did Miss Clarke tell me that? I considered it in all points. She told me either to aid honestly in the effort to catch the thief, or to divert suspicion in another direction. Knowing as much as I did then, I reasoned it was to divert suspicion from you, Mr. Dunston, and from herself possibly. Dineen is in prison, and was there three months before this robbery; I believed she knew that. His pals are the two men in the other room; they are the men who aided Dineen in the robbery of the Hartford bank, with Miss Clarke's assistance; they are the men who robbed the Ralston National with her assistance. She herself indicated her profit from the Hartford robbery to me by a remark she made indicating that she had not found it necessary to work for two years from the time she left the Hartford bank until she became Mr. Fraser's secretary."

There was a pause. Miss Clarke sat sobbing, while Dunston stood near her studying the toe of his shoe. After a while the girl became more calm.

"Miss Clarke, would you like to explain anything?" asked The Thinking Machine. His voice was gentle, even deferential.

"Nothing," she said, "except admit it all—all. I have nothing to conceal. I went to the bank, as I went to the bank in Hartford, for the purpose of robbery, with the assistance of those men in the next room. We have worked together for years. I planned this robbery; I had the opportunity, and availed myself of it, to put a solution on the sockets of the steel bars of the window in Mr. West's room, which would gradually destroy the granite and make it possible to pull out the bars. This took weeks, but I could reach that room safely from Mr. Fraser's.

"I had the opportunity to leave the window unfastened and did so. I dressed in men's clothing and accompanied those two men to the bank. We crept in the window, after pulling the bars out. The men attacked the night watchman and bound him. The handkerchief of Mr. West's I happened to pick up in the office one afternoon a month ago and took it home. There it got the odor of perfume from being in a bureau with my things. On the night we went to the bank I needed something to put about my neck and used it. In the bank I dropped it. We had arranged all details at night, when I met them."

She stopped and looked at Dunston, a long, lingering look, that sent the blood to his face. It was not an appeal; it was nothing save the woman love in her, mingled with desperation.

"I intended to leave the bank in a little while," she went on. "Not immediately, because I was afraid that would attract attention, but after a few weeks. And then, too, I wanted to get forever out of sight of this man," and she indicated Dunston.

"Why?" he asked.

"Because I loved you as no woman ever loved a man before," she said, "and I was not worthy. There was another reason, too—I am married already. This man, Gustave Meyer, is my husband."

She paused and fumbled nervously at the veil fastening at her throat. Silence lay over the room; The Thinking Machine reached behind him and picked up the shabby-looking gripsack which had passed unnoticed.

"Are there any more questions?" the girl asked, at last.

"I think not," said The Thinking Machine.

"And, Mr. Dunston, you will give me credit for some good, won't you—some good in that I loved you?" she pleaded.

"My God!" he exclaimed in a sudden burst of feeling.

"Look out!" shouted The Thinking Machine.

He had seen the girl's hand fly to her hat, saw it drawn suddenly away, saw something slender flash at her breast. But it was too late. She had driven a heavy hat pin straight through her breast, piercing the heart. She died in the arms of the man she loved, with his tears on her face.

Detective Mallory appeared before the two prisoners in an adjoining room.

"Miss Clarke has confessed," he said.

"Well, the little devil!" exclaimed Meyer. "I knew someday she would throw us. I'll kill her!"

"It isn't necessary," remarked Mallory.

———

In the room where the girl lay The Thinking Machine pushed with his foot the shabby-looking grip toward President Fraser and West.

"There's the money," he said.

"Where—how did you get it?"

"Ask Mr. Hatch."

"Professor Van Dusen told me to search the rooms of those men in there, find the shabbiest-looking bag or receptacle that was securely locked, and bring it to him. I—I did so. I found it under the bed, but I didn't know what was in it until he opened it."

The Problem of the Auto Cab

Hutchinson Hatch gathered up his overcoat and took the steps coming down two at a time. There was no car in sight, nothing on wheels—in fact, until—yes, here was an automobile turning the corner, an automobile cab drifting along apparently without purpose. Hatch hailed it.

"Get me out to Commonwealth Avenue and Arden Street in a hurry!" he instructed. "Take a chance with the speed law, and I'll make it worth while. It's important."

He yanked open the door, stepped in, and closed it with a slam. The chauffeur gave a twist to his lever, turned the car almost within its length, and went scuttling off up the street.

Safely inside, Hatch became suddenly aware that he had a fellow passenger. Through the gloom he felt, rather than saw, two inquisitive eyes staring out at him, and there was the faintest odor of violets.

"Hello!" Hatch demanded. "Am I in your way?"

"Not in the slightest," came the voice of a woman. "Am I in yours?"

"Why—I beg your pardon," Hatch stammered. "I thought I had the cab alone—didn't know there was a passenger. Perhaps I'd better get out?"

"No, no!" protested the woman quickly. "Don't think of it."

Then from outside came the bellowing voice of a policeman. "Hey there! I'll report you!"

Glancing back, Hatch saw him standing in the middle of the street jotting down something in a notebook. The chauffeur made a few uncomplimentary remarks about bluecoats in general, swished round a corner, and sped on. With a half smile of appreciation on his lips, Hatch turned back to his unknown companion.

"If you will tell me where you are going," he suggested, "I'll have the chauffeur set you down."

"It's of no consequence," replied the woman a little wearily. "I am going no place particularly—just riding about to collect my thoughts."

A woman unattended, riding about in an automobile at fifteen minutes of eleven o'clock at night to collect her thoughts! And the chauffeur didn't know he had a passenger! The reporter sat oblivious of the bumping, grinding, of the automobile, trying to consider this unexpected incident calmly.

"You are a reporter?" inquired the woman.

"Yes" Hatch replied. "How did you guess it?"

"From seeing you rush out of a newspaper office in such a hurry at this time of night," she replied. "Something important, I dare say?"

"Well, yes," Hatch agreed. "A jewel robbery at a ball. Don't know much about it yet. Just got a police bulletin stating that Mrs. Windsor Dillingham had been robbed of a necklace worth thirty thousand dollars at a big affair she is giving tonight."

The inside of the cab was lighted brilliantly by the electric arc outside, and Hatch had an opportunity of seeing the woman face to face at close range. She was pretty: she was young, and she was well dressed. From her shoulders she was enveloped in some loose cloak of dark material, but it was not drawn together at her throat, and her bare neck gleamed.

There being nothing whatever to say, Hatch sat silently staring out of the window as the automobile whirled into Commonwealth Avenue, and slowed up as it approached Arden Street.

"Will you do me one favor, please?" asked the woman.

"Yes, if I can," was the reporter's reply.

"Allow me, please, to get out of the automobile on the side away from the curb, and be good enough to attract the attention of the chauffeur to yourself while I am doing it. Here is a bill," and she pressed something into Hatch's hand. "You may pay the chauffeur a tip for the passenger he didn't know he had."

Hatch agreed in a dazed sort of way, and the automobile came to a stop. He stepped out on the curb, and slammed the door as the chauffeur leaped down from his seat. From the other side came the answering door slam, as if an echo.

Five minutes later Hatch joined Detective Mallory inside. At just that moment the detective was listening to the story of Mrs. Dillingham's maid.

"There's nothing missing but the necklace," she explained; "so far, at least, as we have been able to find out. Mrs. Dillingham began dressing at about half-past eight o'clock, and I assisted her as usual. I suppose it was half-past nine when she finished. All that time the necklace was in the jewel box on her dressing table. It was the only article of jewelry in the box.

"Well, the butler came up about half-past nine o'clock for his final instructions, and Mrs. Dillingham went into the adjoining room to talk to him. It was not more than a minute later when she sent me down to the conservatory for a rose for her hair. She was still talking to him when I returned five minutes later. I put the rose in her hair, and she sent me into her dressing room for her necklace. When I looked into the jewel box, the necklace was gone. I told Mrs. Dillingham. The butler heard me. That's all I know of it, except that Mrs. Dillingham went into hysterics and fainted, and I telephoned for a doctor."

Detective Mallory regarded the girl coldly. Hatch knew perfectly what was coming. "You are quite sure," asked the detective, "that you did not take the necklace with you when you went down to the conservatory, and pass it to a confederate on the outside?"

The sudden pallor of the girl, her abject, cringing fright, answered the question to Hatch's satisfaction even before she opened her lips with a denial. Hatch himself was about to ask a question, when a footman entered.

"Mrs. Dillingham will see you in her boudoir," he announced.

From the lips of Mrs. Dillingham they heard identically the same story the maid had told. Mrs. Dillingham did not suspect anyone of her household.

For half an hour the detective interrogated her; then there came a rap at the door, and a woman entered.

"Why, Dora!" exclaimed Mrs. Dillingham.

The young woman went straight to her, put her arms about her shoulders protectingly, then turned to glare defiantly at Detective Mallory and Hutchinson Hatch. The reporter gasped—it was the mysterious woman of the automobile. An exclamation was on his lips, but something in her eyes warned him, and he was silent.

When, on the following day, Hutchinson Hatch related the circumstances of the theft of Mrs. Dillingham's necklace to Professor Augustus S. F. X. Van Dusen—The Thinking Machine—he did not mention the mysterious woman in the automobile. However curious those incidents in which he and she had figured were, they were inconsequential, and there was nothing to connect them in any way with the problem in hand. The strange woman's meeting with Mrs. Dillingham in the reporter's presence had convinced him that she was an intimate friend.

"Just what time was the theft discovered?" inquired The Thinking Machine.

"Within a few minutes of half-past nine."

"At what time did most of the guests arrive?"

"Between half-past nine and ten o'clock."

"Then at half-past nine," continued the scientist, "there could have been many persons there?"

"Perhaps a dozen," returned the reporter.

"And who were they?"

"Their names, you mean? I don't know."

"Well, find out," directed The Thinking Machine crustily. "If the servants are removed from the case, and there were a dozen other persons in the house, common sense tells us to find out who and what they were. Suppose, Mr. Hatch, you had attended that ball and stolen that necklace; what would have been your natural inclination afterward?"

Hatch stared at him blankly for a minute, then smiled whimsically. "You mean how would I have tried to get away with it?" he asked.

"Yes. When would you have left the place?"

"That's rather hard to say," Hatch declared thoughtfully. "But I think I should either have gone before anybody else did, through fear of discovery, or else I should have been one of the last, through excess of caution."

"Then proceed along those lines," instructed The Thinking Machine. "You might almost put that down as a law of criminology. It will enable you in the beginning, therefore, to narrow down the dozen or so guests to the first and last who left."

Deeply pondering this little interjection of psychology into a very material affair, Hatch went his way. In the course of events he saw Mrs. Dillingham, who, out of consideration for her guests, flatly refused to give their names.

Luckily for Hatch, the butler didn't feel that way about it at all. This was due partly to the fact that Detective Mallory had given him a miserable half-hour, and partly, perhaps, to the fact that the reporter oiled his greedy palm with a bill of two figures.

"To begin with," said the reporter, "I want to know the names of the first dozen or so persons who arrived here that evening—I mean those who were here when you sent to speak with Mrs. Dillingham."

"I might find out, sir. Their cards were laid on the silver as they arrived, and that silver, I think, has remained undisturbed. Therefore, the first dozen cards on it would give you the names you want."

"Now, that's something like it," commented the reporter enthusiastically. "And do you remember any person who left the house rather early that evening?"

"No, sir," was the reply. Then suddenly there came a flash of remembrance across the stoical face. "But I remember that one gentleman arrived here twice. It was this way. Mr. Hawes Campbell came in about eleven o'clock, and passed by without handing me a card. Then I remembered that he had been here earlier and that I had his card. But I don't recall that anyone went out, and I was at the door all evening except when I was up stairs talking to Mrs. Dillingham."

On a bare chance, Hatch went to find Campbell. Inquiry at his two clubs failed to find him, and finally Hatch called at his home.

At the end of five minutes, perhaps, Hatch caught the swish of skirts in the hallway, then the portiers were thrust aside and—again he was face to face with the mysterious woman of the automobile.

"My brother isn't here," she said calmly, without the slightest sign of any recognition. "Can I do anything for you?"

Her brother! Then she was Miss Campbell, and Mrs. Dillingham had called her Dora—Dora Campbell!

"Well—er——" Hatch faltered a little, "it was a personal matter I wanted to see him about."

"I don't know when he will return," Miss Campbell announced.

Hatch stared at her for a moment; he was making up his mind. At last, he took the bit in his teeth. "We understand, Miss Campbell," he said at last slowly and emphatically, "that your brother, Hawes Campbell, has some information which might be of value in unraveling the mystery surrounding the theft of Mrs. Dillingham's necklace."

Miss Campbell dropped into a chair, and unconsciously Hatch assumed the defensive. "Mrs. Dillingham is very much annoyed, as you must know," Miss Campbell said, "about the publicity given to this affair; particularly as she is confident that the necklace will be returned within a short time. Her only annoyance, beyond the wide publicity, as I said, is that it has not already been returned."

"Returned?" gasped Hatch.

Miss Campbell shrugged her shoulders. "She knows," she continued, "that the necklace is now in safe hands, that there is no danger of its being lost to her, but the situation is such that she cannot demand its return."

"Mrs. Dillingham knows where the necklace is, then?" he asked.

"Yes," replied Miss Campbell.

"Perhaps you know?"

"Perhaps I do," she responded readily. "I can assure you that Mrs. Dillingham is going to take the affair out of the hands of the police, because she knows her property is safe—as safe as if it was in your hands, for instance. It is only a question of time, when it will be returned."

"Where is the necklace?" Hatch demanded suddenly.

Again Miss Campbell shrugged her shoulders.

"And what does your brother know about the affair?"

"I can't answer that question, of course," was the response.

"Well, why did he go to Mrs. Dillingham's early in the evening, then go away, and return about eleven o'clock?" insisted the reporter bluntly.

For the first time there came a change in Miss Campbell's manner, a subtle, indefinable something which the reporter readily saw, but to which he could attach no meaning.

"I can't say more than I have said," she replied after a moment. "Believe me," and there was a note of earnestness in her voice, "it would be far better for you to drop the matter, because otherwise you may be placed in—a ridiculous position."

And that was all—a threat, delicately veiled it is true, but a threat nevertheless. She rose and led the way to the door.

Hatch didn't realize the significance of that remark, then, nor did it occur to him that the mysterious affair in the automobile had not been mentioned between them: for here was material, knotty, incoherent, inexplicable material, for The Thinking Machine, and there he took it. Again he told the story; but this time all of it—every incident from the moment he hailed the automobile in front of his office on the night of the robbery until Miss Campbell closed the door.

"Why didn't you tell me all of it before?" demanded The Thinking Machine irritably.

"I couldn't see that the affair in the automobile had any connection with the robbery," explained the reporter.

"Couldn't see!" stormed the eminent man of science. "Couldn't see! Every trivial happening on this whole round earth bears on every other happening, no matter how vast or how disconnected it may seem; the correlation of facts makes a perpetually unbroken chain. In other words, if Mrs. Leary hadn't kept a cow, Chicago would not have been destroyed by fire. Couldn't see!"

For an instant The Thinking Machine glared at him, and the change from petulant annoyance to deep abstraction, as that singular brain turned to the problem at hand, was almost visible. It was uncanny. Then the scientist dropped back into his chair with eyes turned upward and long slender fingers pressed tip to tip. Ten minutes passed, twenty, thirty, and he turned suddenly to the reporter.

"What was the number of that automobile?" he demanded.

Hatch grinned in sheer triumph. Of all the questions he could have anticipated this was the most unlikely, and yet he had the number set down in his notebook where it would ultimately become a voucher in his expense account. He consulted the book.

"Number 869019," he replied.

"Now find that automobile," directed The Thinking Machine. "It is important that you do so at once."

"You mean that the necklace——" Hatch began breathlessly.

"When you bring the automobile here, I will produce the necklace," declared The Thinking Machine emphatically.

Hatch returned half a dozen hours later with troubled lines in his face. "Automobile No. 869019 has disappeared, evaporated into air," he declared with some heat. "There was one that night, because I was in it, and the highway commission's records show a private cab license granted to John Kilrain under the number, but it has disappeared."

"Where is Kilrain?" inquired The Thinking Machine.

"I didn't see him; but I saw his wife," explained the reporter. "She didn't know anything about the automobile No. 869019, or said she didn't. She said his auto car was——"

"No. 610698," interrupted The Thinking Machine. It was not a question; it was the statement as of one who knew.

Hatch stared from the scientist to the notebook where he had written down the number the woman gave him, and then he looked his utter astonishment.

"Of course, that is the number," continued The Thinking Machine, as if someone had disputed it. "It is past midnight now, and we won't try to find it; but I'll have it here tomorrow at noon. We shall see for ourselves how safely the necklace has been kept."

———

Detective Mallory entered and glanced about inquiringly. He saw only The Thinking Machine and Hutchinson Hatch.

"I sent for you," explained the scientist, "because in half an hour or so I shall either place the Dillingham necklace in your hands, or turn over to you the man who knows where it is. You may use your own discretion as to whether or not you will prosecute. Under all the circumstances, I believe the case is one for a sanitarium, rather than prison. In other words, the person who took the necklace is not wholly responsible."

"Who is it?" demanded the detective.

"You don't happen to know all the facts in this case," continued The Thinking Machine without heeding the question. "I got them all, only after Mr. Hatch, at my suggestion, had located the thief. Originally I began where you left off. I believe you had eliminated the servants, and I presumed there was not a burglary. Ultimately this led to Hawes Campbell in a manner which is no interest to you. Then I got all the facts.

"When Mr. Hatch left his office to go to Mrs. Dillingham's, he took an automobile which happened to be passing," resumed the scientist. "It was a cab No. 869019. Inside that cab he found, much to his astonishment, a woman—a young woman in evening dress. She made the surprising statement that the chauffeur didn't know she was there, and that she was not going anywhere—was merely riding around to collect her thoughts. And this was, please remember, about eleven o'clock at night. On its face this incident had no connection with the jewel theft;

but by a singular chain of coincidences subsequently developed, it seemed that Mr. Hatch had arrived at the solution of the mystery before he even knew the circumstances of the theft."

Detective Mallory nodded doubtfully. "But how does that connect with the——" he began.

"Subsequent developments establish a direct connection," interrupted The Thinking Machine. "We have the woman in the automobile. We shall presume that she must have had some strong motive for leaving a house at that time of night and doing the apparently purposeless things that she did do. We don't know this motive from these facts—we only know there was a motive.

"Now when you and Mr. Hatch were talking to Mrs. Dillingham, a woman entered the room. Mr. Hatch recognized her immediately as the woman in the automobile. Everything indicated that she was an intimate friend of Mrs. Dillingham's. So we pass on to the point where Mr. Hatch found that Hawes Campbell arrived at the ball early, went away again, and returned after eleven o'clock. Mr. Hatch wanted to know why he left, and went to his home to inquire. Campbell's sister met him there. She was the woman he had met in the automobile. So we have Campbell leaving the ball, immediately after the theft, say, and his sister running away from her home sometime between nine-thirty and eleven, and screening herself in an automobile.

"Why? I have said, Mr. Mallory, that imagination—the ability to bridge gaps temporarily—is the most essential part of the logical mind. Now, if we imagine that Campbell stole the necklace, that he went home, that his sister found it out, that there was some sort of scene which terminated in her flight with the necklace, we account for absolutely every incident preceding and following Mr. Hatch's arrival at the Dillingham place.

"I have made inquiries. The Campbells are worth, not thousands, but millions. Therefore, the question. Why should Hawes Campbell steal a necklace. The answer, kleptomania. And again, it was known to the sister, who tried in her own manner to return the stolen property and avoid the scandal. When she was in the automobile, she was trying to collect her thoughts—trying to invent a way to return the necklace. It was the merest chance that Mr. Hatch happened to get into that particular vehicle.

"Now, we come to the most difficult part of the problem," and

The Thinking Machine dropped still further back into the cavernous depths of his chair. "What would a frightened, perhaps hysterical woman do with that necklace? From the fact that it has not been returned, we know that she didn't venture into the house with it, and leave it casually in any one of a hundred places where it might have been discovered without danger to herself. Yet, everything indicates that she had it while she was in the cab, intending to regain possession of it later, and return it. Now, that cab number was 869019. Strangely enough, after Mr. Hatch left the cab, it seems to have disappeared. The chauffeur, John Kilrain, has another cab number now, 610698—that is, auto cab No. 869019 was made to disappear by the simple act of turning over the number board upside down, giving us 610698."

"Well, by George!" exclaimed Detective Mallory. No mere words would convey the reporter's astonishment; he gasped.

"Now," continued The Thinking Machine after a moment, "there are two reasons, both good, why auto cab number 869019 should have disappeared. The vital one, it seems to me, is that Kilrain discovered the necklace inside and kept it; the other is that he was threatened with arrest by the policeman who took his number for speeding, and to avoid a fine, disguised the identity of his cab. There are one or two other possibilities; but if the necklace isn't found in the automobile, I should advise, not arrest, but a close watch on Kilrain, both at his home and in his intercourse with other chauffeurs at the various cab stands."

There was a rap at the door, and Martha appeared. "Did you want an automobile, sir?"

"We'll be right out," returned the scientist.

And so it came about that The Thinking Machine, Detective Mallory, and Hutchinson Hatch searched the very vitals of auto cab No. 869019, temporarily masquerading as No. 610698, while Kilrain stood by in perturbed amazement. At the end he was allowed to go.

"Remember, please, what I advised you to do," The Thinking Machine reminded Detective Mallory.

———

With eyes that were heavy with sleep Hutchinson Hatch crawled out of bed and answered the insistent ringing of his telephone. The crabbed voice of The Thinking Machine came over the wire in a question.

"If Miss Campbell was so anxious to return the necklace that night, she couldn't have done better than to have handed it to a reporter who was going to the house to investigate the robbery?"

"I don't think so," Hatch replied wonderingly.

"Did you have on your overcoat that night?"

"I had it with me."

"Suppose you go look in the pockets, and——"

Hatch dropped the receiver, already inspired by the suggestion, and dragged his overcoat out of the closet. In the left hand lower pocket was a small package. He opened it with trembling fingers. There before his eyes lay the iridescent, gleaming bauble. It had been in his possession from an hour after it was stolen until this very instant. He rushed back to the telephone.

"I've got it!" he shouted.

"Silly of me not to have thought of it in the first place," came the querulous voice of The Thinking Machine. "Good night."

THE SILVER BOX

"Really great criminals are never found out, for the simple reason that the greatest crimes—their crimes—are never discovered," remarked Professor Augustus S. F. X. Van Dusen positively. "There is genius in the perpetration of crime, Mr. Grayson, just as there must be in its detection, unless it is the shallow work of a bungler. In this latter case there have been instances where even the police have uncovered the truth. But the expert criminal, the man of genius—the professional, I may say—regards as perfect only that crime which does not and cannot be made to appear a crime at all; therefore one that can never involve him, or anyone else."

The financier, J. Morgan Grayson, regarded this wizened little man of science—The Thinking Machine—thoughtfully, through the smoke of his cigar.

"It is a strange psychological fact that the casual criminal glories in his crime beforehand and from one to ten minutes afterward," The Thinking Machine continued. "For instance, the man who kills for revenge wants the world to know it is his work; but at the end of ten minutes comes fear, abject terror, and then, paradoxically enough, he will seek to hide his crime and protect himself by some transparent means utterly inadequate, because of what he has said or done in the passion which preceded the act. With fear comes panic, with panic irresponsibility, and then he makes the mistake—hews a pathway which the trained mind follows from motive to a prison cell.

"These are the men who are found out. But there are men of genius, Mr. Grayson, professionally engaged in crime. We never hear of them, because they are never caught, and we never even suspect them, because they make no mistake—they are men of genius. Imagine the great brains as turned to crime. Well, there are today brains as great as any of these which make a profession of it; there is murder and theft and robbery under our noses that we never dream of. If I, for instance, should become an active criminal, can you see——" He paused.

Grayson, with a queer expression on his face, puffed steadily at his cigar.

"I could kill you now, here in this room," The Thinking Machine went on calmly, "and no one would ever know, never even suspect. Why not? Because I would make no mistake. In other words, I would immediately take rank with the criminals of genius who are never found out."

It was not a boast as he said it; it was merely a statement of fact. Grayson appeared to be a little startled. Where there had been only impatient interest in his manner, there was now something else—fascination, perhaps.

"How would you kill me, for instance?" he inquired curiously.

"With any one of a dozen poisons, with virulent germs, or even with a knife or revolver," replied the scientist placidly. "You see, I know how to use poisons. I know how to inoculate with germs; I know how to produce suicidal appearance perfectly with either a revolver or knife. And I never make mistakes, Mr. Grayson. In the sciences we must be exact—not approximately so, but absolutely so. We must know. It isn't like carpentry. A carpenter may make a trivial mistake in a joint, and it will not weaken his house; but if the scientist makes one mistake, the whole structure tumbles down. We must know. Knowledge is progress. We gain knowledge by observation and logic—inevitable logic. And logic tells us that while two and two make four, it is not only sometimes but all the time."

Grayson flicked the ashes of his cigar thoughtfully, and little wrinkles appeared about his eyes as he stared into the drawn, inscrutable face of the scientist. The enormous, straw-yellow head was cushioned against the chair, the squinting, watery blue eyes turned upward, and the slender white fingers at rest, tip to tip. The financier drew a long breath. "I have been informed that you were a remarkable man," he said at last, slowly. "I believe it. Quinton Fraser, the banker who gave me the letter of introduction to you, told me how you once solved a remarkable mystery, in which——"

"Yes, yes," interrupted the scientist shortly, "the Ralston bank robbery—I remember."

"So I came to you to enlist your aid in something which is more inexplicable than that." Grayson went on hesitatingly. "I know that no fee I might offer would influence you, yet it is a case which——"

"State it," interrupted The Thinking Machine again.

"It isn't a crime—that is, a crime that can be reached by law," Grayson hurried on—"but it has cost me millions and——"

For one instant The Thinking Machine lowered his squint eyes to those of his visitor, then raised them again. "Millions!" he repeated. "How many?"

"Six, eight, perhaps ten," was the reply. "Briefly, there is a leak in my office. My plans become known to others almost by the time I have perfected them. My plans are large; I have millions at stake; and the greatest secrecy is absolutely essential. For years I have been able to preserve this secrecy; but half a dozen times in the last eight weeks my plans have become known, and I have been caught. Unless you know the Street, you can't imagine what a tremendous disadvantage it is to have someone know your next move to the minutest detail, and knowing it, defeat you at every turn."

"No, I don't know your world of finance, Mr. Grayson," remarked The Thinking Machine. "Give me an instance."

"Well, take this last case," suggested the financier earnestly. "Briefly, without technicalities, I had planned to unload the securities of the P., Q., and X. railway, protecting myself through brokers, and force the outstanding stock down to a price where other brokers, acting for me, could buy far below the actual value. In this way I intended to get complete control of the stock. But my plans became known, and when I began to unload, everything was snapped up by the opposition, with the result that instead of gaining control of the road I lost heavily. The same thing has happened, with variations, half a dozen times."

"I presume that this is strictly honest?" inquired the scientist mildly.

"Honest?" repeated Grayson. "Certainly—of course. It's business."

"I shall not pretend to understand all that," said The Thinking Machine curtly. "It doesn't seem to matter, anyway. You want to know where the leak is. Is that right?"

"Precisely."

"Well, who is in your confidence?"

"No one, except my stenographer."

"Of course there is an exception. Who is he, please?"

"It's a woman—Miss Evelyn Winthrop. She has been in my employ for six years in the same capacity—more than five years before this leak appeared—and I trust her absolutely."

"No man knows your business?"

"No," replied the financier grimly. "I learned years ago that no one could keep my secrets as I do—there are too many temptations—therefore I never mention my plans to anyone—never—to anyone!"

"Except your stenographer," corrected the scientist.

"I work for days, weeks, sometimes months, perfecting plans, and it's all in my head, not on paper—not a scratch of it," explained Grayson. "Therefore, when I say that she is in my confidence, I mean that she knows my plans only half an hour or less before the machinery is put into motion. For instance, I planned this P., Q., and X. deal. My brokers didn't know of it; Miss Winthrop never heard of it until twenty minutes before the Stock Exchange opened for business. Then I dictated to her, as I always do, some short letters of instructions to my agents. That is all she knew of it."

"You outlined the plan in those letters?"

"No; they merely told my brokers what to do."

"But a shrewd person, knowing the contents of all those letters, could have learned what you intended to do?"

"Yes; but no one person knew the contents of all the letters. No one broker knew what was in the other letters—many of them were unknown to each other. Miss Winthrop and I were the only two human beings who knew all that was in them."

The Thinking Machine sat silent for so long that Grayson began to fidget in his chair. "Who was in the room besides you and Miss Winthrop before the letters were sent?" he asked at last.

"No one," responded Grayson emphatically. "For an hour before I dictated those letters, until at least an hour afterward, after my plans had gone to smash, no one entered that room. Only she and I work there."

"But when she finished the letters, she went out?" insisted The Thinking Machine.

"No," declared the financier. "She didn't even leave her desk."

"Or perhaps sent something out—manifolds of the letters?"

"No."

"Or called up a friend on the telephone?" continued The Thinking Machine quietly.

"Nor that," retorted Grayson.

"Or signaled to some one through the window?"

"No," said the financier again. "She finished the letters, then remained quietly at her desk, reading a book. She didn't move for two hours."

The Thinking Machine lowered his eyes and glared straight into those of the financier. "Someone listened at the window?" he went on after a moment.

"No. It is six stories up, fronting the street, and there is no fire escape."

"Or the door?"

"If you knew the arrangement of my offices, you would see how utterly impossible that would be, because——"

"Nothing is impossible, Mr. Grayson," snapped the scientist abruptly. "It might be improbable, but not impossible. Don't say that. It annoys me exceedingly." He was silent for a moment. Grayson stared at him blankly. "Did either you or she answer a call on the phone?"

"No one called; we called no one."

"Any apertures—holes or cracks in your flooring, or walls or ceilings?" demanded the scientist.

"Private detectives whom I had employed looked for such an opening, and there was none," replied Grayson.

Again The Thinking Machine was silent for a long time. Grayson lighted a fresh cigar and settled back in his chair patiently. Faint cobwebby lines began to appear on the domelike brow of the scientist, and slowly the squint eyes were narrowing.

"The letters you wrote were intercepted?" he suggested at last.

"No," exclaimed Grayson flatly. "Those letters were sent direct to the brokers by a dozen different methods, and every one of them had been delivered by five minutes of ten o'clock, when 'Change begins business. The last one left me at ten minutes of ten."

"Dear me! Dear me!" The Thinking Machine rose and paced the length of the room thrice.

"You don't give me credit for the extraordinary precautions I have taken, particularly in this last P., Q., and X. deal," Grayson continued. "I left positively nothing undone to insure absolute secrecy. And Miss Winthrop I know is innocent of any connection with the affair. The private detectives suspected her at first, as you do, and she was watched in and out of my office for weeks. When she was not under my eyes, she was under the eyes of men to whom I had promised an extravagant sum of money if they found the leak. She didn't know it, and doesn't know it now. I am heartily ashamed of it all, because the investigation proved her absolute loyalty to me. On this last day she was directly under my eyes for two hours; and she didn't make one movement that I didn't note, because the thing means millions to me. That proved beyond all question that it was no fault of hers. What could I do?"

The Thinking Machine didn't say. He paused at a window, and for minute after minute stood motionless there, with eyes narrowed down to mere slits.

"I was on the point of discharging Miss Winthrop," the financier went on, "but her innocence was so thoroughly proved to me by this last affair that it would have been unjust, and so——"

Suddenly the scientist turned upon his visitor. "Do you talk in your sleep?" he demanded.

"No," was the prompt reply. "I had thought of that, too. It is beyond all ordinary things, professor. Yet there is a leak that is costing me millions."

"It comes down to this, Mr. Grayson," The Thinking Machine informed him crabbedly enough. "If only you and Miss Winthrop knew those plans, and no one else, and they did leak, and were not deduced from other things, then either you or she permitted them to leak, intentionally or unintentionally. That is as pure logic as that two and two make four; there is no need to argue it."

"Well, of course, I didn't," said Grayson.

"Then Miss Winthrop did," declared The Thinking Machine finally, positively, "unless we credit the opposition, as you call it, with telepathic gifts hitherto unheard of. By the way, you have referred to the other side only as the opposition. Do the same men, the same clique, appear against you all the time, or is it only one man?"

"It's a clique," explained the financier, "with millions back of it, headed by Ralph Matthews, a young man to whom I give credit for being the prime factor against me." His lips were set sternly.

"Why?" demanded the scientist.

"Because every time he sees me, he grins," was the reply. Grayson seemed suddenly discomfited.

The Thinking Machine went to a desk, addressed an envelope, folded a sheet of paper, placed it inside, then sealed it. At length he turned back to his visitor. "Is Miss Winthrop in your office now?"

"Yes."

"Let us go there, then."

A few minutes later the eminent financier ushered the eminent scientist into his private office on the Street. The only other person there was a young woman—a woman of twenty-six or seven, perhaps—who turned, saw Grayson, and resumed reading. The financier motioned to a seat. Instead of sitting, however, The Thinking Machine went straight to Miss Winthrop and extended a sealed envelope to her.

"Mr. Ralph Matthews asked me to hand you this," he said.

The young woman glanced up into his face frankly, yet with a certain timidity, took the envelope, and turned it curiously in her hand.

"Mr. Ralph Matthews," she repeated, as if the name was a strange one. "I don't think I know him."

The Thinking Machine stood staring at her aggressively, insolently even, as she opened the envelope and drew out the sheet of paper. There was no expression save surprise—bewilderment, rather—to be read on her face.

"Why, it's a blank sheet!" she remarked, puzzled.

The scientist turned away suddenly toward Grayson, who had witnessed the incident with frank astonishment in his eyes. "Your telephone—a moment please," he requested.

"Certainly; here," replied Grayson.

"This will do," remarked the scientist.

He leaned forward over the desk where Miss Winthrop sat, still gazing at him in a sort of bewilderment, picked up the receiver, and held it to his ear. A few moments later he was talking to Hutchinson Hatch, reporter.

"I merely wanted to ask you to meet me at my apartments in an hour," said the scientist. "It is very important."

That was all. He hung up the receiver, paused for a moment to admire an exquisitely wrought silver box—a "vanity" box—on Miss Winthrop's desk, beside the telephone, then took a seat beside Grayson and began to discourse almost pleasantly on the prevailing meteorological conditions. Grayson merely stared; Miss Winthrop continued her reading.

———

Professor Augustus S. F. X. Van Dusen, distinguished scientist, and Hutchinson Hatch, newspaper reporter, were poking round among the chimney pots and other obstructions on the roof of a skyscraper. Far below them the slumber-enshrouded city was spread out like a panorama, streets dotted brilliantly with arc lights, and roofs hazily visible through the mists of night. Above, the infinite blackness hung like a veil, with star points breaking through here and there.

"Here are the wires," Hatch said at last, and he stopped.

The Thinking Machine knelt on the roof beside him, and for several minutes they remained thus in the darkness, with only the glow of an electric flash to indicate their presence. Finally The Thinking Machine rose.

"That's the wire you want, Mr. Hatch," he said. "I'll leave the rest of it to you."

"Are you sure?" asked the reporter.

"I am always sure," was the tart response.

Hatch opened a small hand satchel and removed several queerly shaped tools. These he spread on the roof beside him; then, kneeling again, began his work. For half an hour or so he labored in the gloom, with only the electric flash to aid him, and then he rose.

"It's all right," he said.

The Thinking Machine examined the work that had been done, grunted his satisfaction, and together they went to the skylight, leaving a thin, insulated wire behind them, stringing along to mark their path.

They passed down through the roof, and into the darkness of the hall of the upper story. Here the light was extinguished. From far below came the faint echo of a man's footsteps as the watchman passed through the silent, deserted building.

"Be careful!" warned The Thinking Machine.

Along the hall to a room in the rear they went, and still the wire trailed behind. At the last door they stopped. The Thinking Machine fumbled with some keys, then opened the way. Here an electric light was on. The room was bare of furniture, the only sign of recent occupancy being a telephone instrument on the wall.

Here The Thinking Machine stopped and stared at the spool of wire which he had permitted to wind off as he walked, and his thin face expressed doubt.

"It wouldn't be safe," he said at last, "to leave the wire exposed as we have left it. True, this floor is not occupied; but someone might pass up this way and disturb it. You take the spool, go back to the roof, winding the wire as you go, then swing the spool down to me over the side so I can bring it in the window. That will be best. I shall catch it here, and thus there will be nothing to indicate any connection."

Hatch went out quietly and closed the door.

———

Twice the following day The Thinking Machine spoke to the financier over the telephone. Grayson was in his private office, Miss Winthrop at her desk, when the first call came.

"Be careful in answering my questions," warned The Thinking Machine when Grayson answered. "Do you know how long Miss Winthrop has owned the little silver box which is now on her desk, near the telephone?"

Grayson glanced around involuntarily to where the girl sat idly turning over the leaves of her book. "Yes," he answered; "for seven months. I gave it to her last Christmas."

"Ah!" exclaimed the scientist. "That simplifies matters. Where did you buy it?"

Grayson mentioned the name of a well known jeweler.

"Good by," came the voice of the scientist, and the connection was broken.

Considerably later in the day The Thinking Machine called Grayson to the telephone again.

"What make of typewriter does she use?" came the querulous voice over the wire.

Grayson named it.

"Good by."

While Grayson sat with deeply perplexed lines in his face, the diminutive scientist called upon Hutchinson Hatch at his office. The reporter was just starting out.

"Do you use a typewriter?" demanded The Thinking Machine.

"Yes."

"What kind?"

"Oh, four or five kinds—we have half a dozen varieties in the office. I can use any of them."

They passed along through the city room, at that moment practically deserted, until finally the watery blue eyes settled upon a typewriter with the name emblazoned on the front.

"That's it!" exclaimed The Thinking Machine. "Write something on it," he directed Hatch.

"What shall I write?" inquired the reporter, and he sat down.

"Anything you like," was the terse response. "Just write something."

Hatch drew up a chair and rolled off several lines of the immortal practice sentence beginning, "Now is the time for all good men——"

The Thinking Machine sat beside him, squinting off across the room in deep abstraction, and listening intently. His head was turned away from the reporter, and his ear was within a few inches of the machine. For a minute he sat there listening, then shook his head.

"Strike your vowels," he commanded, "first slowly, then rapidly."

Again Hatch obeyed, while the scientist listened. And again he shook his head. Then in turn every make of machine in the office was tested the same way. At the end The Thinking Machine rose and went his way. There was an expression nearly approaching bewilderment on his face as he went out.

For hour after hour that night The Thinking Machine half lay in a huge chair in his laboratory, with eyes turned uncompromisingly upward, and an expression of complete concentration on his face. There was no change either in his position or his gaze as minute succeeded minute; the brow was deeply wrinkled now, and the thin line of the lips was drawn taut. The tiny clock in the reception room struck ten, eleven, twelve, and finally one. At just half-past one The Thinking Machine rose suddenly.

"Positively, I am getting stupid!" he grumbled half aloud. "Of course! Of course! Why couldn't I have thought of that in the first place!"

So it came about that Grayson did not go to his office on the following morning at the usual time. Instead, he called again upon The Thinking Machine in eager, expectant response to a note which had reached him at his home just before he started to his office.

"Nothing yet," said The Thinking Machine as the financier entered. "But here is something you must do today. What time does the Stock Exchange close?"

"Three o'clock," was the reply.

"Well, at one o'clock," the scientist went on, "you must issue orders for a gigantic deal of some sort; and you must issue them precisely as you have issued them in the past; there must be no variation. Dictate the letters as you have always done to Miss Winthrop; but don't send them. When they come to you, keep them until you see me."

"You mean that the deal must be purely imaginary?" inquired the financier.

"Precisely," was the reply. "But make your instructions circumstantial; give them enough detail to make them absolutely convincing."

"And hold the letters?"

"Hold the letters," the other repeated. "The leak comes before you receive them. I don't want to know or have an idea of what mythical deal it is to be; but issue your orders at one o'clock."

Grayson asked a dozen questions, answer to which was curtly denied, then went to his office. The Thinking Machine again called Hatch to the telephone.

"I've got it," he announced briefly. "I want the best telegraph operator you know. Bring him along and meet me in the room on the top floor where the telephone is, at precisely fifteen minutes of one o'clock today."

"Telegraph operator?" Hatch repeated.

"That's what I said—telegraph operator," replied the scientist irritably. "Good by."

Hatch smiled whimsically at the other end as he heard the receiver banged on the hook—smiled because he knew the eccentric ways of this singular man, whose mind so accurately illuminated every problem to which it was directed. Then he went out to the telegraph room and borrowed the principal operator. They were in the little room on the top floor at precisely fifteen minutes of one.

The operator glanced about in astonishment. The room was still unfurnished, save for the telephone box on the wall.

"What do I do?" he asked.

"I'll tell you when the time comes," responded the scientist, as he glanced at the watch.

At three minutes of one o'clock he handed a sheet of blank paper to the operator, and gave his final instructions. "Hold the telephone receiver to your ear and write on this what you hear," he directed. "It may be several minutes before you hear anything. When you do, tell me so."

There was ludicrous mystification on the operator's face, but he obeyed orders, grinning cheerfully at Hatch as he tilted his cigar up to keep the smoke out of his eyes. The Thinking Machine stood impatiently looking on, watch in hand. Hatch didn't know what was happening; but he was tremendously interested.

And at last the operator heard something. His face suddenly became alert. He continued to listen for a moment, and then came a smile of recognition as he turned to the scientist.

"It's good old Morse, all right," he announced, "but it's the queerest sort of sounder I ever read."

"You mean the Morse telegraphic code?" demanded The Thinking Machine.

"Sure," said the operator.

"Write your message."

———

Within less than ten minutes after Miss Winthrop had handed over the typewritten letters of instruction to Grayson for signature, and while he still sat turning them over in his hands, the door opened and The Thinking Machine entered. He tossed a folded sheet of paper on the desk before Grayson, and went straight to Miss Winthrop.

"So you did know Mr. Ralph Matthews after all?" he inquired.

The girl rose from her desk, and a flash of some subtle emotion passed over her face. "What do you mean, sir?" she demanded.

"You might as well remove the silver box," The Thinking Machine went on mercilessly. "There is no further need for the connection."

Miss Winthrop glanced down at the telephone extension on her desk, and her hand darted toward it. The silver vanity box was underneath the receiver, supporting it, so that all weight was removed from the hook, and the line was open. She snatched the box, the receiver dropped back on the hook, and there was a faint tinkle of a bell somewhere below. The Thinking Machine turned to Grayson.

"It was Miss Winthrop," he said.

"Miss Winthrop!" exclaimed Grayson, and he rose. "I cannot believe it."

"It doesn't matter whether you believe it or not," retorted the scientist. "But if your doubt is very serious, you might ask her."

Grayson turned toward the girl and took a couple of steps forward. There was more than surprise in his face; there was doubt, and perhaps regret.

"I don't know what it's about," she protested feebly.

"Read the paper I gave you, Mr. Grayson," directed The Thinking Machine coldly. "Perhaps that will enlighten her."

The financier opened the sheet, which had remained folded in his hand, and glanced at what was written there. Slowly he read it aloud: "Goldman.—Sell ten thousand shares L. & W. at 97. McCracken Co.—Sell ten thousand shares L. & W. 97." He read on down the list, bewildered. Then gradually, as he realized the import of what he read, there came a hardening of the lines about his mouth.

"I understand, Miss Winthrop," he said at last. "This is the substance of the orders I dictated, and in some way you made them known to persons for whom they were not intended. I don't know how you did it, of course; but I understand that you did do it, so———" He stepped to the door and opened it with grave courtesy. "You may go now. I am sorry."

Miss Winthrop made no plea—simply bowed and went out. Grayson stood staring after her for a moment, then turned to The Thinking Machine, and motioned him to a chair. "What happened?" he asked briskly.

"Miss Winthrop," replied The Thinking Machine, "is a tremendously clever woman. She neglected to tell you, however, that besides being a stenographer and typist, she was a telegraph operator. She is so expert in each of her lines that she combined the two, if I may say it that way. In other words, in writing on the typewriter, she was clever enough to be able to give the click of the machine the sound of the Morse telegraphic code, so that another telegraph operator who heard her machine could translate it into words."

Grayson sat staring at him incredulously.

"I still don't understand," he finally said.

"Here," and The Thinking Machine rose and went to Miss Winthrop's desk—"here is an extension telephone with the receiver on the hook. It just happens that the little silver box which you gave Miss

Winthrop is tall enough to support this receiver clear of the hook, and the minute the receiver is off the hook, the line is open. When you were at your desk and she was here, you couldn't see this telephone; therefore, it was a simple matter for her to lift the receiver, and place the silver box beneath, thus holding the line open permanently. That being true, the sound of the typewriter would go over the open wire to whoever was listening at the other end, wouldn't it? Then, if that typewriter was made to sound the telegraphic code, and an operator held the receiver at the other end, that operator could read a message written at the same moment your letters were being written. That is all. It requires extreme concentration to do the thing—cleverness."

"Oh, I see!" exclaimed Grayson at last.

"When we knew that the leak in your office was not in the usual way," continued The Thinking Machine, "we looked for the unusual. First I was inclined to believe that there was a difference in the sounding keys as they were struck, and someone was clever enough to read that. I had Mr. Hatch make experiments, however, which instantly proved that was out of the question—unless this typewriter had been tuned, I may say. The logic of the thing had convinced me, meanwhile, that the leak must be by way of the telephone line, and Mr. Hatch and I tapped it one night. He is an electrician, as well as a newspaper reporter. Then I saw the possibility of holding the line open, as I explained; but for hour after hour the actual method of communication eluded me. At last I found it—the telegraphic code. Then it was all simple.

"When I telephoned to you to find out how long Miss Winthrop had had the silver box, and you said seven months, I knew that it was always at hand. When I asked you where you got it, I went there and saw a duplicate. There I measured the box and tested my belief that it would just support the receiver clear of the hook. When I requested you to dictate those orders today at one o'clock, I had a telegraph operator listening at a telephone on the top floor of this building. There is nothing very mysterious about it, after all—it's merely clever."

"Clever!" repeated Grayson, and his jaws snapped. "It is more than that. Why, it's criminal! She should be prosecuted."

"I shouldn't advise that, Mr. Grayson," returned the scientist coldly. "If it is honest—merely business—to juggle stocks as you told me you did, this is no more dishonest. And besides, remember that

Miss Winthrop is backed by the people who have made millions out of you, and—well, I wouldn't prosecute. It is betrayal of trust, certainly, but——" He rose as if that was all, and started toward the door. "I would advise you, if you want to stop the leak, to discharge the person in charge of your office exchange here," he said.

"Was she in the scheme?" demanded Grayson. He rushed out of the private office into the main office. At the door he met a clerk coming in.

"Where is Miss Mitchell?" demanded the financier hotly.

"I was just coming to tell you she went out with Miss Winthrop just now without giving any explanation," replied the clerk. "The telephone is without an attendant."

"Good day, Mr. Grayson," said The Thinking Machine.

The financier nodded his thanks, then stalked back into his room, banging the door behind him.

In the course of time The Thinking Machine received a check for ten thousand dollars, signed, "J. Morgan Grayson." He glared at it for a little while, then endorsed it in a crabbed hand, "Pay to Trustees Home for Crippled Children," and sent Martha out to mail it.

THE JACKDAW GIRL

Monsieur Jean Saint Rocheville lived by his wits, and, being rather witty, he lived rather well. In the beginning he hadn't been Monsieur Jean St. Rocheville at all. Born Jones, christened James Aloysius, nick-named Jimmie, he had been, first, a pickpocket. Sheer ability lifted him above that; and it came to pass that he graduated from all the cruder professions—second-story work, burglary, and what not—until now, when we meet him, he was a social brigand famous under many names.

For instance, in two cities of the West he was being industriously sought as Wilhelm Van Der Wyde, and was described as of the aes-thetic, musical type—young, thick-spectacled, clean-shaven, long-haired, and pale blond, speaking English badly and profusely.

In New York, the police knew him as Hubert Montgomery Wade, card sharp and utterer of worthless checks; and described him as tac-iturn, past middle age, with fluffy, iron-gray hair, full iron-gray beard, and a singularly pallid face. As we see him, he seemed about thirty, slim, elegant, aristocratic of feature, with close-cut brown hair, care-fully waxed mustache, and a suggestion of an imperial. Also, he spoke English with a slight accent.

Monsieur St. Rocheville was smiling as he strode through the spa-cious estate of Idlewild, whipping his light cane in the early-morning air of a balmy June day. On the whole, he had little to complain of in the way the world was wagging. True, he had failed, at his first attempt, to possess himself of the superb diamond necklace of his hostess, Mrs. Wardlaw Browne; but it had not been a discreditable failure; there had been no unpleasant features connected therewith, no exposure; not even a shadow of suspicion. Perhaps, after all, he had been hasty. His invitation had several weeks to run; and meanwhile here were all the luxuries of a splendid country place at his command— motors, horses, tennis, golf, to say nothing of a house full of charming women and several execrable players of auction, who insisted on gambling for high stakes. And auction, Monsieur St. Rocheville might have said, was his middle name.

Idly meditating upon all these pleasant things, St. Rocheville dropped down upon a seat in the shade of a hedge overlooking the rose garden, lighted a cigarette, and fell to watching the curious evolutions of three great velvet-black birds swimming in the air above him. Now they rose in a vast spiral, up, up until they were mere specks against the blue void, only to drop sheerly almost to the earth before their wings stayed them; now with motionless pinions, floating away in immense circles; again darting hither and yon swiftly as an arrow flies, weaving strange patterns in the air. Something here for the Wright brothers to learn, Monsieur St. Rocheville thought lazily.

Came finally an odd whistle from the direction of the house behind him. The three birds swooped down with a rush and vanished beyond the hedge. Curiously St. Rocheville peered through the thick-growing screen. On a second-story balcony stood a girl with one of the birds perched upon each shoulder, and the third at rest on her hand.

"Well, by George!" exclaimed St. Rocheville.

As he looked, the girl flipped something into the air. The birds dived for it simultaneously, immediately returning to their perches. Fascinated, he looked on as the trick was repeated. So this was she, to whom he had heard some one refer as the Jackdaw Girl—the young lady he had caught staring at him so oddly the night before, just after her arrival. He had been introduced to her between rubbers—a charming, piquant wisp of a creature, with big, innocent eyes and cameo features, much given to gay little bursts of laughter. Her name? Oh, yes. Fayerwether—Drusila Fayerwether.

St. Rocheville ventured into the open. Miss Fayerwether smiled, and flung a tidbit of some sort directly at his feet. The birds came for it like huge black projectiles. Involuntarily he took a step backward. She laughed.

"They won't hurt you, really," she assured him mockingly. "They are quite tame. Let me show you." She held aloft a slice of toast; the powerful black wings quivered expectantly. "No," she commanded. The toast fell at St. Rocheville's feet. Neither of the birds stirred. "Hold it in your left hand," she directed. Mechanically the astonished young man obeyed. "Extend your right and keep it steady." He did so. "Now, Blitz!"

It was a command. The bird from her left shoulder, the largest of the three, came hurtling toward St. Rocheville with a shrill scream. For an instant the giant wings beat about his ears, then the talons closed on his right hand in no gentle grip, and man and bird stared at each other. To the young man there was something evil and cruel in the beady, fixed eyes; in the poise of the head on the glistening, snake-like neck; in the merciless claws. And, gad, what a beak! It was a thing to tear with, to mutilate, destroy.

St. Rocheville shuddered. The whole performance was creepy and uncanny. It chilled his blood. It seemed out of all proportion, this exquisite, dainty, pink-and-white girl, and the sinister, somber, winged things——

He drew a breath of relief when Blitz, having solemnly gobbled up the toast, flew away to his mistress.

"They are my pets," she said affectionately. "Aren't they beautiful? Blitz and Jack and Jill I call them."

"Strange pets they are, mademoiselle," remarked St. Rocheville gravely. "How did you come to choose them?"

"Why, I've known them always," she replied. "Blitz here is old enough, and I dare say wise enough, to be my grandfather. He is nearly sixty, and was in my family thirty-five years before I was born. He used to stalk solemnly around my cradle like a soldier on guard, and swear dreadfully. He talks a little when he will—half a dozen words or so. Jack and Jill are younger. From their conduct, I should say they haven't yet reached the age of discretion."

"Would you mind telling me," he questioned curiously, "how a person would proceed to tame a—a flock of flying machines like that?"

"Sugar," replied Miss Fayerwether tersely. "They will do anything for sugar."

"Sugar!" Blitz screamed harshly, ruffling his silky plumage. "Sugar!"

Monsieur St. Rocheville went away to keep a tennis engagement. Miss Fayerwether disappeared into her room, leaving the three birds perched on the rail of the balcony. On the court, Rex Miller was waiting for St. Rocheville with a question:

"Meet the new girl last night? Miss Fayerwether?"

"Yes."

"They say she's a bird charmer," Rex went on. "She charmed me, all right. Gad, I always knew I was a bird!"

In his own apartments again, St. Rocheville, hot from his exertions on the tennis court, was preparing for a cold plunge, when Blitz fluttered in at the window and perched himself familiarly on the back of a chair.

"Hello!" said St. Rocheville.

"Hello!" Blitz replied promptly.

Astonished, the young man burst out laughing—a laugh which died under the steady glare of the beady eyes. Again, for some unaccountable reason, he was possessed of that singular feeling of horror he had felt at first. He shook it off impatiently and entered the bathroom, leaving Blitz in possession.

He returned just in time to see the big bird darting through the window with something bright dangling from the powerful beak. He knew instantly what it was—his watch! He had left it on a table, and the bird had taken advantage of his absence to steal it. He started toward the window on a run; but, struck by a sudden thought, he stopped, and stood staring into the open, the while he permitted an idea to seep in. Finally he dropped into a chair, his agile mind teeming with possibilities.

Suppose—just suppose—Blitz had been taught to steal? Absurd, of course! Blitz was probably an upright, moral enough bird according to his own lights; but *couldn't* he be taught to steal? Either Blitz or another bird like him? He had heard somewhere that magpies would filch any glittering thing and secrete it. Why not jackdaws? Weren't they the same thing, after all? He didn't know.

A tame bird, properly trained, cunning, wary, with an innate faculty of making acquaintances, and powerful on the wing!

St. Rocheville forgot all about his watch in contemplation of a new idea. By George, it was worth an experiment, anyway!

There was a light tapping at his door.

"Monsieur St. Rocheville!" someone called.

"Yes?" he answered.

"It is I, Miss Fayerwether. I think I have your watch here. One of my birds came in my window with it from this direction. Your window was open, so I imagine he—he stole it."

St. Rocheville pulled his bathrobe about him and peered out. Miss Fayerwether, with disturbed face, held the watch toward him—the great, solemn-looking bird was perched upon one shoulder.

"Hello!" Blitz greeted him socially.

"It is my watch, yes," said St. Rocheville. "Blitz paid me a visit and took it away with him."

"Naughty, naughty!" and Miss Fayerwether shook one rosy finger under the bird's nose. "He embarrasses me awfully sometimes," she confided. "I can't keep him confined all the time; and he has a trick of picking up any bright thing and bringing it to me."

"Please don't let it disturb you," St. Rocheville begged. "As for you, Monsieur Blitz, I'll keep my eye on you."

Miss Fayerwether vanished down the hall, scolding.

So Blitz had a trick of picking up bright things, eh? Monsieur St. Rocheville was pleased to know it. It was only a question, then, of training the bird to bring the thing he picked up to the right place. Assuredly here was an experiment worth while. In failure or success he was safe. No sane person could blame him for the immoral acts of a bird.

St. Rocheville seemed to have conquered his aversion to Blitz and Jack and Jill, for during the next week he spent hours with them; and hours, too, with their charming mistress. Sometimes he would play games with the birds—curious games—always in the absence of Miss Fayerwether. He would toss bright bits of glass, or even a finger ring, into the grass, or into the open window of his room, and the birds would go hurtling off in search. At length they came to know that there would be a lump of sugar for each on their return, with two pieces for the bird who brought the ring. St. Rocheville found it an absorbing game. He played it for hour after hour, for day after day.

———

All these things immediately preceded the first public knowledge of that series of robberies within a district of which Idlewild was the center. Miss Fayerwether, it seemed, was the first victim. She had either lost, or mislaid, she said, a diamond and ruby bracelet, and asked Mrs. Wardlaw Browne to have her servants look for it. She pooh-poohed the idea of theft. She had been careless, that was all. Yes, the bracelet was quite valuable; but it would doubtless come to light. She wouldn't have mentioned it at all except for the fact that it was an heirloom.

This politely phrased request opened the floodgates of revelation. Rex Miller had lost a rare scarab stickpin; the elderly Mrs. Scott was minus three valuable rings and an aquamarine hair ornament; Claudia Chanoler had been robbed of a rope of pearls worth thousands—robbed was the word she used; an emerald cameo, the property of Agatha Blalock, was missing. Following closely upon these mysterious happenings came word to Mrs. Wardlaw Browne of similar happening at the nearby estates of friends. A dozen valuable trinkets had vanished from the Willows where the Melville Pages had a house party; and at Sagamore, Mrs. Willets was bewailing the loss of an emerald bracelet which represented a small fortune.

The explosion came the night Mrs. Wardlaw Browne's diamond necklace was stolen. There had been an unpleasant scene of some sort in the card room. Rex Miller seemed to think that there was more than luck in the cards Monsieur St. Rocheville held; and he intimated as much. All things considered, Monsieur St. Rocheville behaved superbly. Being the only winner at the table, he tore the score into bits, and it fluttered to the floor. The other gentlemen understood that he disdained to accept money so long as a doubt remained. So the game ended abruptly, and they joined the ladies in the drawing room. Ten minutes later Mrs. Wardlaw Browne's necklace vanished utterly.

So ultimately it came to pass that The Thinking Machine—more properly, Professor Augustus S. F. X. Van Dusen, Ph. D., F. R. S., M. D., LL. D., etc., etc., logician, analyst, and master mind in the sciences—turned his crabbed genius upon the problem. He consented to do so at the request of Hutchinson Hatch, newspaper reporter; and, singularly enough, it was Monsieur Jean St. Rocheville in person who brought the matter to the reporter's attention. Together they went to The Thinking Machine.

"You know," St. Rocheville took the trouble to explain, "every time I read of a robbery of this sort, either in a newspaper or in fiction, some foreign nobleman is always the villain in the piece." He shrugged his shoulders. "It is an honor I do not desire."

"You are a nobleman, then?" queried The Thinking Machine. The narrowed, pale-blue, squinting eyes were fixed tensely upon the young man's face.

"No." St. Rocheville smiled.

"Extraordinary," murmured the little scientist. "And who are you?"

"My father and my father's father are bankers in France." St. Rocheville lied gracefully. "The situation at Idlewild is——"

"Where?" The Thinking Machine interrupted curtly.

"Idlewild."

"I mean, where is your father a banker?"

"Paris."

"In what capacity? What's his position?"

"Managing director."

"What bank?"

"Crédit Lyonnais."

The Thinking Machine nodded his satisfaction and dropped his enormous head, with its thick, straw-colored thatch, back against the chair comfortably, his slim fingers coming to rest precisely tip to tip. Monsieur St. Rocheville stared at him curiously. Obviously here was a person who was not to be trifled with. However, he felt he had passed his preliminary examination, unexpected as it was, with great credit. Not once had he forgotten his dialect; not for a fraction of a second had he hesitated in answering the abrupt questions. Ability to lie readily is a great convenience.

"Now," The Thinking Machine commanded, his squinting eyes turned upward, "what happened at Idlewild?"

Inadvertently or otherwise, St. Rocheville failed to refer, even remotely, to the three great velvet-black birds—Blitz and Jack and Jill—in his narrative of events at Idlewild. It was rather a chronological statement of the thefts as they had been reported, with no suggestion as to the manner in which they might have been committed.

"Now," and St. Rocheville spoke slowly, as one who wanted to be certain of his words, "I come down to those things which happened immediately before the disappearance of Mrs. Wardlaw Browne's necklace. Frankly my own statement will place me in rather a compromising position—that is, my real motive may not be understood— but it is better that I should tell you in the beginning things that you will surely find out."

"Decidedly better," The Thinking Machine agreed dryly. He didn't alter his position.

"Well, you must know that at Idlewild the men play auction a great deal, and——"

"Auction?" The Thinking Machine repeated. "What is auction, Mr. Hatch?"

"Auction bridge," the reporter told him. "A game of cards—a variation of whist."

Monsieur St. Rocheville stared from the wizened little scientist to the reporter incredulously. He would not have believed a person could have lived in a civilized country and not know what auction was. Perhaps he wouldn't have believed, either, that The Thinking Machine never read a newspaper. So circumscribed is our own viewpoint.

"At Idlewild the men play auction a great deal," The Thinking Machine prompted. "Go on."

"Auction, yes," St. Rocheville resumed. "It happens sometimes that the stakes are rather high. On the night Mrs. Wardlaw Browne's necklace was stolen, four of us were playing in the card room—a Mr. Gordon and myself as partners against a Mr. Miller and Franklin Chanoler, the financier." He hesitated slightly. "Mr. Miller had been losing, and in a burst of temper he intimated that—that I—that I—er——"

"Had been cheating," The Thinking Machine supplied crabbedly. "Go on."

"As a result of that little unpleasantness," St. Rocheville continued, "the game ended, and we joined the ladies. Now, please understand that it is not my wish to retaliate upon Mr. Miller. I have explained my motive—I don't want to be made a scapegoat. I do want the actual facts to come out." Some subtle change passed across his face. "Mr. Miller," he said measuredly, "stole Mrs. Wardlaw Browne's necklace!"

"Miller," Hatch repeated. "Do you mean Rex Miller?"

"That's his name, yes—Rex Miller."

"Rex Miller? The son of John W. Miller, the millionaire?" Hatch came to his feet excitedly.

"Rex Miller is his name, yes." St. Rocheville shrugged his shoulders.

"Oh, that's impossible!" Hatch declared.

"Nothing is impossible, Mr. Hatch," interrupted The Thinking Machine tartly. "Sit down. You annoy me." He shifted his pale-blue eyes, and squinted at Monsieur St. Rocheville through his thick spectacles. "How do you *know* Mr. Miller stole the necklace?"

"I saw him slip it into the pocket of his dress coat," St. Rocheville declared flatly. "Naturally, I had an idea that, when he drew Mrs. Wardlaw Browne aside immediately after we came out of the card room, it was his intention to—to denounce me as a card sharp. You may imagine that I was watching them both closely, because my honor was at stake. I wanted to see how she took it. It seems that he said nothing whatever to her about the card game; but he *did* steal the *necklace.* I saw him hiding it."

Fell a long silence. With inscrutable face The Thinking Machine sat staring at the ceiling. Twice St. Rocheville shifted his position uneasily. He was wondering if his story had been convincing. Adroit mixture of truth and falsehood that it was, he failed to see a single defect in it. Hatch, too, was staring curiously at the scientist.

"I understand perfectly your hesitation in going into details," said The Thinking Machine at last. "Under all the circumstances your motive might be misconstrued; but I think you have made me understand." He rose suddenly. "That's all," he said. "I'll look into the matter tomorrow."

Monsieur St. Rocheville was about to take his departure, when The Thinking Machine stopped him for a last question.

"You used a phrase just now," he said. "I am anxious to get it exactly—something about your father and your father's father——"

"Oh! I said"—Monsieur St. Rocheville obliged—"that my father and my father's father were bankers in Paris."

"That's it," said the little scientist. "Thanks. Good day."

Monsieur St. Rocheville went out. The Thinking Machine scribbled something on a sheet of paper and handed it to the reporter.

"Attend to that when you get to your office," he directed. Hatch read it, and his eyes opened wide. "Also, do you happen to know a native Frenchman who speaks perfect English?"

"I do; yes."

"Look him up, and ask him to repeat the phrase, 'My father and my father's father.' "

"Why?" inquired the reporter blankly.

"When he says it you'll know why. Immediately this other matter is attended to, come back here."

———

Monsieur St. Rocheville's troubled meditations were disturbed by the appearance of Miss Fayerwether around a bend in the walk. Fluttering about her were her pets, Blitz and Jack and Jill. One after another they would swoop down, gobble up a beakful of sugar from her open hand, then sail off in a circle. There was something in the sight of Miss Fayerwether to dispel troubled meditations. She was gowned in some filmy white, clinging stuff, with a wide, flapping sun hat, her cheeks glowing with the sun's reflection, her big, innocent eyes repeating the marvelous blue of the sky.

Monsieur St. Rocheville, at sight of her, arose, bowed formally, and made way for her beside him. She sat down, to be instantly submerged in a fluttering cloud of black wings.

"Go away," she ordered. "I have no more sugar. See?" and she extended her empty hands.

The giant birds wandered off seeking what they might find; and for a time the girl and the young man sat silent. Twice Miss Fayerwether's eyes sought St. Rocheville's; twice she caught him staring straight into her face.

"Detectives were here today," she remarked at last.

"Yes, I know," said St. Rocheville.

"They had a long talk with Mrs. Wardlaw Browne, and insisted on searching the house—that is, the rooms of the guests—but she would not permit it."

"She made a mistake."

"You mean that someone of the guests——"

"I mean there is a thief here somewhere," said St. Rocheville; "and he should be unmasked." (And this from Jimmie Jones, erstwhile pickpocket, burglar, and what not—Jimmie Jones, alias Wilhelm Van Der Wyde, alias Hubert Montgomery Wade, alias Jean St. Rocheville.) "I am willing for them to search my room; you are willing for them to search your room—the others should be."

The young man's lips were tightly set; there was an uncompromising glint in his eyes. His simulation had been so perfect that even he was feeling the righteous indignation of the hopelessly moral. Whatever else he felt didn't appear at the moment. Miss Fayerwether was gazing dreamily into the void.

"Have you ever been to Chicago?" she queried irrelevantly at last.

"No," said Monsieur St. Rocheville. As a matter of fact, Chicago was one of the cities in which there was being made even then an industrious search for Wilhelm Van Der Wyde.

"Or Denver?" the girl continued dreamily.

That was another city in which Wilhelm Van Der Wyde was badly wanted. Monsieur St. Rocheville turned upon Miss Fayerwether suspiciously.

"No," he declared. "Why?"

"No reason—I was merely curious," she replied carelessly. And then again irrelevantly: "Nothing has been stolen from you?"

For answer, St. Rocheville held out his left hand. A heavy diamond solitaire which he usually wore on his little finger was missing. The print of the ring on the flesh was still visible.

"Oh!" exclaimed Miss Fayerwether; and again: "Oh!" She looked startled. St. Rocheville didn't recall that he had ever seen just such an expression before. "When was your ring stolen? How?"

"I removed it when I got into my bath," St. Rocheville explained. "My window was closed, but my door was unlocked. When I came out of the bath the ring had disappeared—that's all."

"Well"—and there was a flash of indignation in the girl's eyes— "you can't blame that on Blitz, anyway."

"I'm not trying to," said St. Rocheville. "I said my window was closed. My door was closed but unlocked. I don't think Blitz can open a door, can he?"

Miss Fayerwether didn't answer. Once she was almost on the point of saying something further; and, for an instant, there was mute appeal in the innocent eyes as her slim white hand lay on the young man's arm. Then she changed her mind and went on to her room, the birds fluttering along after.

Strange thoughts came to Monsieur St. Rocheville. The light touch on his arm had thrilled him curiously. He found himself staring off moodily in the direction of her window. Also he caught himself remembering the marvelous blue of her eyes! He didn't recall at the moment that he had ever noticed the color of anyone's eyes before.

'Twas an hour after dinner when The Thinking Machine, accompanied by Detective Mallory, the bright light of the Bureau of Criminal Investigation, and one of his satellites, Blanton by name, with Hutchinson Hatch trailing, appeared at Idlewild. It may have been mere accident that St. Rocheville met them as they stepped out of the automobile.

"I neglected to tell you," he remarked to the scientist, "that young Miller has been losing heavily at auction of late; and I hear that he has had some sort of a row with his father about his allowance."

"I understand." The Thinking Machine nodded.

"Also," St. Rocheville ran on, "there has been at least one other theft here since I saw you. A diamond ring of mine was stolen from my room while I was in the bath. I wouldn't venture to say who took it."

"I know," The Thinking Machine assured him curtly. "I will have it in my hand in ten minutes."

Indignant at the intrusion of the police in what she was pleased to term her personal affairs—the detectives who had been there before were from a private agency—Mrs. Wardlaw Browne bustled into the room where The Thinking Machine and his party waited. Monsieur St. Rocheville effaced himself.

"Pray what does this mean?" Mrs. Wardlaw Browne demanded.

"It means, madam, that we have a search warrant, and intend to go through your house, if necessary," The Thinking Machine informed her crustily. Through the half-open door he caught a glimpse of a slender figure—a mere wisp of a girl with big, wonderstruck eyes. "Mallory, close that door. You, madam,"—this to Mrs. Wardlaw Browne—"can assist us by answering a few questions."

Mrs. Wardlaw Browne was of the tall, gaunt, haughty type; thin to scrawniness, enormously rich, and possessed of all the arrogance that riches bring. She studied the faces of the four men contemptuously; then, with a little resigned expression, sat down.

"Just how did you lose your necklace?" The Thinking Machine began abruptly. "Did you drop it? Was it taken from your neck? Are you sure you had it on?"

"I know I had it on," was the reply. "I did not drop it. It was taken from my neck."

"Did you, by any chance, wear a low-neck gown on the evening it was taken?" The little scientist's squinting eyes were fixed upon her tensely.

"I never wear décolleté," came the frigid response.

With his great head pillowed upon the back of his chair, his thin fingers tip to tip, and his eyes turned upward, The Thinking Machine sat in silence for a minute or more, the while tiny, cobwebby lines appeared in his dome-like brow.

"Can you," he inquired finally, "summon a servant without leaving this room?"

"There is a bell, yes." Mrs. Wardlaw Browne was forgetting to be haughty in a certain fascination which grew upon her as she gazed at this little man.

"Will you ring it, please?"

Mrs. Wardlaw Browne arose, touched a button, and sat down again. A moment later a footman entered.

"Tell Mr. Rex Miller," The Thinking Machine directed, "that Mrs. Wardlaw Browne would like to see him immediately in this room."

The footman bowed and withdrew. Followed an interminable wait—interminable, at least, to Detective Mallory, who impatiently clicked his handcuffs together. Mrs. Wardlaw Browne yawned to hide the curiosity that was consuming her.

The door opened, and Rex Miller entered. He stood for a moment staring at the silent party, and finally:

"Did you send for me, Mrs. Browne?"

"*I* did," said The Thinking Machine. "Sit down, please." Rex sank into a chair mechanically. "Mr. Blanton"—the scientist neither raised his voice nor lowered his eyes—"you will undertake to see that Mr. Miller doesn't leave this room. Mr. Mallory, you will search Mr. Miller's apartments. Somewhere there you will find Mrs. Wardlaw Browne's diamond necklace; also a man's diamond ring."

Rex came to his feet with writhing hands, a thundercloud in his face. Mrs. Wardlaw Browne burst into inarticulate expostulations. Blanton drew a revolver and laid it across his knee. Mallory bustled out. Hatch merely waited. Silence came; a silence so tense, so strained that Mrs. Wardlaw Browne was tempted to scream. At last there were footsteps, the door from the hall was thrown open, and Mallory, triumphant, appeared.

"I have them," he announced grimly. The necklace, a radiant, glittering thing, was dangling from one finger. The ring lay in his open palm. "And now, Mr. Rex Miller"—he fished out his handcuffs and started toward the young man—"if you'll hold out your——"

"Oh, sit down, Mallory!" commanded The Thinking Machine impatiently.

———

Loitering in a hallway, where he could keep an eye on the stairs leading from the lower part of the house, Monsieur St. Rocheville saw Miss Fayerwether creep stealthily up, silent-footed, chalk-white of face, and come racing toward him across the heavy velvet carpet. For the reason that she would surely see him, he walked toward her, amazed and a little perturbed at something in her manner.

"What's the matter?" inquired St. Rocheville calmly.

"Oh, it's you!" Miss Fayerwether's hand flew to her heart. She was frightened, gasping. "Nothing!"

"But something must be the matter," he insisted. "You are white as a sheet."

With an apparent effort the girl regained control of herself, and stood staring at him mutely. 'Twas in that moment that Monsieur St. Rocheville saw for the first time some strange, new expression in the big, innocent eyes—they seemed to grow hard, worldly, all-wise even as he looked.

"There are detectives in the house," she said.

"I know it. What about it?"

"They have a warrant, and intend to search every room."

"Well?" St. Rocheville refused to get excited about it.

"Including, I imagine, yours and mine."

"I'm willing. I dare say you are."

For an instant the girl's self-possession seemed to desert her completely. Her eyes closed as if in pain, and she swayed a little. St. Rocheville thrust out an arm protectingly. When she lifted her face again St. Rocheville read terror therein.

"If—if they search my room," she faltered, "I—I am lost!"

"How? Why? What do you mean?"

"I don't know that I could make anyone else understand," she went on swiftly. "The birds, you know—Blitz and Jack and Jill. You saw, and I explained to you, a trick they have of—of thieving; stealing bright things."

She stopped. In his impatience St. Rocheville seized her by the arm and shook her soundly.

"Well?" he demanded.

"Nearly every jewel that has been stolen is hidden now in my room," she confessed. "I knew nothing of it until yesterday, when I came across them. Then, after all the excitement about the thefts, I was afraid to return the things, and I could think of no way to proceed. So, you see, if they search my room it will——"

St. Rocheville was possessed of an agile mind; resourceful as it was agile. Suddenly he remembered two questions the girl had asked the day before—questions about Chicago and Denver. His teeth snapped. He thrust out a hand, and, opening the nearest door—he didn't happen to know whose room it was—he dragged her in, and turned on the electric light. Then their eyes met squarely.

"You are the thief, then?" he demanded. "Don't lie to me! You are the thief?"

"The things are in my room." She was sobbing a little. "The birds——"

"You are the thief!" There was a curious note of exultation in his voice. "And you *do* know something about Chicago and Denver?"

"I know that you are Wilhelm Van Der Wyde," she flashed defiantly. "I recognized you at once. I saw you in old Charles' 'fence' there once when you were not aware of it. I could never be mistaken in your eyes."

Monsieur St. Rocheville laughed blithely; came a faint answering smile, and he gathered her into his arms.

"I've always needed a partner," he said.

———

"Mr. Miller," The Thinking Machine was saying placidly, "isn't the thief at all." He raised his hand to still a clamor of ejaculation. "Monsieur St. Rocheville, so called, stole the necklace, at least, and concealed it, with a ring from his own finger, in Mr. Miller's apartment." Again he raised his hand. "Mr. Miller caught Monsieur St. Rocheville cheating at cards, and practically denounced him. Monsieur St. Rocheville took his revenge by undertaking to fasten the jewel thefts upon Mr. Miller. He imagined, shallowly enough, that if the necklace should be found in Mr. Miller's room the police would look no further. It is barely possible that the police *wouldn't* have looked further."

Mrs. Wardlaw Browne's aristocratic mouth had dropped open in sheer astonishment. Detective Mallory looked bewildered, dazed. Rex Miller's face was an animated interrogation mark.

"Then who *is* the thief?" Mallory found voice to express the burning question.

"I'm sure I don't know," The Thinking Machine confessed frankly. "I think, perhaps, it was Monsieur St. Rocheville, so called; but there's nothing to connect him—Please sit down, Mallory. You annoy me. It would do no good to search his apartment. If he stole anything, it isn't here now; besides——"

The door opened suddenly, and the footman appeared.

"Miss Fayerwether is badly hurt, ma'am," he explained hurriedly. "She seems to have fallen from her window. We found her outside, unconscious."

Mrs. Wardlaw Browne went out hurriedly. Obeying an almost imperceptible nod of The Thinking Machine's head, Detective Mallory followed her. The scientist turned to Detective Blanton.

"Get St. Rocheville," he directed tersely.

Ten minutes later Mallory returned. In one hand he held a small chamois bag. The contents thereof he spilled upon a table. The Thinking Machine glanced around, saw a glittering heap of jewels, then resumed his steady scrutiny of the ceiling.

"The girl had them?"

"Yes," replied the detective. "She tried to escape from her room by sliding down a rope made of sheets. It broke, and she fell."

"Badly hurt?"

"Only a sprained ankle, and shock."

Blanton flung himself in.

"St. Rocheville's gone," he announced hurriedly. "I imagine he cut for it. Went away in one of the automobiles."

———

When Miss Fayerwether recovered consciousness, and the sharp agony in her ankle had become a mere dull pain, she found herself in some large room, rank with the odor of strange chemical messes. As a matter of fact, it was The Thinking Machine's laboratory; and the three men present were the little scientist in person, Mallory, and Hatch. Blanton had gone on to police headquarters to send out a general alarm for Monsieur St. Rocheville.

"There was no mystery about it," she heard The Thinking Machine saying. "That is, no mystery that the simplest rules of logic wouldn't instantly dissipate. A man, presumably French, but speaking English almost perfectly, comes into this room and betrays himself an imposter five minutes afterward by using, without a trace of accent, the one phrase in all our language which *no* Frenchman, unless he is reared from infancy in an English-speaking country, can pronounce as it should be pronounced. This man used the phrase: 'My father and my father's father;' and he pronounced it as either of us would have pronounced it. The French can master our 'th' only with difficulty, and then only at the beginning of a word; otherwise their 'th' becomes almost like our 'z.'

"From the beginning, therefore, I imagined our so-called Monsieur St. Rocheville an imposter. Being an imposter, he was a liar. I proved he was a liar when I made him state who his father was. At my suggestion, Mr. Hatch cabled to Paris, demonstrated that there is not, and never has been a Monsieur St. Rocheville connected with the Crédit Lyonnais; and, this much established, St. Rocheville's story collapsed utterly. He had been accused of cheating at cards; and in retaliation he tried to shift the thefts upon Mr. Miller. He had seen Mr. Miller, so he said, steal the necklace. His obvious purpose in this was to bring about a search of Mr. Miller's apartment, where he had carefully planted the necklace, also his own ring. The remainder of the story you all know."

Miss Fayerwether had listened breathlessly, with closed eyes. The Thinking Machine arose and came over to her. For an instant his slender, cool hand rested on her brow; and in that instant she fought the fight. She was caught. St. Rocheville, alias Van Der Wyde, was free. He had tried to help her. She was to have gathered the jewels together, escaped through her window to avoid attracting attention, and joined him in the waiting automobile. He was free. She would allow him to remain free. Love, be it said, makes martyrs of us all.

"I stole the jewels," she said quietly. "Monsieur St. Rocheville knew nothing of the thefts. My birds——"

That was all. The door opened and closed. Monsieur St. Rocheville stood before them with a vicious-looking, snub-nosed, automatic pistol in his hand.

"Put up your hands!" he commanded curtly. "You, Mallory, you! Put them up, I say! Put them up!" Mallory put them up. "And you, too! Put them up!" The Thinking Machine and Hutchinson Hatch obeyed unanimously. "Now, Miss Fayerwether, can you walk?"

"I think so." She struggled to her feet.

"Very well." There was a deadly calm in his manner. "Take Mallory's gun, his keys, his handcuffs, and his police whistle. Careful now! Stand on the far side of him. I may have to kill him." The girl obeyed deftly. "Are the handcuffs unlocked? Good! Snap one end around his right wrist. Now, Mallory, lower your right hand!"

"I'll be——" the enraged detective began.

"Lower your right hand." The pistol clicked. "Now, Miss Fayerwether, snap the other end of the handcuff around the leg of his chair, above the rungs." It was done, neatly and quickly. "And I think that will hold you for a few minutes, Mallory. Now, Miss Fayerwether, there's an automobile outside. The motor is running. Get in the car. Take your time. Safely in, honk the horn three times."

The girl hobbled out. Monsieur St. Rocheville took advantage of the pause to sneer a little at the three men—Mallory safely shackled to a heavy chair, which would effectually stop immediate pursuit; Hatch with his hands anxiously stretched into the air; The Thinking Machine placidly meeting his gaze, eye to eye.

"I'll get you yet!" Mallory bellowed in impotent rage.

"Oh, perhaps." Outside, the automobile horn sounded thrice. "Until then, *au revoir!*" and Monsieur St. Rocheville vanished as silently as he had come.

"There's loyalty for you," observed The Thinking Machine, as if astonished.

"Love, not loyalty," Hatch declared. "He's crazy about her. Nothing on earth would have brought him back but love."

"Love!" mused the little scientist. "A most interesting phenomenon. I shall have to look into it some time."

———

As I have said, Monsieur St. Rocheville was a young man of resource and daring. Later that night he burglariously entered the room Miss Fayerwether had occupied at Idlewild, and took Blitz and Jack and Jill away with him, cage and all.

THE BROWN COAT

There was no mystery whatever about the identity of the man who, alone and unaided, robbed the Thirteenth National Bank of $109,437 in cash and $1.29 in postage stamps. It was "Mort" Dolan, an expert safe-cracker albeit a young one, and he had made a clean sweep. Nor yet was there any mystery as to his whereabouts. He was safely in a cell at Police Headquarters, having been captured within less than twelve hours after the robbery was discovered.

Dolan had offered no resistance to the officers when he was cornered, and had attempted no denial when questioned by Detective Mallory. He knew he had been caught fairly and squarely and no argument was possible, so he confessed with a glow of pride at a job well done. It was four or five days after his arrest that the matter came to the attention of The Thinking Machine. Then the problem was—

But perhaps it were better to begin at the beginning.

———

Despite the fact that he was considerably less than thirty years old, "Mort" Dolan was a man for whom the police had a wholesome respect. He had a record, for he had started early. This robbery of the Thirteenth National was his "big" job and was to have been his last. With the proceeds he had intended to take his wife and quietly disappear beneath a full beard and an alias in some place far removed from former haunts. But the mutability of human events is a matter of proverb. While the robbery as a robbery was a thoroughly artistic piece of work and in full accordance with plans which had been worked out to the minutest details months before, he had made one mistake. This was leaving behind him in the bank the can in which the nitroglycerine had been bought. Through this carelessness he had been traced.

Dolan and his wife occupied three poor rooms in a poor tenement house. From the moment the police got a description of the person who bought the explosive they were confident for they knew their men. Therefore four clever men were on watch about the poor tenement. Neither Dolan nor his wife was there then, but from the condition of things in the rooms the police believed that they intended to return so took up positions to watch.

Unsuspecting enough, for his one mistake in the robbery had not occurred to him, Dolan came along just about dusk and started up the five steps to the front door of the tenement. It just happened that he glanced back and saw a head drawn suddenly behind a projecting stoop. But the electric light glared strongly there and Dolan recognized Detective Downey, one of many men who revolved around Detective Mallory within a limited orbit. Dolan paused on the stoop a moment and rolled a cigarette while he thought it over. Perhaps instead of entering, it would be best to stroll on down the street, turn a corner, and make a dash for it. But just at that moment he spied another head in the direction of contemplated flight. That was Detective Blanton.

Deeply thoughtful Dolan smoked half the cigarette and stared blankly in front of him. He knew of a back door opening on an alley. Perhaps the detectives had not thought to guard that! He tossed his cigarette away, entered the house with affected unconcern, and closed the door. Running lightly through the long, unclean hall which extended the full length of the building he flung open the back door. He turned back instantly—just outside he had seen and recognized Detective Cunningham.

Then he had an inspiration! The roof! The building was four stories. He ran up the four flights lightly but rapidly and was half way up the short flight which led to the opening in the roof when he stopped. From above he caught the whiff of a bad cigar, then the measured tread of heavy boots. Another detective! With a sickening depression at his heart Dolan came softly down the stairs again, opened the door of his flat with a latch-key, and entered.

Then and there he sat down to figure it all out. There seemed no escape for him. Every way out was blocked, and it was only a question of time before they would close in on him. He imagined now they were only waiting for his wife's return. He could fight for his freedom of course—even kill one, perhaps two, of the detectives who were waiting for him. But that would only mean his own death. If he tried to run for it past either of the detectives he would get a shot in the back. And besides, murder was repugnant to Dolan's artistic soul. It didn't do any good. But could he warn Isabel, his wife? He feared she would walk into the trap as he had done, and she had had no connection of any sort with the affair.

Then, from a fear that his wife would return, there swiftly came a fear that she would not. He suddenly remembered that it was necessary for him to see her. The police could not connect her with the robbery in any way; they could only hold her for a time and then would be compelled to free her, for her innocence of this particular crime was beyond question. And if he were taken before she returned she would be left penniless; and that was a thing which Dolan dreaded to contemplate. There was a spark of human tenderness in his heart and in prison it would be comforting to know that she was well cared for. If she would only come now he would tell her where the money——!

For ten minutes Dolan considered the question in all possible lights. A letter telling her where the money was? No. It would inevitably fall into the hands of the police. A cipher? She would never get it. How? How? How? Every moment he expected a clamor at the door which would mean that the police had come for him. They knew he was cornered. Whatever he did must be done quickly. Dolan took a long breath and started to roll another cigarette. With the thin white paper held in his left hand and tobacco bag raised in the other he had an inspiration.

For a little more than an hour after that he was left alone. Finally his quick ear caught the shuffle of stealthy feet in the hall, then came an imperative rap on the door. The police had evidently feared to wait longer. Dolan was leaning over a sewing machine when the summons came. Instinctively his hand closed on his revolver, then he tossed it aside and walked to the door.

"Well?" he demanded.

"Let us in, Dolan," came the reply.

"That you, Downey?" Dolan inquired.

"Yes. Now don't make any mistakes, Mort. There are three of us here and Cunningham is in the alley watching your windows. There's no way out."

For one instant—only an instant—Dolan hesitated. It was not that he was repentant; it was not that he feared prison—it was regret at being caught. He had planned it all so differently, and the little woman would be heart-broken. Finally, with a quick backward glance at the sewing machine, he opened the door. Three revolvers were thrust into his face with unanimity that spoke well for the police opinion of the man. Dolan promptly raised his hands over his head.

"Oh, put down your guns," he expostulated. "I'm not crazy. My gun is over on the couch there."

Detective Downey, by a personal search, corroborated this statement then the revolvers were lowered.

"The chief wants you," he said. "It's about that Thirteenth National Bank robbery."

"All right," said Dolan, calmly, and he held out his hands for the steel nippers.

"Now, Mort," said Downey, ingratiatingly, "you can save us a lot of trouble by telling us where the money is."

"Doubtless I could," was the ambiguous response.

Detective Downey looked at him and understood. Cunningham was called in from the alley. He and Downey remained in the apartment and the other two men led Dolan away. In the natural course of events the prisoner appeared before Detective Mallory at Police Headquarters. They were well acquainted, professionally.

Dolan told everything frankly from the inception of the plan to the actual completion of the crime. The detective sat with his feet on his desk listening. At the end he leaned forward toward the prisoner.

"And where is the money?" he asked.

Dolan paused long enough to roll a cigarette.

"That's my business," he responded, pleasantly.

"You might just as well tell us," insisted Detective Mallory. "We will find it, of course, and it will save us trouble."

"I'll just bet you a hat you don't find it," replied Dolan, and there was a glitter of triumph in his eyes. "On the level, between man and man now I will bet you a hat that you never find that money."

"You're on," replied Detective Mallory. He looked keenly at his prisoner and his prisoner stared back without a quiver. "Did your wife get away with it?"

From the question Dolan surmised that she had not been arrested.

"No," he answered.

"Is it in your flat?"

"Downey and Cunningham are searching now," was the rejoinder. "They will report what they find."

There was silence for several minutes as the two men—officer and prisoner—stared each at the other. When a thief takes refuge in a refusal to answer questions he becomes a difficult subject to handle. There was the "third degree" of course, but Dolan was the kind of man who would only laugh at that; the kind of man from whom anything less than physical torture could not bring a statement if he didn't choose to make it. Detective Mallory was perfectly aware of this dogged trait in his character.

"It's this way, chief," explained Dolan at last. "I robbed the bank, I got the money, and it's now where you will never find it. I did it by myself, and am willing to take my medicine. Nobody helped me. My wife—I know your men waited for her before they took me—my wife knows nothing on earth about it. She had no connection with the thing at all and she can prove it. That's all I'm going to say. You might just as well make up your mind to it."

Detective Mallory's eyes snapped.

"You will tell where that money is," he blustered, "or—or I'll see that you get——"

"Twenty years is the absolute limit," interrupted Dolan quietly. "I expect to get twenty years—that's the worst you can do for me."

The Detective stared at him hard.

"And besides," Dolan went on, "I won't be lonesome when I get where you're going to send me. I've got lots of friends there—been there before. One of the jailers is the best pinochle player I ever met."

Like most men who find themselves balked at the outset Detective Mallory sought to appease his indignation by heaping invective upon the prisoner, by threats, by promises, by wheedling, by bluster. It was all the same, Dolan remained silent. Finally he was led away and locked up.

A few minutes later Downey and Cunningham appeared. One glance told their chief that they could not enlighten him as to the whereabouts of the stolen money.

"Do you have any idea where it is?" he demanded.

"No, but I have a very definite idea where it isn't," replied Downey grimly. "It isn't in that flat. There's not one square inch of it that we didn't go over—not one object there that we didn't tear to pieces looking. It simply isn't there. He hid it somewhere before we got him."

"Well take all the men you want and keep at it," instructed Detective Mallory. "One of you, by the way, had better bring in Dolan's wife. I am fairly certain that she had nothing to do with it but she might know something and I can bluff a woman." Detective Mallory announced that accomplishment as if it were a thing to be proud of. "There's nothing to do now but get the money. Meanwhile I'll see that Dolan isn't permitted to communicate with anybody."

"There is always the chance," suggested Downey, "that a man as clever as Dolan could in a cipher letter, or by a chance remark, inform her where the money is if we assume she doesn't know, and that should be guarded against."

"It will be guarded against," declared Detective Mallory emphatically. "Dolan will not be permitted to see or talk to anyone for the present—not even an attorney. He may weaken later on."

But day succeeded day and Dolan showed no signs of weakening. His wife, meanwhile, had been apprehended and subjected to the "third degree." When this ordeal was over, the net result was that Detective Mallory was convinced that she had had nothing whatever to do with the robbery, and had not the faintest idea where the money was. Half a dozen times Dolan asked permission to see her or to write to her. Each time the request was curtly refused.

Newspapermen, with and without inspiration, had sought the money vainly; and the police were now seeking to trace the movements of "Mort" Dolan from the moment of the robbery until the moment of his appearance on the steps of the house where he lived. In this way they hoped to get an inkling of where the money had been hidden, for the idea of the money being in the flat had been abandoned. Dolan simply wouldn't say anything. Finally, one day,

Hutchinson Hatch, reporter, made an exhaustive search of Dolan's flat, for the fourth time, then went over to police headquarters to talk it over with Mallory. While there President Ashe and two directors of the victimized bank appeared. They were worried.

"Is there any trace of the money?" asked Mr. Ashe.

"Not yet," responded Detective Mallory.

"Well, could we talk to Dolan a few minutes?"

"If we didn't get anything out of him you won't," said the detective. "But it won't do any harm. Come along."

Dolan didn't seem particularly glad to see them. He came to the bars of his cell and peered through. It was only when Mr. Ashe was introduced to him as the president of the Thirteenth National that he seemed to take any interest in his visitors. This interest took the form of a grin. Mr. Ashe evidently had something of importance on his mind and was seeking the happiest method of expression. Once or twice he spoke aside to his companions, and Dolan watched them curiously. At last he turned to the prisoner.

"You admit that you robbed the bank?" he asked.

"There's no need of denying it," replied Dolan.

"Well," and Mr. Ashe hesitated a moment, "the board of directors held a meeting this morning, and speaking on their behalf I want to say something. If you will inform us of the whereabouts of the money we will, upon its recovery, exert every effort within our power to have your sentence cut in half. In other words, as I understand it, you have given the police no trouble, you have confessed the crime and this, with the return of the money, would weigh for you when sentence is pronounced. Say the maximum is twenty years, we might be able to get you off with ten if we get the money."

Detective Mallory looked doubtful. He realized, perhaps, the futility of such a promise yet he was silent. The proposition might draw out something on which to proceed.

"Can't see it," said Dolan at last. "It's this way. I'm twenty-seven years old. I'll get twenty years. About two of that'll come off for good behavior, so I'll really get eighteen years. At the end of that time I'll come out with $109,000 odd—rich for life and able to retire at forty-five years. In other words while in prison I'll be working for a good, stiff salary—something really worth while. Very few men are able to retire at forty-five."

Mr. Ashe readily realized the trust of this statement. It was the point of view of a man to whom mere prison has few terrors—a man content to remain immured for twenty years for a consideration. He turned and spoke aside to the two directors again.

"But I'll tell you what I *will* do," said Dolan, after a pause. "If you'll fix it so I get only two years, say, I'll give you half the money."

There was silence. Detective Mallory strolled along the corridor beyond the view of the prisoner and summoned President Ashe to his side by a jerk of his head.

"Agree to that," he said. "Perhaps he'll really give up."

"But it wouldn't be possible to arrange it, would it?" asked Mr. Ashe.

"Certainly not," said the detective, "but agree to it. Get your money and then we'll nail him anyhow."

Mr. Ashe stared at him a moment vaguely indignant at the treachery of the thing, then greed triumphed. He walked back to the cell.

"We'll agree to that, Mr. Dolan," he said briskly. "Fix a two years sentence for you in return for half the money."

Dolan smiled a little.

"All right, go ahead," he said. "When sentence of two years is pronounced and a first-class lawyer arranges it for me so that the matter can never be reopened I'll tell you where you can get your half."

"But of course you must tell us that now," said Mr. Ashe.

Dolan smiled cheerfully. It was a taunting, insinuating, accusing sort of smile and it informed the bank president that the duplicity contemplated was discovered. Mr. Ashe was silent for a moment, then blushed.

"Nothing doing," said Dolan, and he retired into a recess of his cell as if his interest in the matter were at an end.

"But—but we need the money now," stammered Mr. Ashe. "It was a large sum and the theft has crippled us considerably."

"All right," said Dolan carelessly. "The sooner I get two years the sooner you get it."

"How could it be—be fixed?"

"I'll leave that to you."

That was all. The bank president and the two directors went out fuming impotently. Mr. Ashe paused in Detective Mallory's office long enough for a final word.

"Of course it was brilliant work on the part of the police to capture Dolan," he said caustically, "but it isn't doing us a particle of good. All I see now is that we lose a hundred and nine thousand dollars."

"It looks very much like it," assented the detective, "unless we find it."

"Well, why *don't* you find it?"

Detective Mallory had to give it up.

A HUMAN PROBLEM

"What did Dolan do with the money?" Hutchinson Hatch was asking of Professor Augustus S. F. X. Van Dusen—The Thinking Machine. "It isn't in the flat. Everything indicates that it was hidden somewhere else."

"And Dolan's wife?" inquired The Thinking Machine in his perpetually irritated voice. "It seems conclusive that she had no idea where it is?"

"She has been put through the 'third degree,' " explained the reporter, "and if she had known she would probably have told."

"Is she living in the flat now?"

"No. She is stopping with her sister. The flat is under lock and key. Mallory has the key. He has shown the utmost care in everything he has done. Dolan has not been permitted to write to or see his wife for fear he would let her know some way where the money is; he has not been permitted to communicate with anybody at all, not even a lawyer. He did see President Ashe and two directors of the bank but naturally he wouldn't give them a message for his wife."

The Thinking Machine was silent. For five, ten, twenty minutes he sat with long, slender fingers pressed tip to tip, squinting unblinkingly at the ceiling. Hatch waited patiently.

"Of course," said the scientist at last, "$109,000, even in large bills would make a considerable bundle and would be extremely difficult to hide in a place that has been gone over so often. We may suppose, therefore, that it isn't in the flat. What have the detectives learned as to Dolan's whereabouts after the robbery and before he was taken?"

"Nothing," replied Hatch, "nothing, absolutely. He seemed to disappear off the earth for a time. That time, I suppose, was when he was disposing of the money. His plans were evidently well laid."

"It would be possible of course, by the simple rules of logic, to sit still here and ultimately locate the money," remarked The Thinking Machine musingly, "but it would take a long time. We might begin, for instance, with the idea that he contemplated flight. When? By rail or steamer? The answers to those questions would, in a way, enlighten us as to the probable location of the money, because, remember, it would have to be placed where it was readily accessible in case of flight. But the process would be a long one. Perhaps it would be best to make Dolan tell us where he hid it."

"It would if he would tell," agreed the reporter, "but he is reticent to a degree that is maddening when the money is mentioned."

"Naturally," remarked the scientist. "That really doesn't matter. I have no doubt he will inform me."

So Hatch and The Thinking Machine called upon Detective Mallory. They found him in deep abstraction. He glanced up at the intrusion with an appearance, almost, of relief. He knew intuitively what it was.

"If you can find out where that money is, professor," he declared emphatically, "I'll—I'll—well you can't."

The Thinking Machine squinted into the official eyes thoughtfully and the corners of his straight mouth were drawn down disapprovingly.

"I think perhaps there has been a little too much caution here, Mr. Mallory," he said. "I have no doubt Dolan will inform me as to where the money is. As I understand it his wife is practically without means?"

"Yes," was the reply. "She is living with her sister."

"And he has asked several times to be permitted to write to or see her?"

"Yes, dozens of times."

"Well, now suppose you do let him see her," suggested The Thinking Machine.

"Lord, that's just what he wants," blurted the detective. "If he ever sees her I know he will, in some way, by something he says, by a gesture, or a look, inform her where the money is. As it is now I know she doesn't know where it is."

"Well, if he informs her won't he also inform us?" demanded The Thinking Machine tartly. "If Dolan wants to convey knowledge of the whereabouts of the money to his wife let him talk to her—let him give her the information. I dare say if she is clever enough to interpret a word as a clue to where the money is I am too."

The detective thought that over. He knew this crabbed little scientist with the enormous head of old; and he knew, too, some of the amazing results he had achieved by methods wholly unlike those of the police. But in this case he was frankly in doubt.

"This way," The Thinking Machine continued. "Get the wife here, let her pass Dolan's cell and speak to him so that he will know that it is her, then let her carry on a conversation with him while she is beyond his sight. Have a stenographer, without the knowledge of either, take down just what is said, word for word. Give me a transcript of the conversation, and hold the wife on some pretext until I can study it a little. If he gives her a clue I'll get the money."

There was not the slightest trace of egotism in the irritable tone. It seemed merely a statement of fact. Detective Mallory, looking at the wizened face of the logician, was doubtfully hopeful and at last he consented to the experiment. The wife was sent for and came eagerly, a stenographer was placed in the cell adjoining Dolan, and the wife was led along the corridor. As she paused in front of Dolan's cell he started toward her with an exclamation. Then she was led on a little way out of his sight.

With face pressed close against the bars Dolan glowered out upon Detective Mallory and Hatch. An expression of awful ferocity leapt into his eyes.

"What're you doing with her?" he demanded.

"Mort, Mort," she called.

"Belle, is it you?" he asked in turn.

"They told me you wanted to talk to me," explained the wife. She was panting fiercely as she struggled to shake off the hands which held her beyond his reach.

"What sort of a game is this, Mallory?" demanded the prisoner.

"You've wanted to talk to her," Mallory replied, "now go ahead. You may talk, but you must not see her."

"Oh, that's it, eh?" snarled Dolan. "What did you bring her here for then? Is she under arrest?"

"Mort, Mort," came his wife's voice again. "They won't let me come where I can see you."

There was utter silence for a moment. Hatch was overpowered by a feeling that he was intruding upon a family tragedy, and tiptoed beyond reach of Dolan's roving eyes to where The Thinking Machine was sitting on a stool, twiddling his fingers. After a moment the detective joined them.

"Belle?" called Dolan again. It was almost a whisper.

"Don't say anything, Mort," she panted. "Cunningham and Blanton are holding me—the others are listening."

"I don't want to say anything," said Dolan easily. "I did want to see you. I wanted to know if you are getting along all right. Are you still at the flat?"

"No, at my sister's," was the reply. "I have no money—I can't stay at the flat."

"You know they're going to send me away?"

"Yes," and there was almost a sob in the voice. "I—I know it."

"That I'll get the limit—twenty years?"

"Yes."

"Can you—get along?" asked Dolan solicitously. "Is there anything you can do for yourself?"

"I will do something," was the reply. "Oh, Mort, Mort, why——"

"Oh never mind that," he interrupted impatiently. "It doesn't do any good to regret things. It isn't what I planned for, little girl, but it's here so—so I'll meet it. I'll get the good behavior allowance—that'll save two years, and then——"

There was a menace in the tone which was not lost upon the listeners.

"Eighteen years," he heard her moan.

For one instant Dolan's lips were pressed tightly together and in that instant he had a regret—regret that he had not killed Blanton and Cunningham rather than submit to capture. He shook off his anger with an effort.

"I don't know if they'll permit me ever to see you," he said, desperately, "as long as I refuse to tell where the money is hidden, and I know they'll never permit me to write to you for fear I'll tell you where it is. So I suppose the good by'll be like this. I'm sorry, little girl."

He heard her weeping and hurled himself against the bars in a passion; it passed after a moment. He must not forget that she was penniless, and the money—that vast fortune——!

"There's one thing you must do for me, Belle," he said after a moment, more calmly. "This sort of thing doesn't do any good. Brace up, little girl, and wait—wait for me. Eighteen years is not forever, we're both young, and—but never mind that. I wish you would please go up to the flat and—do you remember my heavy, brown coat?"

"Yes, the old one?" she asked.

"That's it," he answered. "It's cold here in this cell. Will you please go up to the flat when they let you loose and sew up that tear under the right arm and send it to me here? It's probably the last favor I'll ask of you for a long time so will you do it this afternoon?"

"Yes," she answered, tearfully.

"The rip is under the right arm, and be certain to sew it up," said Dolan again. "Perhaps, when I am tried, I shall have a chance to see you and——"

The Thinking Machine arose and stretched himself a little.

"That's all that's necessary, Mr. Mallory," he said. "Have her held until I tell you to release her."

Mallory made a motion to Cunningham and Blanton and the woman was led away, screaming. Hatch shuddered a little, and Dolan, not understanding, flung himself against the bars of his cell like a caged animal.

"Clever, aren't you?" he snarled as he caught sight of Detective Mallory. "Thought I'd try to tell her where it was, but I didn't and you never will know where it is—not in a thousand years."

Accompanied by The Thinking Machine and Hatch, the detective went back to his private office. All were silent but the detective glanced from time to time into the eyes of the scientist.

"Now, Mr. Hatch, we have the whereabouts of the money settled," said The Thinking Machine, quietly. "Please go at once to the flat and bring the brown coat Dolan mentioned. I dare say the secret of the hidden money is somewhere in that coat."

"But two of my men have already searched that coat," protested the detective.

"That doesn't make the least difference," snapped the scientist.

The reporter went without a word. Half an hour later he returned with the brown coat. It was a commonplace-looking garment, badly worn and in sad need of repair not only in the rip under the arm but in other places. When he saw it The Thinking Machine nodded his head abruptly as if it were just what he had expected.

"The money can't be in that and I'll bet my head on it," declared Detective Mallory, flatly. "There isn't room for it."

The Thinking Machine gave him a glance in which there was a touch of pity.

"We know," he said, "that the money isn't in this coat. But can't you see that it is perfectly possible that a slip of paper on which Dolan has written down the hiding place of the money can be hidden in it somewhere? Can't you see that he asked for this coat—which is not as good a one as the one he is wearing now—in order to attract his wife's attention to it? Can't you see it is the one definite thing that he mentioned when he knew that in all probability he would not be permitted to see his wife again, at least for a long time?"

Then, seam by seam, the brown coat was ripped to pieces. Each piece in turn was submitted to the sharpest scrutiny. Nothing resulted. Detective Mallory frankly regarded it all as wasted effort and when there remained nothing of the coat save strips of cloth and lining he was inclined to be triumphant. The Thinking Machine was merely thoughtful.

"It went further back than that," the scientist mused, and tiny wrinkles appeared in the dome-like brow. "Ah! Mr. Hatch please go back to the flat, look in the machine drawers, or work basket, and you will find a spool of brown thread. Bring it to me."

"Spool of brown thread?" repeated the detective in amazement. "Have you been through the place?"

"No."

"How do you know there's a spool of brown thread there, then?"

"I know it because Mr. Hatch will bring it back to me," snapped The Thinking Machine. "I know it by the simplest, most rudimentary rules of logic."

Hatch went out again. In half an hour he returned with a spool of brown thread. The Thinking Machine's white fingers seized upon it eagerly, and his watery, squint eyes examined it. A portion of it had been used—the spool was only half gone. But he noted—and as he did his eyes reflected a glitter of triumph—he noted that the paper cap on each end was still in place.

"Now, Mr. Mallory," he said, "I'll demonstrate to you that in Dolan the police are dealing with a man far beyond the ordinary bank thief. In his way he is a genius. Look here!"

With a penknife he ripped off the paper caps and looked through the hole of the spool. For an instant his face showed blank amazement. Then he put the spool down on the table and squinted at it for a moment in absolute silence.

"It must be here," he said at last. "It must be, else why did he—of course!"

With quick fingers he began to unwind the thread. Yard after yard it rolled off in his hand, and finally in the mass of brown on the spool appeared a white strip. In another instant The Thinking Machine held in his hand a tiny, thin sheet of paper—a cigarette paper. It had been wound around the spool and the thread wound over it so smoothly that it was impossible to see that it had ever been removed.

The detective and Hatch were leaning over his shoulder watching him curiously. The tiny paper unfolded—something was written on it. Slowly The Thinking Machine deciphered it.

"47 Causeway Street, basement, tenth flagstone from northeast corner."

And there the money was found—$109,000. The house was unoccupied and within easy reach of a wharf from which a European bound steamer sailed. Within half an hour of sailing time it would have been an easy matter for Dolan to have recovered it all and that without in the least exciting the suspicion of those who might be watching him. For a saloon next door opened into an alley behind, and a broken window in the basement gave quick access to the treasure.

"Dolan reasoned," The Thinking Machine explained, "that even if he was never permitted to see his wife she would probably use that thread and in time find the directions for recovering the money. Further he argued that the police would never suspect that a spool contained the secret for which they sought so long. His conversation with his wife, today, was merely to draw her attention to something which would require her to use the spool of brown thread. The brown coat was all that he could think of. And that's all I think."

Dolan was a sadly surprised man when news of the recovery of the money was broken to him. But a certain quaint philosophy didn't desert him. He gazed at Detective Mallory incredulously as the story was told and at the end went over and sat down on his cell cot.

"Well, chief," he said, "I didn't think it was in you. That makes me owe you a hat."

THE PROBLEM OF THE STOLEN RUBENS

Matthew Kale made fifty million dollars out of axle grease, after which he began to patronize the high arts. It was simple enough: he had the money, and Europe had the old masters. His method of buying was simplicity itself. There were five thousand square yards, more or less, in the huge gallery of his marble mansion which were to be covered, so he bought five thousand yards, more or less, of art. Some of it was good, some of it fair, and much of it bad. The chief picture of the collection was a Rubens, which he had picked up in Rome for fifty thousand dollars.

Soon after acquiring his collection, Kale decided to make certain alterations in the vast room where the pictures hung. They were all taken down and stored in the ballroom, equally vast, with their faces toward the wall. Meanwhile Kale and his family took refuge in a nearby hotel.

It was at this hotel that Kale met Jules de Lesseps. De Lesseps was distinctly French, the sort of Frenchman whose conversation resembles callisthenics. He was nervous, quick, and agile, and he told Kale in confidence that he was not only a painter himself, he was a connoisseur in the high arts. Pompous in the pride of possession, Kale went to a good deal of trouble to exhibit his private collection for de

Lesseps's delectation. It happened in the ballroom, and the true artist's delight shone in the Frenchman's eyes as he handled the pieces which were good. Some of the others made him smile, but it was an inoffensive sort of smile.

With his own hands Kale lifted the precious Rubens and held it before the Frenchman's eyes. It was a Madonna and Child, one of those wonderful creations which have endured through the years with all the sparkle and color beauty of their pristine days. Kale seemed disappointed because de Lesseps was not particularly enthusiastic about the picture.

"Why, it's a Rubens!" he exclaimed.

"Yes, I see," replied de Lesseps.

"It cost me fifty thousand dollars."

"It is perhaps worth more than that," and the Frenchman shrugged his shoulders as he turned away.

Kale looked at him in chagrin. Could it be that de Lesseps did not understand that it was a Rubens, and that Rubens was a painter? Or was it that he had failed to hear him say that it cost him fifty thousand dollars? Kale was accustomed to seeing people bob their heads and open their eyes when he said fifty thousand dollars; therefore, "Don't you like it?" he asked.

"Very much indeed," replied de Lesseps; "but I have seen it before. I saw it in Rome just a week or so before you purchased it."

"They rummaged on through the pictures, and at last a Whistler turned up for their inspection. It was one of the famous Thames series, a water color. De Lesseps's face radiated excitement, and several times he glanced from the water color to the Rubens, as if mentally comparing the exquisitely penciled and colored modern work with the bold, masterly technic of the old.

Kale misunderstood the silence. "I don't think much of this one, myself," he explained apologetically. "It's a Whistler, and all that, and it cost me five thousand dollars, and I sort of had to have it, but still it isn't just the kind of thing that I like. What do you think of it?"

"I think it is perfectly wonderful," replied the Frenchman enthusiastically. "It is the essence, the superlative of modern work. I wonder if it would be possible," and he turned to face Kale, "for me to make a copy of that? I have some slight skill in painting myself, and dare say I could make a fairly creditable copy of it."

Kale was flattered. He was more and more impressed each moment with the picture. "Why, certainly," he replied. "I will have it sent up to the hotel, and you can——"

"No, no, no!" interrupted de Lesseps quickly. "I wouldn't care to accept the responsibility of having the picture in my charge. There is always the danger of fire. But if you would give me permission to come here—this room is large and airy and light, and besides it is quiet——"

"Just as you like," said Kale magnanimously. "I merely thought the other way would be most convenient for you."

De Lesseps drew near, and laid one hand on the millionaire's arm. "My dear friend," he said earnestly, "if these pictures were my pictures, I shouldn't try to accommodate anybody where they were concerned. I dare say the collection as it stands cost you——"

"Six hundred and eighty-seven thousand dollars," volunteered Kale proudly.

"And surely they must be well protected here in your house during your absence?"

"There are about twenty servants in the house while the workmen are making the alterations," said Kale, "and three of them don't do anything but watch this room. No one can go in or out except by the door we entered—the others are locked and barred—and then only with my permission, or a written order from me. No, sir, nobody can get away with anything in this room."

"Excellent—excellent!" said de Lesseps admiringly. He smiled a little bit. "I am afraid I did not give you credit for being the farsighted business man that you are." He turned and glanced over the collection of pictures abstractedly. "A clever thief, though," he ventured, "might cut a valuable painting, for instance the Rubens, out of the frame, roll it up, conceal it under his coat, and escape."

Kale laughed pleasantly and shook his head.

It was a couple of days later at the hotel that de Lesseps brought up the subject of copying the Whistler. He was profuse in his thanks when Kale volunteered to accompany him to the mansion and witness the preliminary stages of the work. They paused at the ballroom door.

"Jennings," said Kale to the liveried servant there, "this is Mr. de Lesseps. He is to come and go as he likes. He is going to do some work in the ballroom here. See that he isn't disturbed."

De Lesseps noticed the Rubens leaning carelessly against some other pictures, with the holy face of the Madonna toward them. "Really, Mr. Kale," he protested, "that picture is too valuable to be left about like that. If you will let your servants bring me some canvas, I shall wrap it and place it up on the table here off the floor. Suppose there were mice here?"

Kale thanked him. The necessary orders were given, and finally the picture was carefully wrapped and placed beyond harm's reach, whereupon de Lesseps adjusted himself, paper, easel, stool and all, and began his work of copying. There Kale left him.

Three days later Kale just happened to drop in, and found the artist still at his labor.

"I just dropped by," he explained, "to see how the work in the gallery was coming along. It will be finished in another week. I hope I am not disturbing you."

"Not at all," said de Lesseps. "I have nearly finished. See how I am getting along?" He turned the easel toward Kale.

The millionaire gazed from that toward the original which stood on a chair nearby, and frank admiration for the artist's efforts was in his eyes. "Why, it's fine!" he exclaimed. "It's just as good as the other one, and I bet you don't want any five thousand dollars for it, eh?"

That was all that was said about it at the time. Kale wandered about the house for an hour or so, then dropped into the ballroom where the artist was just getting his paraphernalia together, and they walked back to the hotel. The artist carried under one arm his copy of the Whistler, loosely rolled up.

Another week passed and the workman who had been engaged in refinishing and decorating the gallery had gone. De Lesseps volunteered to assist in the work of rehanging the pictures, and Kale gladly turned the matter over to him. It was in the afternoon of the day this work began that de Lesseps, chatting pleasantly with Kale, ripped loose the canvas which enshrouded the precious Rubens. Then he paused with an exclamation of dismay. The picture was gone; the frame which had held it was empty. A thin strip of canvas around the inside edge showed that a sharp penknife had been used to cut out the painting.

All of these facts came to the attention of Professor Augustus S. F. X. Van Dusen—The Thinking Machine. This was a day or so after Kale had rushed into Detective Mallory's office at police headquarters, with the statement that his Rubens had been stolen. He banged his fist down on the detective's desk and roared at him.

"It cost me fifty thousand dollars!" he declared violently. "Why don't you do something? What are you sitting there staring at me for?"

"Don't excite yourself, Mr. Kale," the detective advised. "I will put my men at work right now to recover the—the——What is a Rubens, anyway?"

"It's a picture!" bellowed Mr. Kale. "A piece of canvas with some paint on it, and it cost me fifty thousand dollars—don't you forget that!"

So the police machinery was set in motion to recover the painting. And in time the matter fell under the watchful eye of Hutchinson Hatch, reporter. He learned the facts preceding the disappearance of the picture, and then called on de Lesseps. He found the artist in a state of excitement bordering on hysteria; an intimation from the reporter of the object of his visit caused de Lesseps to burst into words.

"*Mon Dieu!* It is outrageous!" he exclaimed. "What can I do? I was the only one in the room for several days. I was the one who took such pains to protect the picture. And now it is gone! The loss is irreparable. What can I do?"

Hatch didn't have any very definite idea as to just what he could do, so he let him go on. "As I understand it, Mr. de Lesseps," he interrupted at last, "no one else was in the room, except you and Mr. Kale, all the time you were there?"

"No one else."

"And I think Mr. Kale said that you were making a copy of some famous water color, weren't you?"

"Yes, a Thames scene. By Whistler," was the reply. "That is it, hanging over the mantel."

Hatch glanced at the picture admiringly. It was an exquisite copy, and showed the deft touch of a man who was himself an artist of great ability.

De Lesseps read the admiration in his face. "It is not bad," he said modestly. "I studied with Carolus Duran."

With all else that was known, and this little additional information, which seemed of no particular value to the reporter, the entire matter was laid before The Thinking Machine. That distinguished man listened from beginning to end without comment.

"Who had access to the room?" he asked finally.

"That is what the police are working on now," was the reply. "There are a couple of dozen servants in the house, and I suppose in spite of Kale's rigid orders there was a certain laxity in their enforcement."

"Of course that makes it more difficult," said The Thinking Machine in the perpetually irritated voice which was so distinctly a part of himself. "Perhaps it would be best for us to go to Mr. Kale's home and personally investigate."

Kale received them with the reserve which all rich men show in the presence of representatives of the press. He stared frankly and somewhat curiously at the diminutive figure of the scientist, who explained the object of their visit.

"I guess you fellows can't do anything with them," the millionaire assured them. "I've got some regular detectives on it."

"Is Mr. Mallory here now?" asked The Thinking Machine curtly.

"Yes, he is upstairs in the servants' quarters."

"May we see the room from which the picture was taken?" inquired the scientist with a suave intonation which Hatch knew well.

Kale granted the permission with a wave of his hand and ushered them into the ballroom, where the pictures had been stored. From the relative center of the room The Thinking Machine surveyed it all. The windows were high. Half a dozen doors leading out into the hallways, to the conservatory, and quiet nooks of the mansion offered innumerable possibilities of access. After this one long comprehensive squint, The Thinking Machine went over and picked up the frame from which the Rubens had been cut. For a long time he examined it. Kale's impatience was painfully evident. Finally the scientist turned to him.

"How well do you know Mr. de Lesseps?" he asked.

"I've known him only for a month or so. Why?"

"Did he bring you letters of introduction, or did you meet him casually?"

Kale regarded him with evident displeasure. "My own personal affairs have nothing whatever to do with this matter," he said pointedly. "Mr. de Lesseps is a gentleman of integrity and certainly he is the last whom I would suspect of any connection with the disappearance of the picture."

"That is usually the case," remarked The Thinking Machine tartly. He turned to Hatch. "Just how good a copy was that he made of the Whistler picture?" he asked.

"I have never seen the original," Hatch replied, "but the workmanship was superb. Perhaps Mr. Kale wouldn't object to our seeing——"

"Oh, of course not," said Kale resignedly. "Come in. It's in the gallery."

Hatch submitted the picture to a careful scrutiny. "I should say that the copy is well nigh perfect," was his verdict. "Of course, in its absence, I couldn't say exactly, but it is certainly a superb piece of work."

The curtains of a wide door almost in front of them were thrown aside suddenly, and Detective Mallory entered. He carried something in his hand, but at the sight of them, concealed it behind himself. Unrepressed triumph was in his face.

"Ah, professor, we meet often, don't we?" he said.

"This reporter here and his friend seem to be trying to drag de Lesseps into this affair somehow," Kale complained to the detective. "I don't want anything like that to happen. He is liable to go out and print anything. They always do."

The Thinking Machine glared at him unwaveringly straight in the eye for an instant, then extended his hand toward Mallory. "Where did you find it?" he asked.

"Sorry to disappoint you, professor," said the detective sarcastically, "but this is the time when you were a little late," and he produced the object which he held behind him. "Here is your picture, Mr. Kale."

Kale gasped a little in relief and astonishment, and held up the canvas with both hands to examine it. "Fine!" he told the detective. "I'll see that you don't lose anything by this. Why, that thing cost me fifty thousand dollars!" Kale didn't seem able to get over that.

The Thinking Machine leaned forward to squint at the upper right-hand corner of the canvas. "Where did you find it?" he asked again.

"Rolled up tight and concealed in the bottom of a trunk in the room of one of the servants," explained Mallory. "The servant's name is Jennings. He is now under arrest."

"Jennings!" exclaimed Kale. "Why, he has been with me for years."

"Did he confess?" asked the scientist imperturbably.

"Of course not," said Mallory. "He says some of the other servants must have put it there."

The Thinking Machine nodded at Hatch. "I think perhaps that is all," he remarked. "I congratulate you, Mr. Mallory, upon bringing the matter to such a quick and satisfactory conclusion."

Ten minutes later they left the house and caught a car for the scientist's home. Hatch was a little chagrined at the unexpected termination of the affair, and was thoughtfully silent for a time.

"Mallory does occasionally show a gleam of human intelligence, doesn't he?" he said at last, quizzically.

"Not that I ever noticed," remarked the scientist.

"But he found the picture," Hatch insisted.

"Of course he found it. It was put there for him to find."

"Put there for him to find," repeated the reporter. "Didn't Jennings steal it?"

"If he did, he's a fool."

"Well, if he didn't steal it, who put it there?"

"De Lesseps."

"De Lesseps!" echoed Hatch. "Why the deuce did he steal a fifty-thousand-dollar picture and put it in a servant's trunk to be found?"

The Thinking Machine twisted around in his seat and squinted at him oddly for a moment. "At times, Mr. Hatch, I am absolutely amazed at your stupidity," he said frankly. "I can understand it in a man like Mallory, but I have always given you credit for being an astute, quick-witted man."

Hatch smiled at the reproach. It was not the first time he had heard of it. But nothing bearing on the problem in hand was said until they reached The Thinking Machine's apartments.

"The only real question in my mind, Mr. Hatch," said the scientist then, "is whether or not I should take the trouble to restore Mr. Kale's picture at all. He is perfectly satisfied, and will probably never know the difference. So——"

Suddenly Hatch saw something. "Great Scott!" he exclaimed. "Do you mean that the picture that Mallory found was——"

"A copy of the original," finished The Thinking Machine. "Personally I know nothing whatever about art, therefore, I could not say from observation that it is a copy, but I know it from the logic of the thing. When the original was cut from the frame, the knife swerved a little at the upper right-hand corner. The canvas remaining in the frame told me that. The picture that Mr. Mallory found did not correspond in this detail with the canvas in the frame. The conclusion is obvious."

"And de Lesseps has the original?"

"De Lesseps has the original. How did he get it? In any one of a dozen ways. He might have rolled it up and stuck it under his coat. He might have had a confederate, but I don't think that any ordinary method of theft would have appealed to him. I am giving him credit for being clever, as I must when we review the whole case——

"For instance, he asked for permission to copy the Whistler, which you saw was the same size as the Rubens. It was granted. He copied it practically under guard, always with the chance that Mr. Kale himself would drop in. It took him three days to copy it, so he says. He was alone in the room all that time. He knew that Mr. Kale had not the faintest idea of art. Taking advantage of that, what would have been simpler than to have copied the Rubens in oil? He could have removed it from the frame immediately after he canvassed it over, and kept it in a position near him where it could be quickly covered if he was interrupted. Remember, the picture is worth fifty thousand dollars, therefore was worth the trouble.

"De Lesseps is an artist—we know that—and dealing with a man who knew nothing whatever of art, he had no fears. We may suppose his idea all along was to use the copy of the Rubens as a sort of decoy after he got away with the original. You saw that Mallory didn't know the difference and it was safe for de Lesseps to suppose that Mr. Kale wouldn't, either. His only danger until he could get away gracefully was of some critic or connoisseur, perhaps, seeing the copy. His boldness we see readily in the fact that he permitted himself to discover the theft, that he discovered it after he had volunteered to assist Mr. Kale in the general work of rehanging the pictures in the gallery. Just how he put the picture in Jennings's trunk, I don't happen to know. We can imagine many ways——" He lay back in his chair for a minute without speaking, eyes steadily turned upward, fingers placed precisely tip to tip.

"The only thing remaining is to go get the picture. It is in de Lesseps's room now—you told me that—and so we know it is safe. I dare say he knows that if he tried to run away, it would inevitably put him under suspicion."

"But how did he take the picture from the Kale home?" asked Hatch.

"He took it with him probably under his arm the day he left the house with Mr. Kale," was the astonishing reply.

Hatch stared at him in amazement. After a moment the scientist rose and passed into the adjoining room, and the telephone bell there jingled. When he joined Hatch again, he picked up his hat and they went out together.

De Lesseps was in when their cards went up, and received them. They conversed of the case generally for ten minutes, while the scientist's eyes were turned inquiringly here and there about the room. At last there came a knock on the door.

"It is Detective Mallory, Mr. Hatch," remarked The Thinking Machine. "Open the door for him."

De Lesseps seemed startled for just one instant, then quickly recovered. Mallory's eyes were full of questions when he entered.

"I should like, Mr. Mallory," began The Thinking Machine quietly, "to call your attention to this copy of Mr. Kale's picture by Whistler—over the mantel here. Isn't it excellent? You have seen the original?"

Mallory grunted. De Lesseps's face, instead of expressing appreciation at the compliment, blanched suddenly, and his hands closed tightly. Again he recovered himself and smiled.

"The beauty of this picture lies not only in its faithfulness to the original," the scientist went on, "but also in the fact that it was painted under extraordinary circumstances. For instance, I don't know if you know, Mr. Mallory, that it is possible so to combine glue and putty and a few other commonplace things into a paste which would effectively blot out an oil painting and offer at the same time an excellent surface for water-color work."

There was a moment's pause, during which the three men stared at him silently—with singularly conflicting emotions depicted on their faces.

"This water color—this copy of Whistler," continued the scientist evenly, "is painted on such a paste as I have described. That paste in turn covers the original Rubens picture. It can be removed with water without damage to the picture, which is in oil, so that instead of a copy of the Whistler painting, we have an original by Rubens, worth fifty thousand dollars. That is true; isn't it, Mr. de Lesseps?"

There was no reply to the question—none was needed. It was an hour later, after de Lesseps was safely in his cell, that Hatch called up The Thinking Machine on the telephone and asked one question.

"How did you know that the water color was painted over the Rubens?"

"Because it was the only absolutely safe way in which the Rubens could be hopelessly lost to those who were looking for it, and at the same time perfectly preserved," was the answer. "I told you de Lesseps was a clever man, and a little logic did the rest. Two and two always makes four, Mr. Hatch, not sometimes, but all the time."

The Fatal Cipher

For the third time Professor Augustus S. F. X. Van Dusen—so-called
The Thinking Machine—read the letter. It was spread out in front of
him on the table, and his blue eyes were narrowed to mere slits as he
studied it through his heavy eyeglasses. The young woman who had
placed the letter in his hands, Miss Elizabeth Devan, sat waiting patiently in the sofa in the little reception room of The Thinking Machine's house. Her blue eyes were opened wide and she stared as if
fascinated at this man who had become so potent a factor in the solution of intangible mysteries.

Here is the letter:

To those concerned:

Tired of it all I seek the end, and am content. Ambition is now
dead; the grave yawns greedily at my feet, and with the labor of
my own hands lost I greet death of my own will, by my own act.

To my son I leave all, and you who maligned me, you who discouraged me, you may read this and know I punish you thus. It's
for him, my son, to forgive.

I dared in life and dare dead your everlasting anger, not alone
that you didn't speak but that you cherished secret, and my ears
are locked forever against you. My vault is my resting place. On

the brightest and dearest page of life I wrote (7) my love for him. Family ties, binding as the Bible itself, bade me give all to my son. Good-bye. I die

POMEROY STOCKTON

"Under just what circumstances did this letter come into your possession, Miss Devan?" The Thinking Machine asked. "Tell me the full story; omit nothing."

The scientist sank back into his chair with his enormous yellow head pillowed comfortably against the cushion and his long, steady fingers pressed tip to tip. He didn't even look at his pretty visitor. She had come to ask for information; he was willing to give it, because it offered another of those abstract problems which he always found interesting. In his own field—the sciences—his fame was world wide. This concentration of a brain which had achieved so much on more material things was perhaps a sort of relaxation.

Miss Devan had a soft, soothing voice, and as she talked it was broken at times by what seemed to be a sob. Her face was flushed a little, and she emphasized her points by a quick clasping and unclasping of her dainty gloved hands.

"My father, or rather, my adopted father, Pomeroy Stockton, was an inventor," she began. "We lived in a great old-fashioned house in Dorchester. We have lived there since I was a child. When I was only five or six years old, I was left an orphan and was adopted by Mr. Stockton, who always treated me as a daughter. His death, therefore, was a great blow to me.

"Mr. Stockton was a widower with only one child of his own, a son, John Stockton, who is now about thirty-one years old. He is a man of irreproachable character, and has always, since I first knew him, been religiously inclined. He is the junior partner in a great commercial company, Dutton and Stockton, leather men. I suppose he has an immense fortune, for he gives largely to charity, and is, too, the active head of a large Sunday school.

"Pomeroy Stockton, my adopted father, almost idolized this son, although there was in his manner toward him something akin to fear. Close work had made my father querulous and irritable. Yet I don't believe a better-hearted man ever lived. He worked most of the time in a little shop, which he had installed in a large back room on the ground floor of the house. He always worked with the door locked.

There were furnaces, moulds, and many things that I didn't know the use of."

"I know who he was," said The Thinking Machine. "He was working to rediscover the secret of hardened copper—a secret which was lost in ancient Egypt. I knew Mr. Stockton very well by reputation. Go on."

Miss Devan resumed: "Whatever it was he worked on, he guarded it very carefully. He would permit no one at all to enter the room. I have never seen more than a glimpse of what was in it. His son, particularly, I have seen barred out of the shop a dozen times and every time there was a quarrel to follow.

"Those were the conditions at the time Mr. Stockton first became ill, six or seven months ago. At that time he double-locked the doors of his shop, retired to his rooms on the second floor, and remained there in practical seclusion for two weeks or more. These rooms adjoined mine, and twice during that time I heard the son and the father talking loudly, as if quarreling. At the end of the two weeks, Mr. Stockton returned to work in the shop and shortly afterward the son, who had also lived in the house, took apartments in Beacon Street and removed his belongings from the house.

"From that time up to last Monday—this is Thursday—I never saw the son in the house. On Monday the father was at work as usual in the shop. He had previously told me that the work he was engaged in was practically ended and he expected a great fortune to result from it. About five o'clock in the afternoon on Monday the son came to the house. No one knows when he went out. It is a fact, however, that Father did not have dinner at the usual time, six-thirty. I presumed he was at work, and did not take time for his dinner. I have known him to do this many times."

For a moment the girl was silent and seemed to be struggling with some deep grief which she could not control.

"And next morning?" asked The Thinking Machine gently.

"Next morning," the girl went on, "Father was found dead in the workshop. There were no marks on his body, nothing to indicate at first the manner of death. It was as if he had sat in his chair beside one of the furnaces and had taken poison and died at once. A small bottle of what I presume to be prussic acid was smashed on the floor, almost beside his chair. We discovered him dead after we had rapped on the door several times and got no answer. Then Montgomery, our butler, smashed in the door, at my request. There we found Father.

"I immediately telephoned to the son, John Stockton, and he came to the house. The letter you now have was found in my father's pocket. It was just as you see it. Mr. Stockton seemed greatly agitated and started to destroy the letter. I induced him to give it to me, because instantly it occurred to me that there was something wrong about all of it. My father had talked too often to me about the future, what he intended to do and his plans for me. There may not be anything wrong. The letter may be just what it purports to be. I hope it is—oh—I hope it is. Yet everything considered——"

"Was there an autopsy?" asked The Thinking Machine.

"No. John Stockton's actions seemed to be directed against any investigation. He told me he thought he could do certain things which would prevent the matter coming to the attention of the police. My father was buried on a death certificate issued by a Dr. Benton, who has been a friend of John Stockton since their college days. In that way the appearance of suicide or anything else was covered up completely.

"Both before and after the funeral John Stockton made me promise to keep this letter hidden or else destroy it. In order to put an end to this I told him I had destroyed the letter. This attitude on his part, the more I thought of it, seemed to confirm my original idea that it had not been suicide. Night after night I thought of this, and finally decided to come to you rather than to the police. I feel that there is some dark mystery behind it all. If you can help me now——"

"Yes, yes," broke in The Thinking Machine. "Where was the key to the workshop? In Pomeroy's pocket? In his room? In the door?"

"Really, I don't know," said Miss Devan. "It hadn't occurred to me."

"Did Mr. Stockton leave a will?"

"Yes, it is with his lawyer, a Mr. Sloane."

"Has it been read? Do you know what is in it?"

"It is to be read in a day or so. Judging from the second paragraph of the letter, I presume he left everything to his son."

For the fourth time The Thinking Machine read the letter. At its end he again looked up at Miss Devan.

"Just what is your interpretation of this letter from one end to the other," he asked.

"Speaking from my knowledge of Mr. Stockton and the circumstances surrounding him," the girl explained, "I should say the letter means just what it says. I should imagine from the first paragraph that something he invented had been taken away from him, stolen perhaps. The second paragraph and the third, I should say, were intended as a rebuke to certain relatives—a brother and two distant cousins—who had always regarded him as a crank and took frequent occasion to tell him so. I don't know a great deal of the history of that other branch of the family. The last two paragraphs explain themselves except———"

"Except the figure 7," interrupted the scientist. "Do you have any idea whatever as to the meaning of that?"

The girl took the letter and studied it closely for a moment.

"Not the slightest," she said. "It does not seem to be connected with anything else in the letter."

"Do you think it possible, Miss Devan, that this letter was written under coercion?"

"I do," said the girl quickly, and her face flamed. "That's just what I do think. From the first I have imagined some ghastly, horrible mystery back of it all."

"Or, perhaps Pomeroy Stockton never saw this letter at all," mused The Thinking Machine. "It may be a forgery?"

"Forgery!" gasped the girl. "Then John Stockton..."

"Whatever it is, forged or genuine," The Thinking Machine went on quietly, "it is a most extraordinary document. It might have been written by a poet: it states things in such a roundabout way. It is not directly to the point, as a practical man would have written."

There was silence for several minutes. The girl sat leaning forward on the table, staring into the inscrutable eyes of the scientist.

"Perhaps, perhaps," she said, "there is a cipher of some sort in it?"

"That is probably correct," said The Thinking Machine emphatically. "There is a cipher in it, and a very ingenious one."

———

It was twenty-four hours later that The Thinking Machine sent for Hutchinson Hatch, reporter, and talked over the matter with him. He had always found Hatch a discreet, resourceful individual, who was willing to aid in any way in his power.

Hatch read the letter, which The Thinking Machine had said contained a cipher, and then the circumstances as related by Miss Devan were retold to the reporter.

"Do you think it is a cipher?" asked Hatch in conclusion.

"It is a cipher," replied The Thinking Machine. "If what Miss Devan has said is correct, John Stockton cannot have said anything about the affair. I want you to go and talk to him, find out all about him and what division of the property is made by the will. Does this will give everything to the son?

"Also find out what personal enmity there is between John Stockton and Miss Devan, and what was the cause of it. Was there a man in it? If so, who? When you have done all this, go to the house in Dorchester and bring me the family Bible, if there is one there. It's probably a big book. If it is not there, let me know immediately by phone. Miss Devan will, I suppose, give it to you, if she has it."

With these instructions Hatch went away. Half an hour later he was in the private office of John Stockton at the latter's place of business. Mr. Stockton was a man of long visage, rather angular and clerical in appearance. There was a smug satisfaction about the man that Hatch didn't quite approve of, and yet it was a trait which found expression only in a soft voice and small acts of needless courtesy.

A deprecatory look passed over Stockton's face when Hatch asked the first question, which bore on his relationship with Pomeroy Stockton.

"I had hoped that this matter would not come to the attention of the press," said Stockton in an oily, gentle tone. "It is something which can only bring disgrace upon my poor father's memory, and his has been a name associated with distinct achievements in the progress of the world. However, if necessary, I will state my knowledge of the affair, and invite the investigation which, frankly, I will say, I tried to stop."

"How much was your father's estate?" asked Hatch.

"Something more than a million," was the reply. "He made most of it through a device for coupling cars. This is now in use on practically all the railroads."

"And the division of this property by will?" asked Hatch.

"I haven't seen the will, but I understand that he left practically everything to me, settling an annuity and the home in Dorchester on Miss Devan, whom he had always regarded as a daughter."

"That would give you then, say, two-thirds or three-quarters of the estate."

"Something like that, possibly eight hundred thousand dollars."

"Where is this will now?"

"I understand in the hands of my father's attorney, Mr. Sloane."

"When is it to be read?"

"It was to have been read today, but there has been some delay about it. The attorney postponed it for a few days."

"What, Mr. Stockton, was the purpose in making it appear that your father died naturally, when obviously he committed suicide and there is even a suggestion of something else?" demanded Hatch.

John Stockton sat up straight in his chair with a startled expression in his eyes. He had been rubbing his hands together complacently; now he stopped and stared at the reporter.

"Something else?" he asked. "Pray what else?"

Hatch shrugged his shoulders, but in his eyes there lay almost an accusation.

"Did any motive ever appear for your father's suicide?"

"I know of none," Stockton replied. "Yet, admitting that this is suicide, without a motive, it seems that the only fault I have committed is that I had a friend report it otherwise and avoided a police inquiry."

"It's just that. Why did you do it?"

"Naturally to save the family name from disgrace. But this something else you spoke of? Do you mean that anyone else thinks that anything other than suicide or natural death is possible?"

As he asked the question there came some subtle change over his face. He leaned forward toward the reporter. All trace of the sanctimonious smirk about the thin-lipped mouth had gone now.

"Miss Devan has produced the letter found on your father at death and has said——" began the reporter.

"Elizabeth! Miss Devan!" exclaimed John Stockton. He arose suddenly, paced several times across the room, then stopped in front of the reporter. "She gave me her word of honor that she would not make the existence of that letter known."

"But she has made it public," said Hatch. "And further she intimates that your father's death was not even what it appeared to be, suicide."

"She's crazy, man, crazy," said Stockton in deep agitation. "Who could have killed my father? What motive could there have been?"

There was a grim twitching of Hatch's lips.

"Was Miss Devan legally adopted by your father?" he asked, irrelevantly.

"Yes."

"In that event, disregarding other relatives, doesn't it seem strange even to you that he gives three-quarters of the estate to you—you have a fortune already—and only a small part to Miss Devan, who has nothing?"

"That's my father's business."

There was a pause. Stockton was still pacing back and forth.

Finally he sank down in his chair at the desk, and sat for a moment looking at the reporter.

"Is that all?" he asked.

"I should like to know, if you don't mind telling me, what direct cause there is for ill feeling between Miss Devan and you?"

"There is no ill feeling. We merely never got along well together. My father and I have had several arguments about her for reasons which it is not necessary to go into."

"Did you have such an argument on the night before your father was found dead?"

"I believe there was something said about her."

"What time did you leave the shop that night?"

"About ten o'clock."

"And you had been in the room with your father since afternoon, had you not?"

"Yes."

"No dinner?"

"No."

"How did you come to neglect that?"

"My father was explaining a recent invention he had perfected, which I was to put on the market."

"I suppose the possibility of suicide or his death in any way had not occurred to you?"

"No, not at all. We were making elaborate plans for the future."

Possibly it was some prejudice against the man's appearance which made Hatch so dissatisfied with the result of the interview. He felt that he had gained nothing, yet Stockton had been absolutely frank, as it seemed. There was one last question.

"Have you any recollection of a large family Bible in your father's house?" he asked.

"I have seen it several times," Stockton said.

"Is it still there?"

"So far as I know, yes."

That was the end of the interview, and Hatch went straight to the house in Dorchester to see Miss Devan. There, in accordance with instructions from The Thinking Machine, he asked for the family Bible.

"There was one here the other day," said Miss Devan, "but it has disappeared."

"Since your father's death?" asked Hatch.

"Yes, the next day."

"Have you any idea who took it?"

"Not unless—unless——"

"John Stockton! Why did he take it?" blurted Hatch.

There was a little resigned movement of the girl's hands, a movement which said, "I don't know."

"He told me, too," said Hatch indignantly, "that he thought the Bible was still here."

The girl drew close to the reporter and laid one white hand on his sleeve. She looked up into his eyes and tears stood in her own. Her lips trembled.

"John Stockton has that book," she said. "He took it away from here the day after my father died, and he did it for a purpose. What, I don't know,"

"Are you absolutely positive he has it?" asked Hatch.

"I saw it in his room, where he had hidden it," replied the girl.

———

Hatch laid the results of the interviews before the scientist at the Beacon Hill home. The Thinking Machine listened without comment up to that point where Miss Devan had said she knew the family Bible to be in the son's possession.

"If Miss Devan and Stockton do not get along well together, why should she visit Stockton's place at all?" demanded The Thinking Machine.

"I don't know," Hatch replied, "except that she thinks he must have had some connection with her father's death, and is investigating on her own account. What has this Bible to do with it anyway?"

"It may have a great deal to do with it," said The Thinking Machine enigmatically. "Now the thing to do is to find out if the girl told the truth and if the Bible is in Stockton's apartment. Now, Mr. Hatch,

I leave that to you. I would like to see that Bible. If you can bring it to me, well and good. If you can't bring it, look at and study the seventh page for any pencil marks in the text, anything whatever. It might even be advisable, if you have the opportunity, to tear out that page and bring it to me. No harm will be done, and it can be returned in proper time."

Perplexed wrinkles were gathering on Hatch's forehead as he listened. What had page 7 of a Bible to do with what seemed to be a murder mystery? Who had said anything about a Bible, anyway? The letter left by Stockton mentioned a Bible, but that didn't seem to mean anything. Then Hatch remembered that the same letter carried a figure seven in parentheses, which had apparently nothing to do and no connection with any other part of the letter. Hatch's introspective study of the affair was interrupted by The Thinking Machine.

"I shall await your report here, Mr. Hatch. If it is what I expect, we shall go out late tonight on a little voyage of discovery. Meanwhile, see that Bible and tell me what you find."

Hatch found the apartments of John Stockton on Beacon Street without any difficulty. In a manner best known to himself, he entered and searched the place. When he came out, there was a look of chagrin on his face as he hurried to the house of The Thinking Machine nearby.

"Well?" asked the scientist.

"I saw the Bible," said Hatch.

"And page 7?"

"Was torn out, missing, gone," replied the reporter.

"Ah," exclaimed the scientist. "I thought so. Tonight we shall make the little trip I spoke of. By the way, did you happen to notice if John Stockton had or used a fountain pen?"

"I didn't see one," said Hatch.

"Well, please see for me if any of his employees have ever noticed one. Then meet me here tonight at ten o'clock."

Thus Hatch was dismissed. A little later he called casually on Stockton again. There, by inquiries, he established to his own satisfaction that Stockton did not own a fountain pen. Then with Stockton himself he took up the matter of the Bible again.

"I understand you to say, Mr. Stockton," he began in his smoothest tone, "that you knew of the existence of a family Bible, but you did not know if it was still at the Dorchester place."

"That's correct," said Stockton.

"How is it then," Hatch resumed, "that that identical Bible is now at your apartments, carefully hidden in a box under a sofa?"

Mr. Stockton seemed to be amazed. He arose suddenly and leaned over toward the reporter with hands clenched. There was glitter of what might have been anger in his eyes.

"What do you know about this? What are you talking about?" he demanded.

"I mean you had said you did not know where this book was and meanwhile have it hidden. Why?"

"Have you seen the Bible in my rooms?" asked Stockton.

"I have," said the reporter coolly.

Now a new determination came over the face of the merchant. The oiliness of his manner was gone, the sanctimonious smirk had been obliterated, the thin lips closed into a straight rigid line.

"I shall have nothing further to say," he declared almost fiercely.

"Will you tell me why you tore out the seventh page of the Bible?" asked Hatch.

Stockton stared at him dully, as if dazed for a moment. All the color left his face. There came a startling pallor instead. When next he spoke, his voice was tense and strained.

"Is—is—the seventh page missing?"

"Yes," Hatch replied. "Where is it?"

"I'll have nothing further to say under any circumstances. That's all."

With not the slightest idea of what it might mean or what bearing it had on the matter, Hatch had brought out statements which were wholly at variance with facts. Why was Stockton so affected by the statement that page 7 was gone? Why had the Bible been taken from the Dorchester home? Why had it been so carefully hidden? How did Miss Devan know it was there?

These were only a few of the questions that were racing through the reporter's mind. He did not seem to be able to grasp anything tangible. If there were a cipher hidden in the letter, what was it? What bearing did it have on the case?

Seeking a possible answer to some of these questions, Hatch took a cab and was soon back at the Dorchester house. He was somewhat surprised to see The Thinking Machine standing on the stoop waiting to be admitted. The scientist took his presence as a matter of course.

"What did you find out about Stockton's fountain pen?" he asked.

"I satisfied myself that he had not owned a fountain pen, at least recently enough for the pen to have been used in writing that letter. I presume that's what inquiries in that direction mean."

The two men were admitted to the house and after a few minutes Miss Devan entered. She understood when The Thinking Machine explained that they merely wished to see the shop in which Mr. Stockton had been found dead.

"And also if you have a sample of Mr. Stockton's handwriting," asked the scientist.

"It's rather peculiar," Miss Devan explained, "but I doubt if there is an authentic example in existence, large enough, that is, to be compared with the letter. He had a certain amount of correspondence, but this I did for him on the typewriter. Occasionally he would prepare an article for a scientific journal, but these were also dictated to me. He has been in the habit of doing so for years."

"This letter seems to be all there is?"

"Of course the signature appears on checks and in other places. I can produce some of those for you. I don't think, however, that there is the slightest doubt that he wrote this letter. It is his handwriting."

"I suppose he never used a fountain pen?" asked The Thinking Machine.

"Not that I know of."

"Do you own one?"

"Yes," the girl replied, and she took a pen out of a little gold fascinator she wore at her bosom.

The scientist pressed the point of the pen against his thumbnail, and a tiny drop of blue ink appeared. The letter was written in black. The Thinking Machine seemed satisfied.

"And now the shop," he suggested.

Miss Devan led the way through the long wide hall to the back of the building. There she opened a door, which showed signs of having been battered in, and admitted them. Then at the request of The Thinking Machine she rehearsed the story in full, showed him where Stockton had been found, where the bottle of prussic acid had been broken, where the servant, Montgomery, had broken in the door at her request.

"Did you ever find the key to the door?"

"No. I can't imagine what became of it."

"Is this room precisely as it was when the body was found? That is, has anything been removed from it?"

"Nothing," replied the girl.

"Have the servants taken anything out? Did they have access to this room?"

"They have not been permitted to enter it at all. The body was removed, and the fragments of the acid bottle were taken away, but nothing else."

"Have you ever known of pen and ink being in this room?"

"I hadn't thought of it."

"You haven't taken them out since the body was found, have you?"

"I—I—have not," the girl stammered.

Miss Devan left the room and for an hour Hatch and The Thinking Machine conducted their search.

"Find a pen and ink," The Thinking Machine instructed.

They were not found.

———

At midnight, which was six hours later, The Thinking Machine and Hutchinson Hatch were groping through the cellar of the Dorchester house with the aid of a small electric lamp which shot a straight beam aggressively through the murky, damp air. Finally the ray fell on a tiny door set in the solid wall of the cellar.

There was a slight exclamation from The Thinking Machine, and this was followed by the sharp, unmistakable click of a revolver somewhere behind them in the dark.

"Down, quick," gasped Hatch, and with a sudden blow he dashed aside the electric light, extinguishing it. Simultaneously with this came a revolver shot, and a bullet struck the wall behind Hatch's head.

The reverberation of the pistol shot was still ringing in Hatch's ears when he felt the hand of The Thinking Machine on his arm, and then through the utter blackness of the cellar came the irritable voice of the scientist:

"To your right, to your right," it said sharply.

Then, contrary to this advice Hatch felt the scientist drawing him to the left. In another moment there came a second shot, and by the flash Hatch could see that it was aimed at a point a dozen feet to the right of the point they had been when the first shot was fired. The person with the revolver had heard the scientist and had been duped.

Firmly the scientist drew Hatch on until they were almost to the cellar steps. There, outlined against a dim light which came down the stairs, they could see a tall figure peering through the darkness toward a spot opposite where they stood. Hatch saw only one thing to do and did it. He leaped forward and landed on the back of the figure, bearing the man to the ground. An instant later his hand closed on the revolver, and he wrested it away.

"All right," he sang out, "I've got it."

The electric light which he had dashed from the hand of The Thinking Machine gleamed again through the cellar and fell upon the face of John Stockton, still helpless and gasping in the hands of the reporter.

"Well?" asked Stockton calmly. "Are you burglars or what?"

"Let's go upstairs, to the light," suggested The Thinking Machine.

It was under these peculiar circumstances that the scientist came face to face for the first time with John Stockton. Hatch introduced the two men in a most matter-of-fact tone and restored to Stockton his revolver. This was suggested by a nod of the scientist's head. Stockton laid the revolver on a table.

"Why did you try to kill us?" asked The Thinking Machine.

"I presumed you were burglars," was the reply. "I heard the noise down stairs and came down to investigate."

"I thought you lived on Beacon Street," said the scientist.

"I do, but I came here tonight on a little business which is all my own, and happened to hear you. What were you doing in the cellar?"

"How long have you been here?"

"Five or ten minutes."

"Have you a key to this house?"

"I have had one for many years. What is all this, anyway? How did you get in this house? What right had you here?"

"Is Miss Devan in the house tonight?" asked The Thinking Machine, entirely disregarding the other's questions.

"I don't know. I suppose so."

"You haven't seen her, of course?"

"Certainly not."

"And you came here secretly without her knowledge?"

Stockton shrugged his shoulders and was silent. The Thinking Machine raised himself on the chair on which he had been sitting and squinted steadily into Stockton's eyes. When he spoke it was to Hatch, but his gaze did not waver.

"Arouse the servants, find where Miss Devan's room is, and see if anything has happened to her," he directed.

"I think that will be unwise," broke in Stockton quickly.

"Why?"

"If I may put it on personal grounds," said Stockton. "I would ask as a favor that you do not make known my visit here, or your own, for that matter, to Miss Devan."

There was a certain uneasiness in the man's attitude, a certain eagerness to keep things away from Miss Devan that spurred Hatch to instant action. He went out of the room hurriedly and ten minutes later Miss Devan, who had dressed quickly, came into the room with him. The servants stood outside in the hall, all curiosity. The closed door barred them from knowledge of what was happening.

There was a little dramatic pause as Miss Devan entered and Stockton arose from his seat. The Thinking Machine glanced from one to the other. He noted the pallor of the girl's face and the frank embarrassment of Stockton.

"What is it?" asked Miss Devan, and her voice trembled a little. "Why are you all here? What has happened?"

"Mr. Stockton came here tonight," The Thinking Machine began quietly, "to remove the contents from the locked vault in the cellar. He came without your knowledge and found us ahead of him. Mr. Hatch and myself are here in the course of our inquiry into the matter which you placed in my hands. We also came without your knowledge. I considered this best. Mr. Stockton was very anxious that his visit should be kept from you. Have you anything to say now?"

The girl turned on Stockton with magnificent scorn. Accusation was in her very attitude. Her small hand was pointed directly at Stockton and into his face came a strange emotion, which he struggled to repress.

"Murderer! Thief!" the girl almost hissed.

"Do you know why he came?" asked The Thinking Machine.

"He came to rob the vault, as you said," said the girl fiercely. "It was because my father would not give him the secret of his last invention that this man killed him. How he compelled him to write that letter I don't know."

"Elizabeth, for God's sake what are you saying?" asked Stockton with ashen face.

"His greed is so great that he wanted all of my father's estate," the girl went on impetuously. "He was not content that I should get even a small part of it."

"Elizabeth, Elizabeth!" said Stockton, as he leaned forward with his head in his hands.

"What do you know about this secret vault?" asked the scientist.

"I—I—have always thought there was a secret vault in the cellar," the girl explained. "I may say I know there was one because those things my father took the greatest care of were always disposed of by him somewhere in the house. I can imagine no other place than the cellar."

There was a long pause. The girl stood rigid, staring down at the bowed figure of Stockton with not a gleam of pity in her face. Hatch caught the expression and it occurred to him for the first time that Miss Devan was vindictive. He was more convinced than ever that there had been some long-standing feud between these two. The Thinking Machine broke the long silence.

Do you happen to know, Miss Devan, that page 7 of the Bible which you found hidden in Mr. Stockton's place is missing?"

"I didn't notice," said the girl.

Stockton had arisen with the words and now stood with white face listening intently.

"Did you ever happen to see a page 7 in that Bible?" the scientist asked.

"I don't recall."

"What were you doing in my rooms?" demanded Stockton of the girl.

"Why did you tear out page 7?" asked The Thinking Machine.

Stockton thought the question was addressed to him and turned to answer. Then he saw it unmistakably a question to Miss Devan and turned again to her.

"I didn't tear it out," exclaimed Miss Devan. "I never saw it. I don't know what you mean."

The Thinking Machine made an impatient gesture with his hands; his next question was to Stockton.

"Have you a sample of your father's handwriting?"

"Several," said Stockton. "Here are three or four letters from him."

Miss Devan gasped a little as if startled and Stockton produced the letters and handed them to The Thinking Machine. The latter glanced over two of them.

"I thought, Miss Devan, you said your father always dictated his letters to you?"

"I did say so," said the girl. "I didn't know of the existence of these."

"May I have these?" asked The Thinking Machine.

"Yes. They are of no consequence."

"Now let's see what is in the secret vault," the scientist went on.

He arose and led the way again into the cellar, lighting his path with the electric bulb. Stockton followed immediately behind, then came Miss Devan, her white dressing gown trailing mystically in the dim light, and last came Hatch. The Thinking Machine went straight to that spot where he and Hatch had been when Stockton had fired at them. Again the rays of the light revealed the tiny door set into the walls of the cellar. The door opened readily enough at his touch; the small vault was empty.

Intent on his examination of this, The Thinking Machine was oblivious for a moment to what was happening. Suddenly there came again a pistol shot, followed instantly by a woman's scream.

"My God, he's killed himself! He's killed himself!"

It was Miss Devan's voice.

———

When The Thinking Machine flashed his light back into the gloom of the cellar, he saw Miss Devan and Hatch leaning over the prostrate figure of John Stockton. The latter's face was perfectly white save just at the edge of his hair, where there was a trickle of red. In his right hand he clasped a revolver.

"Dear me! Dear me!" exclaimed the scientist. "What is it?"

"Stockton shot himself," said Hatch, and there was excitement in his tone.

On his knees the scientist made a hurried examination of the wounded man, then suddenly—it may have been inadvertently—he flashed the light in the face of Miss Devan.

"Where were you?" he demanded quickly.

"Just behind him," said the girl. "Will he die? Is it fatal?"

"Hopeless," said the scientist. "Let us carry him upstairs."

The unconscious man was lifted and with Hatch leading was again taken to the room which they had left only a few minutes before. Hatch stood by helplessly while The Thinking Machine, in his capacity of physician, made a more minute examination of the wound.

The bullet mark just above the right temple was almost bloodless; around it there were the unmistakeable marks of burned powder.

"Help me just a moment, Miss Devan," requested The Thinking Machine, as he bound an improvised handkerchief bandage about the head. Miss Devan tied the final knots of the bandage and The Thinking Machine studied her hands closely as she did so. When the work was completed, he turned to her in a most matter-of-fact way.

"Why did you shoot him?" he asked.

"I—I——" stammered the girl. "I didn't shoot him. He shot himself."

"How came those powder marks on your right hand?"

Miss Devan glanced down at her right hand, and the color which had been in her face faded as if by magic. There was fear, now, in her manner.

"I—I don't know," she stammered. "Surely you don't think that I——"

"Mr. Hatch, phone at once for an ambulance and then see if it is possible to get Detective Mallory here immediately. I shall give Miss Devan into custody on the charge of shooting this man."

The girl stared at him dully for a moment and then dropped back into a chair with dead white face and fear-distended eyes. Hatch went out, seeking a telephone, and for a time Miss Devan sat silent, as if dazed. Finally, with an effort, she aroused herself and facing The Thinking Machine defiantly burst out:

"I didn't shoot him. I didn't. I didn't. He did it himself."

The long slender fingers of The Thinking Machine closed on the revolver and gently removed it from the hand of the wounded man.

"Ah, I was mistaken," he said suddenly, "he is not as badly wounded as I thought. See! he is reviving."

"Reviving!" exclaimed Miss Devan. "Won't he die, then?"

"Why?" asked The Thinking Machine sharply.

"It seems so pitiful, almost a confession of guilt," she hurriedly exclaimed. "Won't he die?"

Gradually the color was coming back into Stockton's face. The Thinking Machine bending over him, with one hand on the heart, saw the eyelids quiver, and then slowly the eyes opened. Almost immediately the strength of the heartbeat grew perceptibly stronger. Stockton stared at him a moment, then wearily his eyelids drooped again.

"Why did Miss Devan shoot you?" The Thinking Machine demanded.

There was a pause and the eyes opened for the second time. Miss Devan stood within range of the glance, her hands outstretched entreatingly toward Stockton.

"Why did she shoot you?" repeated The Thinking Machine.

"She—did—not," said Stockton slowly. "I—did—it—myself."

For an instant there was a little wrinkle of perplexity on the brow of The Thinking Machine and then it passed.

"Purposely?" he asked.

"I did it myself."

Again the eyes closed and Stockton seemed to be passing into unconsciousness. The Thinking Machine glanced up to find an infinite expression of relief on Miss Devan's face. His own manner changed; he became almost abject, in fact, as he turned to her again.

"I beg your pardon," he said. "I made a mistake."

"Will he die?"

"No, that was another mistake. He will recover."

Within a few minutes a City Hospital ambulance rattled up to the door and John Stockton was removed. It was with a feeling of pity that Hatch assisted Miss Devan, now almost in fainting condition, to her room. The Thinking Machine had previously given her a slight stimulant. Detective Mallory had not answered the call by phone.

The Thinking Machine and Hatch returned to Boston. At the Park Street subway they separated, after The Thinking Machine had given certain instructions. Hatch spent most of the following day carrying out these instructions. First he went to see Dr. Benton, the physician who had issued the death certificate on which Pomeroy Stockton had been buried. Dr. Benton was considerably alarmed when the reporter broached the subject of his visit. After a time he talked freely of the case.

"I have known John Stockton since we were in college together," he said, "and I believe him to be one of the few really good men I know. I can't believe otherwise. Singularly enough, he is also one of the few good men who have made their own fortunes. There is nothing hypocritical about him.

"Immediately after his father was found dead, he phoned to me and I went out to the house in Dorchester. He explained then that it was apparent that Pomeroy Stockton had committed suicide. He dreaded the disgrace that public knowledge would bring on an honored name, and asked me what could be done. I suggested the only thing I knew— that was the issuance of a death certificate specifying natural causes— heart disease, I said. This act was due entirely to my friendship for him.

"I examined the body and found a trace of prussic acid on Pomeroy's tongue. Beside the chair on which he sat a bottle of prussic acid had been broken. I made no autopsy. Of course, ethically I may have sinned, but I feel that no real harm has been done. Of course, now that you know the real facts, my entire career is at stake."

"There is no question in your mind but that it was suicide?" asked Hatch.

"Not the slightest. Then, too, there was the letter, which was found in Pomeroy's pocket. I saw that and if there had been any doubt then it was removed. This letter, I think, was then in Miss Devan's possession. I presume it is still."

"Do you know anything about Miss Devan?"

"Nothing, except that she is an adopted daughter who for some reason retained her own family name. Three or four years ago she had a little love affair, to which John Stockton objected. I believe he was the cause of it being broken off. As a matter of fact, I think at one time he was himself in love with her and she refused to accept him as a suitor. Since that time there has been some slight friction, but I know nothing of this except in a general way, from what he has said to me."

Then Hatch proceeded to carry out the other part of The Thinking Machine's instructions. This was to see the attorney in whose possession Pomeroy Stockton's will was supposed to be and to ask him why there had been a delay in the reading of the will.

Hatch found the attorney, Frederick Sloane, without difficulty. Without reservation Hatch laid all the circumstances as he knew them before Mr. Sloane. Then came the question of why the will had not been read. Mr. Sloane, too, was frank.

"It's because the will is not now in my possession," he said. "It has either been mislaid, lost, or possibly stolen. I did not care for the family to know this just now, and delayed the reading of the will while I made a search for it. Thus far I have found not a trace. I haven't even the remotest idea where it is."

"What does the will provide?" asked Hatch.

"It leaves the bulk of the estate to John Stockton, settles an annuity of five thousand dollars a year on Miss Devan, gives her the Dorchester house, and specifically cuts off other relatives whom Pomeroy Stockton once accused of stealing an invention he made. The letter, found after Mr. Stockton's death——"

"You knew of that letter, too?" Hatch interrupted.

"Oh, yes, this letter confirms the will, except, in general terms, it also cuts off Miss Devan."

"Would it not be to the interest of the other immediate relatives of Stockton, those who were specifically cut off, to get possession of that will and destroy it?"

"Of course, it might be, but there has been no communication between the two branches of the family for several years. That branch lives in the Far West and I have taken particular pains to ascertain that they could not have had anything to do with the disappearance of the will."

With these new facts in his possession, Hatch started to report to The Thinking Machine. He had to wait half an hour or so. At last the scientist came in.

"I've been attending an autopsy," he said.

"An autopsy? Whose?"

"On the body of Pomeroy Stockton."

"Why, I had thought he had been buried."

"No, only placed in a receiving vault. I had to call the attention of the Medical Examiner to the case in order to get permission to make an autopsy. We did it together."

"What did you find?" asked Hatch.

"What did *you* find?" asked The Thinking Machine, in turn.

Briefly Hatch told him of the interview with Dr. Benton and Mr. Sloane. The scientist listened without comment and at the end sat back in his big chair squinting at the ceiling.

"That seems to finish it," he said. "These are the questions which were presented: First, in what manner did Pomeroy Stockton die? Second, if not suicide, as appeared, what motive was there for anything else? Third, if there was a motive, to whom does it lead? Fourth, what was in the cipher letter? Now, Mr. Hatch, I think I may make all of it clear. There was a cipher in the letter—what may be described as a cipher in five, the figure five being the key to it.

———

"First, Mr. Hatch," The Thinking Machine resumed, as he drew out and spread on a table the letter which had been originally placed in his hands by Miss Devan, "the question of whether there was a cipher in this letter was to be definitely decided.

"There are a thousand different kinds of ciphers. One of them, which we will call the arbitrary cipher, is excellently illustrated in Poe's story, 'The Gold Bug.' In that cipher, a figure or symbol is made to represent each letter of the alphabet.

"Then, there are book ciphers, which are perhaps the safest of all ciphers, because without a clue to the book from which words may be chosen and designated by numbers, no one can solve it.

"It would be useless for me to go into the matter at any length, so let us consider this particular letter as a cipher possibility. A careful study of the letter develops three possible starting points. The first of these is the general tone of the letter. It is not a direct, straight-away statement such as a man about to commit suicide would write unless he had a purpose—that is, a purpose beyond the mere apparent meaning of the surface text itself. Therefore we will suppose there was another purpose hidden behind a cipher.

"The second starting point is that offered by the absence of one word. You will see that the word 'in' should appear between the word 'cherished' and 'secret.' This, of course, may have been an oversight in writing, the sort of thing anyone might do. But further down we find the third starting point.

"This is the figure 7 in parentheses. It apparently has no connection whatever with what precedes or follows. It could not have been an accident. Therefore what did it mean? Was it a crude outward indication of a hurriedly constructed cipher?

"I took the figure 7 at first to be a sort of key to the entire letter, always presuming there was a cipher. I counted seven words down from that figure and found the word 'binding.' Seven words from that down made the next word 'give.' Together the two words seemed to mean something.

"I stopped there and started back. The seventh word up is 'and'. The seventh word from 'and,' still counting backwards, seemed meaningless. I pursued that theory of seven all the way through the letter and found only a jumble of words. It was the same way counting seven letters. These letters meant nothing unless each letter was arbitrarily taken to represent another letter. This immediately led to intracacies. I always believe in exhausting simple possibilities first, so I started over again.

"Now what word nearest to the seven meant anything when taken together with it? Not 'family,' not 'Bible,' not 'son,' as the vital words appear from the seven down. Going up from the seven, I did find a word which applied to it and meant something. That was the word 'page.' 'Page' was the fifth word up from the seven.

"What was the next fifth word, still going up? This was 'on.' Then I had 'on page 7'—connected words appearing in order, each being the fifth from the other. The fifth word down from seven I found was 'family'; the next fifth word was 'Bible.' Thus I had 'on page 7 family Bible.'

"It is unnecessary to go further into the study I made of the cipher. I worked upward from the seven, taking each fifth word, until I had all the cipher words. I have underscored them here. Read the words underscored and you have the cipher."

Hatch took the letter marked as follows:

To those concerned:
    Tired of it all <u>I</u> seek the end, and <u>AM</u> content. Ambition is <u>DEAD</u>; the grave yawns greedily <u>AT</u> my feet, and with <u>THE</u> labor of my own <u>HANDS</u> lost I greet death <u>OF</u> my own will, by <u>MY</u> own act.
    To my <u>SON</u> I leave all, and <u>YOU</u> who maligned me, you <u>WHO</u> discouraged me, you may <u>READ</u> this and know I <u>PUNISH</u> you thus. It's for <u>HIM</u>, my son, to forgive.
    <u>I</u> dared in life and <u>DARE</u> dead your everlasting anger, <u>NOT</u> alone that you didn't <u>SPEAK</u>, but that you cherished <u>SECRET</u>, and my ears are <u>LOCKED</u> forever against you. My <u>VAULT</u> is my resting place.
    <u>ON</u> the brightest and dearest <u>PAGE</u> of life I wrote <u>(7)</u> my love for him. <u>FAMILY</u> ties, binding as the <u>BIBLE</u> itself, bade me give all to my son.
    Good-bye. I die.
                                Pomeroy Stockton

Slowly Hatch read this: "I am dead at the hands of my son. You who read punish him. I dare not speak. Secret locked vault on page 7 family Bible."

"Well, by George!" exclaimed the reporter. It was a tribute to The Thinking Machine, as well as an expression of amazement at what he read.

"You see," explained The Thinking Machine. "If the word 'in' had appeared between 'cherished' and 'secret,' as it would naturally have done, it would have lost the order of the cipher, therefore it was purposely left out."

"It's enough to send Stockton to the electric chair," said Hatch.

"It would be if it were not a forgery," said the scientist testily.

"A forgery," gasped Hatch. "Didn't Pomeroy Stockton write it?"

"No."

"Surely not John Stockton?"

"No."

"Well, who then?"

"Miss Devan."

"Miss Devan!" Hatch repeated in amazement. "Then, Miss Devan killed Pomeroy Stockton?"

"No, he died a natural death."

Hatch's head was whirling. A thousand questions demanded an immediate answer. He stared mouth agape at The Thinking Machine. All his ideas of the case were tumbling about him. Nothing remained.

"Briefly, here is what happened," said The Thinking Machine. "Pomeroy Stockton died a natural death of heart disease. Miss Devan found him dead, wrote this letter, put it in his pocket, put a drop of prussic acid on his tongue, smashed the bottle of acid, left the room, locked the door, and next day had it broken down.

"It was she who shot John Stockton. It was she who tore out page 7 of that family Bible, and then hid the book in Stockton's room. It was she who in some way got hold of the will. She either has it or has destroyed it. It was she who took advantage of her aged benefactor's sudden death to further as weird and inhuman a plot against another as a woman can devise. There is nothing on God's earth as bad as a bad woman. I think that has been said before."

"But as to this case," Hatch interrupted. "How? What? Why?"

"I read the cipher within a few hours after I got the letter," replied The Thinking Machine. "Naturally I wanted to find out then who and what this son was.

"I had Miss Devan's story, of course—a short story of disagreement between father and son, quarreling and all that. It was also a story which showed a certain underlying animosity despite Miss Devan's cleverness. She had so mingled fact with fiction that it was not altogether easy to weed out the truth, therefore I believed what I chose.

"Miss Devan's idea, as expressed to me, was that the letter was written under coercion. Men who are being murdered don't write cipher letters as intricate as that; and men who are committing suicide have no obvious reasons for writing such letters. The line 'I dare not speak' was silly. Pomeroy Stockton was not a prisoner. If he had feared a conspiracy to kill him, why shouldn't he speak?

"All these things were in my mind when I asked you to see John Stockton. I was particularly anxious to hear what he had to say as to the family Bible. And yet I may say I knew that page 7 had been torn out of the book and was then in Miss Devan's possession.

"I may say, too, that I knew that the secret vault was empty. Whatever these two things contained, supposing she wrote the cipher, had been removed or she would not have called attention to them in the cipher. I had an idea that she might have written it from the mere fact that it was she who first called my attention to the possibility of a cipher.

"Assuming then that the cipher was a forgery, that she wrote it, that it directly accused John Stockton, that she brought it to me, I had fairly conclusive proof that if Pomeroy Stockton had been murdered, she had had a hand in it. John Stockton's motive in trying to suppress the fact of a suicide, as he thought it, was perfectly clear. It was, as he said, to avoid disgrace. Such things are done frequently.

"From the moment you told him of the possibility of murder, he suspected Miss Devan. Why? Because, above all, she had the opportunity, because there was some animosity against John Stockton.

"This now proves to have been a broken-off love affair. John Stockton broke it off. He himself had loved Miss Devan. She had refused him. Later, when he broke off the love affair, she hated him.

"Her plan for revenge was almost diabolical. It was intended to give her full revenge and the estate at the same time. She hoped, she knew, that I would read that cipher. She planned that it would send John Stockton to the electric chair."

"Horrible," commented Hatch with a little shudder.

"It was a fear that this plan might go wrong that induced her to try to kill Stockton by shooting him. The cellar was dark, but she forgot that ninety-nine revolvers out of a hundred leave slight powder stains on the hand of the person who fires them. Stockton said that she did not shoot him, because of that inexplicable loyalty which some men show to a woman they love or have loved.

"Stockton made his secret visit to the house that night to get what was in that vault without her knowledge. He knew of its existence. His father had probably told him. The thing that appeared on page 7 of the family Bible was in all probability the copper hardening process he was perfecting. I should think it had been written there in invisible ink. John Stockton knew this was there. His father told him. If his father told it, Miss Devan probably overheard it. She knew it, too.

"Now the actual circumstances of the death. The girl must have had and used a key to the workroom. After John Stockton left the house that Monday night she entered that room. She found his father dead of heart disease. The autopsy proved this.

"Then the whole scheme was clear to her. She forged that cipher letter—as Pomeroy Stockton's secretary she probably knew the handwriting better than anyone else in the world—placed it in his pocket, and the rest of it you know."

"But the Bible in John Stockton's room?" asked Hatch.

"Was placed there by Miss Devan," replied The Thinking Machine. "It was a part of the general scheme to hopelessly implicate Stockton. She is a clever woman. She showed that when she produced the fountain pen, having carefully filled it with blue instead of black ink."

"What was in the locked vault?"

"That I can only conjecture. It is not impossible that the inventor had only part of the formula he so closely guarded written on the Bible leaf, and the other part of it in that vault, together with other valuable documents.

"I may add that the letters which John Stockton had were not forged. They were written without Miss Devan's knowledge. There was a vast difference in the handwriting of the cipher letter which she wrote and those others which the father wrote.

"Of course it is obvious that the missing will is now, or was, in Miss Devan's possession. How she got it, I don't know. With that out of the way and this cipher unravelled apparently proving the son's guilt, at least half, possibly all, of the estate would have gone to her."

Hatch lighted a cigarette thoughtfully and was silent for a moment.

"What will be the end of it all?" he asked. "Of course, I understand that John Stockton will recover."

"The result will be that the world will lose a great scientific achievement—the secret of hardening copper, which Pomeroy Stockton had rediscovered. I think it safe to say that Miss Devan has burned every scrap of this."

"But what will become of her?"

"She knows nothing of this. I believe she will disappear before Stockton recovers. He wouldn't prosecute anyway. Remember he loved her once."

———

John Stockton was convalescent two weeks later, when a nurse in the City Hospital placed an envelope in his hands. He opened it and a little cloud of ashes filtered through his fingers onto the bed clothing. He sank back on his pillow, weeping.

The Superfluous Finger

She drew off her left glove, a delicate, crinkled suede affair, and offered her bare hand to the surgeon.

An artist would have called it beautiful, perfect, even; the surgeon, professionally enough, set it down as an excellent structural specimen. From the polished pink nails of the tapering fingers to the firm, well-molded wrist, it was distinctly the hand of a woman of ease—one that had never known labor, a pampered hand, Dr. Prescott told himself.

"The forefinger," she exclaimed calmly. "I should like to have it amputated at the first joint, please."

"Amputated?" gasped Dr. Prescott. He stared into the pretty face of his caller. It was flushed softly, and the red lips were parted in a slight smile. It seemed quite an ordinary affair to her. The surgeon bent over the hand with quick interest. "Amputated!" he repeated.

"I came to you," she went on with a nod, "because I have been informed that you are one of the most skillful men of your profession, and the cost of the operation is quite immaterial."

Dr. Prescott pressed the pink nail of the forefinger, then permitted the blood to rush back into it. Several times he did this, then he turned the hand over and scrutinized it closely inside from the delicately lined palm to the tips of the fingers. When he looked up at last there was an expression of frank bewilderment on his face.

"What's the matter with it?" he asked.

"Nothing," the woman replied pleasantly. "I merely want it off from the first joint."

The surgeon leaned back in his chair with a frown of perplexity on his brow, and his visitor was subjected to a sharp, professional stare. She bore it unflinchingly and even smiled a little at his obvious perturbation.

"Why do you want it off?" he demanded.

The woman shrugged her shoulders a little impatiently.

"I can't tell you that," she replied. "It really is not necessary that you should know. You are a surgeon, I want an operation performed. That is all."

There was a long pause; the mutual stare didn't waver.

"You must understand, Miss—Miss—er——" began Dr. Prescott at last. "By the way, you have not introduced yourself?" She was silent. "May I ask your name?"

"My name is of no consequence," she replied calmly. "I might, of course, give you a name, but it would not be mine, therefore any name would be superfluous."

Again the surgeon stared.

"When do you want the operation performed?" he inquired.

"Now," she replied. "I am ready."

"You must understand," he said severely, "that surgery is a profession for the relief of human suffering, not for mutilation—willful mutilation I might say."

"I understand that perfectly," she said. "But where a person submits of her own desire to—to mutilation as you call it, I can see no valid objection on your part."

"It would be criminal to remove a finger where there is no necessity for it," continued the surgeon bluntly. "No good end could be served."

A trace of disappointment showed in the young woman's face, and again she shrugged her shoulders.

"The question after all," she said finally, "is not one of ethics but is simply whether or not you will perform the operation. Would you do it for, say, a thousand dollars?"

"Not for five thousand dollars," blurted the surgeon.

"Well, for ten thousand then?" she asked, quite casually.

All sorts of questions were pounding in Dr. Prescott's mind. Why did a young and beautiful woman desire—why was she anxious even—to sacrifice a perfectly healthy finger? What possible purpose would it serve to mar a hand which was as nearly perfect as any he had ever seen? Was it some insane caprice? Staring deeply into her steady, quiet eyes he could only be convinced of her sanity. Then what?

"No, madam," he said at last, vehemently, "I would not perform the operation for any sum you might mention, unless I was first convinced that the removal of that finger was absolutely necessary. That, I think, is all."

He arose as if to end the consultation. The woman remained seated and continued thoughtful for a minute.

"As I understand it," she said, "you *would* perform the operation if I could convince you that it was absolutely necessary?"

"Certainly," he replied promptly, almost eagerly. His curiosity was aroused. "Then it would come within the range of my professional duties."

"Won't you take my word that it is necessary, and that it is impossible for me to explain why?"

"No. I must know why."

The woman arose and stood facing him. The disappointment had gone from her face now.

"Very well," she remarked steadily. "You *will* perform the operation if it is necessary, therefore if I should shoot the finger off, perhaps———?"

"Shoot it off?" exclaimed Dr. Prescott in amazement. "Shoot it off?"

"That is what I said," she replied calmly. "If I should shoot the finger off you would consent to dress the wound? You would make any necessary amputation?"

She held up the finger under discussion and looked at it curiously. Dr. Prescott himself stared at it with a sudden new interest.

"Shoot it off?" he repeated. "Why you must be mad to contemplate such a thing," he exploded, and his face flushed in sheer anger. "I—I will have nothing whatever to do with the affair, madam. Good day."

"I should have to be very careful, of course," she mused, "but I think perhaps one shot would be sufficient; then I should come to you and demand that you dress it?"

There was a question in the tone. Dr. Prescott stared at her for a full minute, then walked over and opened the door.

"In my profession, madam," he said coldly, "there is too much possibility of doing good and relieving actual suffering for me to consider this matter or discuss it further with you. There are three persons now waiting in the ante-room who *need* my services. I shall be compelled to ask you to excuse me."

"But you will dress the wound?" the woman insisted, undaunted by his forbidding tone and manner.

"I shall have nothing whatever to do with it," declared the surgeon, positively, finally. "If you need the services of any medical man permit me to suggest that it is an alienist and not a surgeon."

The woman didn't appear to take offense.

"Someone would have to dress it," she continued insistently. "I should much prefer that it be a man of undisputed skill—you I mean; therefore I shall call again. Good day."

There was a rustle of silken skirts and she was gone. Dr. Prescott stood for an instant gazing after her in frank wonder and annoyance in his eyes, his attitude, then he went back and sat down at the desk. The crinkled suede glove still lay where she had left it. He examined it gingerly then with a final shake of his head dismissed the affair and turned to other things.

Early next afternoon Dr. Prescott was sitting in his office writing when the door from the ante-room where patients awaited his leisure was thrown open and the young man in attendance rushed in.

"A lady has fainted, sir," he said hurriedly. "She seems to be hurt."

Dr. Prescott arose quickly and strode out. There, lying helplessly back in her chair with white face and closed eyes, was his visitor of the day before. He stepped toward her quickly, then hesitated as he recalled their conversation. Finally, however, professional instinct, the desire to relieve suffering, and perhaps curiosity, too, caused him to go to her. The left hand was wrapped in an improvised bandage through which there was a trickle of blood. He glared at it with incredulous eyes.

"Hanged if she didn't do it," he blurted angrily.

The fainting spell, Dr. Prescott saw, was due only to loss of blood and physical pain, and he busied himself trying to restore her to consciousness. Meanwhile he gave some hurried instructions to the young man who was in attendance in the ante-room.

"Call up Professor Van Dusen on the 'phone," he directed, "and ask him if he can assist me in a minor operation. Tell him it's rather a curious case and I am sure it will interest him."

It was in this manner that the problem of the superfluous finger first came to the attention of The Thinking Machine. He arrived just as the mysterious woman was opening her eyes to consciousness from the fainting spell. She stared at him glassily, unrecognizingly; then her glance wandered to Dr. Prescott. She smiled.

"I knew you'd have to do it," she murmured weakly.

After the ether had been administered for the operation, a simple and an easy one, Dr. Prescott stated the circumstances of the case to The Thinking Machine. The scientist stood with his long, slender fingers resting lightly on the young woman's pulse, listening in silence.

"What do you make of it?" demanded the surgeon.

The Thinking Machine didn't say. At the moment he was leaning over the unconscious woman, squinting at her forehead. With his disengaged hand he stroked the delicately penciled eyebrows several times the wrong way, and again at close range squinted at them. Dr. Prescott saw and seeing, understood.

"No, it isn't that," he said and he shuddered a little. "I thought of it myself. Her bodily condition is excellent, splendid."

It was some time later when the young woman was sleeping lightly, placidly under the influence of a soothing potion, that The Thinking Machine spoke of the peculiar events which had preceded the operation. Then he was sitting in Dr. Prescott's private office. He had picked up a woman's glove from the desk.

"This is the glove she left when she first called, isn't it?" he inquired.

"Yes."

"Did you happen to see her remove it?"

"Yes."

The Thinking Machine curiously examined the dainty, perfumed trifle, then, arising suddenly, went into the adjoining room where the woman lay asleep. He stood for an instant gazing down admiringly at the exquisite, slender figure; then, bending over, he looked closely at her left hand. When at last he straightened up, it seemed that some unspoken question in his mind had been answered. He rejoined Dr. Prescott.

"It's difficult to say what motive is back of her desire to have the finger amputated," he said musingly. "I could perhaps venture a conjecture but if the matter is of no importance to you beyond mere curiosity I should not like to do so. Within a few months from now, I daresay, important developments will result and I should like to find out something more about her. That I can do when she returns to wherever she is stopping in the city. I'll 'phone to Mr. Hatch and have him ascertain for me where she goes, her name and other things which may throw a light on the matter."

"He will follow her?"

"Yes, precisely. Now we only seem to know two facts in connection with her. First, she is English."

"Yes," Dr. Prescott agreed. "Her accent, her appearance, everything about her suggests that."

"And the second fact is of no consequence at the moment," resumed The Thinking Machine. "Let me use your 'phone please."

———

Hutchinson Hatch, reporter, was talking.

"When the young woman left Dr. Prescott's, she took the cab which had been ordered for her and told the driver to go ahead until she stopped him. I got a good look at her, by the way. I managed to pass just as she entered the cab and walking on down got into another cab, which was waiting for me. Her cab drove for three or four blocks aimlessly, and finally stopped. The driver stooped down as if to listen to someone inside, and my cab passed. Then the other cab turned across a side street and after going eight or ten blocks, pulled up in front of an apartment house. The young woman got out and went inside. Her cab went away. Inside I found out that she was Mrs. Frederick Chevedon Morey. She came there last Tuesday—this is Friday—with her husband, and they engaged——"

"Yes, I knew she had a husband," interrupted The Thinking Machine.

"——engaged apartments for three months. When I had learned this much I remembered your instructions as to steamers from Europe landing on the day they took apartments or possibly a day or so before. I was just going out when Mrs. Morey stepped out of the elevator and preceded me to the door. She had changed her clothing and wore a different hat.

"It didn't seem to be necessary then to find out where she was going, for I knew I could find her when I wanted to, so I went down and made inquiries at the steamship offices. I found, after a great deal of work, that none of the three steamers which arrived the day the apartments were rented had brought a Mr. and Mrs. Morey, but a steamer on the day before had brought a Mr. and Mrs. David Girardeau from Liverpool. Mrs. Girardeau answered Mrs. Morey's description to the minutest detail, even to the gown she wore when she left the steamer. It was the same gown she wore when she left Dr. Prescott's after the operation."

That was all. The Thinking Machine sat with his enormous yellow head pillowed against a high-backed chair and his long slender fingers pressed tip to tip. He asked no questions and made no comment for a long time, then:

"About how many minutes was it from the time she entered the house until she came out again?"

"Not more than ten or fifteen," was the reply. "I was still talking casually to the people down stairs trying to find out something about her."

"What do they pay for their apartment?" asked the scientist, irrelevantly.

"Three hundred dollars a month."

The Thinking Machine's squint eyes were fixed immovably on a small discolored spot on the ceiling of his laboratory.

"Whatever else may develop in this matter, Mr. Hatch," he said after a time, "we must admit that we have met a woman with extraordinary courage—nerve, I dare say you'd call it. When Mrs. Morey left Dr. Prescott's operating room, she was so ill and weak from the shock that she could hardly stand, and now you tell me she changed her dress and went out immediately after she returned home."

"Well, of course——" Hatch said, apologetically.

"In that event," resumed the scientist, "we must assume also that the matter is one of the utmost importance to her, and yet the nature of the case had led me to believe that it might be months, perhaps, before there would be any particular development in it."

"What? How?" asked the reporter.

"The final development doesn't seem, from what I know, to belong on this side of the ocean at all," explained The Thinking Machine. "I imagine it is a case for Scotland Yard. The problem of course is: What made it necessary for her to get rid of that finger? If we admit her sanity, we can count the possible answers to this question on one hand, and at least three of these answers take the case back to

England." He paused. "By the way, was Mrs. Morey's hand bound up in the same way when you saw her the second time?"

"Her left hand was in a muff," explained the reporter. "I couldn't see, but it seems to me that she wouldn't have had time to change the manner of its dressing."

"It's extraordinary," commented the scientist. He arose and paced back and forth across the room. "Extraordinary," he repeated. "One can't help but admire the fortitude of women under certain circumstances, Mr. Hatch. I think perhaps this particular case had better be called to the attention of Scotland Yard, but first I think it would be best for you to call on the Moreys tomorrow—you can find some pretext—and see what you can learn about them. You are an ingenious young man—I'll leave it all to you."

Hatch did call at the Morey apartments on the morrow, but under circumstances which were not at all what he expected. He went there with Detective Mallory, and Detective Mallory went there in a cab at full speed because the manager of the apartment house had 'phoned that Mrs. Frederick Chevedon Morey had been found murdered in her apartments. The detective ran up two flights of stairs and blundered, heavy-footed, into the rooms, and there he paused in the presence of death.

The body of the woman lay on the floor and some one had mercifully covered it with a cloth from the bed. Detective Mallory drew the covering down from over the face and Hatch stared with a feeling of awe at the beautiful countenance which had, on the day before, been so radiant with life. Now it was distorted into an expression of awful agony and the limbs were drawn up convulsively. The mark of the murderer was at the white, exquisitely rounded throat—great black bruises where powerful, merciless fingers had sunk deeply into the soft flesh.

A physician in the house had preceded the police. After one glance at the woman and a swift, comprehensive look about the room Detective Mallory turned to him inquiringly.

"She has been dead for several hours," the doctor volunteered, "possibly since early last night. It appears that some virulent, burning poison was administered and then she was choked. I gather this from an examination of her mouth."

These things were readily to be seen; also it was plainly evident for many reasons that the finger marks at the throat were those of a man, but each step beyond these obvious facts only served further to bewilder the investigators. First was the statement of the night elevator boy.

"Mr. and Mrs. Morey left here last night about eleven o'clock," he said. "I know because I telephoned for a cab, and later brought them down from the third floor. They went into the manager's office leaving two suit cases in the hall. When they came out I took the suit cases to a cab that was waiting. They got in it and drove away."

"When did they return?" inquired the detective.

"They didn't return, sir," responded the boy. "I was on duty until six o'clock this morning. It just happened that no one came in after they went out until I was off duty at six."

The detective turned to the physician again.

"Then she couldn't have been dead since early last night," he said.

"She has been dead for several hours—at least twelve, possibly longer," said the physician firmly. "There's no possible argument about that."

The detective stared at him scornfully for an instant, then looked at the manager of the house.

"What was said when Mr. and Mrs. Morey entered your office last night?" he asked. "Were you there?"

"I was there, yes," was the reply. "Mr. Morey explained that they had been called away for a few days unexpectedly and left the keys of the apartment with me. That was all that was said; I saw the elevator boy take the suit cases out for them as they went to the cab."

"How did it come, then, if you knew they were away that some one entered here this morning, and so found the body?"

"I discovered the body myself," replied the manager. "There was some electric wiring to be done in here and I thought their absence would be a good time for it. I came up to see about it and saw—that."

He glanced at the covered body with a little shiver and a grimace. Detective Mallory was deeply thoughtful for several minutes.

"The woman is here and she's dead," he said finally. "If she is here, she came back here, dead or alive last night between the time she went out with her husband and the time her body was found this morning. Now that's an absolute fact. But *how* did she come here?"

Of the three employees of the apartment house only the elevator boy on duty had not spoken. Now he spoke because the detective glared at him fiercely.

"I didn't see either Mr. or Mrs. Morey come in this morning," he explained hastily. "Nobody came in at all except the postman and some delivery wagon drivers up to the time the body was found."

Again Detective Mallory turned on the manager.

"Does any window of this apartment open on a fire escape?" he demanded.

"Yes—this way."

They passed through the short hallway to the back. Both the windows were locked on the inside, so it appeared that even if the woman had been brought into the room that way, the windows would not have been fastened unless her murderer went out of the house the front way. When Detective Mallory reached this stage of the investigation, he sat down and stared from one to the other of the silent little party as if he considered the entire matter some affair which they had perpetrated to annoy him.

Hutchinson Hatch started to say something, then thought better of it and turning, went to the telephone below. Within a few minutes The Thinking Machine stepped out of a cab in front and paused in the lower hall long enough to listen to the facts developed. There was a perfect network of wrinkles in the dome-like brow when the reporter concluded.

"It's merely a transfer of the final development in the affair from England to this country," he said enigmatically. "Please 'phone for Dr. Prescott to come here immediately."

He went on to the Morey apartments. With only a curt nod for Detective Mallory, the only one of the small party who knew him, he proceeded to the body of the dead woman and squinted down without a trace of emotion into the white pallid face. After a moment he dropped on his knees beside the inert body and examined the mouth and the finger marks about the white throat.

"Carbolic acid and strangulation," he remarked tersely to Detective Mallory who was leaning over watching him with something of hopeful eagerness in his stolid face. The Thinking Machine glanced past him to the manager of the house. "Mr. Morey is a powerful, athletic man in appearance?" he asked.

"Oh, no," was the reply. "He's short and slight, only a little larger than you are."

The scientist squinted aggressively at the manager as if the description were not quite what he expected. Then the slightly puzzled expression passed.

"Oh, I see," he remarked. "Played the piano." This was not a question; it was a statement.

"Yes, a great deal," was the reply, "so much so in fact that twice we had complaints from other persons in the house despite the fact that they had been here only a few days."

"Of course," mused the scientist abstractedly. "Of course. Perhaps Mrs. Morey did not play at all?"

"I believe she told me she did not."

The Thinking Machine drew down the thin cloth which had been thrown over the body and glanced at the left hand.

"Dear me! Dear me!" he exclaimed suddenly, and he arose. "Dear me!" he repeated. "That's the——" He turned to the manager and the two elevator boys. "This is Mrs. Morey beyond any question?"

The answer was a chorus of affirmation accompanied by some startling facial expressions.

"Did Mr. and Mrs. Morey employ any servants?"

"No," was the reply. "They had their meals in the café below most of the time. There is no housekeeping in these apartments at all."

"How many persons live in the building?"

"A hundred, I should say."

"There is a great deal of passing to and fro, then?"

"Certainly. It was rather unusual that so few persons passed in and out last night and this morning, and certainly Mrs. Morey and her husband were not among them, if that's what you're trying to find out."

The Thinking Machine glanced at the physician who was standing by silently.

"How long do you make it that she's been dead?" he asked.

"At least twelve hours," replied the physician. "Possibly longer."

"Yes, nearer fourteen, I imagine."

Abruptly he left the group and walked through the apartment and back again slowly. As he re-entered the room where the body lay, the door from the hall opened and Dr. Prescott entered, followed by Hutchinson Hatch. The Thinking Machine led the surgeon straight to the body and drew the cloth down from the face. Dr. Prescott started back with an exclamation of astonishment, recognition.

"There's no doubt about it at all in your mind?" inquired the scientist.

"Not the slightest," replied Dr. Prescott positively. "It's the same woman."

"Yet, look here!"

With a quick movement The Thinking Machine drew down the cloth still more. Dr. Prescott together with those who had no idea of what to expect, peered down at the body. After one glance the surgeon dropped on his knees and examined closely the dead left hand. The forefinger was off at the first joint. Dr. Prescott stared, stared incredulously. After a moment his eyes left the maimed hand and settled again on her face.

"I have never seen—never dreamed—of such a startling——" he began.

"That settles it all, of course," interrupted The Thinking Machine. "It solves and proves the problem at once. Now, Mr. Mallory, if we can go to your office or some place where we will be undisturbed I will——"

"But who killed her?" demanded the detective abruptly.

"Let us find a quiet place," said The Thinking Machine in his usual irritable manner.

———

Detective Mallory, Dr. Prescott, The Thinking Machine, Hutchinson Hatch, and the apartment-house physician were seated in the front room of the Morey apartments with all doors closed against prying, inquisitive eyes. At the scientist's request Dr. Prescott repeated the circumstances leading up to the removal of a woman's left forefinger, and there The Thinking Machine took up the story.

"Suppose, Mr. Mallory," and the scientist turned to the detective, "a woman should walk into *your* office and say she must have a finger cut off, what would you think?"

"I'd think she was crazy," was the prompt reply.

"Naturally, in your position," The Thinking Machine went on, "you are acquainted with many strange happenings. Wouldn't this one instantly suggest something to you? Something that was to happen months off?"

Detective Mallory considered it wisely, but was silent.

"Well, here," declared The Thinking Machine. "A woman whom

we now know to be Mrs. Morey wanted her finger cut off. It instantly suggested three, four, five, a dozen possibilities. Of course, only one, or possibly two in combination, could be true. Therefore which one? A little logic now to prove that two and two always make four—not *some* times but *all* the time.

"Naturally the first supposition was insanity. We pass that as absurd on its face. Then disease—a taint of leprosy perhaps which had been visible on the left forefinger. I tested for that, and that was eliminated. Three strong reasons for desiring the finger off, either of which is strongly probable, remained. The fact that the woman was unmistakably English was obvious. From the mark of a wedding ring on her glove and a corresponding mark on her finger—she wore no such ring—we could safely surmise that she was married. These were the two first facts I learned. Substantiative evidence that she was married and not a widow came partly from her extreme youth and the lack of mourning in her attire.

"Then Mr. Hatch followed her, learned her name, where she lived, and later the fact that she had arrived with her husband on a steamer a day or so before they took apartments here. This was proof that she was English, and proof that she had a husband. They came over on the steamer as Mr. and Mrs. David Girardeau—here they were Mr. and Mrs. Frederick Chevedon Morey. Why this difference in name? The circumstance in itself pointed to irregularity—crime committed or contemplated. Other things made me think it was merely contemplated and that it could be prevented; for then absence of every fact gave me no intimation that there would be murder. Then came the murder presumably of—Mrs. Morey?"

"Isn't it Mrs. Morey?" demanded the detective.

"Mr. Hatch recognized the woman as the one he had followed, I recognized her as the one on which there had been an operation, Dr. Prescott also recognized her," continued The Thinking Machine. "To convince myself, after I had found the manner of death, that it was the woman, I looked at her left hand. I found that the forefinger was gone—it had been removed by a skilled surgeon at the first joint. And this fact instantly showed me that the dead woman was not Mrs. Morey at all, but somebody else; and incidentally cleared up the entire affair."

"How?" demanded the detective. "I thought you just said that you had helped cut off her forefinger?"

"Dr. Prescott and I cut off that finger yesterday," replied The Thinking Machine calmly. "The finger of the dead woman had been cut off months, perhaps years, ago."

There was blank amazement on Detective Mallory's face, and Hatch was staring straight into the squint eyes of the scientist. Vaguely, as through a mist, he was beginning to account for many things which had been hitherto inexplicable.

"The perfectly healed wound on the hand eliminated every possibility but one," The Thinking Machine resumed. "Previously I had been informed that Mrs. Morey did not—or said she did not—play the piano. I had seen the bare possibility of an immense insurance on her hands, and some trick to defraud the insurance company by marring one. Of course, against this was the fact that she had offered to pay a large sum for the operation; that their expenses here must have been enormous, so I was beginning to doubt the tenability of this supposition. The fact that the dead woman's finger was off removed that possibility completely, as it also removed the possibility of a crime of some sort in which there might have been left behind a telltale print of that forefinger. If there had been a serious crime with the trace of the finger as evidence, its removal would have been necessary to her.

"Then the one thing remained—that is that Mrs. Morey or whatever her name is—was in a conspiracy with her husband to get possession of certain properties, perhaps a title—remember she is English—by sacrificing that finger so that identification might be in accordance with the description of an heir whom she was to impersonate. We may well believe that she was provided with the necessary documentary evidence, and we know conclusively—we don't conjecture but we *know*—that the dead woman in there is the woman whose rights were to have been stolen by the so-called Mrs. Morey."

"But that is Mrs. Morey, isn't it?" demanded the detective again.

"No," was the sharp retort. "The perfect resemblance to Mrs. Morey and the finger removed long ago makes that clear. There is, I imagine, a relationship between them—perhaps they are cousins. I can hardly believe they are twins because the necessity, then, of one impersonating the other to obtain either money or a title, would not have existed so palpably, although it is possible that Mrs. Morey, if disinherited or disowned, would have resorted to such a course. This dead woman is Miss—Miss—" and he glanced at the back of a photograph, "Miss Evelyn Rossmore, and she has evidently been living in this city for some time. This is her picture and it was made at least a year ago by Harkinson here. Perhaps he can give you her address as well."

There was silence for several minutes. Each member of the little group was turning over the stated facts mentally.

"But how did she come here—like this?" Hatch inquired.

"You remember, Mr. Hatch, when you followed Mrs. Morey here you told me she dressed again and went out?" asked the scientist in turn. "It was not Mrs. Morey you saw then—she was ill and I knew it from the operation—it was Miss Rossmore. The manager says a hundred persons live in this house—that there is a great deal of passing in and out. Can't you see that when there is such a startling resemblance Miss Rossmore could pass in and out at will and always be mistaken for Mrs. Morey? That no one would ever notice the difference?"

"But who killed her?" asked Detective Mallory, curiously. "How? Why?"

"Morey killed her," said The Thinking Machine flatly. "How did he kill her? We can fairly presume that first he tricked her into drinking the acid, then perhaps she was screaming with the pain of it, and he choked her to death. I imagined first he was a large, powerful man, because his grip on her throat was so powerful that he ruptured the jugular inside; but instead of that he plays the piano a great deal, which would give him the hand-power to choke her. And why? We can suppose only that it was because she had in some way learned of their purpose. That would have established the motive. The crowning delicacy of the affair was Morey's act in leaving his keys with the manager here. He did not anticipate that the apartments would be entered for several days—after they were safely away—while there was a chance that if neither of them had been seen here and their disappearance was unexplained the rooms would have been opened to ascertain why. That is all, I think."

"Except to catch Morey and his wife," said the detective grimly.

"Easily done," said The Thinking Machine. "I imagine, if this murder is kept out of the newspapers for a couple of hours you can find them about to sail for Europe. Suppose you try the line they came over on?"

It was just three hours later that the accused man and wife were taken prisoner. They had just engaged passage on the steamer which sailed at half-past four o'clock.

Their trial was a famous one and resulted in conviction after an astonishing story of an attempt to seize an estate and title belonging rightfully to a Miss Evelyn Rossmore who had mysteriously disappeared years before, and was identified with the dead woman.

THE MOTOR BOAT

Captain Hank Barber, master mariner, gripped the bow-rail of the *Liddy Ann* and peered off through the semi-fog of the early morning at a dark streak slashing along through the gray-green waters. It was a motor boat of long, graceful lines; and a single figure, that of a man, sat upright at her helm staring uncompromisingly ahead. She nosed through a roller, staggered a little, righted herself and sped on as a sheet of spray swept over her. The helmsman sat motionless, heedless of the stinging splash of wind-driven water in his face.

"She sure is a-goin' some," remarked Captain Hank, reflectively. "By Ginger! If she keeps it up into Boston Harbor, she won't stop this side o' the Public Gardens."

Captain Hank watched the boat curiously until she was swallowed up, lost in the mist, then turned to his own affairs. He was a couple of miles out of Boston Harbor, going in; it was six o'clock of a gray morning. A few minutes after the disappearance of the motor boat Captain Hank's attention was attracted by the hoarse shriek of a whistle two hundred yards away. He dimly traced through the mist the gigantic lines of a great vessel—it seemed to be a ship of war.

It was only a few minutes after Captain Hank lost sight of the motor boat that she was again sighted, this time as she flashed into Boston Harbor at full speed. She fled past, almost under the prow of a pilot boat, going out, and was hailed. At the mess table later the pilot's man on watch made a remark about her.

"Goin'! Well, wasn't she though! Never saw one thing pass so close to another in my life without scrubbin' the paint offen it. She was so close up I could spit in her, and when I spoke the feller didn't even look up—just kept a-goin'. I told *him* a few things that was good for his soul."

Inside Boston Harbor the motor boat performed a miracle. Pursuing a course which was singularly erratic and at a speed more than dangerous she reeled on through the surge of the sea regardless alike of fog, the proximity of other vessels and the heavy wash from larger craft. Here she narrowly missed a tug; there she skimmed by a slow-moving tramp and a warning shout was raised; a fisherman swore at her as only a fisherman can. And finally when she passed into a clear space, seemingly headed for a dock at top speed, she was the most unanimously damned craft that ever came into Boston Harbor.

"Guess that's a through boat," remarked an aged salt, facetiously, as he gazed at her from a dock. "If that durned fool don't take some o' the speed offen her she'll go through all right—wharf an' all."

Still the man in the boat made no motion; the whizz of her motor, plainly heard in a sudden silence, was undiminished. Suddenly the tumult of warning was renewed. Only a chance would prevent a smash. Then Big John Dawson appeared on the string piece of the dock. Big John had a voice that was noted from Newfoundland to Norfolk for its depth and width, and possessed objurgatory powers which were at once the awe and admiration of the fishing fleet.

"You ijit!" he bellowed at the impassive helmsman. "Shut off that power an' throw yer hellum."

There was no response; the boat came on directly toward the dock where Big John and his fellows were gathered. The fishermen and loungers saw that a crash was coming and scattered from the string piece.

"The *durned* fool," said Big John, resignedly.

Then came the crash, the rending of timbers, and silence save for the grinding whir of the motor. Big John ran to the end of the wharf and peered down. The speed of the motor had driven the boat half way upon a float which careened perilously. The man had been thrown forward and lay huddled up face downward and motionless on the float. The dirty water lapped at him greedily.

Big John was the first man on the float. He crept cautiously to the huddled figure and turned it face upward. He gazed for an instant into wide staring eyes then turned to the curious ones peering down from the dock.

"No wonder he didn't stop," he said in an awed tone. "The durned fool is dead."

Willing hands gave aid and after a minute the lifeless figure lay on the dock. It was that of a man in uniform—the uniform of a foreign navy. He was apparently forty-five years old, large and powerful of frame with the sun-browned face of a seaman. The jet black of mustache and goatee was startling against the dead color of the face. The hair was tinged with gray; and on the back of the left hand was a single letter—"D"—tattooed in blue.

"He's French," said Big John authoritatively, "an' that's the uniform of a Cap'n in the French Navy." He looked puzzled a moment as he stared at the figure. "An' they ain't been a French man-o'-war in Boston Harbor for six months."

After a while the police came and with them Detective Mallory, the big man of the Bureau of Criminal Investigation; and finally Dr. Clough, Medical Examiner. While the detective questioned the fishermen and those who had witnessed the crash, Dr. Clough examined the body.

"An autopsy will be necessary," he announced as he arose.

"How long has he been dead?" asked the detective.

"Eight or ten hours, I should say. The cause of death doesn't appear. There is no shot or knife wound so far as I can see."

Detective Mallory closely examined the dead man's clothing. There was no name or tailor mark; the linen was new; the name of the maker of the shoes had been ripped out with a knife. There was nothing in the pockets, not a piece of paper or even a vagrant coin.

Then Detective Mallory turned his attention to the boat. Both hull and motor were of French manufacture. Long, deep scratches on each side showed how the name had been removed. Inside the boat the detective saw something white and picked it up. It was a handkerchief—a woman's handkerchief, with the initials "E. M. B." in a corner.

"Ah, a woman's in it!" he soliloquized.

Then the body was removed and carefully secluded from the prying eyes of the press. Thus no picture of the dead man appeared. Hutchinson Hatch, reporter, and others asked many questions. Detective Mallory hinted vaguely at international questions—the dead man was a French officer, he said, and there might be something back of it.

"I can't tell you all of it," he said wisely, "but my theory is complete. It is murder. The victim was captain of a French man-of-war. His body was placed in a motor boat, possibly a part of the fittings of the warship, and the boat set adrift. I can say no more."

"Your theory is complete then," Hatch remarked casually, "except the name of the man, the manner of death, the motive, the name of his ship, the presence of the handkerchief, and the precise reason why the body should be disposed of in this fashion instead of being cast into the sea."

The detective snorted. Hatch went away to make some inquiries on his own account. Within half a dozen hours he had satisfied himself by telegraph that no French war craft had been within five hundred miles of Boston for six months. Thus the mystery grew deeper; a thousand questions to which there seemed no answer arose.

At this point, the day following the events related, the problem of the motor boat came to the attention of Professor Augustus S. F. X. Van Dusen, The Thinking Machine. The scientist listened closely but petulantly to the story Hatch told.

"Has there been an autopsy yet?" he asked at last.

"It is set for eleven o'clock today," replied the reporter. "It is now after ten."

"I shall attend it," said the scientist.

Medical Examiner Clough welcomed the eminent Professor Van Dusen's proffer of assistance in his capacity of M. D., while Hatch and other reporters impatiently cooled their toes on the curb. In two hours the autopsy had been completed. The Thinking Machine amused himself by studying the insignia on the dead man's uniform, leaving it to Dr. Clough to make a startling statement to the press. The man had not been murdered; he had died of heart failure. There was no poison in the stomach, nor was there a knife or pistol wound.

Then the inquisitive press poured in a flood of questions. Who had scratched off the name of the boat? Dr. Clough didn't know. Why had it been scratched off? Still he didn't know. How did it happen that the name of the maker of the shoes had been ripped out? He shrugged his shoulders. What did the handkerchief have to do with it? Really he couldn't conjecture. Was there any inkling of the dead man's identity? Not so far as he knew. Any scar on the body which might lead to identification? No.

Hatch made a few mental comments on officials in general and skilfully steered The Thinking Machine away from the other reporters.

"Did that man die of heart failure?" he asked, flatly.

"He did not," was the curt reply. "It was poison."

"But the medical examiner specifically stated that there was no poison in the stomach," persisted the reporter.

The scientist did not reply. Hatch struggled with and suppressed a desire to ask more questions. On reaching home the scientist's first act was to consult an encyclopedia. After several minutes he turned to the reporter with an inscrutable face.

"Of course the idea of a natural death in this case is absurd," he said, shortly. "Every fact is against it. Now, Mr. Hatch, please get for me all the local and New York newspapers of the day the body was found—not the day after. Send or bring them to me, then come again at five this afternoon."

"But—but——" Hatch blurted.

"I can say nothing until I know all the facts," interrupted The Thinking Machine.

Hatch personally delivered the specified newspapers into the hands of The Thinking Machine—this man who never read newspapers—and went away. It was an afternoon of agony; an agony of impatience. Promptly at five o'clock he was ushered into Professor Van Dusen's laboratory. The scientist sat half smothered in newspapers, and popped up out of the heap aggressively.

"It was murder, Mr. Hatch," he exclaimed, suddenly. "Murder by an extraordinary method."

"Who—who is the man? How was he killed?" asked Hatch.

"His name is——" the scientist began, then paused. "I presume your office has the book *Who's Who In America*? Please 'phone and ask them to give you the record of Langham Dudley."

"Is he the dead man?" Hatch demanded quickly.

"I don't know," was the reply.

Hatch went to the telephone. Ten minutes later he returned to find The Thinking Machine dressed to go out.

"Langham Dudley is a ship owner, fifty-one years old," the reporter read from notes he had taken. "He was once a sailor before the mast and later became a ship owner in a small way. He was successful in his small undertakings and for fifteen years has been a millionaire. He has a certain social position, partly through his wife whom he married a year and a half ago. She was Edith Marston Belding, a daughter of the famous Belding family. He has an estate on the North Shore."

"Very good," commented the scientist. "Now we will find out something about how this man was killed."

At North Station they took train for a small place on the North Shore, thirty-five miles from Boston. There The Thinking Machine made some inquiries and finally they entered a lumbersome carry-all. After a drive of half an hour through the dark they saw the lights of what seemed to be a pretentious country place. Somewhere off to the right Hatch heard the roar of the restless ocean.

"Wait for us," commanded The Thinking Machine as the carry-all stopped.

THE WOMAN IN THE CASE

The Thinking Machine ascended the steps, followed by Hatch, and rang. After a minute or so the door was opened and the light flooded out. Standing before them was a Japanese—a man of indeterminate age with the graven face of his race.

"Is Mr. Dudley in?" asked The Thinking Machine.

"He has not that pleasure," replied the Japanese, and Hatch smiled at the queerly turned phrase.

"Mrs. Dudley?" asked the scientist.

"Mrs. Dudley is attiring herself in clothing," replied the Japanese. "If you will be pleased to enter."

The Thinking Machine handed him a card and was shown into a reception room. The Japanese placed chairs for them with courteous precision and disappeared. After a short pause there was a rustle of silken skirts on the stairs, and a woman—Mrs. Dudley—entered. She was not pretty; she was stunning rather, tall, of superb figure and crowned with a glory of black hair.

"Mr. Van Dusen?" she asked as she glanced at the card.

The Thinking Machine bowed low, albeit awkwardly. Mrs. Dudley sank down on a couch and the two men resumed their seats. There was a little pause; Mrs. Dudley broke the silence at last.

"Well, Mr. Van Dusen, if you——" she began.

"You have not seen a newspaper for several days?" asked The Thinking Machine, abruptly.

"No," she replied, wonderingly, almost smiling. "Why?"

"Can you tell me just where your husband is?"

The Thinking Machine squinted at her in that aggressive way which was habitual. A quick flush crept into her face, and grew deeper at the sharp scrutiny. Inquiry lay in her eyes.

"I don't know," she replied at last. "In Boston, I presume."

"You haven't seen him since the night of the ball?"

"No. I think it was half-past one o'clock that night."

"Is his motor boat here?"

"Really, I don't know. I presume it is. May I ask the purpose of this questioning?"

The Thinking Machine squinted hard at her for half a minute. Hatch was uncomfortable, half resentful even, at the agitation of the woman and the sharp, cold tone of his companion.

"On the night of the ball," the scientist went on, passing the question, "Mr. Dudley cut his left arm just above the wrist. It was only a slight wound. A piece of court plaster was put on it. Do you know if he put it on himself? If not, who did?"

"I put it on," replied Mrs. Dudley, unhesitatingly, wonderingly.

"And whose court plaster was it?"

"Mine—some I had in my dressing room. Why?"

The scientist arose and paced across the floor, glancing once out the hall door. Mrs. Dudley looked at Hatch inquiringly and was about to speak when The Thinking Machine stopped beside her and placed his slim fingers on her wrist. She did not resent the action; was only curious if one might judge from her eyes.

"Are you prepared for a shock?" the scientist asked.

"What is it?" she demanded in sudden terror. "This suspense——"

"Your husband is dead—murdered—poisoned!" said the scientist with sudden brutality. His fingers still lay on her pulse. "The court plaster which you put on his arm and which came from your room was covered with a virulent poison which was instantly transfused into his blood."

Mrs. Dudley did not start or scream. Instead she stared up at The Thinking Machine a moment, her face became pallid, a little shiver passed over her. Then she fell back on the couch in a dead faint.

"Good!" remarked The Thinking Machine complacently. And then as Hatch started up suddenly: "Shut that door," he commanded.

The reporter did so. When he turned back, his companion was leaning over the unconscious woman. After a moment he left her and went to a window where he stood looking out. As Hatch watched he saw the color coming back into Mrs. Dudley's face. At last she opened her eyes.

"Don't get hysterical," The Thinking Machine directed calmly. "I know you had nothing whatever to do with your husband's death. I want only a little assistance to find out who killed him."

"Oh, my God!" exclaimed Mrs. Dudley. "Dead! Dead!"

Suddenly tears leaped from her eyes and for several minutes the two men respected her grief. When at last she raised her face her eyes were red, but there was a rigid expression about the mouth.

"If I can be of any service——" she began.

"Is this the boat house I see from this window?" asked The Thinking Machine. "That long, low building with the light over the door?"

"Yes," replied Mrs. Dudley.

"You say you don't know if the motor boat is there now?"

"No, I don't."

"Will you ask your Japanese servant, and if he doesn't know, let him go see, please?"

Mrs. Dudley arose and touched an electric button. After a moment the Japanese appeared at the door.

"Osaka, do you know if Mr. Dudley's motor boat is in the boat house?" she asked.

"No, honorable lady."

"Will you go yourself and see?"

Osaka bowed low and left the room, closing the door gently behind him. The Thinking Machine again crossed to the window and sat down staring out into the night. Mrs. Dudley asked questions, scores of them, and he answered them in order until she knew the details of the finding of her husband's body—that is, the details the public knew. She was interrupted by the reappearance of Osaka.

"I do not find the motor boat in the house, honorable lady."

"That is all," said the scientist.

Again Osaka bowed and retired.

"Now, Mrs. Dudley," resumed The Thinking Machine almost gently, "we know your husband wore a French naval costume at the masked ball. May I ask what you wore?"

"It was a Queen Elizabeth costume," replied Mrs. Dudley, "very heavy with a long train."

"And if you could give me a photograph of Mr. Dudley?"

Mrs. Dudley left the room an instant and returned with a cabinet photograph. Hatch and the scientist looked at it together; it was unmistakably the man in the motor boat.

"You can do nothing yourself," said The Thinking Machine at last, and he moved as if to go. "Within a few hours we will have the guilty person. You may rest assured that your name will be in no way brought into the matter unpleasantly."

Hatch glanced at his companion; he thought he detected a sinister note in the soothing voice, but the face expressed nothing. Mrs. Dudley ushered them into the hall; Osaka stood at the front door. They passed out and the door closed behind them.

Hatch started down the steps but The Thinking Machine stopped at the door and tramped up and down. The reporter turned back in astonishment. In the dim reflected light he saw the scientist's finger raised, enjoining silence, then saw him lean forward suddenly with his ear pressed to the door. After a little he rapped gently. The door was opened by Osaka, who obeyed a beckoning motion of the scientist's hand and came out. Silently he was led off the veranda into the yard; he appeared in no way surprised.

"Your master, Mr. Dudley, has been murdered," declared The Thinking Machine quietly, to Osaka. "We know that Mrs. Dudley killed him," he went on as Hatch stared, "but I have told her she is not suspected. We are not officers and cannot arrest her. Can you go with us to Boston, without the knowledge of anyone here and tell what you know of the quarrel between husband and wife to the police?"

Osaka looked placidly into the eager face.

"I had the honor to believe that the circumstances would not be recognized," he said finally. "Since you know, I will go."

"We will drive down a little way and wait for you."

The Japanese disappeared into the house again. Hatch was too astounded to speak, but followed The Thinking Machine into the carry-all. It drove away a hundred yards and stopped. After a few minutes an impalpable shadow came toward them through the night. The scientist peered out as it came up.

"Osaka?" he asked softly.

"Yes."

An hour later the three men were on a train, Boston bound. Once comfortably settled the scientist turned to the Japanese.

"Now if you will please tell me just what happened the night of the ball?" he asked, "and the incidents leading up to the disagreement between Mr. and Mrs. Dudley?"

"He drank elaborately," Osaka explained reluctantly, in his quaint English, "and when drinking he was brutal to the honorable lady. Twice with my own eyes I saw him strike her—once in Japan where I entered his service while they were on a wedding journey, and once here. On the night of the ball he was immeasurably intoxicated, and when he danced, he fell down to the floor. The honorable lady was chagrined and angry—she had been angry before. There was some quarrel which I am not comprehensive of. They had been widely divergent for several months. It was, of course, not prominent in the presence of others."

"And the cut on his arm where the court plaster was applied?" asked the scientist. "Just how did he get that?"

"It was when he fell down," continued the Japanese. "He reached to embrace a carved chair and the carved wood cut his arm. I assisted him to his feet and the honorable lady sent me to her room to get court plaster. I acquired it from her dressing table and she placed it on the cut."

"That makes the evidence against her absolutely conclusive," remarked The Thinking Machine, as if finally. There was a little pause, and then: "Do you happen to know just how Mrs. Dudley placed the body in the boat?"

"I have not that honor," said Osaka. "Indeed I am not comprehensive of anything that happened after the court plaster was put on except that Mr. Dudley was affected some way and went out of the house. Mrs. Dudley, too, was not in the ballroom for ten minutes or so afterwards."

Hutchinson Hatch stared frankly into the face of The Thinking Machine; there was nothing to be read there. Still deeply thoughtful, Hatch heard the brakeman bawl "Boston" and mechanically followed the scientist and Osaka out of the station into a cab. They were driven immediately to Police Headquarters. Detective Mallory was just about to go home when they entered his office.

"It may enlighten you, Mr. Mallory," announced the scientist coldly, "to know that the man in the motor boat was not a French naval officer who died of natural causes—he was Langham Dudley, a millionaire ship owner. He was murdered. It just happens that I know the person who did it."

The detective arose in astonishment and stared at the slight figure before him inquiringly; he knew the man too well to dispute any assertion he might make.

"Who is the murderer?" he asked.

The Thinking Machine closed the door and the spring lock clicked.

"That man there," he remarked calmly, turning on Osaka.

For one brief moment there was a pause and silence; then the detective advanced upon the Japanese with hand outstretched. The agile Osaka leapt suddenly, as a snake strikes; there was a quick, fierce struggle and Detective Mallory sprawled on the floor. There had been just a twist of the wrist—a trick of jiu jitsu—and Osaka had flung himself at the locked door. As he fumbled there, Hatch, deliberately and without compunction, raised a chair and brought it down on his head. Osaka sank down without a sound.

It was an hour before they brought him around again. Meanwhile the detective had patted and petted half a dozen suddenly acquired bruises, and had then searched Osaka. He found nothing to interest him save a small bottle. He uncorked it and started to smell it when The Thinking Machine snatched it away.

"You fool, that'll kill you!" he exclaimed.

—

Osaka sat, lashed hand and foot to a chair, in Detective Mallory's office—so placed by the detective for safe keeping. His face was no longer expressionless; there were fear and treachery and cunning there. So he listened, perforce, to the statement of the case by The Thinking Machine who leaned back in his chair, squinting steadily upward and with his long, slender fingers pressed together.

"Two and two make four, not *some*times but *all* the time," he began at last as if disputing some previous assertion. "As the figure 'two,' wholly disconnected from any other, gives small indication of a result, so is an isolated fact of little consequence. Yet that fact added to another, and the resulting fact added to a third, and so on, will give a final result. That result, if every fact is considered, *must* be correct. Thus any problem may be solved by logic; logic is inevitable.

"In this case the facts, considered singly, might have been compatible with either a natural death, suicide, or murder—considered together they proved murder. The climax of this proof was the removal of the maker's name from the dead man's shoes, and a fact strongly contributory was the attempt to destroy the identity of the boat. A subtle mind lay back of it all."

"I so regarded it," said Detective Mallory. "I was confident of murder until the medical examiner——"

"We prove a murder," The Thinking Machine went on serenely. "The method? I was with Dr. Clough at the autopsy. There was no shot, or knife wound, no poison in the stomach. Knowing there was murder I sought further. Then I found the method in a slight, jagged wound on the left arm. It had been covered with court plaster. The heart showed constriction without apparent cause, and while Dr. Clough examined it I took off this court plaster. Its odor, an unusual one, told me that poison had been transfused into the blood through the wound. So two and two had made four.

"Then—what poison? A knowledge of botany aided me. I recognized faintly the trace of an odor of an herb which is not only indigenous to, but grows exclusively in Japan. Thus a Japanese poison. Analysis later in my laboratory proved it was a Japanese poison, virulent, and necessarily slow to act unless it is placed directly in an artery. The poison on the court plaster and that you took from Osaka is identical."

The scientist uncorked the bottle and permitted a single drop of a green liquid to fall on his handkerchief. He allowed a minute or more for evaporation, then handed it to Detective Mallory who sniffed at it from a respectful distance. Then The Thinking Machine produced the bit of court plaster he had taken from the dead man's arm, and again the detective sniffed.

"The same," the scientist resumed as he touched a lighted match to the handkerchief and watched it crumble to ashes, "and so powerful that in its pure state mere inhalation is fatal. I permitted Dr. Clough to make public his opinion—heart failure—after the autopsy for obvious reasons. It would reassure the murderer for instance if he saw it printed, and besides Dudley did die from heart failure; the poison caused it.

"Next came identification. Mr. Hatch learned that no French warship had been within hundreds of miles of Boston for months. The one seen by Captain Barber might have been one of our own. This man was supposed to be a French naval officer, and had been dead less than eight hours. Obviously he did not come from a ship of his own country. Then from where?

"I know nothing of uniforms, yet I examined the insignia on the arms and shoulders closely after which I consulted my encyclopedia. I learned that while the uniform was more French than anything else, it was really the uniform of *no country,* because it was not correct. The insignia were mixed.

"Then what? There were several possibilities, among them a fancy dress ball was probable. Absolute accuracy would not be essential there. Where had there been a fancy dress ball? I trusted to the newspapers to tell me that. They did. A short dispatch from a place on the North Shore stated that on the night before the man was found dead there had been a fancy dress ball at the Langham Dudley estate.

"Now it is as necessary to remember *every* fact in solving a problem as it is to consider every figure in arithmetic. Dudley! Here was the 'D' tattooed on the dead man's hand. *Who's Who* showed that Langham Dudley married Edith Marston Belding. Here was the 'E. M. B.' on the handkerchief in the boat. Langham Dudley was a ship owner, had been a sailor, was a millionaire. Possibly this was his own boat built in France."

Detective Mallory was staring into the eyes of The Thinking Machine in frank admiration; Osaka, to whom the narrative had thus far been impersonal, gazed, gazed as if fascinated. Hutchinson Hatch, reporter, was drinking in every word greedily.

"We went to the Dudley place," the scientist resumed after a moment. "This Japanese opened the door. Japanese poison! Two and two were still making four. But I was first interested in Mrs. Dudley. She showed no agitation and told me frankly that she placed the court plaster on her husband's arm, and that it came from her room. There was instantly a doubt as to her connection with the murder; her immediate frankness aroused it.

"Finally, with my hand on her pulse—which was normal—I told her as brutally as I could that her husband had been murdered. Her pulse jumped frightfully and as I told her the cause of death it wavered, weakened and she fainted. Now if she had known her husband was dead—even if she had killed him—a mere statement of his death would not have caused that pulse. Further I doubt if she could have disposed of her husband's body in the motor boat. He was a large man and the manner of her dress even, was against this. Therefore she was innocent.

"And then? The Japanese, Osaka, here. I could see the door of the boat house from the room where we were. Mrs. Dudley asked Osaka if Mr. Dudley's boat were in the house. He said he didn't know. Then she sent him to see. He returned and said the boat was not there, *yet he had not gone to the boat house at all.* Ergo, he knew the boat was not there. He may have learned it from another servant, still it was a point against him."

Again the scientist paused and squinted at the Japanese. For a moment Osaka withstood the gaze, then his eyes shifted and he moved uncomfortably.

"I tricked Osaka into coming here by a ludicrously simple expedient," The Thinking Machine went on steadily. "On the train I asked if he knew just how Mrs. Dudley got the body of her husband into the boat. Remember at this point he was not supposed to know that the body had been in a boat at all. He said he didn't know and by that very answer admitted that he knew the body had been placed in the boat. He knew because he put it there himself. He didn't merely throw it in the water because he had sense enough to know if the tide didn't take it out, it would rise, and possibly be found.

"After the slight injury Mr. Dudley evidently wandered out toward the boat house. The poison was working, and perhaps he fell. Then this man removed all identifying marks, even to the name in the shoes, put the body in the boat and turned on full power. He had a right to assume that the boat would be lost, or that the dead man would be thrown out. Wind and tide and a loose rudder brought it into Boston Harbor. I do not attempt to account for the presence of Mrs. Dudley's handkerchief in the boat. It might have gotten there in one of a hundred ways."

"How did you know husband and wife had quarreled?" asked Hatch.

"Surmise to account for her not knowing where he was," replied The Thinking Machine. "If they had had a violent disagreement it was possible that he would have gone away without telling her, and she would not have been particularly worried, at least up to the time we saw her. As it was, she presumed he was in Boston; perhaps Osaka here gave her that impression?"

The Thinking Machine turned and stared at the Japanese curiously.

"Is that correct?" he asked.

Osaka did not answer.

"And the motive?" asked Detective Mallory, at last.

"Will you tell us just why you killed Mr. Dudley?" asked The Thinking Machine of the Japanese.

"I will not," exclaimed Osaka, suddenly. It was the first time he had spoken.

"It probably had to do with a girl in Japan," explained The Thinking Machine, easily. "The murder had been a long-cherished project, such a one as revenge through love would have inspired."

It was a day or so later that Hutchinson Hatch called to inform The Thinking Machine that Osaka had confessed and had given the motive for the murder. It was not a nice story.

"One of the most astonishing things to me," Hatch added, "is the complete case of circumstantial evidence against Mrs. Dudley, beginning with the quarrel and leading to the application of the poison with her own hands. I believe she would have been convicted on the actual circumstantial evidence had you not shown conclusively that Osaka did it."

"Circumstantial fiddlesticks!" snapped The Thinking Machine. "I wouldn't convict a dog of stealing jam on circumstantial evidence alone, even if he had jam all over his nose." He squinted truculently at Hatch for a moment. "In the first place well-behaved dogs don't eat jam," he added more mildly.

THE PROBLEM OF THE BROKEN BRACELET

The girl in the green mask leaned against the foot of the bed and idly fingered a revolver which lay in the palm of her daintily gloved hand. The dim glow of the night lamp enveloped her softly, and added a sinister glint to the bright steel of the weapon. Cowering in the bed was another figure, the figure of a woman. Sheets and blankets were drawn up tightly to her chin, and startled eyes peered anxiously, as if fascinated at the revolver.

"Now please don't scream!" warned the masked girl. Her voice was quite casual, the tone in which one might have discussed an affair of far removed personal interest. "It would be perfectly useless, and besides, dangerous."

"Who are you?" gasped the woman in the bed, staring horror-stricken at the inscrutable mask of her visitor. "What do you want?"

A faint flicker of amusement lay in the shadowy eyes of the masked girl, and her red lips twitched slightly. "I don't think I can be mistaken," she said inquiringly. "This is Miss Isabel Leigh Harding?"

"Y-yes," was the chattering reply.

"Originally of Virginia?"

"Yes."

"Great-granddaughter of William Tremaine Harding, an officer in the Continental Army about 1775?"

The inflection of the questioning voice had risen almost imperceptibly; but the tone remained coldly, exquisitely courteous. At the last question the masked girl leaned forward a little expectantly.

"Yes," faltered Miss Harding faintly.

"Good, very good," commented the masked girl and there was a note of repressed triumph in her voice. "I congratulate you, Miss Harding, on your self-possession. Under the same circumstances most women would have begun by screaming. I should have myself."

"But who are you?" demanded Miss Harding again. "How did you get in here? What do you want?"

She sat bolt upright in bed, with less of fear now than curiosity in her manner, and her luxuriant hair tumbled about her semi-bare shoulders in profuse dishevelment.

At the sudden movement the masked girl took a firmer grip on the revolver, and moved it forward a little threateningly. "Now please don't make any mistake!" she advised Miss Harding pleasantly. "You will notice that I have drawn the bell rope up beyond your reach and knotted it. The servants are on the floor above in the extreme rear, and I doubt if they could hear a scream. Your companion is away for the night, and besides there is this." She tapped her weapon significantly. "Furthermore, you may notice that the lamp is beyond your reach; so that you cannot extinguish it as long as you remain in bed."

Miss Harding noticed all these things, and was convinced.

"Now as to your question," continued the masked girl quietly. "My identity is of absolutely no concern or importance to you. You would not even recognize my name if I gave it to you. How did I get here? By opening an unfastened window in the drawing room on the first floor and walking in. I shall leave it unlatched when I go; so perhaps you had better have some one fasten it, otherwise thieves may enter." She smiled a little at the astonishment in Miss Harding's face. "Now as to why I am here and what I want."

She sat down on the foot of the bed, drew her cloak more closely about her, and folded her hands in her lap. Miss Harding placed a pillow and lounged against it comfortably, watching her visitor in astonishment. Except for the mask and the revolver, it might have been a cosy chat in any woman's boudoir.

"I came here to borrow from you—borrow, understand," the masked girl went on, "the least valuable article in your jewel box."

"My jewel box!" gasped Miss Harding suddenly. She had just thought of it, and glanced around at the table where it lay open.

"Don't alarm yourself," the masked girl remarked reassuringly. "I have removed nothing from it."

The light of the lamp fell full upon the open casket whence radiated multicolored flashes of gems. Miss Harding craned her neck a little to see, and seeing sank back against her pillow with a sigh of relief.

"As I said, I came to borrow one thing," the masked girl continued evenly. "If I cannot borrow it, I shall take it."

Miss Harding sat for a moment in mute contemplation of her visitor. She was searching her mind for some tangible explanation of this nightmarish thing. After a while she shook her head, meaning thereby that even conjecture was futile. "What particular article do you want?" she asked finally.

"Specifically by letter, from the prison in which he was executed by order of the British commander, your great-grandfather, William Tremaine Harding, left a gold bracelet, a plain band, to your grandfather," the masked girl explained. "Your grandfather, at that time a child, received the bracelet, when twenty-one years old, from the persons who held it in trust for him, and on his death, March 25, 1853, left it to your father. Your father died intestate in April, 1898, and the bracelet passed into your mother's keeping, there being no son. Your mother died within the last year. Therefore, the bracelet is now, or should be, in your possession. You see," she concluded, "I have taken some pains to acquaint myself with your family history."

"You have," Miss Harding assented. "And may I ask why you want this bracelet?"

"I should answer that it was no concern of yours."

"You said borrow it, I believe?"

"Either I will borrow it or take it."

"Is there any certainty that it will ever be returned? And if so, when?"

"You will have to take my word for that, of course," replied the masked girl. "I shall return it within a few days."

Miss Harding glanced at her jewel box. "Have you looked there?" she inquired.

"Yes," replied the masked girl. "It isn't there."

"Not there?" repeated Miss Harding.

"If it had been there, I should have taken it and gone away without disturbing you," the masked girl went on. "Its absence is what caused me to wake you."

"Not there!" said Miss Harding again wonderingly, and she moved as if to get up.

"Don't do that, please!" warned the masked girl quickly. "I shall hand you the box if you like."

She rose and passed the casket to Miss Harding, who spilled out its contents on her lap.

"Why, it is gone!" she exclaimed.

"Yes, from there," said the other a little grimly. "Now please tell me immediately where it is. It will save trouble."

"I don't know," replied Miss Harding hopelessly.

The masked girl stared at her coldly for a moment, then drew back the hammer of the revolver until it clicked.

Miss Harding stared in sudden terror.

"All this is merely time wasted," said the masked girl sternly, coldly. "Either the bracelet or this!" Again she tapped the revolver.

"If it is not here, I don't know where it is," Miss Harding rushed on desperately. "I placed it here at ten o'clock last night—here in this box—when I undressed. I don't know—I can't imagine———"

The masked girl tapped the revolver again several times with one gloved finger. "The bracelet!" she demanded impatiently.

Fear was in Miss Harding's eyes now, and she made a helpless, pleading gesture with both white hands. "You wouldn't kill me— murder me!" she gasped. "I don't know. I—here, take the other jewels. I can't tell you."

"The other jewels are of absolutely no use to me," said the girl coldly. "I want only the bracelet."

"On my honor," faltered Miss Harding, "I don't know where it is. I can't imagine what has happened to it. I—I———" she stopped helplessly.

The masked girl raised the weapon threateningly, and Miss Harding stared in terror.

"Please, please, I don't know!" she pleaded hysterically.

For a little while the masked girl was thoughtfully silent. One shoe tapped the floor rhythmically; the eyes were contracted. "I believe you," she said slowly at last. She rose suddenly and drew her coat closely about her. "Good night," she added as she started toward the door. There she turned back. "It would not be wise for you to give an alarm for at least half an hour. Then you had better have some one latch the window in the drawing room. I shall leave it unfastened. Good night."

And she was gone.

———

Hutchinson Hatch, reporter, had just finished relating the story to The Thinking Machine, incident by incident, as it had been reported to Chief of Detectives Mallory, when the eminent scientist's aged servant, Martha, tapped on the door of the reception room and entered with a card.

"A lady to see you, sir," she announced.

The scientist extended one slender white hand, took the card, and glanced at it.

"Your story is merely what Miss Harding told the police?" he inquired of the reporter. "You didn't get it from Miss Harding herself?"

"No, I didn't see her."

"Show the lady in, Martha," directed The Thinking Machine. She turned and went out, and he passed the card to the reporter.

"By George! It's Miss Harding herself," Hatch exclaimed. "Now we can get it all straight!"

There was a little pause, and Martha ushered a young woman into the room. She was girlish, slender, daintily yet immaculately attired, with deep brown eyes, firmly molded chin and mouth, and wavy hair. Hatch's expression of curiosity gave way to one of frank admiration as he regarded her. There was only the most impersonal sort of interest in the watery blue eyes of The Thinking Machine. She stood for a moment with gaze alternating between the distinguished man of science and the reporter.

"I am Mr. Van Dusen," explained The Thinking Machine. "Allow me, Miss Harding—Mr. Hatch."

The girl smiled and offered a gloved hand cordially to each of the two men. The Thinking Machine merely touched it respectfully; Hatch shook it warmly. The eyes were veiled demurely for an instant, then the lids were lifted suddenly, and she favored the newspaperman with a gaze that sent the blood to his cheeks.

"Be seated, Miss Harding," the scientist invited.

"I hardly know just what I came to say, and just how to say it," she began uncertainly, and smiled a little. "And anyway I had hoped that you were alone; so———"

"You may speak with perfect freedom before Mr. Hatch," interrupted The Thinking Machine. "Perhaps I shall be able to help you; but first will you repeat the history of the bracelet as nearly as you can in the words of the masked woman who called upon you so—so unconventionally."

The girl's brows were lifted inquiringly, with a sort of start.

"We were discussing the case when your card was brought in," continued The Thinking Machine tersely. "We shall continue from that point, if you will be so good."

The young woman recited the history of the bracelet slowly and carefully.

"And that statement of the case is correct?" queried the scientist.

"Absolutely, so far as I know," was the reply.

"And as I understand it, you were in the house alone; that is, alone except for the servants?"

"Yes. I live there alone, except for a companion and two servants. The servants were not within the sound of my voice, even if I had screamed, and Miss Tablott, my companion, it happened, was out for the night."

The Thinking Machine had dropped back into his chair, with squint eyes turned upward, and long white fingers pressed tip to tip. He sat thus silently for a long time. The girl at last broke the silence.

"Naturally I was a little surprised," she remarked falteringly, "that I should have appeared just in time to interrupt a discussion of the singular happenings in my home last night, but really———"

"This bracelet," interrupted the little scientist again. "It was of oval form, perhaps, with no stones set in it, or anything of that sort, merely a band that fastened with an invisible hinge. That's right, I believe?"

"Quite right, yes," replied the girl readily.

It occurred to Hatch suddenly that he himself did not know—in fact, had not inquired—the shape of the bracelet. He knew only that it was gold and of no great value. Knowing nothing about what it looked like, he had not described it to The Thinking Machine, therefore he raised his eyes inquiringly now. The drawn face of the scientist was inscrutable.

"As I started to say," the girl went on, "the bracelet and the events of last night have no direct connection with the purpose of my visit here."

"Indeed?" commented the scientist.

"No. I came to see if you would assist me in another way. For instance," and she fumbled in her pocketbook, "I happened to know, Professor Van Dusen, of some of the remarkable things you have accomplished, and I should like to ask if you can throw any light on this for me."

She drew from the pocketbook a crumpled, yellow sheet of paper—a strip perhaps an inch wide, thin as tissue, glazed, and extraordinarily wrinkled. The Thinking Machine squinted at its manifold irregularities for an instant curiously, nodded, sniffed at it, then slowly began to unfold it, smoothing it out carefully as he went. Hatch leaned forward eagerly and stared. He was a little more than astonished at the end to find that the sheet was blank. The Thinking Machine examined both sides of the paper thoughtfully.

"And where did you find the bracelet at last?" he inquired casually.

"I have reason to believe," the girl rushed on suddenly, regardless of the question, "that this strip of paper has been substituted for one of real value—I may say one of great value—and I don't know how to proceed, unless——"

"Where did you find the bracelet?" demanded The Thinking Machine again, impatiently.

Hatch would have hesitated a long time before he would have said the girl was disconcerted at the question, or that there had been any real change in the expression of her pretty face. And yet——

"After the masked woman had gone," she went on calmly, "I summoned the servants and we made a search. We found the bracelet at last. I thought I had tossed it into my jewel box when I removed it last night; but it seems I was careless enough to let it fall down behind my dressing table, and it was there all the time the—masked woman was in my room."

"And when did you make this discovery?" asked The Thinking Machine.

"Within a few minutes after she went out."

"In making your search, you were guided, perhaps, by a belief that in the natural course of events the bracelet could not have disappeared from your jewel box unless some one had entered the room before the masked woman entered; and further that if anyone had entered you would have been awakened?"

"Precisely." There was another pause. "And now please," she went on, "what does this blank strip of paper mean?"

"You had expected something with writing on it, of course?"

"That's just what I had expected," and she laughed nervously. "You may rest assured I was considerably surprised at finding that."

"I can imagine you were," remarked the scientist dryly.

The conversation had reached a point where Hatch was hopelessly lost. The young woman and the scientist were talking with mutual understanding of things that seemed to have no connection with anything that had gone before. What was the paper anyway? Where did it come from? What connection did it have with the affairs of the previous night? How did——

"Mr. Hatch, a match, please," requested The Thinking Machine.

Wonderingly the reporter produced one and handed it over. The imperturbable man of science lighted it and thrust the mysterious paper into the blaze. The girl rose with a sudden, startled cry, and snatched at the paper desperately, extinguishing the match as she did so. The Thinking Machine turned disapproving eyes on her.

"I thought you were going to burn it!" she gasped.

"There is not the slightest danger of that, Miss Harding," declared The Thinking Machine coldly. He examined the blank sheet again. "This way, please."

He rose and led the way into his tiny laboratory across the narrow hall, with the girl following. Hatch trailed behind, wondering vaguely what it was all about. A small brazier flashed into flame as The Thinking Machine applied a match, and curious eyes peered over his shoulders as he held the blank strip, now smoothed out, so that the rising heat would strike it.

For a long time three pairs of eyes were fastened on the mysterious paper, all with understanding now; but nothing appeared. Hatch glanced round at the young woman. Her face wore an expression of tense excitement. The red lips were slightly parted in anticipation, the eyes sparkling, and the cheeks flushed deeply. In staring at her the reporter forgot for the instant everything else, until suddenly:

"There! There! Do you see?"

The exclamation burst from her triumphantly, as faint, scrawly lines grew on the strip suspended over the brazier. Totally oblivious of their presence apparently, The Thinking Machine was squinting steadily at the paper, which was slowly crinkling up into wavy lines under the influence of the heat. Gradually the edges were charring, and the odor of scorched paper filled the room. Still the scientist held the paper over the fire. Just as it seemed inevitable that it would burst into flame, he withdrew it and turned to the girl.

"There was no substitution," he remarked tersely. "It is sympathetic ink."

"What does it say?" demanded the young woman abruptly. "What does it mean?"

The Thinking Machine spread the scorched strip of paper on the table before them carefully, and for a long time studied it minutely.

"Really, my dear young woman, I don't know," he said crabbedly at last. "It may take days to find out what it means."

"But something is written there! Read it!" the girl insisted.

"Read it for yourself," said the scientist impatiently. "I am frank to say it's beyond me as it is now. No, don't touch it. It will crumble to pieces."

Faintly, yet decipherable under a magnifying glass, the three were able to make out this on the paper:

Stonehedge—idim-serpa'l ed serueh soirt a tnaeG ed eteT al rap eetej erbmo'l ed etniop al srevart a sro U'd rehcoR ud eueuq al ed dron ua sdeip tnec.

"What does it mean? What does it mean?" demanded the young woman impatiently. "What does it mean?"

The sudden hardening of her tone caused both Hatch and The Thinking Machine to turn and stare at her. Some strange change had come over her face. There was chagrin, perhaps, and there was more than that—a merciless glitter in the brown eyes, a grim expression about the chin and mouth, a greedy closing and unclosing of the small, well-shaped hands.

"I presume it's a cipher of some sort," remarked The Thinking Machine curtly. "It may take time to read it and to learn definitely just where the treasure is hidden, and you may have to wait for——"

"Treasure!" exclaimed the girl. "Did you say treasure? There is treasure, then?"

The Thinking Machine shrugged his shoulders. "What else?" he asked. "Now, please, let me see the bracelet."

"The bracelet!" the girl repeated, and again Hatch noted that quick change of expression on her pretty face. "I—er—must you see it? I—er——" And she stopped.

"It is absolutely necessary, if I make anything of this," and the scientist indicated the charred paper. "You have it in your pocketbook, of course."

The girl stepped forward suddenly and leaned over the laboratory table, intently studying the mysterious strip of paper. At last she raised her head as if she had reached a decision.

"I have only a—a part of the bracelet," she announced, "only half. It was unavoidably broken, and——"

"Only half?" interrupted The Thinking Machine and he squinted coldly into the young woman's eyes.

"Here it is," she said at last, desperately almost. "I don't know where the other half is; it would be useless to ask me."

She drew an aged, badly scratched half circlet of gold from her pocketbook, handed it to the scientist, then went and looked out the window. The Thinking Machine examined it—the delicate decorative tracings, then the invisible hinge where the bracelet had been rudely torn apart. Twice he raised his squint eyes and stared at the girl as she stood silhouetted against the light of the window. When he spoke again, there was a deeper note in his voice—a singular softening, an unusual deference.

"I shall read the cipher, of course, Miss Harding," he said slowly. "It may take an hour, or it may take a week, I don't know." Again he scrutinized the charred paper. "Do you speak French?" he inquired suddenly.

"Enough to understand and to make myself understood," replied the girl. "Why?"

The Thinking Machine scribbled off a copy of the cipher and handed it to her.

"I'll communicate with you when I reach a conclusion," he remarked. "Please leave your address on your card here," and he handed her the card and pencil.

"You know my home address," she said. "Perhaps it would be better for me to call this afternoon late, or tomorrow."

"I'd prefer to have your address," said the scientist. "As I say, I don't know when I shall be able to speak definitely."

The girl paused for a moment and tapped the blunt end of the pencil against her white teeth thoughtfully with her left hand. "As a matter of fact," she said at last, "I am not returning home now. The events of last night have shaken me considerably, and I am now on my way to Blank Rock, a little seashore town where I shall remain for a few days. My address there will be the High Towers."

"Write it down, please!" directed The Thinking Machine tersely. The girl stared at him strangely, with a challenge in her eyes, then leaned over the table to write. Before the pencil had touched the card, however, she changed her mind and handed both to Hatch, with a smile.

"Please write it for me," she requested. "I write a wretched hand, anyway, and besides I have on my gloves." She turned again to the little scientist, who stood squinting over her head. "Thank you so much for your trouble," she said in conclusion. "You can reach me at this address, either by wire or letter, for the next fortnight."

And a few minutes later she was gone. For a while The Thinking Machine was silent as he again studied the faint writing on the strip of paper.

"The cipher," he remarked to Hatch at last, "is no cipher at all; it's so simple. But there are some other things I shall have to find out first, and—suppose you drop by early tomorrow to see me."

Half an hour later The Thinking Machine went to the telephone, and after running through the book, called a number.

"Is Miss Harding home yet?" he demanded, when an answer came.

"No, sir," was the reply, in a woman's voice.

"Would you mind telling me, please, if she is left-handed?"

"Why, no, sir. She's right-handed. Who is this?"

"I knew it, of course. Good by."

———

The Thinking Machine was squinting into the inquiring eyes of Hutchinson Hatch.

"The reason why the police are so frequently unsuccessful in explaining the mysteries of crime," he remarked, "is not through lack of natural intelligence, or through lack of a birth-given aptitude for the work, but through the lack of an absolutely accurate knowledge which is wide enough to enable them to proceed. Now here is a case in point. It starts with a cipher, goes into an intricate astronomical calculation, and from that into simple geometry. The difficulty with the detectives is not that they could not work out each of these as it was presented, perhaps with the aid of some outsider, but that they would not recognize the existence of the three phases of the problem in the first place.

"You have heard me say frequently, Mr. Hatch, that logic is inevitable—as inevitable as that two and two make four not *some*times, but *all* the time. That is true; but it must have an indisputable starting point—the one unit which is unassailable. In this case unit produces unit in order, and the proper array of these units gives a coherent answer. Let me demonstrate briefly just what I mean.

"A masked woman, employing the methods at least of a thief, demands a certain bracelet of this Miss Harding. She doesn't want jewels; she wants that bracelet. Whatever other conjectures may be advanced, the one dominant fact is that that bracelet, itself of little comparative value, is worth more than all the rest to her—the masked woman, I mean—and she has endangered her liberty and perhaps life to get it. Why? The history of the bracelet as she herself stated it to Miss Harding gives the answer. A man in prison, under sentence of death, had that bracelet at one time. We can conjecture immediately, therefore, that the masked woman knew that the fact of its having been in this man's possession gave him an opportunity at least of so marking the bracelet—or of confiding in it, I may say, a valuable secret. One's first thought, therefore, is of treasure—hidden treasure. We shall go further and say treasure hidden by a Continental officer to prevent its falling into other hands as loot. This officer under sentence of death, and therefore cut off from all communication with the outside, took a desperate means of communicating the location of the treasure to his heirs. That is clear, isn't it?"

The reporter nodded.

"I described the bracelet—you heard me—and yet I had never seen it, nor had I a description of it. That description was merely a forward step, a preliminary test of the truth of the first assumptions. I reasoned that the bracelet must be of a type which could be employed to carry a message safely past prying eyes; and there is really only one sort which is feasible, and that is the one I described. These bracelets are always hollow, the invisible hinges hold them together on one side, and they lock in the other. It would be perfectly possible, therefore, to write the message the prisoner wanted to send out on a strip of tissue paper, or any other thin paper, and cram it into the bracelet at the back end. In that event it would certainly pass inspection; the only difficulty would be for the outside person to find it. That was a chance; but it was all a chance anyway.

"When the young woman came here and produced a strip of thin paper, apparently blank, with the multitude of wrinkles in it, I immediately saw that that paper had been recovered from the bracelet. It was old, yellow and worn. Therefore, blank or not, that was the message which the prisoner had sent out. You saw me hold it over the brazier, and saw the characters appear. It was sympathetic ink, of course.

"Hard to make in prison, you say? Not at all. Writing either with lemon juice or milk, once dry, is perfectly invisible on paper; but when exposed to heat at any time afterward, it will appear. That is a chemical truth.

"Now the thing that appeared was a cipher—an absurd one, still a cipher. Extraordinary precaution of the prisoner who was about to die! This cipher—let me see exactly," and the scientist spelled it out:

Stonehedge—idim-serpa'l ed serueh soirt a tnaeG ed eteT al rap eetej erbmo'l ed etniop al srevart a sro U'd rehcoR ud eueuq al ed dron ua sdeip tnec.

"If you know anything of languages, Mr. Hatch," he continued, "you know that French is the only common language where the apostrophe and the accent marks play a very important part. A moment's study of this particular cipher therefore convinced me that it was in French. I tried the simple expedient of reading it backward, with this result

Stonehedge. Hundred feet due north from the tail of Bear Rock through apex (or point) of shadow cast by Giant's Head. Three P.M.

"I had read the cipher and knew the English clear version before I gave a copy of it to the young woman who was here. I specifically asked her if she knew French, to give her a clue by which she might interpret the cipher herself. And thus I blazed the way within a few minutes to the point where astronomical and geometrical calculations were next. Please bear in mind that this message from the dead was not dated.

"Now, about the young woman herself," continued the scientist after a moment. "The statement of how she came to find the bracelet was obviously untrue; particularly are we convinced of this when she cannot, or will not, explain how it was broken. Therefore, another field is open for scrutiny. The bracelet was broken. If we assume that it is *the* bracelet, and there is no reason to doubt it, and we know that it is in her possession, we know also that more than one person had been searching for it. We know positively that that other person—not the masked girl, but the girl who had preceded her to Miss Harding's room on the same night—got the bracelet from Miss Harding, and we are safe in assuming that it passed out of that other person's hand by force. The bracelet had been literally torn apart at the hinge. In other words, there had been a physical contest, and one piece of the circlet, the piece with the message, passed out of the hands of the person who had preceded the masked woman and stolen the bracelet.

"But this is by the way. Stonehedge is the name of the old Tremaine Harding estate, about twenty miles out, and there the Tremaine Harding family valuables were hidden by William Tremaine Harding, who died by bullet, a martyr to the cause of freedom. We shall get the treasure this afternoon after I have settled one or two dates and made the astronomical and geometrical calculations which are necessary."

—

There was silence for a minute or more, broken at last by the impatient "Honk, honk!" of an automobile outside.

"We'll go now," announced The Thinking Machine as he rose. "There is a car for us."

He led the way out, Hatch following. A heavy touring car, with three seats, driven by a young woman, was waiting at the door. The woman was a stranger to the reporter, but there was no introduction.

"Did you get the date of Captain Harding's imprisonment?" asked The Thinking Machine.

"Yes," was the reply. "June 3, 1776."

The Thinking Machine clambered in, Hatch following silently, and the car rushed away. It paused in a suburb long enough to pick up two workmen with picks and shovels, who took their places in the back seat, and then the automobile with its strange company—a pretty woman, a newspaper reporter, a distinguished scientist, and two laborers—proceeded on its way. Hatch, alone in the second seat, heard only one remark by the scientist, and this was:

"Of course she was clever enough to read the cipher, after I gave her the hint that it was in French; so we shall find that the place has been dug over, but there is only one chance in 365 that the treasure was found. I give her credit for extraordinary cleverness, but not enough to make the necessary astronomical calculations."

A run of an hour and a half brought them to Stonehedge, a huge old estate with ramshackle dwelling and acres of rock-ridden ground. Away off in the northwest corner were two large stones—Bear Rock and Giant's Head—rising fifteen or twenty feet above the ground. The car was driven over a rough road and stopped near them.

"You see, she did read the cipher," remarked the scientist placidly. "Workmen have already been here."

Straight ahead of them was an excavation ten feet or more square. Hatch peered into it, while The Thinking Machine busied himself by plunging a stake at the so-called tail of Bear Rock. Then he glanced at his watch—it was half-past two o'clock—and sat down with the young woman in the shadow of Giant's Head. Hatch lounged on the ground near them, and the workmen made themselves comfortable in their own way.

"We can't do anything till three o'clock," remarked The Thinking Machine.

"And just what shall we do then?" inquired the young woman expectantly. It was the first time she had spoken since they started.

"It is rather difficult to explain," said The Thinking Machine. "The hole over there proves that the young woman read the cipher, of course. Now here briefly is why the treasure was not found. Today is September 17. A measurement was made, according to instructions, from the tail of Bear Rock through the apex of the shadow of Giant's Head precisely at three o'clock yesterday one hundred feet due north, or as near north as possible. The hole shows the end of the hundred-foot line. Now we know that Captain Harding was imprisoned on June 3, 1776. We know he buried the treasure before that date; we have a right to assume it was only shortly before. On June 3 of any year the apex of the shadow will be in a totally different place from September 17, because of the movement of the earth about the sun and the relative changes in the sun's position. What we must do now is to find precisely where the shadow falls at three o'clock today, then make our calculations to show where it will fall say one week before June 3. Do you follow me? In other words, a difference of half a foot in the location of the apex of the shadow will make a difference of many feet at the end of one hundred feet when we follow the cipher."

At precisely three o'clock The Thinking Machine noted the position of the shadow, and then began a calculation which covered two sheets of blank paper which Hatch had had in his pocket.

"This is correct," said The Thinking Machine at last as he rose and planted another stake in the ground. "There is a chance, of course, that we miss fire the first time because of a change in the surface of the ground, or a few days' error in the assumed date, but this is mathematically correct."

Then, with the assistance of the newspaper man and the young woman, he drew his hundred-foot line, and planted a third stake.

"Dig here!" he told the workmen.

One hour later the long-lost family plate and jewels of the ancient Harding family had been unearthed. The Thinking Machine and the others stooped over the rotting box which had been brought to the surface and noted the contents. Roughly the value was above two hundred thousand dollars.

"And I think that is all, Miss Harding," said the scientist at last. "It is yours. Load it into your car there, and drive home."

"Miss Harding!" Hatch repeated quickly, with a glance at the young woman. "Miss Harding!"

The Thinking Machine turned and squinted at the reporter for a moment. "Didn't you know that the young woman who called on me was not Miss Harding?" he demanded. "It was evident in her every act—in her failing to explain the broken bracelet, and in the fact that she was left-handed. You must have noticed that. Well, this is Miss Harding, and she is right-handed."

The girl smiled at Hatch's astonishment.

"Then the other woman merely impersonated Miss Harding?" he asked at last.

"That is all, and cleverly," replied The Thinking Machine. "She merely wanted me to read the cipher for her. I put her on the track of reading it herself purposely, and she and the persons associated with her are responsible for the excavation over there."

"But who is the other young woman?"

"She is the one who visited Miss Harding, wearing a mask."

"But what is her name? And who is the third woman? And how did this all come about now?"

"I'm sure I haven't the faintest idea," responded the little scientist shortly. "We have the masked woman to thank, however, for placing the solution of the affair into our hands. Who she is, and what she is, is of no real consequence now, particularly as Miss Harding has this."

The scientist indicated the box with one small foot, and then turned and clambered into the waiting automobile.

THE PROBLEM OF THE CROSS MARK

It was an unsolved mystery, apparently a riddle without an answer, in which Watson Richards, the distinguished character actor, happened to play a principal part. The story was told at the Mummers Club one dull afternoon. Richards's listeners were three other actors, a celebrated poet, and a newspaper reporter named Hutchinson Hatch.

"You know there are few men in the profession today who really amount to anything, who haven't had their hard knocks. Well, my hard times came early, and lasted a long time. So it was just about three years ago to a day that a real crisis came in my affairs. It seemed the end. I had gone one day without food, had bunked in the park that night, and here it was two o'clock in the afternoon of another day. It was dismal enough.

"I was standing on a corner, gazing moodily across the street at the display window of a restaurant, rapidly approaching the don't care stage. Someone came up behind and touched me on the shoulder. I turned listlessly enough, and found myself facing a stranger—a clean-cut, well-groomed man of some forty years.

" 'Is this Mr. Watson Richards, the character actor?' he asked.

" 'Yes,' I replied.

" 'I have been looking for you everywhere,' he explained briefly. 'I want to engage you to do a part for one performance. Are you at liberty?'

"You chaps know what that meant to me just at that moment. Certainly the words dispelled some unpleasant possibilities I had been considering.

" 'I am at liberty—yes,' I replied, 'Be glad to do it. What sort of part is it?'

" 'An old man,' he informed me. 'Just one performance, you know. Perhaps you'd better come up town with me and see Mr. Hallman right now.'

"I agreed with a readiness which approached eagerness, and he called a passing cab. Hallman was perhaps the manager, or stage manager, I thought. We had driven on for a block in the general direction of up town, my companion chatting pleasantly. Finally he offered me a cigar. I accepted it. I know now that the cigar was drugged, because I had hardly taken more than two or three puffs from it when I lost myself completely.

"The next thing I remember distinctly was of stepping out of the cab—I think the stranger assisted me—and going into a house. I don't know where it was—I didn't know then—didn't know even the street. I was dizzy, giddy. And suddenly I stood before a tall, keen-faced, clean-shaven man. He was Hallman. The stranger introduced me and then left the room. Hallman regarded me keenly for several minutes, and somehow under that scrutiny my dormant faculties were aroused. I had thrown away the cigar at the door.

" 'You play character parts?' Hallman began.

" 'Yes, all the usual things,' I told him. 'I'm rather obscure, but——'

" 'I know,' he interrupted, 'but I have seen your work, and like it. I have been told too that you are remarkably clever at make-up.'

"I think I blushed—I hope I did, anyway—I know I nodded. He paused to stare at me for a long time.

" 'For instance,' he went on finally, 'you would have no difficulty at all in making up as a man of seventy-five years?'

" 'Not the slightest,' " I answered. 'I have played such parts.'

" 'Yes, yes, I know,' and he seemed a little impatient. 'Well, your make-up is the matter which is most important here. I want you for only one performance; but the make-up must be perfect, you understand." Again he stopped and stared at me. 'The pay will be one hundred dollars for the one performance.'

"He drew out a drawer of a desk and produced a photograph. He looked at it, then at me, several times, and finally placed it in my hands.

" 'Can you make-up to look precisely like that?' he asked quietly.

"I studied the photograph closely. It was that of a man about seventy-five years old, of rather a long cast of features, not unlike the general shape of my own face. He had white hair, and was clean-shaven. It was simple enough, with the proper wig, a make-up box, and a mirror.

" 'I can,' I told Hallman.

" 'Would you mind putting on the make-up here now for my inspection?' he inquired.

" 'Certainly not,' I replied. It did not strike me at the moment as unusual. 'But I'll need the wig and paints.'

" 'Here they are,' said Hallman abruptly and produced them. 'There's a mirror in front of you. Go ahead.'

"I examined the wig and compared it with the photograph. It was as near perfect as I had ever seen. The make-up box was new and the most complete I ever saw. It didn't occur to me until a long time afterward that it had never been used before. So I went to work. Hallman paced up and down nervously behind me. At the end of twenty minutes I turned upon him a face which was so much like the photograph that I might have posed for it. He stared at me in amazement.

" 'By George,' he exclaimed. 'That's it! It's marvelous!' Then he turned and opened the door. 'Come in Frank,' he called, and the man who had conducted me there entered. Hallman indicated me with a wave of his hand . . .

" 'How is it?' he asked.

"Frank, whoever he was, also seemed astonished. Then that passed and a queer expression appeared on his face. You may imagine that I awaited their verdict anxiously.

" 'Perfect—absolutely perfect,' said Frank at last.

" 'Perhaps the only thing,' Hallman mused critically, 'is that it isn't quite pale enough.'

" 'Easily remedied,' I replied and turned again to the make-up box. A moment later I turned back to the two men. Simple enough, you know—it was one of those pallid, pasty-faced make-ups—the old man on the verge of the grave, and all that sort of thing—good deal of pearl powder.

" 'That's it!' exclaimed the two men.

"The man Frank looked at Hallman inquiringly.

" 'Go ahead,' said Hallman, and Frank left the room.

"Hallman went over, closed and locked the door, after which he came back and sat down in front of me, staring at me for a long time in silence. At length he opened an upper drawer of the desk and glanced in. A revolver lay there, right under his hand. I know now he intended that I should see it.

" 'Now, Mr. Richards,' he said at last very slowly, 'what we want you to do is very simple, and as I said there's a hundred dollars in it. I know your circumstances perfectly—you need the hundred dollars.' He offered me a cigar, and foolishly enough I accepted it. 'The part you are to play is that of an old man, who is ill in bed, speechless, utterly helpless. You are dying, and you are to play the part. Use your eyes all you want; but don't speak!'

"Gradually the dizziness I had felt before was coming upon me again. As I said, I know now it was the cigar; but I kept on smoking.

" 'There will be no rehearsal,' Hallman went on, and now I knew he was fingering the revolver I had seen in the desk, but it made no particular impression on me. 'If I ask you questions, you may nod an affirmative, but don't speak! Do only what I say, and nothing else!'

"Full realization was upon me now; but everything was growing hazy again. I remember I fought the feeling for a moment; then it seemed to overwhelm me, and I was utterly helpless under the dominating power of that man.

" 'When am I to play the part?' I remember asking.

" 'Now!' said Hallman suddenly, and he rose. 'I'm afraid you don't fully understand me yet, Mr. Richards. If you play the part properly, you get the hundred dollars; if you don't, this!'

"He meant the revolver. I stared at it dumbly, overcome by a helpless terror, and tried to stand up. Then there came a blank, for how long I don't know. The next thing I remember I was lying in bed propped up against several pillows. I opened my eyes feebly enough, and there wasn't any acting about it either, because whoever drugged those cigars knew his business.

"There in front of me was Hallman, with a grief-stricken expression on his face which made all my art seem amateurish. There was another man there (not Frank) and a woman who seemed to be about forty years old. I couldn't see their faces—I wouldn't even be able to suggest a description of them, because the room was almost dark. Just the faintest flicker of light came through in low tones—sickroom voices—but I couldn't hear and doubt if I could have followed their conversation if I had heard.

"Finally the door opened and a girl entered. I have seen many women, but—well she was peculiarly fascinating. She gave one little cry, rushed toward the bed impulsively, dropped on her knees beside it, and buried her face in the sheets. She was shaking with sobs.

"Then I knew—intuitively, perhaps, but I knew—that in some way I was being used to injure that girl. A sudden feeling of fearful anger seized upon me, but I couldn't move to save my soul. Hallman must have caught the blaze in my eyes, for he came forward on the other side of the bed, and, under cover of a handkerchief which he had been using rather ostentatiously, pressed the revolver against my side.

"But I wouldn't be made a tool of. In my dazed condition I know I was seized with a desperate desire to fight it out—to make him kill me if he had to, but I would not deceive the girl. I knew if I could jerk my head down on the pillow it would disarrange the wig, and perhaps she would see. I couldn't. I might pass my hands across my make-up and smear it. But I couldn't lift my hands. I was struggling to speak, and couldn't.

"Then somehow I lost myself again. Hazily I remember that somebody placed a paper in front of me on a book—a legal-looking document—and guided my hand across it; but that isn't clear. I was helpless, inert, so much clay in the hands of this man Hallman. Then everything faded—slowly, slowly. My impression was that I was actually dying; my eyelids closed of themselves and the last thing I saw was the shining gold of that girl's hair as she sobbed there beside me.

"That's all of it. When I became fully conscious again a policeman was shaking me. I was sitting on a bench in the park. He swore at me volubly, and I got up and moved slowly along the path with my hands in my pockets. Something was clenched in one hand. I drew it out and looked at it. It was a hundred-dollar bill. I remember I got something to eat; and I woke up in a hospital.

"Well, that's the story. Make what you like of it. It can never be solved, of course. It was three years ago. You fellows know what I have done in that time. Well, I'd give it all, every bit of it, to meet that girl again (I should know her), tell her what I know, and make her believe that it was no fault of mine."

———

Hutchinson Hatch related the circumstances casually one afternoon a day or so later to Professor Augustus S. F. X. Van Dusen—The Thinking Machine.

That eminent man of science listened petulantly, as he listened to all things. "It happened in this city?" he inquired at the end.

"Yes."

"But Richards has no idea what part of the city?"

"Not the slightest. I imagine that the drugged cigar and a naturally weakened condition made him lose his bearings while in the cab."

"I dare say," commented the scientist. "And of course he has never seen Hallman again?"

"No—he would have mentioned it if he had."

"Does Richards remember the exact date of the affair?"

"I dare say he does, though he didn't mention it," replied the reporter.

"Suppose you see Richards and get the date—exactly, if possible," remarked The Thinking Machine. "You might telephone it to me. Perhaps———" and he shrugged his slender shoulders.

"You think there is a possibility of solving the riddle?" demanded the reporter eagerly.

"Certainly," snapped The Thinking Machine. "It requires no solution. It is ridiculously simple—obvious, I might say—and yet I dare say the girl Richards referred to has been the victim of some huge plot. It's worth looking into for her sake."

"Remember, it happened three years ago," Hatch suggested tentatively.

"It wouldn't matter particularly if it happened thirty years ago," declared the scientist. "Logic, Mr. Hatch, remains the same through all the ages—from Adam and Eve to us. Two and two made four in the Garden of Eden just as they do now in a counting house. Therefore, the solution, I say, is absurdly simple. The only problem is to discover the identity of the principals in the affair—and a child could do that."

Later that afternoon Hatch telephoned to The Thinking Machine from the Mummers Club.

"That date you asked for was May 19, three years ago," said the reporter.

"Very well," commented The Thinking Machine. "Drop by tomorrow afternoon. Perhaps we can solve the riddle for Richards."

Hatch called late the following afternoon, as directed, but The Thinking Machine was not in.

"He went out about nine o'clock and hasn't returned yet," the scientist's aged servant, Martha, informed him.

That night about ten o'clock Hatch used the telephone in a second attempt to reach The Thinking Machine.

"He hasn't come in yet," Martha told him over the wire. "He said he would be back for luncheon; but he isn't here yet."

Hatch replaced the receiver thoughtfully on the hook. Early the next morning he again used the telephone, and there was a note of anxiety in Martha's voice when she answered.

"He hasn't come yet, sir," she explained. "Please, what ought I to do? I'm afraid something has happened to him."

"Don't do anything yet," replied Hatch. "I dare say he'll return today."

Again at noon, at six o'clock, and at eleven that night Hatch called Martha on the telephone. Still the scientist had not appeared. Hatch, too, was worried now; yet how should he proceed? He didn't know, and he hesitated to think of the possibilities. On the morrow, however, something must be done—he would take the matter to Detective Mallory at police headquarters if necessary.

But this was made unnecessary unexpectedly by the arrival next morning of a letter from The Thinking Machine. As he read, an expression of bewilderment spread over Hatch's face. Tersely, the letter was like this:

> Employ an expert burglar, a careful, clever man. At two o'clock of the night following the receipt of this letter, go with him to the alley which runs behind No. 810 Blank St. Enter this house with him from the rear, go up two flights of stairs, and let him pick the lock of the third door on the left from the head of the stairs. Silence above everything. Don't shoot if possible to avoid it.
>
> VAN DUSEN

P.S. Put some ham sandwiches in your pocket.

Hatch stared at the note in blank bewilderment for a long time, but he obeyed orders. Thus it came to pass that at ten minutes of two o'clock that night he boosted the notorious Blindy Bates—a man of rare accomplishments in his profession, who at the moment happened to be out of prison—to the top of the rear fence of No. 810 Blank St. Bates hauled up the reporter and they leaped down lightly inside the yard.

The back door was simplicity itself to the gifted Bates, and yielded in less than sixty seconds from the moment he laid his hand on it. Then came a sneaking, noiseless advance along the lower hall, to the accompaniment of innumerable thrills up and down Hatch's spinal column; up the first flight safely, with Blindy Bates leading the way; then along the hall and up the second flight. There was absolutely not a sound in the house—they moved like ghosts.

At the top of the second flight Bates shot a gleam of light from his dark lantern along the hall. The third door it was. And a moment later he was concentrating every faculty on the three locks of this door. Still there had been not the slightest sound. The one spot in the darkness was the bull's eye of the lantern as it illuminated the lock. The first lock was unfastened, then the second, and finally the third. Bates didn't open the door—he merely stepped back—and the door opened as of its own volition. Involuntarily Hatch's hand closed fiercely on his revolver, and Bates's ready weapon glittered a little in the darkness.

"Thanks," came after a moment, in the quiet, querulous voice of The Thinking Machine. "Mr. Hatch, did you bring those sandwiches?"

Half an hour later The Thinking Machine and Hatch appeared at police headquarters. Being naturally of a retiring, unostentatious disposition, Bates did not accompany them. Instead, he went his way fingering a bill of moderately large denomination.

Detective Mallory was at home in bed; but Detective Cunningham, another shining light, received his distinguished visitor and Hatch.

"There's a man named Howard Guerin now asleep in his state room aboard the steamer *Austriana*, which sails at five o'clock this morning—just an hour and a half from now—for Hamburg," began The Thinking Machine without any preface. "Please have him arrested immediately."

"What charge?" asked the detective.

"Really, it's of no consequence," replied The Thinking Machine. "Attempted murder, conspiracy, embezzlement, fraud—whatever you like. I can prove any or all of them."

"I'll go after him myself," said the detective.

"And there is also a young woman aboard," continued The Thinking Machine, "a Miss Hilda Fanshawe. Please have her detained, not arrested, and keep a close guard on her—not to prevent escape, but to protect her."

"Tell us some of the particulars of it," asked the detective.

"I haven't slept in more than forty-eight hours," replied The Thinking Machine. "I'll explain it all this afternoon, after I've rested a while."

———

The Thinking Machine, for the benefit of Detective Mallory and his satellites, recited briefly the salient points of the story told by the actor, Watson Richards. His listeners were Howard Guerin, tall, keen-faced, and clean-shaven; Miss Hilda Fanshawe, whose pretty face reflected her every thought; Hutchinson Hatch, and three or four headquarters men. Every eye was upon the drawn face of the diminutive scientist, as he sat far back in his chair, with squint eyes turned upward, and fingertips pressed together.

"From the facts as he stated them, we know beyond all question, in the very beginning, that Mr. Richards was used as a tool to further some conspiracy or fraud," explained The Thinking Machine. "That was obvious. So the first thing to do was to learn the identity of those persons who played the principal parts in it. From Mr. Richards' story we apparently had nothing, yet it gave us practically the names and addresses of the persons at the bottom of the thing.

"How? To find how, we'll have to consider the purpose of the conspiracy. An actor—an artist in facial impersonation, we might say—is picked up in the street and compelled to go through the mummery of a death bed scene while stupefied with drugs. Obviously this was arranged for the benefit of some person who must be convinced that he or she had witnessed a dissolution and the signature of a will, perhaps—and a will signed under the eyes of that person for whose benefit the farce was acted.

"So we assume a will was signed. We know, within reason, that the mummery was arranged for the benefit of a young woman—Miss

Fanshawe here. From the intricacy and daring of the plot, it was pretty safe to assume that a large sum of money was involved. As a matter of fact, there was—more than a million. Now, here is where we take an abstract problem and establish the identity of the actors in it. That will was signed by compulsory forgery, if I may use the phrase, by an utter stranger—a man who could not have known the handwriting of the man whose name he signed, and who was in a condition that makes it preposterous to imagine that he even attempted to sign that name. Yet the will was signed, and the conspirators had to have a signature that would bear inspection. Now, what have we left?

"When a person is incapable of signing his or her name, physically or by reason of no education, the law accepts a cross mark as a signature, when properly witnessed. We know Mr. Richards couldn't have known or imitated the signature of the old man he impersonated; but he did sign—therefore a cross mark, which could have been established beyond question in a court of law. Now, you see how I established the identity of the persons in this fraud. I got the date of the incident from Mr. Richards, then a trip to the surrogate's office told me all I wanted to know. What will had been filed for probate about that date which bore the cross mark as a signature? The records answered the question instantly—John Wallace Lawrence.

"I glanced over the will. It specifically allowed Miss Hilda Fanshawe a trivial thousand dollars a year, and yet she was Lawrence's adopted daughter. See how the joints began to fit together? Further, the will left the bulk of the property to Howard Guerin, a Mrs. Francis—since deceased, by the way—and one Frank Hughes. The men were his nephews, the woman his niece. The joints continued to fit nicely, therefore the problem was solved. It was an easy matter to find these people, once I knew their names. I found Guerin—Mr. Richards knew him as Hallman—and asked him about the matter. From the fact that he locked me up in a room of his house and kept me prisoner for two days, I was convinced that he was the principal conspirator. And so it proves."

Again there was silence. Detective Mallory took three long breaths, and asked a question. "But where was John Wallace Lawrence when this thing happened?"

"Miss Fanshawe had been in Europe, and was rushing home, knowing that her adopted father was dying," The Thinking Machine explained. "As a matter of fact, when she returned, Mr. Lawrence was dead—he died the day before the farce which had been arranged for her benefit, and at the moment his body lay in an upstairs room. He was buried two days later—a day after the imposture—and she attended his funeral. You see, there was no reason why she should have suspected anything. I don't happen to know the provisions of Lawrence's real will, but I dare say it left practically everything to her. The thousand-dollar allowance by the conspirators was a sop to stop possible legal action."

The door of the room opened, and a uniformed man thrust his head in. "Mr. Richards wants to see Professor Van Dusen," he announced.

Immediately behind him came the actor. He stopped in the door and stared at Guerin for a moment.

"Why, hello Hallman!" he remarked pleasantly. Then his eyes fell upon the girl, and a flash of recognition lighted them.

"Miss Fanshawe, permit me, Mr. Richards," said The Thinking Machine. "You have met before. This is the gentleman you saw die."

"And where is Frank Hughes?" asked Detective Mallory.

"In South Africa," replied the scientist. "I learned a great deal while I was a prisoner."

———

A deeply troubled expression suddenly appeared on Hutchinson Hatch's face that night when he was writing the story for his newspaper, and he went to the telephone and called The Thinking Machine.

"If you were guarded so closely as a prisoner in that room, how on earth did you mail that letter to me?" he inquired.

"Guerin came in to say some unpleasant things," came the reply, "and placed several letters he intended to post on the table for a moment. The letter for you was already written and stamped, and I was seeking a way to mail it, so I put it with his letters and he mailed it for me."

Hatch burst out laughing.

THE ROSWELL TIARA

Had it not been for the personal interest of a fellow savant in the case, it is hardly likely that the problem of the Roswell tiara would ever have come to the attention of The Thinking Machine. And had the problem not come to his attention, it would inevitably have gone to the police. Then there would have been a scandal in high places, a disrupted home and everlasting unhappiness to at least four persons. Perhaps it was an inkling of this latter possibility that led The Thinking Machine to take initial steps in the solution of a mystery which seemed to have only an obvious ending.

When he was first approached in the matter, The Thinking Machine was in his small laboratory, from which had gone forth truths that shocked and partially readjusted at least three of the exact sciences. His enormous head, with its long yellow hair, bobbed up and down over a little world of chemical apparatus, and the narrow, squint eyes peered with disagreeable satisfaction at a blue flame which spouted from a brazier. Martha, an aged woman who was the scientist's household staff, entered. She was not tall yet she towered commandingly above the slight figure of her eminent master. Professor Van Dusen turned to her impatiently.

"Well? Well?" he demanded shortly.

Martha handed him two cards. On one was the name Charles Wingate Field, and on the other Mrs. Richard Watson Roswell. Charles Wingate Field was a name to juggle with in astronomy—The Thinking Machine knew him well; the name of the woman was strange to him.

"The gentleman said it was very important," Martha explained, "and the poor lady was crying."

"What about?" snapped the scientist.

"Lord, sir, I didn't ask her," exclaimed Martha.

"I'll be there in a moment."

A few minutes later The Thinking Machine appeared at the door of the little reception room, which he regarded as a sort of useless glory, and the two persons there arose to meet him. One was a woman apparently of forty-five years, richly gowned, splendid of figure and with a distinct, matured beauty. Her eyes showed she had been weeping but now her tears were dried and she caught herself staring curiously at the pallid face, the keen blue eyes and the long slender hands of the scientist. The other person was Mr. Field.

There was an introduction and the scientist motioned them to seats. He himself dropped into a large cushioned chair, and looked from one to the other with a question in his eyes.

"I have been telling Mrs. Roswell some of the things you have done, Van Dusen," began Mr. Field. "I have brought her to you because this is a mystery, a problem, an abstruse problem, and it isn't the kind of thing one cares to take to the police. If you——"

"If Mrs. Roswell will tell me about it?" interrupted the scientist. He seemed to withdraw even further into the big chair. With head tilted back, eyes squinting steadily upward and white fingers pressed tip to tip he waited.

"Briefly," said Mrs. Roswell, "it has to do with the disappearance of a single small gem from a diamond tiara which I had locked in a vault—a vault of which no living person knew the combination except myself. Because of family reasons I could not go to the police, and——"

"Please begin at the beginning," requested The Thinking Machine. "Remember I know nothing whatever of you or your circumstances."

It was not unnatural that Mrs. Roswell should be surprised. Her social reign was supreme, her name was constantly to be seen in the newspapers, her entertainments were gorgeous, her social doings on an elaborate scale. She glanced at Mr. Field inquiringly, and he nodded.

"My first husband was Sidney Grantham, an Englishman," she explained. "Seven years ago he left me a widow with one child—a son Arthur—now twenty-two years old and just out of Harvard. Mr. Grantham died intestate and his whole fortune, together with the family jewels, came to me and my son. The tiara was among these jewels.

"A year ago I was married to Mr. Roswell. He, too, is a man of wealth, with one daughter, Jeanette, now nineteen years old. We live on Commonwealth Avenue and while there are many servants I know it is impossible——"

"Nothing is impossible, madam," interposed The Thinking Machine positively. "Don't say that please. It annoys me exceedingly."

Mrs. Roswell stared at him a moment then resumed:

"My bedroom is on the second floor. Adjoining and connecting with it is the bedroom of my step-daughter. This connecting door is always left unlocked because she is timid and nervous. I keep the door from my room into the hall bolted at night and Jeanette keeps the hall door of her room similarly fastened. The windows, too, are always secured at night in both rooms.

"My maid and my daughter's maid both sleep in the servant's quarters. I arranged for this because, as I was about to state, I keep about half a million dollars worth of jewels in my bedroom, locked in a small vault built into the wall. This little vault opens with a combination. Not one person knows that combination except myself. It so happens that the man who set it is dead.

"Last night, Thursday, I attended a reception and wore the tiara. My daughter remained at home. At four o'clock this morning I returned. The maids had retired; Jeanette was sleeping soundly. I took off the tiara and placed it, with my other jewels, in the vault. I know that the small diamond now missing was in its setting at that time. I locked the vault, shot the bolt, and turned the combination. Afterwards I tried the vault door to make certain it was fastened. It was then—then——"

For no apparent reason Mrs. Roswell suddenly burst into tears. The two men were silent and The Thinking Machine looked at her uneasily. He was not accustomed to women anyway, and women who wept were hopelessly beyond him.

"Well, well, what happened?" he asked brusquely at last.

"It was perhaps five o'clock when I fell asleep," Mrs. Roswell continued after a moment. "About twenty minutes later I was aroused by a scream of 'Jeanette, Jeanette, Jeanette.' Instantly I was fully awake. The screaming was that of a cockatoo which I have kept in my room for many years. It was in its usual place on a perch near the window, and seemed greatly disturbed.

"My first impression was that Jeanette had been in the room. I went into her room and even shook her gently. She was asleep so far as I could ascertain. I returned to my own room and then was amazed to see the vault door standing open. All the jewels and papers from the vault were scattered over the floor. My first thought was of burglars who had been frightened away by the cockatoo. I tried every door and every window in both Jeanette's room and mine. Everything was securely fastened.

"When I picked up the tiara, I found that a diamond was missing. It had evidently been torn out of the setting. I searched for it on the floor and inside the vault. I found nothing. Then of course I could only associate its disappearance with some act of—of my stepdaughter's. I don't believe the cockatoo would have called her name if she had not been in my room. Certainly the bird could not have opened the vault. Therefore I—I——"

There was a fresh burst of tears and for a long time no one spoke.

"Do you burn a night lamp?" asked The Thinking Machine finally.

"Yes," replied Mrs. Roswell.

"Did the bird ever disturb you at any time previous to last night—that is, I mean, at night?"

"No."

"Has it any habit of speaking the word 'Jeanette.' "

"No. I don't think I ever heard it pronounce the word more than three or four times before. It is stupid and seems to dislike her."

The Thinking Machine took down a volume of an encyclopedia which he studied for a moment.

"Have you any record anywhere of that combination?" he inquired.

"Yes, but it would have been impossi——"

The scientist made a little impatient gesture with his hands.

"Where is this record?"

"The combination begins with the figure 3," Mrs. Roswell hastened to explain. "I jotted it down in a French copy of *Les Misérables* which I keep in my room with a few other books. The first number, 3, appears on page 3, the second on page 33, and the third on page 333. The combination in full is 3-14-9. No person could possibly associate the numbers in the book with the combination even if he should notice them."

Again there was the quick, impatient gesture of the scientist's hands. Mr. Field interpreted it aright as annoyance.

"You say your daughter is nervous," The Thinking Machine said. "Is it serious? Is there any somnambulistic tendency that you know of?"

Mrs. Roswell flushed a little.

"She has a nervous disorder," she confessed at last. "But I know of no somnambulistic tendency. She has been treated by half a dozen specialists. Two or three times we feared—feared——"

She faltered and stopped. The Thinking Machine squinted at her oddly, then turned his eyes toward the ceiling again.

"I understand," he said. "You feared for her sanity. And she may have the sleep-walking habit without your knowledge?"

"Yes, she may have," faltered Mrs. Roswell.

"And now your son. Tell me something about him. He has an allowance, I suppose? Is he inclined to be studious or otherwise? Has he any love affair?"

Again Mrs. Roswell flushed. Her entire manner resented this connection of her son's name with the affair. She looked inquiringly at Mr. Field.

"I don't see——" Mr. Field began, remonstratingly.

"My son could have nothing——" Mrs. Roswell interrupted.

"Madam, you have presented an abstract problem," broke in The Thinking Machine impatiently. "I presumed you wanted a solution. Of course, if you do not——" and he made as if to arise.

"Please pardon me," said Mrs. Roswell quickly, almost tearfully. "My son has an allowance of ten thousand a year; my daughter has the same. My son is inclined to be studious along political lines, while my daughter is interested in charity. He has no love affair except—except a deep attachment for his step-sister. It is rather unfortunate——"

"I know, I know," interrupted the scientist again. "Naturally you object to any affection in that direction because of a fear for the girl's mental condition. May I ask if there is any further prejudice on your part to the girl?"

"Not the slightest," said Mrs. Roswell quickly. "I am deeply attached to her. It is only a fear for my son's happiness."

"I presume your son understands your attitude in the matter?"

"I have tried to intimate it to him without saying it openly," she explained. "I don't think he knows how serious her condition has been, and is, for that matter."

"Of your knowledge has either your son or the girl ever handled or looked into the book where the combination is written?"

"Not that I know of, or ever heard of."

"Or any of your servants?"

"No."

"Does it happen that you have this tiara with you?"

Mrs. Roswell produced it from her hand bag. It was a glittering, glistening thing, a triumph of the jeweler's art, intricate and marvelously delicate in conception yet wonderfully heavy with the dead weight of pure gold. A single splendid diamond of four or five carats blazed at its apex, and radiating from this were strings of smaller stones. One was missing from its setting. The prongs which had held it were almost straight from the force used to pry out the stone. The Thinking Machine studied the gorgeous ornament in silence.

"It is possible for you to clear up this matter without my active interference," he said at last. "You do not want it to become known outside your own family, therefore you must watch for this thief—yourself in person. Take no one into your confidence, least of all your son and step-daughter. Given the same circumstances, the A B C rules of logic—and logic is inevitable—indicate that another may disappear."

Mrs. Roswell was frankly startled, and Mr. Field leaned forward with eager interest.

"If you see how this second stone disappears," continued The Thinking Machine musingly, without heeding in the slightest the effect of his words on the others, "you will know what became of the first and will be able to recover both."

"If another attempt is to be made," exclaimed Mrs. Roswell apprehensively, "would it not be better to send the jewels to a safe deposit? Would I not be in danger myself?"

"It is perfectly possible that if the jewels were removed, the vault would be opened just the same," said The Thinking Machine quietly, enigmatically, while his visitors stared. "Leave the jewels where they are. You may be assured that you are in no personal danger whatever. If you learn what you seek, you need not communicate with me again. If you do not, I will personally investigate the matter. On no condition whatever interrupt or attempt to prevent anything that may happen."

Mr. Field arose; the interview seemed to be at an end. He had one last question.

"Have you any theory of what actually happened?" he asked. "How was the jewel taken?"

"If I told you, you wouldn't believe it," said The Thinking Machine, curtly. "Good day."

It was on the third day following that Mrs. Roswell hurriedly summoned The Thinking Machine to her home. When he arrived she was deeply agitated.

"Another of the small stones has been stolen from the tiara," she told him hurriedly. "The circumstances were identical with those of the first theft, even to the screaming of the cockatoo. I watched as you suggested, have been watching each night but last night was so weary that I fell asleep. The cockatoo awoke me. Why would Jeanette——"

"Let me see the apartments," suggested the scientist.

Thus he was ushered into the room which was the center of the mystery. Again he examined the tiara, then studied the door of the vault. Afterwards he casually picked up and verified the record of the combination, locked and unlocked the vault twice, after which he examined the fastenings of the door and the windows. This done he went over and peered inquisitively at the cockatoo on its perch.

The bird was a giant of its species, pure white, with a yellow crest which drooped in exaggerated melancholy. The cockatoo resented the impertinence and had not The Thinking Machine moved quickly, would have torn off his spectacles.

A door from another room opened and a girl—Jeanette—entered. She was tall, slender, and exquisitely proportioned with a great cloud of ruddy gold hair. Her face was white with the dead white of illness and infinite weariness was in her eyes. She was startled at sight of a stranger.

"I beg your pardon," she said. "I didn't know——" and started to retire.

Professor Van Dusen acknowledged an introduction to her by a glance and a nod then turned quickly and looked at the cockatoo which was quarreling volubly with crest upraised. Mrs. Roswell's attention, too, was attracted by the angry attitude of her pet. She grasped the scientist's arm quickly.

"The bird!" she exclaimed.

"Jeanette, Jeanette, Jeanette," screamed the cockatoo, shrilly.

Jeanette dropped wearily into a chair, heeding neither the tense attitude of her step-mother nor the quarrelings of the cockatoo.

"You don't sleep well, Miss Roswell?" asked The Thinking Machine.

"Oh, yes," the girl replied. "I seem to sleep enough, but I am always very tired. And I dream constantly, nearly always my dreams are of the cockatoo. I imagine he calls my name."

Mrs. Roswell looked quickly at Professor Van Dusen. He crossed to the girl and examined her pulse.

"Do you read much?" he asked. "Did you ever read this?" and he held up the copy of *Les Misérables*.

"I don't read French well enough," she replied. "I have read it in English."

The conversation was desultory for a time and finally The Thinking Machine arose. In the drawing room down stairs he gave Mrs. Roswell some instructions which amazed her exceedingly, and went his way.

Jeanette retired about eleven o'clock that night and in an hour was sleeping soundly. But Mrs. Roswell was up when the clock struck one. She had previously bolted the doors of the two rooms and fastened the windows. Now she arose from her seat, picked up a small jar from her table, and crept cautiously, even stealthily to the bed whereon Jeanette lay, pale almost as the sheets. The girl's hands were outstretched in an attitude of utter exhaustion. Mrs. Roswell bent low over them a moment, then stole back to her own room. Half an hour later she was asleep.

A FOOL OF GOOD INTENTION

Early next morning Mrs. Roswell 'phoned to The Thinking Machine, and they talked for fifteen minutes. She was apparently explaining something and the scientist gave crisp, monosyllabic answers. When the wire was disconnected he called up two other persons on the 'phone. One of them was Dr. Henderson, noted alienist; the other was Dr. Forrester, a nerve specialist of international repute. To both he said:

"I want to show you the most extraordinary thing you have ever seen."

———

The dim light of the night lamp cast strange, unexpected shadows, half revealing yet half hiding, the various objects in Mrs. Roswell's room. The bed made a great white splotch in the shadows, and the only other conspicuous point was the bright silver dial of the jewel vault. From the utter darkness of Jeanette Roswell's room came the steady, regular breathing of a person asleep; the cockatoo was gone from his perch. Outside was the faint night-throb of a city at rest. In the distance a clock boomed four times.

Finally the stillness was broken by a faint creaking, the tread of a light foot, and Jeanette, robed mystically in white, appeared in the door of her room. Her eyes were wide open, staring, her face was chalk-like, her hair tumbled in confusion about her head and here and there was flecked with the glint of the night-light.

The girl paused and from somewhere in the shadows came a quick gasp, instantly stifled. Then, unhearing, she moved slowly but without hesitation across the room to a table whereon lay several books. She stooped over this and when she straightened up again she held *Les Misérables* in her hand. Several times the leaves fluttered through her fingers, and thrice she held the book close to her eyes in the uncertain light, then nodded as if satisfied and carefully replaced it as she had found it.

From the table she went straight toward the silver dial which gleamed a reflection of light. As she went, another figure detached itself noiselessly from the shadows and crept toward her from behind. As the girl leaned forward to place her hand on the dial a steady ray of light from an electric bulb struck her full in the face. She did not flinch nor by the slightest sign show that she was aware of it. From her face the light traveled to each of her hands in turn.

The dial whirled in her fingers several times and then stopped with a click, the bolt snapped and the vault door opened. Conspicuously in front lay the tiara glittering mockingly. Again from the shadows there came a quick gasp as the girl lifted the regal toy and tumbled it on the floor. Again the gasp was stifled.

With quick-moving, nervous hands she dragged the jewels out, permitting them to fall. She seemed to be seeking something else, seeking vainly, apparently, for after a while she rose with a sigh, staring into the vault hopelessly. She stood thus for a dozen heartbeats, then the low, guarded voice of the second figure was heard—low yet singularly clear of enunciation.

"What is it you seek?"

"The letters," she replied dreamily yet distinctly. There was a pause and she turned suddenly as if to re-enter her room. As she did so the light again flashed in her glassy eyes, and the second figure laid a detaining hand on her arm. She started a little, staggered, her eyes closed suddenly to open again in abject terror as she stared into the face before her. She screamed wildly, piercingly, gazed a moment then sank down fainting.

"Dr. Forrester, she needs you now."

It was the calm, unexcited, impersonal voice of The Thinking Machine. He touched a button in the wall and the room was flooded with light. Drs. Forrester and Henderson, suddenly revealed with Mr. and Mrs. Roswell and Arthur Grantham, came forward and lifted the senseless body. Grantham, too, rushed to her with pained, horror-stricken face. Mrs. Roswell dropped limply into a chair; her husband stood beside her helplessly stroking her hair.

"It's all right," said The Thinking Machine. "It's only shock."

Grantham turned on him savagely, impetuously, and danger lay in the boyish eyes.

"It's a lie!" he said fiercely. "She didn't steal those diamonds."

"How do you know?" asked The Thinking Machine coldly.

"Because—because I took them myself," the young man blurted. "If I had known there was to be any such trick as this, I should never have consented to it."

His mother stared up at him in open-eyed wonder.

"How did you remove the jewels from the setting?" asked The Thinking Machine, still quietly.

"I—I did it with my fingers."

"Take out one of these for me," and The Thinking Machine offered him the tiara.

Grantham snatched it from his hand and tugged at it frantically while the others stared, but each jewel remained in its setting. Finally he sank down on the bed beside the still figure of the girl he loved. His face was crimson.

"Your intentions are good, but you're a fool," commented The Thinking Machine tartly. "I know you did not take the jewels—you have proven it yourself—and I may add that Miss Roswell did not take them."

The stupefied look on Grantham's face was reflected in those of his mother and step-father. Drs. Forrester and Henderson were busy with the girl, heedless of the others.

"Then where are the jewels?" Mrs. Roswell demanded.

The Thinking Machine turned and squinted at her with a slight suggestion of irritable reproach in his manner.

"Safe and easily found," he replied impatiently. He lifted the unconscious girl's hand and allowed his fingers to rest on her pulse for a moment, then turned to the medical men. "Would you have believed that somnambulistic sub-consciousness would have taken just this form?" he asked curtly.

"Not unless I had seen it," replied Dr. Henderson, frankly.

"It's a remarkable mental condition—remarkable," commented Dr. Forrester.

———

It was a weirdly simple recital of the facts as he had found them that The Thinking Machine told downstairs in the drawing room an hour later. Dawn was breaking over the city, and the faces of those who had waited and watched for just what had happened showed weariness. Yet they listened, listened with all their faculties as the eminent scientist talked. Young Grantham sat white-faced and nervous; Jeanette was sleeping quietly upstairs with her maid on watch.

"The problem in itself was not a difficult one," The Thinking Machine began as he lounged in a big chair with eyes upturned. "The unusual, not to say strange, features, which seemed to make it more difficult served to simplify it as a matter of fact. When I had all the facts, I had the solution in the main. It was adding a fact to a fact to get a good result as one might add two and two to get four.

"In the first place burglars were instantly removed as a possibility. They would have taken everything, not one small stone. Then what? Mr. Grantham here? His mother assured me that he was quiet and studious of habit, and had an allowance of ten thousand a year. Then remember always that he no more than anyone else could have entered the rooms. The barred doors excluded the servants too.

"Then we had only you, Mrs. Roswell, and your step-daughter. There would have been no motive for you to remove the jewel unless your object was to throw suspicion on the girl. I didn't believe you capable of this. So there was left somnambulism or a willful act of your step-daughter's. There was no motive for the last—your daughter has ten thousand a year. Then sleep-walking alone remained. Sleep-walking it was. I am speaking now of the opening of the vault."

Grantham leaned forward in his chair gripping its arms fiercely. The mother saw, and one of her white hands was laid gently on his. He glanced at her impatiently then turned to The Thinking Machine. Mr. Roswell, the alienist, and the specialist, followed the cold clear logic as if fascinated.

"If somnambulism, then who was the somnambulist?" The Thinking Machine resumed after a moment. "It did not seem to be you, Mrs. Roswell. You are not of a nervous temperament; you are a normal healthy woman. If we accept as true your statement that you were aroused in bed by the cockatoo screaming 'Jeanette' we prove that you were not the somnambulist. Your step-daughter? She suffered from a nervous disorder so pronounced that you had fears for her mental condition. With everyone else removed, she was the somnambulist. Even the cockatoo said that.

"Now let us see how it would have been possible to open the vault. We admit that no one except yourself knew the combination. But a record of that combination did appear; therefore it was possible for some one else to learn it. Your step-daughter does not know that combination when she is in a normal condition. I won't say that she knows it when in the somnambulistic state, but I will say that when in that condition *she knows where there is a record of it*. How she learned this I don't know. It is not a legitimate part of the problem.

"Be that as it may she was firmly convinced that something she was seeking, something of deep concern to her, was in that vault. It might *not* have been in the vault but in her abnormal condition she thought it was. She was not after jewels—her every act even tonight showed that. What else? Letters. I knew it was a letter, or letters, before she said so herself. What was in these letters is of no consequence here. You, Mrs. Roswell considered it your duty to hide them—possibly destroy them."

Both husband and son turned on Mrs. Roswell inquiringly. She stared from one to the other helplessly, pleadingly.

"The letters contained——" she started to explain.

"Never mind that, it's none of our business," curtly interrupted The Thinking Machine. "If there is a family skeleton, it's yours.

"Even with the practical certain knowledge that Miss Roswell *did* open the vault," The Thinking Machine resumed placidly, "and that she opened it in precisely the manner you saw tonight, I took one more step to prove it. This was after the second stone had disappeared. I instructed Mrs. Roswell to place a little strawberry jam on her step-daughter's hands while she was sleeping. If this jam appeared on the book the next time the vault was found open, it proved finally and conclusively that Miss Roswell opened it. I chose strawberry jam because it was unusual. I dare say no one who might have a purpose in opening that vault would go around with strawberry jam on his hands. This jam did appear on the book, and then I summoned you, Dr. Forrester, and you, Dr. Henderson. You know the rest. I may add that Mr. Grantham in attempting to take the theft upon himself merely made a fool of himself. No person with bare fingers could have torn out one of the stones."

There was a long pause, and deep silence while the problem as seen by The Thinking Machine was considered in the minds of his hearers. Grantham at last broke the silence.

"Where are the two stones that are missing?"

"Oh yes," said The Thinking Machine easily, as if that trivial point had escaped him. "Mrs. Roswell, will you please have the cockatoo brought in?" he asked, and then explained to the others: "I had the bird removed from the room tonight for fear it would interrupt at the wrong moment."

Mrs. Roswell arose and gave some instructions to a servant who was waiting outside. He went away and returned later with a startled expression on his graven face.

"The bird is dead, madam," he reported.

"Dead!" repeated Mrs. Roswell.

"Good!" said The Thinking Machine, rubbing his hands briskly together. "Bring it in anyhow."

"Why, what could have killed it?" asked Mrs. Roswell, bewildered.

"Indigestion," replied the scientist. "Here is the thief."

He turned suddenly to the servant who had entered bearing the cockatoo in state on a silver tray.

"Who? I?" gasped the astonished servant.

"No, this fellow," replied The Thinking Machine as he picked up the dead bird. "He had the opportunity; he had the pointed instrument necessary to pry out a stone—note the sharp hooked bill; and he had the strength to do it. Besides all that he confessed a fondness for bright things when he tried to snatch my eyeglasses. He saw Miss Roswell drop the tiara on the floor; its brightness fascinated him. He pried out the stone and swallowed it. It pained him, and he screamed 'Jeanette.' This same thing happened on two occasions. Your encyclopedia will tell you that the cockatoo has more strength in that sharp beak than you could possibly exercise with two fingers unless you had a steel instrument."

Later that day The Thinking Machine sent to Mrs. Roswell the two missing diamonds, the glass head of a hat pin and a crystal shoe button which he had recovered from the dead bird. His diagnosis of the case was acute indigestion.

The Problem of the Red Rose

Through the open windows of a pleasantly sunny little sitting room a lazy breath of early summer drifted in, and gently stirred the wayward hair of a girl who leaned forward over a small writing desk with her head resting upon one white forearm, and her face hidden. Her attitude was one of utter collapse, complete abandonment perhaps to grief or perhaps to actual physical suffering; yet there was no movement of the slender, graceful body, nothing to indicate even a passive interest in her surroundings—just this silent, motionless figure, alone.

One arm, the left, swung down listlessly at her side, and in that hand she held a single red rose, a splendid, full-blown crimson blossom. The thorny stem touched the floor, and the leaves swayed rhythmically, playthings of the caressing breeze. On the green stem, just below the girl's tightly clenched hand, was a single stain—a drop of blood—as if the thorn had pierced the delicate flesh. On the desk, from which dainty writing trinkets had been pushed back, was a florist's box, open. It was from this box evidently that the red rose had been taken. The wax paper which had been wrapped round the flower was torn.

A Dresden clock on the mantel whirred faintly and chimed the hour of five; but the girl gave not the slightest indication of having heard. And then after a moment a door opened and a maid appeared. She paused as her eyes fell upon the figure of the young woman, made as if to speak, then instead silently withdrew, leaving the door slightly open. She did not seem surprised that no notice was taken of her. A dozen times she had found her young mistress like this, and it was always after the box had come from the florist's with the single red rose. She sighed a little as she went out.

The hands of the clock crept on round the dial slowly, to five minutes past the hour, then to ten, and finally to fifteen. Then there came a scampering of soft feet along the hall, and a white, shaggy little dog thrust his head in at the door inquisitively. Helterskelter he came tumbling in and planted two soiled forefeet in the girl's lap as he awaited the caress which was always ready for him. Now it didn't come. He backed away and regarded her thoughtfully. It must be some new sort of game she was playing. He crouched on the floor and barked playfully; but she didn't look round.

Evidently this was not what was expected of him. He scampered back and forth across the room twice, then returned to the motionless figure and placed his feet in her lap again. She wouldn't look. He barked, whined softly, then off like the wind round the room again. He stopped on her left side this time—the side where the arm swung down, and the hand clutched the rose. His moist tongue caressed the closed hand, and sniffed at it insistently. Suddenly he seemed dazed, and reeled uncertainly as if from an unexpected blow. He whined again as if choking; there was a rattle in his shaggy throat; and then began a violent whirling, twisting, which continued till he fell. After a while he lay still with all four feet turned upward and glazed, staring eyes. And yet the girl hadn't moved.

The hands of the clock crept on. At five minutes of six o'clock the maid appeared at the door again, paused for a moment, then ventured in. "Will you dress for dinner, ma'am?" she inquired.

The girl didn't answer.

"It's nearly six o'clock, ma'am," said the maid.

Still there was no answer.

The maid approached her young mistress and touched her lightly on the shoulder. "You'll be late, unless——" she began.

And then something about the unresisting, impassive figure frightened her. She shook the girl sharply and called her name many times. Finally with an effort she raised the shapely head. What she saw in the upturned face wrung scream after scream from her lips, now suddenly ashen, and turning she staggered toward the door with unutterable horror in her widely distended eyes. She clutched at the door frame to steady herself, screamed again, and fell forward, fainting. There they found them: Miss Edna Burdock dead with hideously distorted face—a face upon which was written some awful agony—and the rose still clasped so fiercely in her hand that the thorns had pierced the palm; her little dog Tatters dead beside her; and the maid, Goodwin, unconscious. For half an hour two servants worked over the maid; but when at last she opened her eyes she only screamed and babbled incoherently. There were no marks on Miss Burdock's body save the prick of thorns in her left hand—nothing that would indicate the manner of death; nor was there the slightest thing to explain the death of the dog.

———

"The police are not at all certain that Miss Burdock's death was due to anything more mysterious than heart failure," Hutchinson Hatch, reporter, was explaining. "In that event, of course———"

"In that event, of course," interrupted Professor Augustus S. F. X. Van Dusen—The Thinking Machine—crabbedly, "their theory must be that the pet dog died at the same time of the same disease?"

"That seems to be about the way they look at it, although there are several curious features," the reporter went on; "for instance, the expression on her face." He shuddered a little. "I saw her. It was awful. The dog too. There was not a mark or scratch on the dog—not even the prick of a thorn like that in the girl's palm, therefore heart failure seems to be the only thing that will cover the case, unless———"

"Fidldesticks!" exclaimed the irritable little scientist. "Persons who die of heart failure don't show suffering in their faces, and little dogs don't have heart failure. What did the autopsy show?"

"Nothing illuminating," responded the reporter. "There was no trace of poison in Miss Burdock's system; a blood test showed her blood to be about normal, and yet she was dead. There was a peculiar constriction of the heart, and the same thing was true of the dog. The medical examiner's report brought out these facts; but there was no poison—they were just dead."

"When did this happen, Mr. Hatch?"

"Yesterday afternoon, Monday."

"You tell me the maid found the body. Has she said anything about noticing any odor when she entered the room?"

"Not a word; but there are curious things——"

"In a minute, Mr. Hatch," interrupted The Thinking Machine impatiently. "Were the windows open?"

"Yes," replied the reporter. "She was sitting at her desk, between two open windows."

The man of science dropped back in his chair, and for a long time sat silent with the perpetually squinting eyes turned upward, and slender white fingers pressed tip to tip. Hatch lighted a cigarette, smoked it, and threw the butt away before he spoke.

"There are peaches in the market, I think, Mr. Hatch," said the scientist at last. "When you go out, buy one, cut the meat off, crush the kernel, take it to the maid, and ask her to smell it. Ask her if she noticed yesterday any odor similar to that when she entered the room and was near the girl's body."

Hatch absorbed the instructions wonderingly, then ventured a remark. "I presume you are thinking of poison. Isn't there a chance that despite the normal condition of her blood some sort of poison was introduced into her system—I mean that the thorns of the rose might have been poisoned, for instance."

"You say there was no scratch or thorn prick on the dog?" asked The Thinking Machine in answer.

"No mark of any sort."

"And the dog is dead. That answers your question, Mr. Hatch." He relapsed into silence.

"Poison on the thorns could not have killed both of them, because only the woman's hand showed the marks?" Hatch asked.

"Precisely," was the reply. "Unless we allow for coincidence, and that has never been reduced to a scientific law, we must say that both the woman and the dog died of the same cause. When we know that, we prove that the thorn prick had nothing to do with the woman's death. Two and two make four, Mr. Hatch, not sometimes but all the time. And so what have we left?"

"I don't see that we have anything left," remarked Hatch frankly. "If there is no outward cause, how can we——"

"The mere fact that there is no apparent cause, or outward cause, as you term it, makes the manner of death of both the woman and the dog perfectly plain," declared The Thinking Machine belligerently.

"There is no mystery about that at all—it's obvious. Our problem is not what killed her, but who killed her."

"Yes, that seems quite clear," the reporter admitted.

Minute after minute passed while the scientist sat staring upward. Finally he lowered his eyes to the face of the newspaperman. "Where did this red rose come from?" he demanded.

"I was going to tell you about that," responded Hatch. "It came from Lamperti's, a florist. The police are investigating it now. It seems, according to a statement of the manager of the shop, that on June 16 he received a special delivery letter from Washington with only a typewritten, unsigned slip of paper enclosed. This directed that one dozen red roses be sent to Miss Burdock, one at a time on specified days, Mondays, Wednesdays, and Saturdays. They accepted the order—there was no way to return the money anyway—and so——"

He paused to gaze curiously into the eyes of The Thinking Machine. They were drawn down to mere slits of watery blue and some subtle change had altered the straight line of the lips.

"Well, well!" grumbled the scientist. "Go on!"

"As a rule the long box with the one rose was delivered at the house by one of the wagons of the company," the reporter continued; "but some days when the wagon was not going in that direction the box was sent by a messenger boy. This last rose went to her by messenger."

"And have all the roses been sent?"

"So the manager says."

"And where is the red rose—the one she had in her hand when found?"

"Detective Mallory has it in charge, I suppose," explained the reporter. "He has an idea that Miss Burdock was killed by poison on the thorns; so he stripped them off and sent them to a chemist to see if any trace of poison could be found. I presume he kept the flower and the box it came in."

"That's just like Mallory," commented the scientist testily. "Whenever the police want to keep a cat's teeth from falling out they cut off its tail. Now tell me something about Miss Burdock herself. Who was she? What was she? What were her circumstances?" He settled back in his chair for a categorical answer.

"She was the only daughter of Plympton Burdock; a man who is not wealthy, but who is well to do," answered Hatch. "She lived at home with her father, her mother, and a younger brother, a chap about eighteen or nineteen years old. She was something of a social favorite, although not yet quite twenty-one, and went about a great deal; so——"

"So naturally a great many men, some of whom admired her," The Thinking Machine finished for him. "Now who are the men? Tell me about her love affairs."

"It hasn't appeared yet that there was a love affair, in the sense you mean. At least, if there was, no one knew of it."

"Doesn't the maid, Goodwin, know?" insisted the scientist.

"She says she doesn't."

"But somebody sent the rose. The mere fact that she received the one rose a dozen times indicates that someone was interested in her. Therefore, who was it? Who?"

"That's what the police are trying to find out now."

The Thinking Machine arose suddenly, picked up his hat and planted it aggressively on his enormous yellow head. "I'm going to the florist's," he said. "You get the peach and see the maid Goodwin. Meet me at police headquarters in an hour."

It required ten minutes for The Thinking Machine to reach the florist's shop, and in five minutes more the manager was at liberty.

"All I want to know," the scientist explained, "is the day you sent the first rose of that dozen to Miss Burdock, and I should like to see your records of delivery. That is, when a package is delivered either by your wagon or by messenger you get a receipt for it? Yes. I should like to see those, please."

The manager obligingly consulted his records. "The letter with the enclosure was received on June 16," he explained as he ran his finger down the book. "It came in the morning mail. June 16 was Monday; therefore the first rose of the dozen was sent that afternoon, Monday."

"Are you absolutely certain of that?" demanded The Thinking Machine. "A—a person's life may depend on that record."

The manager stared at him in frank astonishment, then arose. "I can make sure," he said. He went to a cabinet and took out another book—a delivery receipt book, and fluttered the leaves through his fingers. At last he laid it before The Thinking Machine and indicated an entry with his finger. "There it is," he said. "Monday, June 16, at five-thirty in the afternoon. The book was signed by Edna Burdock in person. See."

The Thinking Machine squinted down at the entry for a minute or more in silence. "From that date forward one rose was sent every Monday, Wednesday, and Saturday without a break until the dozen were delivered?" he asked at last.

"Yes; that was the direction. Run through the book on the dates it should have been sent and see, if you like."

The scientist heeded the suggestion, and for ten minutes or so was engrossed in the record. "These slips?" he inquired, as he looked up. "I find three of them."

"Those were the occasions when we didn't happen to have a wagon going in that direction," the manager explained; "so the box was sent by special messenger. Each messenger took a receipt and returned it here. In that way those receipts became a part of our record."

The Thinking Machine scrutinized the slips carefully, made a note of the dates on them, then closed the record book. That seemed to be all. Fifteen minutes later Plympton Burdock, father of the dead girl, received a card from a servant, glanced at it, nodded, and The Thinking Machine was ushered in.

"I should not have disturbed you, believe me, if the necessity for it had not been pressing in the interest of justice," the scientist apologized. "Just one or two questions, please."

Burdock regarded the little man curiously, and motioned to a seat.

"First," began The Thinking Machine, "was your daughter engaged to be married at the time of her—her death?"

"No," replied Burdock.

"She did receive attention, however?"

"Certainly. All girls of her age do. Really, Mr.—Mr.—" and he glanced at the card—"Mr. Van Dusen, this matter is entirely beyond discussion. We believe, my wife and I, that death was due to natural causes, and have so informed the police. I hope it may go no further."

The Thinking Machine looked at him sharply with some strange new expression in his squint eyes. "The investigation won't stop now, Mr. Burdock," he said coldly. "I don't know your object in—in seeking to stop it."

"I don't want to stop it," declared Burdock quickly. "We are convinced that no good can come of an investigation, because there is no ground for suspicion, and certainly it is not pleasant to have one's family affairs constantly pawed over when it is a foregone conclusion that nothing will result except unpleasant notoriety which merely adds to the burden that we now have to bear."

The Thinking Machine understood and nodded. It was almost an apology. "Well, just one more question, please," he said. "What is the name of the man whose attentions to your daughter you in person forbade?"

"How do you know of that?" blazed Burdock quickly.

"What is his name?" repeated The Thinking Machine.

"I will not discuss the matter further with you," was the reply.

"In the interests of justice I demand his name!" The Thinking Machine insisted.

Burdock stared at the slight figure before him with growing horror in his face. "You don't mean to say you suspect——" He stopped. "My God! if I thought that I'd——How was she killed, if she was killed?" he concluded.

"His name, please," urged The Thinking Machine. "If you don't give it to me, you will place me under the necessity of asking the police to compel you to give it. I'd prefer not to."

Burdock seemed not to heed the speech. His face had gone perfectly white, and he stood staring past the scientist, out the window. His hands were clenched tightly and the fingers were working. "If he did! If he did!" he repeated fiercely. Suddenly he recovered himself and glared down at his visitor. "I beg your pardon," he said simply. His name is—is Paul K. Darrow."

"Of this city," said The Thinking Machine. It was not a question; it was a statement of fact.

"Of this city," repeated Burdock—"at least formerly of this city. He left here, I am informed, four or five weeks ago."

The Thinking Machine went his way, leaving Burdock sitting with his face in his hands. A few minutes later he appeared in Detective Mallory's office at police headquarters. The officer was sitting with his feet on his desk, smoking furiously, with a dozen deep wrinkles in his brow. He hailed the scientist almost cordially, something unusual for him.

"What do you make of it?" he demanded as he arose.

"Let me see your directory for a moment, please," replied The Thinking Machine. He bent over the book, ran down a page or so of the D's, then finally looked up.

"We don't seem to be able to establish a crime, even," Detective Mallory confessed. "I had the thorns examined, and the chemist reports that there is not a trace of poison about them."

"Silly in the first place," remarked The Thinking Machine ungraciously enough. "Is the rose here?"

The detective produced it from a drawer of his desk, whereupon The Thinking Machine did several things with it which he didn't understand. First he waved it about in the air at arm's length, then took two steps forward and sniffed. Then he waved it about much closer to him and sniffed. Detective Mallory looked on in mingled curiosity and disgust. Finally the scientist held it close to his nose and sniffed, then examined the petals closely, after which he laid it on the desk again.

"And the box the rose was delivered in?" queried the scientist.

Silently the detective produced that. The Thinking Machine sniffed at it cautiously, then turned it over to examine the handwriting on the address.

"Know who wrote this?" he inquired.

"Someone at the florist's," was the reply.

"Can you lend me a man for half an hour or so?" asked the scientist next.

"Oh, I suppose so," grumbled Detective Mallory. "But what's it all about, anyway?"

"Perhaps I may be able to tell you at the end of the half hour," The Thinking Machine assured him. "Meanwhile lend me the man you said I could have."

Detective Downey was called in, and the diminutive scientist led him into the hall, where he gave him some definite directions. Downey went out the front door at full speed. The Thinking Machine returned to Detective Mallory's private room, to find the officer sulking, like a boy.

"Where'd you send him?" he growled.

"Wait till he comes back and I'll tell you," was the reply. "It isn't necessary to get excited about something that we know nothing of. I'm saving you some excitement."

He dropped back into a chair and sat there idly twiddling his thumbs while Detective Mallory glared at him. After a few minutes the door was thrown open violently and Hutchinson Hatch entered. He was frankly excited.

"Well?" demanded The Thinking Machine without looking round.

"When she smelled that crushed kernel she fainted!" said Hatch explosively.

"Fainted?" repeated the scientist. "Fainted?" The tone was hardly one of surprise, and yet——

"Yes, she took one whiff, and screamed and went right over," the reporter rushed on.

"Dear me! Dear me!" commented The Thinking Machine. He sat still looking up. "Wait a few minutes," he advised. "Let's see what Downey gets."

At the end of fifteen minutes Downey returned. His chief glared at him curiously as he entered and as he handed a piece of paper to The Thinking Machine. That imperturbable man of science examined the paper closely, then handed it to Detective Mallory.

"Is that the handwriting on the flower box?" he asked.

Mallory, Downey, and Hatch compared it together. The verdict was unanimous: "Yes."

"Then the man who wrote it is the man you want," declared The Thinking Machine flatly. "His name is Paul K. Darrow. Detective Downey knows his address."

———

Two days passed. Professor Van Dusen stood beside his laboratory table poking idly at the dismembered legs of a frog with a short copper wire. Each time the point touched the flesh there was a spasmodic twitching of the limbs, a simulation of living contraction and extension. There beside the table Hutchinson Hatch found him.

"Watch this a moment, Mr. Hatch," requested the scientist. "It bears, in a way, on our problem in hand."

Then began a rhythmic swinging of his slender hand, not unlike the beat of the musician's baton, the wire touching the frog's legs at each downward swing. Hatch had seen a similar demonstration before.

"Watch the strokes," said the scientist, "and watch the legs after the twentieth."

"Fourteen, fifteen, sixteen," Hatch counted. Each time the wire touched, and each time came the spasmodic motion. "Seventeen, eighteen, nineteen, twenty."

The Thinking Machine, instead of touching the twenty-first time, held the wire aloft. At the instant it would have touched the flesh, according to the beat, there came the same quick, spasmodic twitch, and then the legs were still.

"You see the effect is precisely as if I had touched them the twenty-first time," explained The Thinking Machine, "and that, Mr. Hatch, is one of the things science doesn't attempt to explain. It can be explained some day—it will be explained, but——" He paused. "Darrow hasn't been captured yet?" he said.

"No; no trace of him yet," was the reply. "The police have sent out a general alarm for him all over the country, and today Burdock increased the reward he offered from five thousand to ten thousand dollars."

"One of my objections to dealing with the police is that they are prone to jump at conclusions," remarked The Thinking Machine. "I didn't say, of course, that Darrow was a murderer. He may have killed Miss Burdock—he probably did—but it isn't conclusive at all. Still he is the next link in the chain, so his presence is necessary."

Hatch gazed at him in amazement, and a hundred questions rushed to his lips. They were stilled by the sudden appearance in the doorway of a young man. A soft hat was pulled down over his eyes, and he was crouching as if about to spring. One hand, the right, was in his coat pocket, clutching something fiercely. His face was perfectly pallid, and roving, glittering eyes blazed with madness.

"Come in," suggested The Thinking Machine calmly.

"I—I must talk to you, quick!" the young man burst out. "It's a matter of the most vital importance, and——"

"I'm at your service, Mr. Darrow," remarked The Thinking Machine pleasantly. "Have a seat."

Darrow! Hatch was startled, made speechless, by the uncanny appearance of this man whom the police of the entire continent were seeking. Darrow was still crouching there in the doorway, staring at them.

"I risked everything to come here," declared the young man—and there was a menace in his tone. "I was on the stoop about to ring the bell when I glanced back and saw Detective Mallory turn the corner. I didn't wait to ring—the door was unfastened and I came on in. Mallory is probably coming here. I must talk to you—and I won't be taken alive. Do you understand what I say?"

"Perfectly," replied The Thinking Machine. "Mr. Mallory won't see you. Come in out of the door."

"No tricks!" warned Darrow fiercely.

"No tricks. Sit down."

With furtive glances to right and left along the hall, the young man entered and dropped into a seat in a corner, facing them. There was a long, tense silence, and finally the doorbell rang. Darrow half rose and made as if to take his right hand from his pocket.

"That's Mallory," remarked The Thinking Machine, and he started toward the door.

Darrow took one step forward, blocking his way. "Understand, please," he began in a low, even voice. "I am utterly desperate, and I won't be taken! If you attempt to betray me, I——" He stopped.

The Thinking Machine walked round him to the door leading into the hall. Martha, his aged servant, was just passing.

"Mr. Mallory is at the door, Martha," said the scientist. "Tell him I am not in; but that I shall be at police headquarters within an hour, and Mr. Darrow will come with me."

He stepped back into the laboratory and closed the door, without even a glance at his visitor. They heard Martha open the front door, then they heard Mallory's heavy voice, finally Martha's answer, then the door was closed, and Martha's footsteps passed along the hall. Darrow suddenly rushed to the window and glanced out.

"All right, Mr. Darrow," remarked the little scientist, as he sat down. "I know now you are innocent; I know why you have been hiding out, I know why you came here to see me, and I understand too your deep grief; so we can come immediately to the vital things."

The young man turned and glared at the small, impassive figure. "You said I would be at police headquarters with you in an hour," he said accusingly.

"Certainly," agreed the scientist impatiently. "As an innocent man you will go there of your own free will, with me."

The young man dropped into a chair and sat there for a long time with his face in his hands. After a while Hatch saw a teardrop trickle through the unsteady fingers, and the shoulders moved convulsively. The Thinking Machine sat with head tilted back, squinting upward and fingers at rest, tip to tip.

"This trouble between you and Mr. Burdock?" suggested the scientist at last.

"You don't know the malignant hatred he has for me," said Darrow suddenly. "He is not a man of great wealth, but he is a man of great power, great influence, and if I should fall into the hands of the police with the circumstantial case against me that now exists he would bring all that power and influence to bear against me, with the result that I should be railroaded to a felon's grave. I don't know just how he would do it; but he would do it. I'm afraid of him—that's why I came here to see you when I wouldn't dare go to the police. I won't be taken by the police until I know I can prove my innocence; then I will surrender."

The Thinking Machine nodded.

"The enmity existing between us is of years' standing, and is not of importance here," Darrow went on. "But I know this man's power—I have felt it all my life—he has brought me to the edge of starvation half a dozen times, pursued me in every walk of life, until now—now if I should have to commit murder, he would be the victim. I'm telling you this because——"

"All this is of no consequence," interrupted The Thinking Machine shortly. "Who poisoned the rose?"

"I don't know," replied Darrow helplessly.

"You must have some idea," insisted The Thinking Machine.

"I did have an idea," was the reply. "I went this morning to a place to see a—a person whom I intended to accuse openly of the crime, taking the chance of capture myself, much as I dreaded it; but there was no one there. The door was locked; a servant connected with the apartment house told me that the—the person had not been there for a day or so."

The Thinking Machine turned quickly in his chair and glared at Darrow curiously.

"What's her name?" he demanded sharply.

"I don't know that she could have had anything to do with it," warned Darrow. "It seems awful to suggest such a thing, and yet——" He stopped. "I will go there with you to see her if you wish."

"Mr. Hatch," directed The Thinking Machine, "step into the next room there and telephone for a cab." He turned again to Darrow. "She threatened you, or Miss Burdock, I imagine?"

"Yes," said Darrow reluctantly.

"And now, please, one last question," said the little scientist. "What relation existed between you and Miss Burdock?"

"She was my wife," Darrow replied in a low voice. "We were secretly married four months ago."

"Um-m," mused the scientist. "I imagined as much."

———

Detective Mallory impatiently strode back and forth across his private office, his brain turbulent with conjecture. The telephone bell rang; The Thinking Machine was at the other end of the wire.

"Come at once and bring the medical examiner to the Craddock apartments!" commanded the irritable voice of the little scientist.

"Another murder?" demanded the detective, aghast.

"No, a suicide," was the reply. "Good by."

Detective Mallory and Medical Examiner Francis found The Thinking Machine, Hutchinson Hatch, and Paul K. Darrow in the sitting room of a small apartment on the fourth floor. Some sinister thing lay outstretched on a couch, covered with a sheet.

"Mr. Mallory, this is Mr. Darrow," the scientist remarked. "And here," he indicated the couch, "is the woman who murdered Miss Burdock, or rather Mrs. Darrow. Her name is Maria di Peculini. Here is a full confession in her own handwriting," he passed an envelope to the detective, "and here are several torn pieces of paper which show how assiduously she practiced before she forged Mr. Darrow's handwriting in addressing the box in which the red rose was sent to Miss—I should say Mrs. Darrow. I may add that Signorina di Peculini killed herself by inhaling hydrocyanic acid—perhaps you know it better as prussic acid—in a bottle from which came the single drop, allowed to settle in the bloom of the rose, which killed Mrs. Darrow."

Detective Mallory remained standing still for a long time to take it all in. At last he opened the confession—only a dozen lines—and read it from end to end. It was a pitiful, disjointed, almost incoherent, revelation of a woman's distorted soul. She too had loved Darrow, and this had changed to hate when he drifted away from her. Then, when by her own hand she had removed the woman he had made his wife, and had sought subtly to place the blame on him by the little forgery—then had come a revulsion of feeling. She loved again, and overcome by remorse sought relief in death.

"There was no mystery whatever as to the cause of death," The

Thinking Machine told Detective Mallory and Hatch a little while later. "Murder by poison was obvious from the fact that both the woman and the dog were dead; and when we knew that there was no mark or scratch on the dog, and the autopsy revealed nothing, we knew by the simplest rule of logic that the poison had been inhaled. The most powerful poison to inhale is hydrocyanic acid—it kills instantly—therefore it occurred to me first. It is so powerful that it is never made pure, at least in this country. The strongest you can buy in a drug store, for instance, is about a two per cent solution. One drop of a stronger solution than that, on a rose bloom, would have killed Miss Burdock, and the dog if he sniffed at it, as he must have.

"Therefore, from the very first, we knew the manner of death. When we knew further that hydrocyanic acid is extremely volatile, we see how that single drop on the rose evaporated, was dissipated in the air, as the windows of the room where the young woman was found were open. Still there was a faint odor of it left—it smells precisely like crushed peach kernels—and the maid Goodwin was unconsciously affected by it.

"Knowing these things," he continued, "I went to the florist's. Only twelve roses had been bought, paid for, and delivered from there, and the rose that killed Miss Burdock was the thirteenth rose. The roses went from the florist's Mondays, Wednesdays, and Saturdays for four weeks, making twelve roses. They had all been delivered, as the receipt books there showed; but Miss Burdock was killed on Monday; therefore that was the thirteenth rose, and it didn't come direct from the florist's. It was sent by messenger, and the date didn't correspond with any date in the receipt book; therefore it came from another source.

"Incidentally the fact that the roses were sent in that way—that is, one at a time without a card or suggestion of by whom they were sent—suggested a clandestine arrangement with the girl. In other words, the roses were being sent by someone she knew, in all probability; but no one else must know. It was, I saw, a method of correspondence, I might say a love token of some sort, which would not attract attention at her home as a letter would.

"Thus I established a relationship between Miss Burdock and someone else—unknown. The logic of it all informed me that the reason that unknown didn't communicate with her was because of some objection in her home. Her father! Do you see? I simply asked him about it, and instantly his hatred for a single individual came out, that individual being Mr. Darrow. Thus, things pointed toward Mr. Darrow, who was away. The letter to the florist was from Washington. The joints were fitting nicely.

"At police headquarters I saw the rose, and by cautious experiments detected a faint odor of peach kernels. Then I saw the handwriting on the box. It seemed to be a man's; yet I knew by the receipt book there that it did not come from the florist's, therefore was not addressed by anyone there. Did Mr. Darrow address it? Mr. Downey got for me a sample of Mr. Darrow's writing (I don't know how he got it), and the two were compared. They seemed to be the same. This fact was connecting with all the others. Clandestine communication—poison—Darrow! Do you see? This development made Darrow's presence necessary, and I told you, Mr. Mallory, that he was the man we must find. Yet, from the fact that the handwriting on the box was his I had a first suggestion that he was not guilty of the crime. No intelligent man would address a box like that in his own handwriting.

"The matter rested at this point. Mr. Burdock accepted a murder theory and offered rewards, and then Mr. Darrow in person came to see me. The moment he stepped inside my door, to tell me an improbable story, I knew he was innocent. Mr. Burdock's hatred of him (the cause of the feud between them is not of consequence) told me why he had disappeared; and his mere appearance before me accounted for his not going to the police. So—so that's all. He told me of calling to see Signorina di Peculini, and she was not in. We came here, found the door locked, went in with a pass key, and found the things as I delivered them to you, Mr. Mallory." He stopped and sat silently staring for a little while.

"Briefly," he supplemented, "the woman who killed herself knew of the rose being sent regularly, then determined on revenge, bought one, and sent it herself after dropping a single drop of poison in the bloom. The wax paper which surrounded the flower prevented evaporation, and when it was opened——We know the rest."

Neither Detective Mallory nor Hatch spoke for a long time. But the reporter had one more question to ask; and at last he put it.

"That peach kernel that you sent me to Goodwin with——" he began.

"Oh, yes," interrupted The Thinking Machine. "That was a little psychological experiment, and the result of it disconcerted me a little. It is one of the many things science doesn't fully understand, Mr. Hatch—like the little experiment with the frog. For instance, nitrite of amyl is a powerful heart stimulant. It smells precisely like banana oil. A person who has used nitrite of amyl, or to whom it has been administered without their knowledge by inhalation, is momentarily affected the same way when they come suddenly upon the odor of banana oil. Prussic acid has an odor like a peach kernel. I sent you to Goodwin, therefore, to prove definitely whether or not prussic acid had been used, and if she had inhaled it unconsciously. The result gave the proof I wanted."

The Man Who Was Lost

I

Here are the facts in the case as they were known in the beginning to Professor Augustus S. F. X. Van Dusen, scientist and logician. After hearing a statement of the problem from the lips of its principal he declared it to be one of the most engaging that had ever come to his attention, and——

But let me begin at the beginning:

——

The Thinking Machine was in the small laboratory of his modest apartments at two o'clock in the afternoon. Martha, the scientist's only servant, appeared at the door with a puzzled expression on her wrinkled face.

"A gentleman to see you, sir," she said.

"Name?" inquired The Thinking Machine, without turning.

"He—he didn't give it, sir," she stammered.

"I have told you always, Martha, to ask names of callers."

"I did ask his name, sir, and—and he said he didn't know it."

The Thinking Machine was never surprised, yet now he turned on

Martha in perplexity and squinted at her fiercely through his thick glasses.

"Don't know his own name?" he repeated. "Dear me! How careless! Show the gentleman into the reception room immediately."

With no more introduction to the problem than this, therefore, The Thinking Machine passed into the other room. A stranger arose and came forward. He was tall, of apparently thirty-five years, clean-shaven and had the keen, alert face of a man of affairs. He would have been handsome had it not been for dark rings under the eyes and the unusual white of his face. He was immaculately dressed from top to toe; altogether a man who would attract attention.

For a moment he regarded the scientist curiously; perhaps there was a trace of well-bred astonishment in his manner. He gazed curiously at the enormous head, with its shock of yellow hair, and noted, too, the droop in the thin shoulders. Thus for a moment they stood, face to face, the tall stranger making The Thinking Machine dwarf-like by comparison.

"Well?" asked the scientist.

The stranger turned as if to pace back and forth across the room, then instead dropped into a chair which the scientist indicated.

"I have heard a great deal about you, Professor," he began, in a well-modulated voice, "and at last it occurred to me to come to you for advice. I am in a most remarkable position—and I'm not insane. Don't think that, please. But unless I see some way out of this amazing predicament I shall be. As it is now, my nerves have gone; I am not myself."

"Your story? What is it? How can I help you?"

"I am lost, hopelessly lost," the stranger resumed. "I know neither my home, my business, nor even my name. I know nothing whatever of myself or my life; what it was or what it might have been previous to four weeks ago. I am seeking light on my identity. Now, if there is any fee——"

"Never mind that," the scientist put in, and he squinted steadily into the eyes of the visitor. "What *do* you know? From the time you remember things tell me all of it."

He sank back into his chair, squinting steadily upward. The stranger arose, paced back and forth across the room several times and then dropped into his chair again.

"It's perfectly incomprehensible," he said. "It's precisely as if I, full grown, had been born into a world of which I knew nothing except its language. The ordinary things, chairs, tables, and such things, are perfectly familiar, but who I am, where I came from, why I came—of these I have no idea. I will tell you just as my impressions came to me when I awoke one morning, four weeks ago.

"It was eight or nine o'clock, I suppose. I was in a room. I knew instantly it was a hotel, but had not the faintest idea of how I got there, or of ever having seen the room before. I didn't even know my own clothing when I started to dress. I glanced out of my window; the scene was wholly strange to me.

"For half an hour or so I remained in my room, dressing and wondering what it meant. Then, suddenly, in the midst of my other worries, it came home to me that I didn't know my own name, the place where I lived nor anything about myself. I didn't know what hotel I was in. In terror I looked into a mirror. The face reflected at me was not one I knew. It didn't seem to be the face of a stranger; it was merely not a face that I knew.

"The thing was unbelievable. Then I began a search of my clothing for some trace of my identity. I found nothing whatever that would enlighten me—not a scrap of paper of any kind, no personal or business card."

"Have a watch?" asked The Thinking Machine.

"No."

"Any money?"

"Yes, money," said the stranger. "There was a bundle of more than ten thousand dollars in my pocket, in one-hundred-dollar bills. Whose it is or where it came from I don't know. I have been living on it since, and shall continue to do so, but I don't know if it is mine. I knew it was money when I saw it, but did not recollect ever having seen any previously."

"Any jewelry?"

"These cuff buttons," and the stranger exhibited a pair which he drew from his pocket.

"Go on."

"I finally finished dressing and went down to the office. It was my purpose to find out the name of the hotel and who I was. I knew I could learn some of this from the hotel register without attracting any attention or making anyone think I was insane. I had noted the number of my room. It was twenty-seven.

"I looked over the hotel register casually. I saw I was at the Hotel Yarmouth in Boston. I looked carefully down the pages until I came to the number of my room. Opposite this number was a name—John Doane, but where the name of the city should have been there was only a dash."

"You realize that it is perfectly possible that John Doane is your name?" asked The Thinking Machine.

"Certainly," was the reply. "But I have no recollection of ever having heard it before. This register showed that I had arrived at the hotel the night before—or rather that John Doane had arrived and been assigned to Room 27, and I was the John Doane, presumably. From that moment to this the hotel people have known me as John Doane, as have other people whom I have met during the four weeks since I awoke."

"Did the handwriting recall nothing?"

"Nothing whatever."

"Is it anything like the handwriting you write now?"

"Identical, so far as I can see."

"Did you have any baggage or checks for baggage?"

"No. All I had was the money and this clothing I stand in. Of course, since then I have bought necessities."

Both were silent for a long time and finally the stranger—Doane—arose and began pacing nervously again.

"That a tailor-made suit?" asked the scientist.

"Yes," said Doane, quickly. "I know what you mean. Tailor-made garments have linen strips sewed inside the pockets on which are the names of the manufacturers and the name of the man for whom the clothes were made, together with the date. I looked for those. They had been removed, cut out."

"Ah!" exclaimed The Thinking Machine suddenly. "No laundry marks on your linen either, I suppose?"

"No. It was all perfectly new."

"Name of the maker on it?"

"No. That had been cut out, too."

Doane was pacing back and forth across the reception room; the scientist lay back in his chair.

"Do you know the circumstances of your arrival at the hotel?" he asked at last.

"Yes. I asked, guardedly enough, you may be sure, hinting to the clerk that I had been drunk so as not to make him think I was insane. He said I came in about eleven o'clock at night, without any baggage, paid for my room with a one-hundred-dollar bill, which he changed. I registered and went upstairs. I said nothing that he recalls beyond making a request for a room."

"The name Doane is not familiar to you?"

"No."

"You can't recall a wife or children?"

"No."

"Do you speak any foreign language?"

"No."

"Is your mind clear now? Do you remember things?"

"I remember perfectly every incident since I awoke in the hotel," said Doane. "I seem to remember with remarkable clearness, and somehow I attach the gravest importance to the most trivial incidents."

The Thinking Machine arose and motioned to Doane to sit down. He dropped back into a seat wearily. Then the scientist's long, slender fingers ran lightly, deftly through the abundant black hair of his visitor. Finally they passed down from the hair and along the firm jaws; thence they went to the arms, where they pressed upon good, substantial muscles. At last the hands, well shaped and white, were examined minutely. A magnifying glass was used to facilitate this examination. Finally The Thinking Machine stared into the quick-moving, nervous eyes of the stranger.

"Any marks at all on your body?" he asked at last.

"No," Doane responded. "I had thought of that and sought for an hour for some sort of mark. There's nothing—nothing." The eyes glittered a little and finally, in a burst of nervousness, he struggled to his feet. "My God!" he exclaimed. "Is there nothing you can do? What is it all, anyway?"

"Seems to be a remarkable form of aphasia," replied The Thinking Machine. "That's not an uncommon disease among people whose minds and nerves are overwrought. You've simply lost yourself—lost your identity. If it is aphasia, you will recover in time. When, I don't know."

"And meantime?"

"Let me see the money you found."

With trembling hands Doane produced a large roll of bills, principally hundreds, many of them perfectly new. The Thinking Machine examined them minutely, and finally made some memoranda on a slip of paper. The money was then returned to Doane.

"Now, what shall I do?" asked the latter.

"Don't worry," advised the scientist. "I'll do what I can."

"And—tell me who and what I am?"

"Oh, I can find that out all right," remarked The Thinking Machine. "But there's a possibility that you wouldn't recall even if I told you all about yourself."

I I

When John Doane of Nowhere—to all practical purposes—left the home of The Thinking Machine he bore instructions of divers kinds. First he was to get a large map of the United States and study it closely, reading over and pronouncing aloud the name of every city, town and village he found. After an hour of this he was to take a city directory and read over the names, pronouncing them aloud as he did so. Then he was to make out a list of the various professions and higher commercial pursuits, and pronounce these. All these things were calculated, obviously, to arouse the sleeping brain. After Doane had gone The Thinking Machine called up Hutchinson Hatch, reporter, on the 'phone.

"Come up immediately," he requested. "There's something that will interest you."

"A mystery?" Hatch inquired, eagerly.

"One of the most engaging problems that has ever come to my attention," replied the scientist.

It was only a question of a few minutes before Hatch was ushered in. He was a living interrogation point, and repressed a rush of questions with a distinct effort. The Thinking Machine finally told what he knew.

"Now it seems to be," said The Thinking Machine, and he emphasized the "seems," "it seems to be a case of aphasia. You know, of course, what that is. The man simply doesn't know himself. I examined him closely. I went over his head for a sign of a possible depression, or abnormality. It didn't appear. I examined his muscles. He has biceps of great power, is evidently now or has been athletic. His hands are white, well cared for and have no marks on them. They are not the hands of a man who has ever done physical work. The money in his pocket tends to confirm the fact that he is not of that sphere.

"Then what is he? Lawyer? Banker? Financier? What? He might be either, yet he impressed me as being rather of the business than the professional school. He has a good, square-cut jaw—the jaw of a fighting man—and his poise gives one the impression that whatever he has been doing he has been foremost in it. Being foremost in it, he would naturally drift to a city, a big city. He is typically a city man.

"Now, please, to aid me, communicate with your correspondents in the large cities and find if such a name as John Doane appears in any directory. Is he at home now? Has he a family? All about him."

"Do you believe that John Doane is his name?" asked the reporter.

"No reason why it shouldn't be," said The Thinking Machine. "Yet it might not be."

"How about inquiries in this city?"

"He can't well be a local man," was the reply. "He has been wandering about the streets for four weeks, and if he had lived here he would have met someone who knew him."

"But the money?"

"I'll probably be able to locate him through that," said The Thinking Machine. "The matter is not at all clear to me now, but it occurs to me that he is a man of consequence, and that it was possibly necessary for some one to get rid of him for a time."

"Well, if it's plain aphasia, as you say," the reporter put in, "it seems rather difficult to imagine that the attack came at a moment when it was necessary to get rid of him."

"I say it *seems* like aphasia," said the scientist, crustily. "There are known drugs which will produce the identical effect if properly administered."

"Oh," said Hatch. He was beginning to see.

"There is one drug particularly, made in India, and not unlike hasheesh. In a case of this kind anything is possible. Tomorrow I shall ask you to take Mr. Doane down through the financial district, as an experiment. When you go there I want you particularly to get him to the sound of the 'ticker.' It will be an interesting experiment."

The reporter went away and The Thinking Machine sent a telegram to the Blank National Bank of Butte, Montana:

"To whom did you issue hundred-dollar bills, series B, numbering 846380 to 846395 inclusive? Please answer."

It was ten o'clock next day when Hatch called on The Thinking Machine. There he was introduced to John Doane, the man who was lost. The Thinking Machine was asking questions of Mr. Doane when Hatch was ushered in.

"Did the map recall nothing?"

"Nothing."

"Montana, Montana, Montana," the scientist repeated monotonously; "think of it. Butte, Montana."

Doane shook his head hopelessly, sadly.

"Cowboy, cowboy. Did you ever see a cowboy?"

Again the head shake.

"Coyote—something like a wolf—coyote. Don't you recall ever having seen one?"

"I'm afraid it's hopeless," remarked the other.

There was a note of more than ordinary irritation in The Thinking Machine's voice when he turned to Hatch.

"Mr. Hatch, will you walk through the financial district with Mr. Doane?" he asked. "Please go to the places I suggested."

So it came to pass that the reporter and Doane went out together, walking through the crowded, hurrying, bustling financial district. The first place visited was a private room where market quotations were displayed on a blackboard. Mr. Doane was interested, but the scene seemed to suggest nothing. He looked upon it all as any stranger might have done. After a time they passed out. Suddenly a man came running toward them—evidently a broker.

"What's the matter?" asked another.

"Montana copper's gone to smash," was the reply.

"Copper! Copper!" gasped Doane suddenly.

Hatch looked around quickly at his companion. Doane's face was a study. On it was half realization and a deep perplexed wrinkle, a glimmer even of excitement.

"Copper!" he repeated.

"Does the word mean anything to you?" asked Hatch quickly. "Copper—metal, you know."

"Copper, copper, copper," the other repeated. Then, as Hatch looked, the queer expression faded; there came again utter hopelessness.

There are many men with powerful names who operate in the Street—some of them in copper. Hatch led Doane straight to the office of one of these men and there introduced him to a partner in the business.

"We want to talk about copper a little," Hatch explained, still eying his companion.

"Do you want to buy or sell?" asked the broker.

"Sell," said Doane suddenly. "Sell, sell, sell copper. That's it—copper."

He turned to Hatch, stared at him dully a moment, a deathly pallor came over his face, then, with upraised hands, fell senseless.

III

Still unconscious, the man of mystery was removed to the home of The Thinking Machine and there stretched out on a sofa. The Thinking Machine was bending over him, this time in his capacity of physician, making an examination. Hatch stood by, looking on curiously.

"I never saw anything like it," Hatch remarked. "He just threw up his hands and collapsed. He hasn't been conscious since."

"It may be that when he comes to he will have recovered his memory, and in that event he will have absolutely no recollection whatever of you and me," explained The Thinking Machine.

Doane moved a little at last, and under a stimulant the color began to creep back into his pallid face.

"Just what was said, Mr. Hatch, before he collapsed?" asked the scientist.

Hatch explained, repeating the conversation as he remembered it.

"And he said 'sell,'" mused The Thinking Machine. "In other words, he thinks—or imagines he knows—that copper is to drop. I believe the first remark he heard was that copper had gone to smash—down, I presume that means?"

"Yes," the reporter replied.

Half an hour later John Doane sat up on the couch and looked about the room.

"Ah, professor," he remarked. "I fainted, didn't I?"

The Thinking Machine was disappointed because his patient had not recovered memory with consciousness. The remark showed that he was still in the same mental condition—the man who was lost.

"Sell copper, sell, sell, sell," repeated The Thinking Machine, commandingly.

"Yes, yes, sell," was the reply.

The reflection of some great mental struggle was on Doane's face; he was seeking to recall something which persistently eluded him.

"Copper, copper," the scientist repeated, and he exhibited a penny.

"Yes, copper," said Doane. "I know. A penny."

"Why did you say sell copper?"

"I don't know," was the weary reply. "It seemed to be an unconscious act entirely. I don't know."

He clasped and unclasped his hands nervously and sat for a long time dully staring at the floor. The fight for memory was a dramatic one.

"It seemed to me," Doane explained after a while, "that the word copper touched some responsive chord in my memory, then it was lost again. Some time in the past, I think, I must have had something to do with copper."

"Yes," said The Thinking Machine, and he rubbed his slender fingers briskly. "Now you are coming around again."

His remarks were interrupted by the appearance of Martha at the door with a telegram. The Thinking Machine opened it hastily. What he saw perplexed him again.

"Dear me! Most extraordinary!" he exclaimed.

"What is it?" asked Hatch, curiously.

The scientist turned to Doane again.

"Do you happen to remember Preston Bell?" he demanded, emphasizing the name explosively.

"Preston Bell?" the other repeated, and again the mental struggle was apparent on his face. "Preston Bell!"

"Cashier of the Blank National Bank of Butte, Montana?" urged the other, still in an emphatic tone. "Cashier Bell?"

He leaned forward eagerly and watched the face of his patient; Hatch unconsciously did the same. Once there was almost realization, and seeing it The Thinking Machine sought to bring back full memory.

"Bell, cashier, copper," he repeated, time after time.

The flash of realization which had been on Doane's face passed, and there came infinite weariness—the weariness of one who is ill.

"I don't remember," he said at last. "I'm very tired."

"Stretch out there on the couch and go to sleep," advised The Thinking Machine, and he arose to arrange a pillow. "Sleep will do you more good than anything else right now. But before you lie down, let me have, please, a few of those hundred-dollar bills you found."

Doane extended the roll of money, and then slept like a child. It was uncanny to Hatch, who had been a deeply interested spectator.

The Thinking Machine ran over the bills and finally selected fifteen of them—bills that were new and crisp. They were of an issue by the Blank National Bank of Butte, Montana. The Thinking Machine stared at the money closely, then handed it to Hatch.

"Does that look like counterfeit to you?" he asked.

"Counterfeit?" gasped Hatch. "Counterfeit?" he repeated. He took the bills and examined them. "So far as I can see they seem to be good," he went on, "though I have never had enough experience with one-hundred-dollar bills to qualify as an expert."

"Do you know an expert?"

"Yes."

"See him immediately. Take fifteen bills and ask him to pass on them, each and every one. Tell him you have reason—excellent reason—to believe that they are counterfeit. When he gives his opinion come back to me."

Hatch went away with the money in his pocket. Then The Thinking Machine wrote another telegram, addressed to President Bell, cashier of the Butte Bank. It was as follows:

Please send me full details of the manner in which money previously described was lost, with names of all persons who might have had any knowledge of the matter. Highly important to your bank and to justice. Will communicate in detail on receipt of your answer.

Then, while his visitor slept, The Thinking Machine quietly removed his shoes and examined them. He found, almost worn away, the name of the maker. This was subjected to close scrutiny under the magnifying glass, after which The Thinking Machine arose with a perceptible expression of relief on his face.

"Why didn't I think of that before?" he demanded of himself.

Then other telegrams went into the West. One was to a customs shoemaker in Denver, Colorado:

To what financier or banker have you sold within three months a pair of shoes, Senate brand, calfskin blucher, number 8, D last? Do you know John Doane?

A second telegram went to the Chief of Police of Denver. It was:

Please wire if any financier, banker or business man has been out of your city for five weeks or more, presumably on business trip. Do you know John Doane?

Then The Thinking Machine sat down to wait. At last the door bell rang and Hatch entered.

"Well?" demanded the scientist, impatiently.

"The expert declares those are not counterfeit," said Hatch.

Now The Thinking Machine was surprised. It was shown clearly by the quick lifting of the eyebrows, by the sudden snap of his jaws, by a quick forward movement of the yellow head.

"Well, well, well!" he exclaimed at last. Then again: "Well, well!"

"What is it?"

"See here," and The Thinking Machine took the hundred-dollar bills in his own hands. "These bills, perfectly new and crisp, were issued by the Blank National Bank of Butte, and the fact that they are in proper sequence would indicate that they were issued to one individual at the same time, probably recently. There can be no doubt of that. The numbers run from 846380 to 846395, all series B."

"I see," said Hatch.

"Now read that," and the scientist extended to the reporter the telegram Martha had brought in just before Hatch had gone away. Hatch read this:

Series B, hundred-dollar bills 846380 to 846395 issued by this bank are not in existence. Were destroyed by fire, together with twenty-seven others of the same series. Government has been asked to grant permission to reissue these numbers.

PRESTON BELL, Cashier.

The reporter looked up with a question in his eyes.

"It means," said The Thinking Machine, "that this man is either a thief or the victim of some sort of financial jugglery."

"In that case is he what he pretends to be—a man who doesn't know himself?" asked the reporter.

"That remains to be seen."

IV

Event followed event with startling rapidity during the next few hours. First came a message from the chief of police of Denver. No capitalist or financier of consequence was out of Denver at the moment, so far as his men could ascertain. Longer search might be fruitful. He did not know John Doane. One John Doane in the directory was a teamster.

Then from the Blank National Bank came another telegram signed "Preston Bell, Cashier," reciting the circumstances of the disappearance of the hundred-dollar bills. The Blank National Bank had moved into a new structure; within a week there had been a fire which destroyed it. Several packages of money, including one package of hundred-dollar bills, among them those specified by The Thinking Machine, had been burned. President Harrison of the bank immediately made affidavit to the Government that these bills were left in his office.

The Thinking Machine studied this telegram carefully and from time to time glanced at it while Hatch made his report. This was as to the work of the correspondents who had been seeking John Doane. They found many men of the name and reported at length on each. One by one The Thinking Machine heard the reports, then shook his head.

Finally he reverted again to the telegram, and after consideration sent another—this time to the chief of police of Butte. In it he asked these questions:

Has there ever been any financial trouble in Blank National Bank? Was there an embezzlement or shortage at any time? What is reputation of President Harrison? What is reputation of Cashier Bell? Do you know John Doane?

In due course of events the answer came. It was brief and to the point. It said:

Harrison recently embezzled $175,000 and disappeared. Bell's reputation excellent; now out of city. Don't know John Doane. If you have any trace of Harrison, wire quick.

This answer came just after Doane awoke, apparently greatly refreshed, but himself again—that is, himself insofar as he was still lost. For an hour The Thinking Machine pounded him with questions— questions of all sorts, serious, religious and at times seemingly silly. They apparently aroused no trace of memory, save when the name Preston Bell was mentioned; then there was the strange, puzzled expression on Doane's face.

"Harrison—do you know him?" asked the scientist. "President of the Blank National Bank of Butte?"

There was only an uncomprehending stare for an answer. After a long time of this The Thinking Machine instructed Hatch and Doane to go for a walk. He had still a faint hope that someone might recognize Doane and speak to him. As they wandered aimlessly on, two persons spoke to him. One was a man who nodded and passed on.

"Who was that?" asked Hatch quickly. "Do you remember ever having seen him before?"

"Oh, yes," was the reply. "He stops at my hotel. He knows me as Doane."

It was just a few minutes before six o'clock when, walking slowly, they passed a great office building. Coming toward them was a well-dressed, active man of thirty-five years or so. As he approached he removed a cigar from his lips.

"Hello, Harry!" he exclaimed, and reached for Doane's hand.

"Hello," said Doane, but there was no trace of recognition in his voice.

"How's Pittsburgh?" asked the stranger.

"Oh, all right, I guess," said Doane, and there came new wrinkles of perplexity in his brow. "Allow me, Mr.—Mr.—really I have forgotten your name——"

"Manning," laughed the other.

"Mr. Hatch, Mr. Manning."

The reporter shook hands with Manning eagerly; he saw now a

new line of possibilities suddenly revealed. Here was a man who knew Doane as Harry—and then Pittsburgh, too.

"Last time I saw you was in Pittsburgh, wasn't it?" Manning rattled on, as he led the way into a nearby café. "By George, that was a stiff game that night! Remember that jack full I held? It cost me nineteen hundred dollars," he added, ruefully.

"Yes, I remember," said Doane, but Hatch knew that he did not. And meanwhile a thousand questions were surging through the reporter's brain.

"Poker hands as expensive as that are liable to be long remembered," remarked Hatch, casually. "How long ago was that?"

"Three years, wasn't it, Harry?" asked Manning.

"All of that, I should say," was the reply.

"Twenty hours at the table," said Manning, and again he laughed cheerfully. "I was woozy when we finished."

Inside the café they sought out a table in a corner. No one else was near. When the waiter had gone, Hatch leaned over and looked Doane straight in the eyes.

"Shall I ask some questions?" he inquired.

"Yes, yes," said the other eagerly.

"What—what is it?" asked Manning.

"It's a remarkably strange chain of circumstances," said Hatch, in explanation. "This man whom you call Harry, we know as John Doane. What is his real name? Harry what?"

Manning stared at the reporter for a moment in amazement, then gradually a smile came to his lips.

"What are you trying to do?" he asked. "Is this a joke?"

"No, my God, man, can't you see?" exclaimed Doane, fiercely. "I'm ill, sick, something. I've lost my memory, all of my past. I don't remember anything about myself. What is my name?"

"Well, by George!" exclaimed Manning. "By George! I don't believe I know your full name. Harry—Harry—what?"

He drew from his pocket several letters and half a dozen scraps of paper and ran over them. Then he looked carefully through a worn notebook.

"I don't know," he confessed. "I had your name and address in an old notebook, but I suppose I burned it. I remember, though, I met you in the Lincoln Club in Pittsburg three years ago. I called you Harry because everyone was calling everyone else by his first name.

Your last name made no impression on me at all. By George!" he concluded, in a new burst of amazement.

"What were the circumstances, exactly?" asked Hatch.

"I'm a traveling man," Manning explained. "I go everywhere. A friend gave me a card to the Lincoln Club in Pittsburgh and I went there. There were five or six of us playing poker, among them Mr.— Mr. Doane here. I sat at the same table with him for twenty hours or so, but I can't recall his last name to save me. It isn't Doane, I'm positive. I have an excellent memory for faces, and I know you're the man. Don't you remember me?"

"I haven't the slightest recollection of ever having seen you before in my life," was Doane's slow reply. "I have no recollection of ever having been in Pittsburgh—no recollection of anything."

"Do you know if Mr. Doane is a resident of Pittsburgh?" Hatch inquired. "Or was he there as a visitor, as you were?"

"Couldn't tell you to save my life," replied Manning. "Lord, it's amazing, isn't it? You don't remember me? You called me Bill all evening."

The other man shook his head.

"Well, say, is there anything I can do for you?"

"Nothing, thanks," said Doane. "Only tell me my name, and who I am."

"Lord, I don't know."

"What sort of a club is the Lincoln?" asked Hatch.

"It's a sort of a millionaire's club," Manning explained. "Lots of iron men belong to it. I had considerable business with them—that's what took me to Pittsburgh."

"And you are absolutely positive this is the man you met there?"

"Why, I *know* it. I never forget faces; it's my business to remember them."

"Did he say anything about a family?"

"Not that I recall. A man doesn't usually speak of his family at a poker table."

"Do you remember the exact date or the month?"

"I think it was in January or February possibly," was the reply. "It was bitterly cold and the snow was all smoked up. Yes, I'm positive it was in January, three years ago."

After a while the men separated. Manning was stopping at the Hotel Teutonic and willingly gave his name and permanent address to Hatch, explaining at the same time that he would be in the city for several days and was perfectly willing to help in any way he could. He took also the address of The Thinking Machine.

From the café Hatch and Doane returned to the scientist. They found him with two telegrams spread out on a table before him. Briefly Hatch told the story of the meeting with Manning, while Doane sank down with his head in his hands. The Thinking Machine listened without comment.

"Here," he said, at the conclusion of the recital, and he offered one of the telegrams to Hatch. "I got the name of a shoemaker from Mr. Doane's shoe and wired to him in Denver, asking if he had a record of the sale. This is the answer. Read it aloud."

Hatch did so.

"Shoes such as described made nine weeks ago for Preston Bell, cashier Blank National Bank of Butte. Don't know John Doane."

"Well—what——" Doane began, bewildered.

"*It means that you are Preston Bell,*" said Hatch, emphatically.

"No," said The Thinking Machine, quickly. "It means that there is only a strong probability of it."

———

The door bell rang. After a moment Martha appeared.

"A lady to see you, sir," she said.

"Her name?"

"Mrs. John Doane."

"Gentlemen, kindly step into the next room," requested The Thinking Machine.

Together Hatch and Doane passed through the door. There was an expression of—of—no man may say what—on Doane's face as he went.

"Show her in here, Martha," instructed the scientist.

There was a rustle of silk in the hall, the curtains on the door were pulled apart quickly and a richly gowned woman rushed into the room.

"My husband? Is he here?" she demanded, breathlessly. "I went to the hotel; they said he came here for treatment. Please, please, is he here?"

"A moment, madam," said The Thinking Machine. He stepped to

the door through which Hatch and Doane had gone, and said something. One of them appeared in the door. It was Hutchinson Hatch.

"John, John, my darling husband," and the woman flung her arms about Hatch's neck. "Don't you know me?"

With blushing face Hatch looked over her shoulder into the eyes of The Thinking Machine, who stood briskly rubbing his hands. Never before in his long acquaintance with the scientist had Hatch seen him smile.

V

For a time there was silence, broken only by sobs, as the woman clung frantically to Hatch, with her face buried on his shoulder. Then:

"Don't you remember me?" she asked again and again. "Your wife? Don't you remember me?"

Hatch could still see the trace of a smile on the scientist's face, and said nothing.

"You are positive this gentleman is your husband?" inquired The Thinking Machine, finally.

"Oh, I know," the woman sobbed. "Oh, John, don't you remember me?" She drew away a little and looked deeply into the reporter's eyes. "Don't you remember me, John?"

"Can't say that I ever saw you before," said Hatch, truthfully enough. "I—I—fact is——"

"Mr. Doane's memory is wholly gone now," explained The Thinking Machine. "Meanwhile, perhaps you would tell me something about him. He is my patient. I am particularly interested."

The voice was soothing; it had lost for the moment its perpetual irritation. The woman sat down beside Hatch. Her face, pretty enough in a bold sort of way, was turned to The Thinking Machine inquiringly. With one hand she stroked that of the reporter.

"Where are you from?" began the scientist. "I mean where is the home of John Doane?"

"In Buffalo," she replied, glibly. "Didn't he even remember that?"

"And what's his business?"

"His health has been bad for some time and recently he gave up active business," said the woman. "Previously he was connected with a bank."

"When did you see him last?"

"Six weeks ago. He left the house one day and I have never heard from him since. I had Pinkerton men searching and at last they reported he was at the Yarmouth Hotel. I came on immediately. And now we shall go back to Buffalo." She turned to Hatch with a languishing glance. "Shall we not, dear?"

"Whatever Professor Van Dusen thinks best," was the equivocal reply.

Slowly the glimmer of amusement was passing out of the squint eyes of The Thinking Machine; as Hatch looked he saw a hardening of the lines of the mouth. There was an explosion coming. He knew it. Yet when the scientist spoke his voice was more velvety than ever.

"Mrs. Doane, do you happen to be acquainted with a drug which produces temporary loss of memory?"

She stared at him, but did not lose her self-possession.

"No," she said finally. "Why?"

"You know, of course, that this man is *not* your husband?"

This time the question had its effect. The woman arose suddenly, stared at the two men, and her face went white.

"Not?—not?—what do you mean?"

"I mean," and the voice reassumed its tone of irritation, "I mean that I shall send for the police and give you in their charge unless you tell me the truth about this affair. Is that perfectly clear to you?"

The woman's lips were pressed tightly together. She saw that she had fallen into some sort of a trap; her gloved hands were clenched fiercely; the pallor faded and a flush of anger came.

"Further, for fear you don't quite follow me even now," explained The Thinking Machine, "I will say that I know all about this copper deal of which this so-called John Doane was the victim. *I know his condition now.* If you tell the truth you may escape prison—if you don't, there is a long term, not only for you, but for your fellow-conspirators. Now will you talk?"

"No," said the woman. She arose as if to go out.

"Never mind that," said The Thinking Machine. "You had better stay where you are. You will be locked up at the proper moment. Mr. Hatch, please 'phone for Detective Mallory."

Hatch arose and passed into the adjoining room.

"You tricked me," the woman screamed suddenly, fiercely.

"Yes," the other agreed, complacently. "Next time be sure you know your own husband. Meanwhile where is Harrison?"

"Not another word," was the quick reply.

"Very well," said the scientist, calmly. "Detective Mallory will be here in a few minutes. Meanwhile I'll lock this door."

"You have no right——" the woman began.

Without heeding the remark, The Thinking Machine passed into the adjoining room. There for half an hour he talked earnestly to Hatch and Doane. At the end of that time he sent a telegram to the manager of the Lincoln Club in Pittsburgh, as follows:

Does your visitors' book show any man, registered there in the month of January three years ago, whose first name is Harry or Henry? If so, please wire name and description, also name of man whose guest he was.

This telegram was dispatched. A few minutes later the door bell rang and Detective Mallory entered.

"What is it?" he inquired.

"A prisoner for you in the next room," was the reply. "A woman. I charge her with conspiracy to defraud a man who for the present we will call John Doane. That may or may not be his name."

"What do you know about it?" asked the detective.

"A great deal now——more after a while. I shall tell you then. Meanwhile take this woman. You gentlemen, I should suggest, might go out somewhere this evening. If you drop by afterwards there may be an answer to a few telegrams which will make this matter clear."

Protestingly the mysterious woman was led away by Detective Mallory; and Doane and Hatch followed shortly after. The next act of The Thinking Machine was to write a telegram addressed to Mrs. Preston Bell, Butte, Montana. Here it is:

Your husband suffering temporary mental trouble here. Can you come on immediately? Answer.

When the messenger boy came for the telegram he found a man on the stoop. The Thinking Machine received the telegram, and the man, who gave to Martha the name of Manning, was announced.

"Manning, too," mused the scientist. "Show him in."

"I don't know if you know why I am here," explained Manning.

"Oh, yes," said the scientist. "You have remembered Doane's name. What is it, please?"

Manning was too frankly surprised to answer and only stared at the scientist.

"Yes, that's right," he said finally, and he smiled. "His name is Pillsbury. I recall it now."

"And what made you recall it?"

"I noticed an advertisement in a magazine with the name in large letters. It instantly came to me that that was Doane's real name."

"Thanks," remarked the scientist. "And the woman—who is she?"

"What woman?" asked Manning.

"Never mind, then. I am deeply obliged for your information. I don't suppose you know anything else about it?"

"No," said Manning. He was a little bewildered, and after a while went away.

For an hour or more The Thinking Machine sat with finger tips pressed together staring at the ceiling. His meditations were interrupted by Martha.

"Another telegram, sir."

The Thinking Machine took it eagerly. It was from the manager of the Lincoln Club in Pittsburgh:

Henry C. Carney, Harry Meltz, Henry Blake, Henry W. Tolman, Harry Pillsbury, Henry Calvert, and Henry Louis Smith all visitors to club in month you name. Which do you want to learn more about?

It took more than an hour for The Thinking Machine to establish long distance connection by 'phone with Pittsburgh. When he had finished talking he seemed satisfied.

"Now," he mused. "The answer from Mrs. Preston."

It was nearly midnight when that came. Hatch and Doane had returned from a theater and were talking to the scientist when the telegram was brought in.

"Anything important?" asked Doane, anxiously.

"Yes," said the scientist, and he slipped a finger beneath the flap of the envelope. "It's clear now. It was an engaging problem from first to last, and now——"

He opened the telegram and glanced at it; then with bewilderment on his face and mouth slightly open he sank down at the table and leaned forward with his head on his arms. The message fluttered to the table and Hatch read this:

Man in Boston can't be my husband. He is now in Honolulu. I received cablegram from him today.

MRS. PRESTON BELL.

VI

It was thirty-six hours later that the three men met again. The Thinking Machine had abruptly dismissed Hatch and Doane the last time. The reporter knew that something wholly unexpected had happened. He could only conjecture that this had to do with Preston Bell. When the three met again it was in Detective Mallory's office at police headquarters. The mysterious woman who had claimed Doane for her husband was present, as were Mallory, Hatch, Doane and The Thinking Machine.

"Has this woman given any name?" was the scientist's first question.

"Mary Jones," replied the detective, with a grin.

"And address?"

"No."

"Is her picture in the Rogues' Gallery?"

"No. I looked carefully."

"Anybody called to ask about her?"

"A man—yes. That is, he didn't ask about her—he merely asked some general questions, which now we believe were to find out about her."

The Thinking Machine arose and walked over to the woman. She looked up at him defiantly.

"There has been a mistake made, Mr. Mallory," said the scientist. "It's my fault entirely. Let this woman go. I am sorry to have done her so grave an injustice."

Instantly the woman was on her feet, her face radiant. A look of disgust crept into Mallory's face.

"I can't let her go now without arraignment," the detective growled. "It ain't regular."

"You must let her go, Mr. Mallory," commanded The Thinking Machine, and over the woman's shoulder the detective saw an astonishing thing. The Thinking Machine winked. It was a decided, long, pronounced wink.

"Oh, all right," he said, "but it ain't regular at that."

The woman passed out of the room hurriedly, her silken skirts rustling loudly. She was free again. Immediately she disappeared The Thinking Machine's entire manner changed.

"Put your best man to follow her," he directed rapidly. "Let him go to her home and arrest the man who is with her as her husband. Then bring them both back here, after searching their rooms for money."

"Why—what—what is all this?" demanded Mallory, amazed.

"The man who inquired for her, who is with her, is wanted for a $175,000 embezzlement in Butte, Montana. Don't let your man lose sight of her."

The detective left the room hurriedly. Ten minutes later he returned to find The Thinking Machine leaning back in his chair with eyes upturned. Hatch and Doane were waiting, both impatiently.

"Now, Mr. Mallory," said the scientist, "I shall try to make this matter as clear to you as it is to me. By the time I finish I expect your man will be back here with this woman and the embezzler. His name is Harrison; I don't know hers. I can't believe she is Mrs. Harrison, yet he has, I suppose, a wife. But here's the story. It is the chaining together of fact after fact; a necessary logical sequence to a series of incidents, which are, separately, deeply puzzling."

The detective lighted a cigar and the others disposed themselves comfortably to listen.

"This gentleman came to me," began The Thinking Machine, "with a story of loss of memory. He told me that he knew neither his name, home, occupation, nor anything whatever about himself. At the moment it struck me as a case for a mental expert; still I was interested. It seemed to be a remarkable case of aphasia, and I so regarded it until he told me that he had ten thousand dollars in bills, that he had no watch, that everything which might possibly be of value in establishing his identity had been removed from his clothing. This included even the names of the makers of his linen. That showed intent, deliberation.

"Then I knew it could *not* be aphasia. That disease strikes a man suddenly as he walks the street, as he sleeps, as he works, but never gives any desire to remove traces of one's identity. On the contrary, a man is still apparently sound mentally—he has merely forgotten something—and usually his first desire is to find out who he is. This gentleman had that desire, and in trying to find some clew he showed a mind capable of grasping at every possible opportunity. Nearly every question I asked had been anticipated. Thus I recognized that he must be a more than usually astute man.

"But if not aphasia, what was it? What caused his condition? A drug? I remembered that there was such a drug in India, not unlike hasheesh. Therefore for the moment I assumed a drug. It gave me a working basis. Then what did I have? A man of striking mentality who was the victim of some sort of plot, who had been drugged until he lost himself, and in that way disposed of. The handwriting might be the same, for handwriting is rarely affected by a mental disorder; it is a physical function.

"So far, so good. I examined his head for a possible accident. Nothing. His hands were white and in no way callused. Seeking to reconcile the fact that he had been a man of strong mentality, with all other things a financier or banker, occurred to me. The same things might have indicated a lawyer, but the poise of this man, his elaborate care in dress, all these things made me think him the financier rather than the lawyer.

"Then I examined some money he had when he awoke. Fifteen or sixteen of the hundred-dollar bills were new and in sequence. They were issued by a national bank. To whom? The possibilities were that the bank would have a record. I wired, asking about this, and also asked Mr. Hatch to have his correspondents make inquiries in various cities for a John Doane. It was not impossible that John Doane was his name. Now I believe it will be safe for me to say that when he registered at the hotel he was drugged, his own name slipped his mind, and he signed John Doane—the first name that came to him. That is *not* his name.

"While waiting an answer from the bank I tried to arouse his memory by referring to things in the West. It appeared possible that he might have brought the money from the West with him. Then, still with the idea that he was a financier, I sent him to the financial district. There was a result. The word 'copper' aroused him so that he fainted after shouting, 'Sell copper, sell, sell, sell.'

"In a way my estimate of the man was confirmed. He was or had been in a copper deal, selling copper in the market, or planning to do so. I know nothing of the intricacies of the stock market. But there came instantly to me the thought that a man who would faint away in such a case must be vitally interested as well as ill. Thus I had a financier, in a copper deal, drugged as result of a conspiracy. Do you follow me, Mr. Mallory?"

"Sure," was the reply.

"At this point I received a telegram from the Butte bank telling me that the hundred-dollar bills I asked about had been burned. This telegram was signed 'Preston Bell, Cashier.' If that were true, the bills this man had were counterfeit. There were no ifs about that. I asked him if he knew Preston Bell. It was the only name of a person to arouse him in any way. A man knows his own name better than anything in the world. Therefore was it his? For a moment I presumed it was.

"Thus the case stood: Preston Bell, cashier of the Butte bank, had been drugged, was the victim of a conspiracy, which was probably a part of some great move in copper. But if this man were *Preston Bell,* how came the signature there? Part of the office regulation? It happens hundreds of times that a name is so used, particularly on telegrams.

"Well, this man who was lost—Doane, or Preston Bell—went to sleep in my apartments. At that time I believed it fully possible that he was a counterfeiter, as the bills were supposedly burned, and sent Mr. Hatch to consult an expert. I also wired for details of the fire loss in Butte and names of persons who had any knowledge of the matter. This done, I removed and examined this gentleman's shoes for the name of the maker. I found it. The shoes were of fine quality, probably made to order for him.

"Remember, at this time I believed this gentleman to be Preston Bell, for reasons I have stated. I wired to the maker or retailer to know if he had a record of a sale of the shoes, describing them in detail, to any financier or banker. I also wired to the Denver police to know if any financier or banker had been away from there for four or five weeks. Then came the somewhat startling information, through

Mr. Hatch, that the hundred-dollar bills were genuine. That answer meant that Preston Bell—as I had begun to think of him—was either a thief or the victim of some sort of financial conspiracy."

During the silence which followed every eye was turned on the man who was lost—Doane or Preston Bell. He sat staring straight ahead of him with hands nervously clenched. On his face was written the sign of a desperate mental struggle. He was still trying to recall the past.

"Then," The Thinking Machine resumed, "I heard from the Denver police. There was no leading financier or banker out of the city so far as they could learn hurriedly. It was not conclusive, but it aided me. Also I received another telegram from Butte, signed Preston Bell, telling me the circumstances of the supposed burning of the hundred-dollar bills. It did not show that they were burned at all; it was merely an assumption that they had been. They were last seen in President Harrison's office."

"Harrison, Harrison, Harrison," repeated Doane.

"Vaguely I could see the possibility of something financially wrong in the bank. Possibly Harrison, even Mr. Bell here, knew of it. Banks do not apply for permission to reissue bills unless they are positive of the original loss. Yet here were the bills. Obviously some sort of jugglery. I wired to the police of Butte, asking some questions. The answer was that Harrison had embezzled $175,000 and had disappeared. Now I knew he had part of the missing, supposedly burned, bills with him. It was obvious. Was Bell also a thief?

"The same telegram said that Mr. Bell's reputation was of the best, and he was out of the city. That confirmed my belief that it was an office rule to sign telegrams with the cashier's name, and further made me positive that this man was Preston Bell. The chain of circumstances was complete. It was two and two—inevitable result, four.

"Now, what was the plot? Something to do with copper, and there was an embezzlement. Then, still seeking a man who knew Bell personally, I sent him out walking with Hatch. I had done so before. Suddenly another figure came into the mystery—a confusing one at the moment. This was a Mr. Manning, who knew Doane, or Bell, as Harry—something; met him in Pittsburgh three years ago, in the Lincoln Club.

"It was just after Mr. Hatch told me of this man that I received a telegram from the shoemaker in Denver. It said that he had made a shoe such as I described within a few months for Preston Bell. I had asked if a sale had been made to a financier or banker; I got the name back by wire.

"At this point a woman appeared to claim John Doane as her husband. With no definite purpose, save general precaution, I asked Mr. Hatch to see her first. She imagined he was Doane and embraced him, calling him John. Therefore she was a fraud. She did not know John Doane, or Preston Bell, by sight. Was she acting under the direction of someone else? If so, whose?"

There was a pause as The Thinking Machine readjusted himself in the chair. After a time he went on:

"There are shades of emotion, intuition, call it what you will, so subtle that it is difficult to express them in words. As I had instinctively associated Harrison with Bell's present condition I instinctively associated this woman with Harrison. For not a word of the affair had appeared in a newspaper; only a very few persons knew of it. Was it possible that the stranger Manning was backing the woman in an effort to get the ten thousand dollars? That remained to be seen. I questioned the woman; she would say nothing. She is clever, but she blundered badly in claiming Mr. Hatch for a husband."

The reporter blushed modestly.

"I asked her flatly about a drug. She was quite calm and her manner indicated that she knew nothing of it. Yet I presume she did. Then I sprung the bombshell, and she saw she had made a mistake. I gave her over to Detective Mallory and she was locked up. This done, I wired to the Lincoln Club in Pittsburgh to find out about this mysterious 'Harry' who had come into the case. I was so confident then that I also wired to Mrs. Bell in Butte, presuming that there was a Mrs. Bell, asking about her husband.

"Then Manning came to see me. I knew he came because he had remembered the name he knew you by," and The Thinking Machine turned to the central figure in this strange entanglement of identity, "although he seemed surprised when I told him as much. He knew you as Harry Pillsbury. I asked him who the woman was. His manner told me that he knew nothing whatever of her. Then it came back to her as an associate of Harrison, your enemy for some reason, and I could see it in no other light. It was her purpose to get hold of you and possibly keep you a prisoner, at least until some gigantic deal in which copper figured was disposed of. That was what I surmised.

"Then another telegram came from the Lincoln Club in Pittsburgh. The name of Harry Pillsbury appeared as a visitor in the book in January, three years ago. It was you—Manning is not the sort of man to be mistaken—and then there remained only one point to be solved as I then saw the case. That was an answer from Mrs. Preston Bell, if there was a Mrs. Bell. She would know where her husband was."

Again there was silence. A thousand things were running through Bell's mind. The story had been told so pointedly, and was so vitally a part of him, that semi-recollection was again on his face.

"That telegram said that Preston Bell was in Honolulu; that the wife had received a cable dispatch that day. Then, frankly, I was puzzled; so puzzled, in fact, that the entire fabric I had constructed seemed to melt away before my eyes. It took me hours to readjust it. I tried it all over in detail, and then the theory which would reconcile every fact in the case was evolved. That theory is right—as right as that two and two make four. It's logic."

It was half an hour later when a detective entered and spoke to Detective Mallory aside.

"Fine!" said Mallory. "Bring 'em in."

Then there reappeared the woman who had been a prisoner and a man of fifty years.

"Harrison!" exclaimed Bell, suddenly. He staggered to his feet with outstretched hands. "Harrison! I know! I know!"

"Good, good, very good," said The Thinking Machine.

Bell's nervously twitching hands were reaching for Harrison's throat when he was pushed aside by Detective Mallory. He stood pallid for a moment, then sank down on the floor in a heap. He was senseless. The Thinking Machine made a hurried examination.

"Good!" he remarked again. "When he recovers he will remember everything except what has happened since he has been in Boston. Meanwhile, Mr. Harrison, we know all about the little affair of the drug, the battle for new copper workings in Honolulu, and your partner there has been arrested. Your drug didn't do its work well enough. Have you anything to add?"

The prisoner was silent.

"Did you search his rooms?" asked The Thinking Machine of the detective who had made the double arrest.

"Yes, and found this."

It was a large roll of money. The Thinking Machine ran over it lightly—seventy thousand dollars—scanning the numbers of the bills. At last he held forth half a dozen. They were among the twenty-seven reported to have been burned in the bank fire in Butte.

Harrison and the woman were led away. Subsequently it developed that he had been systematically robbing the bank of which he was president for years; was responsible for the fire, at which time he had evidently expected to make a great haul; and that the woman was not his wife. Following his arrest this entire story came out; also the facts of the gigantic copper deal, in which he had rid himself of Bell, who was his partner, and had sent another man to Honolulu in Bell's name to buy up options on some valuable copper property there. This confederate in Honolulu had sent the cable dispatches to the wife in Butte. She accepted them without question.

It was a day or so later that Hatch dropped in to see The Thinking Machine and asked a few questions.

"How did Bell happen to have that ten thousand dollars?"

"It was given to him, probably, because it was safer to have him rambling about the country, not knowing who he was, than to kill him."

"And how did he happen to be here?"

"That question may be answered at the trial."

"And how did it come that Bell was once known as Harry Pillsbury?"

"Bell is a director in United States Steel, I have since learned. There was a secret meeting of this board in Pittsburgh three years ago. He went incog. to attend that meeting and was introduced at the Lincoln Club as Harry Pillsbury."

"Oh!" exclaimed Hatch.

A Piece of String

It was just midnight. Somewhere near the center of a cloud of tobacco smoke, which hovered over one corner of the long editorial room, Hutchinson Hatch, reporter, was writing. The rapid click-click of his typewriter went on and on, broken only when he laid aside one sheet to put in another. The finished pages were seized upon one at a time by an office boy and rushed off to the city editor. That astute person glanced at them for information and sent them on to the copy desk, whence they were shot down into that noisy, chaotic wilderness, the composing room.

The story was what the phlegmatic head of the copy desk, speaking in the vernacular, would have called a "beaut." It was about the kidnapping that afternoon of Walter Francis, the four-year-old son of a wealthy young broker, Stanley Francis. An alternative to the abduction had been proposed in the form of a gift to certain persons, identity unknown, of fifty thousand dollars. Francis, not unnaturally, objected to the bestowal of so vast a sum upon anyone. So he told the police, and while they were making up their minds the child was stolen. It happened in the usual way—closed carriage, and all that sort of thing.

Hatch was telling the story graphically, as he could tell a story when there was one to be told. He glanced at the clock, jerked out another sheet of copy, and the office boy scuttled away with it.

"How much more?" called the city editor.

"Just a paragraph," Hatch answered.

His typewriter clicked on merrily for a couple of minutes and then stopped. The last sheet of copy was taken away, and he rose and stretched his legs.

"Some guy wants yer at the 'phone," an office boy told him.

"Who is it?" asked Hatch.

"Search me," replied the boy. "Talks like he'd been eatin' pickles."

Hatch went into the booth indicated. The man at the other end was Professor Augustus S. F. X. Van Dusen. The reporter instantly recognized the crabbed, perpetually irritated voice of the noted scientist, The Thinking Machine.

"That you, Mr. Hatch?" came over the wire.

"Yes."

"Can you do something for me immediately?" he queried. "It is very important."

"Certainly."

"Now listen closely," directed The Thinking Machine. "Take a car from Park Square, the one that goes toward Worcester through Brookline. About two miles beyond Brookline is Randall's Crossing. Get off there and go to your right until you come to a small white house. In front of this house, a little to the left and across an open field, is a large tree. It stands just at the edge of a dense wood. It might be better to approach it *through* the wood, so as not to attract attention. Do you follow me?"

"Yes," Hatch replied. His imagination was leading him a chase.

"Go to this tree now, immediately, tonight," continued The Thinking Machine. "You will find a small hole in it near the level of your eye. Feel in that hole, and see what is there—no matter what it is—then return to Brookline and telephone me. It is of the greatest importance."

The reporter was thoughtful for a moment; it sounded like a page from a Dumas romance.

"What's it all about?" he asked curiously.

"Will you go?" came the counter question.

"Yes, certainly."

"Good by."

Hatch heard a click as the receiver was hung up at the other end. He shrugged his shoulders, said "Good night" to the city editor, and went out. An hour later he was at Randall's Crossing. The night was dark—so dark that the road was barely visible. The car whirled on, and as its lights were swallowed up Hatch set out to find the white house. He came upon it at last, and, turning, faced across an open field toward the wood. Far away over there, outlined vaguely against the distant glow of the city, was a tall tree.

Having fixed its location, the reporter moved along for a hundred yards or more to where the wood ran down to the road. Here he climbed a fence and stumbled on through the dark, doing sundry injuries to his shins. After a disagreeable ten minutes he reached the tree.

With a small electric flash light he found the hole. It was only a little larger than his hand, a place where decay had eaten its way into the tree trunk. For just a moment he hesitated about putting his hand into it—he didn't know what might be there. Then, with a grim smile, he obeyed orders.

He felt nothing save crumblings of decayed wood, and finally dragged out a handful, only to spill it on the ground. That couldn't be what was meant. For the second time he thrust in his hand, and after a deal of grabbing about produced—a piece of string. It was just a plain, ordinary, common piece of string—white string. He stared at it and smiled.

"I wonder what Van Dusen will make of that?" he asked himself.

Again his hand was thrust into the hole. But that was all—the piece of string. Then came another thought and, with that due regard for detail which made him a good reporter, he went looking around the big tree for a possible second opening of some sort. He found none.

About three quarters of an hour later he stepped into an all-night drugstore in Brookline and 'phoned to The Thinking Machine. There was an instant response to his ring.

"Well, well, what did you find?" came the query.

"Nothing to interest you, I imagine," replied the reporter grimly. "Just a piece of string."

"Good, good!" exclaimed The Thinking Machine. "What does it look like?"

"Well," replied the newspaper man judicially, "it's just a piece of white string—cotton, I imagine—about six inches long."

"Any knots in it?"

"Wait till I see."

He was reaching into his pocket to take it out, when the startled voice of The Thinking Machine came over the line.

"Didn't you leave it there?" it demanded.

"No; I have it in my pocket."

"Dear me!" exclaimed the scientist irritably. "That's bad. Well, has it any knots in it?" he asked with marked resignation.

Hatch felt that he had committed the unpardonable sin. "Yes," he replied after an examination. "It has two knots in it—just plain knots—about two inches apart."

"Single or double knots?"

"Single knots."

"Excellent! Now, Mr. Hatch, listen. Untie one of those knots—it doesn't matter which one—and carefully smooth out the string. Then take it and put it back where you found it. 'Phone me as soon after that as you can."

"Now, tonight?"

"Now, immediately."

"But—but——" began the astonished reporter.

"It is a matter of the utmost consequence," the irritated voice assured him. "You should not have taken the string. I told you merely to see what was there. But as you have brought it away you must put it back as soon as possible. Believe me, it is of the highest importance. And don't forget to 'phone me."

The sharp, commanding tone stirred the reporter to new action and interest. A streetcar was just going past the door, outward bound. He raced for it and got aboard. Once settled, he untied one of the knots, straightened out the string, and fell to wondering what sort of fool's errand he was on.

"Randall's Crossing!" called the conductor at last.

Hatch left the car and retraced his tortuous way along the road and through the wood to the tall tree, found the hole, and had just thrust in his hand to replace the string when he heard a woman's voice directly behind him, almost in his ear. It was a calm, placid, convincing sort of voice. It said:

"Hands up!"

Hatch was a rational human being with ambitions and hopes for the future; therefore his hands went up without hesitation. "I knew something would happen," he told himself.

He turned to see the woman. In the darkness he could only dimly trace a tall, slender figure. Steadily poised just a couple of dozen inches from his nose was a revolver. He could see that without any difficulty. It glinted a little, even in the gloom, and made itself conspicuous.

"Well," asked the reporter at last, as he stood reaching upward, "it's your move."

"Who are you?" asked the woman. Her voice was steady and rather pleasant.

The reporter considered the question in the light of all he didn't know. He felt it wouldn't be a sensible thing to say just who he was. Somewhere at the end of this thing The Thinking Machine was working on a problem; he was presumably helping in a modest, unobtrusive sort of way; therefore he would be cautious.

"My name is Williams," he said promptly. "Jim Williams," he added circumstantially.

"What are you doing here?"

Another subject for thought. That was a question he couldn't answer; he didn't know what he was doing there; he was wondering himself. He could only hazard a guess, and he did that with trepidation.

"I came from him," he said with deep meaning.

"Who?" demanded the woman suspiciously.

"It would be useless to name him," replied the reporter.

"Yes, yes, of course," the woman mused. "I understand."

There was a little pause. Hatch was still watching the revolver. He had a lively interest in it. It had not moved a hair's breadth since he first looked at it; hanging up there in the night it fairly stared him out of countenance.

"And the string?" asked the woman at last.

Now the reporter felt that he was in the mire. The woman herself relieved this new embarrassment.

"Is it in the tree?" she went on.

"Yes."

"How many knots are in it?"

"One."

"One?" she repeated eagerly. "Put your hand in there and hand me the string. No tricks, now!"

Hatch complied with a certain deprecatory manner which he intended should convey to her the impression that there would be no tricks. As she took the string her fingers brushed against his. They were smooth and delicate. He knew that even in the dark.

"And what did he say?" she went on.

Having gone this far without falling into anything, the reporter was willing to plunge—felt that he had to, as a matter of fact.

"He said yes," he murmured without shifting his eyes from the revolver.

"Yes?" the woman repeated again eagerly. "Are you sure?"

"Yes," said the reporter again. The thought flashed through his mind that he was tangling up somebody's affairs badly—he didn't know whose. Anyhow, it was a matter of no consequence to him, as long as that revolver stared at him that way.

"Where is it?" asked the woman.

Then the earth slipped out from under him. "I don't know," he replied weakly.

"Didn't he give it to you?"

"Oh, no. He—he wouldn't trust me with it."

"How can I get it, then?"

"Oh, he'll fix it all right," Hatch assured her soothingly. "I think he said something about tomorrow night."

"Where?"

"Here."

"Thank God!" the woman gasped suddenly. Her tone betrayed deep emotion; but it wasn't so deep that she lowered the revolver.

There was a long pause. Hatch was figuring possibilities. How to get possession of the revolver seemed the imminent problem. His hands were still in the air, and there was nothing to indicate that they were not to remain there indefinitely. The woman finally broke the silence.

"Are you armed?"

"Oh, no."

"Truthfully?"

"Truthfully."

"You may lower your hands," she said, as if satisfied; "then go on ahead of me straight across the field to the road. Turn to your left there. Don't look back under any circumstances. I shall be behind you with this revolver pointing at your head. If you attempt to escape or make any outcry I shall shoot. Do you believe me?"

The reporter considered it for a moment. "I'm firmly convinced of it," he said at last.

They stumbled on to the road, and there Hatch turned as directed. Walking along in the shadows with the tread of small feet behind him he first contemplated a dash for liberty; but that would mean giving up the adventure, whatever it was. He had no fear for his personal safety as long as he obeyed orders, and he intended to do that implicitly. And besides, The Thinking Machine had his slender finger in the pie somewhere. Hatch knew that, and knowing it was a source of deep gratification.

Just now he was taking things at face value, hoping that with their arrival at whatever place they were bound for he would be further enlightened. Once he thought he heard the woman sobbing, and started to look back. Then he remembered her warning, and thought better of it. Had he looked back he would have seen her stumbling along, weeping, with the revolver dangling limply at her side.

At last, a mile or more farther on, they began to arrive somewhere. A house sat back some distance from the road.

"Go in there!" commanded his captor.

He turned in at the gate, and five minutes later stood in a comfortably furnished room on the ground floor of a small house. A dim light was burning. The woman turned it up. Then almost defiantly she threw aside her veil and hat and stood before him. Hatch gasped. She was pretty—bewilderingly pretty—and young and graceful and all that a young woman should be. Her cheeks were flushed.

"You know me, I suppose?" she exclaimed.

"Oh yes, certainly," Hatch assured her.

And saying that, he knew he had never seen her before.

"I suppose you thought it perfectly horrid of me to keep you with your hands up like that all the time; but I was dreadfully frightened," the woman went on, and she smiled a little uncertainly. "But there wasn't anything else to do."

"It was the only thing," Hatch agreed.

"Now I'm going to ask you to write and tell him just what happened," she resumed. "And tell him, too, that the other matter must be arranged immediately. I'll see that your letter is delivered. Sit here!"

She picked up the revolver from the table beside her and placed a chair in position. Hatch walked to the table and sat down. Pen and ink lay before him. He knew now he was trapped. He couldn't write a letter to that vague "him" of whom he had talked so glibly, about that still more vague "it"—whatever that might be. He sat dumbly staring at the paper.

"Well?" she demanded suspiciously.

"I—I can't write it," he confessed suddenly.

She stared at him coldly for a moment as if she had suspected just that, and he in turn stared at the revolver with a new and vital interest. He felt the tension, but saw no way to relieve it.

"You are an imposter!" she blurted out at last. "A detective?"

Hatch didn't deny it. She backed away toward a bell call near the door, watching him closely, and rang vigorously several times. After a little pause the door opened, and two men, evidently servants, entered.

"Take this gentleman to the rear room upstairs," she commanded without giving them a glance, "and lock him up. Keep him under close guard. If he attempts to escape, stop him! That's all."

Here was another page from a Dumas romance. The reporter started to explain; but there was a merciless gleam, danger even, in the woman's eyes, and he submitted to orders. So, he was led upstairs a captive, and one of the men took a place on guard inside the room.

The dawn was creeping on when Hatch fell asleep. It was about ten o'clock when he awoke, and the sun was high. His guard, wide eyed and alert, still sat beside the door. For several minutes the reporter lay still, seeking vainly some sort of explanation of what was happening. Then, cheerfully:

"Good morning."

The guard merely glared at him.

"May I inquire your name?" the reporter asked.

There was no answer.

"Or the lady's name?"

No answer.

"Or why I am where I am?"

Still no answer.

"What would you do," Hatch went on casually, "if I should try to get out of here?"

The guard handled his revolver carelessly. The reporter was satisfied. "He is not deaf, that's certain," he told himself.

He spent the remainder of the morning yawning and wondering what The Thinking Machine was about; also he had a few casual reflections as to the mental state of his city editor at his failure to appear and follow up the kidnapping story. He finally dismissed all these ideas with a shrug of his shoulders, and sat down to wait for whatever was coming.

It was in the early afternoon that he heard laughter in the next room. First there was a woman's voice, then the shrill cackle of a child. Finally he distinguished some words.

"You ticky!" exclaimed the child, and again there was the laugh.

The reporter understood "you ticky," coupled with the subsequent peal, to be a sort of abbreviated English for "you tickle." After a while the merriment died away and he heard the child's insistent demand for something else.

"You be hossie."

"No, no," the woman expostulated.

"Yes, you be hossie."

"No, let Morris be hossie."

"No, no. You be hossie."

That was all. Evidently some one was "hossie," because there was a sound of romping; but finally even that died away. Hatch yawned away another hour or so under the constant eye of his guard, and then began to grow restless. He turned on the guard savagely.

"Isn't anything ever going to happen?" he demanded.

The guard didn't say.

"You'll never convict yourself on your own statement," Hatch burst out again in disgust.

He stretched out on a couch, bored by the sameness which had characterized the last few hours of his adventure. His attention was attracted by some movement at the door, and he looked up. His guard heard, too, and with revolver in hand went to the door, carefully unlocking it. After a few hurriedly whispered words he left the room, and Hatch was meditating an instant rush for a window, when the woman entered. She had the revolver now. She was deathly white and gripped the weapon menacingly. She did not lock the door—only closed it—but with her own person and the attention-compelling revolver she blocked the way.

"What is it now?" asked Hatch wearily.

"You must not speak or call, or make the slightest sound," she whispered tensely. "If you do, I'll kill you. Do you understand?"

Hatch confessed by a nod that he understood. He also imagined that he understood this sudden change in guard, and the warning. It was because someone was about to enter or had entered the house. His conjecture was partially confirmed instantly by a distant rapping on a door.

"Not a sound, now!" whispered the woman.

From somewhere below he heard the sound of steps as one of the servants answered the knock. After a short wait he heard two voices mumbling. Suddenly one was raised clearly.

"Why, Worcester can't be that far," it protested irritably.

Hatch knew. It was The Thinking Machine. The woman noted a change in his manner and drew back the hammer of the revolver. The reporter saw the idea. He didn't dare call. That would be suicide. Perhaps he could attract attention, though; drop a key, for instance. The sound might reach The Thinking Machine and be interpreted aright. One hand was in a pocket, and slowly he was drawing out a key. He would risk it. Maybe——

Then came a new sound. It was the patter of small feet. The guarded door was pushed open and a tousle-headed child, a boy, ran in.

"Mama, mama!" he called loudly. He ran to the woman and clutched at her skirts.

"Oh, my baby! What have you done?" she asked piteously. "We are lost, lost!"

"Me 'faid," the child went on.

With the door—his avenue of possible escape—open, Hatch did not drop the key. Instead, he gazed at the woman, then down at the child. From below he again heard The Thinking Machine.

"How far is the streetcar track, then?"

The servant answered something. There was a sound of steps, and the front door closed. Hatch knew that The Thinking Machine had come and gone; yet he was strangely calm about it, quite himself, despite the fact that a nervous finger still lay on the trigger of the pistol.

From his refuge behind his mother's skirts the boy peered around at Hatch shyly. The reporter gazed, gazed, all eyes, and then was convinced. The boy was Walter Francis, the kidnapped boy whose pictures were being published in every newspaper of a dozen cities. Here was a story—*the* story—the superlative story.

"Mrs. Francis, if you wouldn't mind letting down that hammer——" he suggested modestly. "I assure you I contemplate no harm, and you—you are very nervous."

"You know me, then?" she asked.

"Only because the child there, Walter, called you mama."

Mrs. Francis lowered the revolver hammer so recklessly that Hatch involuntarily dodged. And then came a scene, a scene with tears in it, and all those things which stir men, even reporters. Finally the woman dropped the revolver on the floor and swept the boy up in her arms with a gesture of infinite tenderness. He cuddled there, content. At that moment Hatch could have walked out the door, but instead he sat down. He was just beginning to get interested.

"They sha'n't take you!" sobbed the mother.

"There is no immediate danger," the reporter assured her. "The man who came here for that purpose has gone. Meanwhile, if you will tell me the facts, perhaps—perhaps I may be able to be of some assistance."

Mrs. Francis looked at him, startled. "Help me?"

"If you will explain, perhaps I can do something," said Hatch again.

Somewhere back in a remote recess of his brain he was remembering. And as it became clearer he was surprised that he had not remembered sooner. It was a story of marital infelicity, and its principals were Stanley Francis and his wife—this bewilderingly pretty young woman before him. It had been only eight or nine months back.

Technically she had deserted Stanley Francis. There had been some violent scene and she left their home and little son. Soon afterward she went to Europe. It had been rumored that divorce proceedings would follow, or at least a legal separation, but nothing had ever come of the rumors. All this Mrs. Francis told to Hatch in little incoherent bursts, punctuated with sobs and tears.

"He struck me, he struck me!" she declared with a flush of anger and shame, "and I went then on impulse. I was desperate. Later, even before I went to Europe, I knew the legal status of the affair; but the thought of my boy lingered, and I resolved to come back and get him—abduct him, if necessary. I did that, and I will keep him if I have to kill the one who opposes me."

Hatch saw the mother instinct here, that tigerish ferocity of love which stops at nothing.

"I conceived the plan of demanding fifty thousand dollars of my husband under threat of abduction," Mrs. Francis went on. "My purpose was to make it appear that the plot was that of professional— what would you call it?—kidnappers. But I did not send the letter demanding this until I had perfected all my plans and knew I could get the boy. I wanted my husband to think it was the work of others, at least until we were safe in Europe, because even then I imagined there would be a long legal fight.

"After I stole the boy and he recognized me, I wanted him as my own, absolutely safe from legal action by his father. Then I wrote to Mr. Francis, telling him I had Walter, and asking that in pity to me he legally give me the boy by a document of some sort. In that letter I told how he might signify his willingness to do this; but of course I would not give my address. I placed a string, the one you saw, in that tree after having tied two knots in it. It was a silly, romantic means of communication he and I used years ago in my girlhood when we both lived near here. If he agreed that I should have the child, he was to come or send someone last night and untie one of the two knots."

Then, to Hatch, the intricacies passed away. He understood clearly. Instead of going to the police with the second letter from his wife, Francis had gone to The Thinking Machine. The Thinking Machine sent the reporter to untie the knot, which was an answer of "Yes" to Mrs. Francis's request for the child. Then she would have written, giving her address, and there would have been a clue to the child's whereabouts. It was all perfectly clear now.

"Did you specifically mention a string in your letter?" he asked.

"No. I merely stated that I would expect his answer in that place, and would leave something there by which he could signify 'Yes' or 'No,' as he did years ago. The string was one of the odd little ideas of my girlhood. Two knots meant 'No'; one knot meant 'Yes'; and if the string was found by anyone else it meant nothing."

This, then, was why The Thinking Machine did not tell him at first that he would find a string and instruct him to untie one of the knots in it. The scientist had seen that it might have been one of the other tokens of the old romantic days.

"When I met you there," Mrs. Francis resumed. "I believed you were an imposter—I don't know why, I just believed it—yet your answers were in a way correct. For fear you were not what you seemed—that you were a detective—I brought you here to keep you until I got the child's release. You know the rest."

The reporter picked up the revolver and whirled it in his fingers. The action, apparently, did not disturb Mrs. Francis.

"Why did you remain here so long after you got the child?" asked Hatch.

"I believed it was safer than in a city," she answered frankly. "The steamer on which I planned to sail for Europe with my boy leaves tomorrow. I had intended going to New York tonight to catch it; but now——"

The reporter glanced down at the child. He had fallen asleep in his mother's arms. His tiny hand clung to her. The picture was a pretty one. Hatch made up his mind.

"Well, you'd better pack up," he said. "I'll go with you to New York and do all I can."

It was on the New York–bound train several hours later that Hatch turned to Mrs. Francis with an odd smile.

"Why didn't you load that revolver?" he asked.

"Because I was horribly afraid someone would get hurt with it," she replied laughingly.

She was gay with that gentle happiness of possession which blesses woman for the agonies of motherhood, and glanced from time to time at the berth across the aisle where her baby was asleep. Looking upon it all, Hatch was content. He didn't know his exact position in law; but that didn't matter, after all.

———

Hutchinson Hatch's exclusive story of the escape to Europe of Mrs. Francis and her boy was remarkably complete; but all the facts were not in it. It was a week or so later that he detailed them to The Thinking Machine.

"I knew it," said the scientist at the end. "Francis came to me, and I interested myself in the case, practically knowing every fact from his statement. When you heard me speak in the house where you were a prisoner I was there merely to convince myself that the mother did have the baby. I heard it call her and went away satisfied. I knew you were there, too, because you had failed to 'phone me the second time as I expected, and I knew intuitively what you would do when you got the real facts about Mrs. Francis and her baby. I went away so that the field might be clear for you to act. Francis himself is a detestable puppy. I told him so."

And that was all that was ever said about it.

The Problem of the Deserted House

The telephone bell rang sharply, twice. Professor Augustus S. F. X. Van Dusen—The Thinking Machine—opened his eyes from a sound sleep, rose from the bed, turned on an electric light, and squinted at the clock on the table. It was just half-past one; he had been asleep for only a little more than an hour. He slid his small feet into a pair of soft slippers and went to the telephone.

"Hello!" he called irritably.

"Is that Professor Van Dusen?" came the answer in a man's voice—a voice tense with nervous excitement, and so quick in enunciation that the words tumbled over one another.

"Yes," replied the scientist. "What is it?"

"It's a matter of life and death!" came the hurried response in the same hasty tone. "Can you come at once and——" The instrument buzzed and sputtered incoherently, and the remainder of the question was lost.

For an instant The Thinking Machine listened intently, seeking to interpret the interruption; then the sputtering ceased and the wire was silent. "Who is this talking?" he demanded.

The answer was almost a shout; it was as if the speaker was strangling, and the words came explosively, with a distinct effort. "My name is——"

And that was all. The voice was swallowed up suddenly in the deafening crack of an explosion of some sort—a pistol shot! Involuntarily The Thinking Machine dodged. The receiver sang shrilly in his ear, and the transmitter vibrated audibly; then the instrument was mute again—the connection was broken.

"Hello, hello!" the scientist called again and again; but there was no answer. He moved the hook up and down several times to attract Central's attention. But that brought no response. Whatever had happened had at least temporarily rendered his own line lifeless. "Dear me! Dear me!" he grumbled petulantly. "Most extraordinary!"

For a time he stood thoughtfully staring at the instrument; then went over and sat down on the edge of the bed. Sleep was banished now. Here was a problem, and a strange one! Every faculty of his wonderful brain was concentrated upon it. The minutes sped on as he sat there turning it all over in his mind, analyzing it, regarding it from every possible viewpoint, while tiny wrinkles were growing in the enormous brow. Finally he concluded to try the telephone again. Perhaps it had only been momentarily deadened by the shock. He returned to the instrument and picked up the receiver. The rhythmic buzz of the wire told him instantly that the line was working. Central answered promptly.

"Can you tell me the number which was just connected with this?" he inquired. "We were interrupted."

"I'll see if I can get it," was the reply.

"It's of the utmost importance," he went on to explain tersely; "a matter of life and death, even."

"I'll do what I can," Central assured him; "but there is no record of the calls, you know, and there may have been fifty in the last ten or fifteen minutes, and of course the operators don't remember them." She obligingly gave him a quarter of an hour as she sought some clue to the number.

The Thinking Machine waited patiently for the report, staring dumbly at the transmitter meanwhile, and at last it came. No one remembered the number; there was no record of it. Central was sorry. With a curt word of thanks the scientist called for one of the big newspaper offices and asked for Hutchinson Hatch, reporter.

"Mr. Hatch isn't in," came the response.

"Do you know where he is?" queried the scientist, and there was a shadow of anxiety in the perpetually irritated voice.

"No; home, I suppose."

The man of science drew a long, quick breath—it might have been one of uneasiness—and called the newspaperman's home number. Of course the mysterious message over the telephone had not been from Hatch. It was not the reporter's voice, he was positive of that, and yet there was the bare chance that—

"Hello!" Hatch growled amiably but sleepily over the wire.

The Thinking Machine's drawn face showed a vague relief as he recognized the tone. "That you, Mr. Hatch?" he asked.

"Yes."

"In any trouble?"

"Trouble?" repeated the reporter in evident surprise. "No. Who is this?"

"Van Dusen," was the response. "Good night."

Mechanically, unconsciously almost, The Thinking Machine began dressing. The ever active, resourceful brain, plunged so suddenly into this maze of mystery, was fully awake now and was groping through the fog of possibilities and conjecture, feeling for some starting point in this singular problem which had been thrust upon it so strangely. And evidently at last there came some inspiration; for the eminent scientist started hurriedly out the front door into the night, pausing on the steps to remember that in his haste he had forgotten to exchange his slippers for shoes, and that he was bare headed.

Fifteen minutes later the night operator in chief at the branch telephone exchange was favored with a personal call from Professor Augustus S. F. X. Van Dusen. There was a conference of five minutes or so, after which the scientist was led back through the operating room and ushered into a long high-ceilinged apartment where thousands of telephone wires were centered—a web woven of thin strands, each of which led ultimately to the long table where a dozen or more girls were on watch. He went into that room at five minutes of two o'clock; he came out at seventeen minutes after four and appeared before the night operator in the outer office.

"I found it," he announced shortly. "Please, now, let me speak to police headquarters—either Detective Mallory or Detective Cunningham."

Detective Cunningham answered.

"This is Van Dusen," the scientist told him. "I should like to know if any murder or attempted murder has been reported to the police tonight?"

"No," replied the detective. "Why?"

"I was afraid not," mused The Thinking Machine enigmatically. "Has there been any call for police assistance anywhere?"

"No."

"Between one and two o'clock?" insisted the scientist.

"There hasn't been a call tonight," was the reply. "What's it all about?"

"I don't know—yet," said the scientist. "Good night."

The Thinking Machine went out after a few minutes, pausing on the curb in the brilliant glare of a street lamp to jot down a number on his cuff. When he looked up, a cab was just passing. He hailed it, gave an address to the driver, and a moment later the vehicle went clattering down the street. When it stopped at last before a dark, four-story house, the cabman sat still for a moment expecting his passenger to alight. But nothing happened; so he jumped down and peered into the gloom of the vehicle. Dimly he was able to make out the small figure of the scientist huddled up in a corner of the cab with his huge yellow head thrown back, and slender white fingers pressed tip to tip.

"Here we are, sir," announced the driver.

"Yes, yes, to be sure!" exclaimed the scientist hurriedly. "I quite forgot. You needn't wait."

The vehicle was driven off as The Thinking Machine ascended the brown stone steps of the house and pulled the bell. There was no answer, no sound inside, and he pulled it the second time, then the third. Finally, leaning forward with his ear pressed against the door, he pulled the bell the fourth time. This evidently convinced him that the cord inside was disconnected, and he tried the door. It was locked.

Without an instant's hesitation he ran down the steps to the basement entrance in an areaway. There was no bell there, and he tried the knob tentatively. It turned, and he stepped into a damp, smelly hallway, unrelieved by one glint of light. He closed the door noiselessly behind him, and stood for a little while listening. Then he did a peculiar thing. He produced a small electric pocket lamp, and holding it as far to the left as he could reach, with the lens pointing ahead of him, pressed the button. A single white ray cleft the darkness, revealing a bare, littered floor, moldy walls, a couple of doors, and stairs leading up.

He spent perhaps five cautious minutes in the basement. There was no sign of recent human habitation, nothing but accumulated litter, and dust and dirt. Then he went up the stairs to the floor above. Here he spent another five minutes, with only an occasional flash of light, always at arm's length to extreme right or left, to tell him there was yet no sign of occupancy. Then another flight of stairs to the second floor. Still there was no sound, no trace of anyone, no indication of a living thing.

His first glimpse of the third floor confirmed at first glance all those impressions of desertion he had gathered below. The front room was identical with the one below, the front hall room was identical; but there was a difference in the large rear room. The dust and litter of the floor seemed worn into a sort of path from the top of the stairs, and following this path toward the back he came upon—a telephone!

"Forty-one-seventeen," he read, as the instrument stood revealed, bathed in the light from the electric bulb. Then he glanced down at his cuff and repeated, "Forty-one-seventeen."

With every sense alert for one disturbing sound, he spent two full minutes examining the instrument. He seemed to be seeking some mark upon it,—the scar of a bullet, perhaps—and as the scrutiny continued fruitless, the tiny wrinkles, which had momentarily disappeared from his face, appeared there again, and deepened perceptibly. The receiver was on the hook, the transmitter seemed to be in perfect condition, and the walls round the box were smooth. Finally he allowed the light to fade, then picked up the receiver and held it to his ear. His sensitive fingers instantly became aware of tiny particles of dust on the smooth black surface; and the line was dead. Central did not answer. Yet this was the telephone from which he had been called!

Again he examined the instrument under the light, with something akin to perplexity on his drawn face; then allowed his eyes to follow the silken wire as it led up, across the room, and out the window. Did it go up or down? Probably up, possibly down. He had just taken two steps toward that window, with the purpose of answering this question definitely, when he heard a sound somewhere off in the house and stopped.

The light faded, and utter gloom swooped down upon him as he listened. What he heard apparently was the tread of feet at a distance, somewhere below. They seemed to be approaching. Now they were in the lower hall, and grew clatteringly distinct in the emptiness of the house; then the tread sounded on the stairs, the certain, quick step of one who knew his way perfectly. Now the sound was at the door—now finally in the room. Yet there was not one ray of light.

For a little time The Thinking Machine stood motionless, invisible in the enshrouding darkness, until the footsteps seemed almost upon him. Then suddenly his right arm was extended full length from his body, the electric bulb blazed in his hand, and slashed around the room. By every evidence of the sense of sound the flash should have revealed something—perhaps the figure of a man. But there was nothing! The room was vacant, save for himself. And even while the light flared he heard the steps again. The light went out, he took four quick, noiseless steps to his left, and stood there for a moment puzzled.

Then he understood. The mysterious tread was stilled now, as if the person had stopped, and it remained still for several minutes. The Thinking Machine crept silently, cautiously, toward the door and stepped out into the hall. Leaning over the stair rail, he listened. And after a while the tread sounded again. He drew back into the shadow of a linen closet as the sound grew nearer—stood stock-still staring into blank nothingness as it was almost upon him; then the footsteps receded gradually along the hall, down the stairs, growing fainter, until the receding echo was lost in the silence of the night.

Whereupon The Thinking Machine went boldly up the stairs to the fourth floor, the top. He mounted confidently, as if expecting something to reward his scrutiny; but his eyes rested only upon the bleak desolation of unoccupied apartments. He went straight to the rear room, above the one he had just left, and directly across to one of the windows. Faint, rosy streaks of dawn slashed the east—just enough natural light to show dimly a silken wire hanging down from the middle of the window outside. He opened the window, drew in the wire, and examined it carefully under the electric light, and nodded as if he understood.

Finally he turned abruptly and retraced his steps to the first floor. There he paused to examine the knob of the front door; then went on down into the basement. Instead of examining the door there, however, he turned back under the stairs. There he found another door— a door to the subcellar, standing open a scant few inches. A damp, moldy smell came up. After a moment he pushed the door open slowly and ventured one foot forward in the darkness. It found a step, and he began to descend. The fourth step down creaked suddenly, and he paused to listen intently. Utter silence!

Then on down, ten, eleven, twelve, fourteen, steps, and his foot struck soft, yielding earth. Safely on the ground again, in the protecting gloom, he stood still for a long time, peering blindly around him. At last a blaze of light leaped from the electric bulb, which was extended far from the body to the right, and The Thinking Machine drew a quick breath. It might have been surprise; for within the glow of the light lay the figure of a young man, a boy almost, flat on his back on the muddy earth, with eyes blinking in the glare. His feet were bound tight together with a rope, and his hands were evidently fastened behind him.

"Are you the gentleman who telephoned for me?" inquired The Thinking Machine calmly.

There was no answer, and yet the prostrate man was fully conscious, as proved by the moving eyes and a twitching of his limbs.

"Well?" demanded the scientist impatiently. "Can't you talk?"

His answer was a flash of flame, the crash of a revolver at short range, and the light dropped, automatically extinguished as the pressure on the button was removed. Upon this came the sound of a body falling. There was a long drawn gasp, and again silence.

"For God's sake, Cranston!" came the explosive voice of a man after a moment. "You've killed him!"

"Well, I'm not in this game to spend the rest of my life in jail," was the answer, almost a snarl. "I didn't want to kill anybody; but if I had to, all right. If it hadn't been for this kid here, we'd have been all right anyway. I've got a good mind to give him one too, while I'm at it!"

"Well, why don't you?" came a third voice. It was taunting, cold, unafraid.

"Oh, shut up!"

Feet moved uncertainly, feelingly, over the soft earth and stumbled upon the inert, limp figure of The Thinking Machine, lying face down on the ground, almost at the feet of the bound man. One of the men who had spoken stooped, and his fingers touched the still, slim body. He withdrew his hands quickly.

"Is he dead?" some one asked.

"My God, man! Why did you do it?" exclaimed the man who had spoken first, and there was a passionate undertone in his voice. "I never dreamed that this thing would lead to—to murder!"

"It hardly seems to be a time to debate why I did it," was the brutal response, "so much as it is to decide what we'll do now that it is done. We might drop this body in the coal bin in the basement until we finish up here; but what shall we do with the boy? We are both guilty—he saw it. He wanted to tell the other. What will he do now?"

"He'll tell it just so surely as he lives," the bound man answered for himself.

"In that case there's only one thing to do," declared Cranston flatly. "We'd better make a double job of this, leave them both here, and get away."

"Don't kill me—don't kill me!" whined the young man suddenly. "I won't ever tell—I promise! Don't kill me!"

"Oh, shut up!" snarled Cranston. "We'll attend to you later. Got a match?"

"Don't strike a light," commanded the other man sharply, fearfully. "No, don't! Why, man, suppose—suppose your shot had struck him in—in the face. God!"

"Well, help me lift it," asked Cranston shortly.

And between them they carried the child-like body of the eminent man of science through the darkness to the stairs, up the stairs and through the basement to the back. The dawn was growing now, and the pallid, drawn face of The Thinking Machine was dimly visible by a light from the window. The eyes were wide open, glassy; the mouth agape slightly. Overcome by a newborn terror—hideous fear—the two men flung the body brutally into an open coal bin, slammed down the cover, and went stumbling, clattering, out of the room.

It was something less than half an hour later that the lid of the coal bin was raised from inside, and The Thinking Machine clambered out. He paused for a moment, to rub his knees and elbows ruefully and stretch his cramped limbs.

"Dear me! Dear me!" he grumbled to himself. "I really must be more careful."

And then straight back to the entrance of the subcellar he went. It was lighter outside now, and he walked with the assurance of one who saw where he went, yet noiselessly. But the door of the stairs leading down still revealed only a yawning, black hole. He went on without the slightest hesitation, remembering to step over the fourth step, which had squeaked once before. In the gloom below, standing on the earth again, he listened for many minutes.

Assured at last that he was alone, he groped about the floor for his electric light, and finally found it. Without fear or apparent caution he examined the huge, dark, damp room. On each side were thrown up banks of dirt that seemed to have been dug recently, and here before him was where the bound man had lain. And over there—he started forward eagerly when he saw it—was a telephone! The transmitter box had been wrecked by what seemed to be a bullet. As he saw it he nodded his head comprehendingly.

From there he went on around some masonry. Here was a passage of some sort. He flashed the light into it. It had been dug out of the solid earth, and its existence evidently accounted for the heaps of dirt in the subcellar. Still he didn't hesitate. Straight along the passage he went, wary of step, and stooping occasionally to avoid striking his head against the earth above him. Ten, fifteen, twenty feet he went, and still the gloomy, foul-smelling hole lay ahead of him, leading to—what? At about thirty-five feet from the subcellar there was a sharp turn—he thought at first it was the end of the tunnel—then the passage straightened out again, and there was another fifteen or twenty feet, growing smaller and smaller as he went forward.

Suddenly the tunnel stopped. The Thinking Machine found himself flattening his nose against a door of some sort. He allowed his light to fade, then dimly, through a cranny, he saw a faint glow outside. This seemed to be his destination, wherever it was—and he paused thoughtfully. Obviously the light outside was electric, and if electric light, might not someone be in there? A subterranean chamber of some sort, perhaps? His fingers ran around the edge of the door, loosened a fastening, and he peered out. Then, assured again, he opened the door wide, and stepped out into a brilliant glare.

He was in the subway. He stood blinking incredulously. Here to his right the shining rails went winding off round a curve in the far distance; and to the left was a quicker turn in the line of the excavation. In neither direction was there anything that looked like a station.

"Really, this is most extraordinary!" he exclaimed.

Then and there the eminent man of science paused to consider this weird thing from all possible viewpoints. It was unbelievable, positively nightmarish; yet true enough, for here he stood in the subway. There was no question about that; for in the distance was the roar of a train, and he discreetly withdrew into the little door, closing it carefully behind him until it had passed.

Finally he popped out again, closed the door behind him, paused only to admire the skill with which a portion of the tiling in the tunnel had been utilized as a door, then went on across the tracks. It was still early morning; the trains were as yet few and far between; so he had a little leisure for the minute examination he made of the tiled walls opposite the closed door. It was perhaps ten minutes before he found a tile that was loose. He hauled at it until it came out in his hand, revealing a dark aperture beyond.

Within fifteen minutes, therefore, from the time he undertook the search for the second door he was standing in another narrow, earthy tunnel which beckoned him on. With the ever-ready light to guide him, and still proceeding with caution, he advanced for possibly thirty feet; then came a turn. Round the turn he found himself in a sort of room—another cellar, perhaps. He permitted his light to go out, and stood listening, straining his squint eyes. After a time he was satisfied and flashed his light again.

Directly before him were half a dozen rough steps, leading up to what seemed to be a trap door. He had barely time to notice this and to see that the trap door was hanging open, when there came a cyclonic rush toward him out of the darkness, from the direction of his right, something whizzed past his head, causing him to drop the precious light, and instinctively he ran up the steps. The gloom above was no more dangerous, he thought, than the gloom below, and he went on, finally passing through the trap and standing on a hard floor above.

There was the sound of a fierce, desperate struggle down there somewhere, cursing, blasphemy, then the noise of feet on the steps coming toward him, and the trap door closed with the heavy, resonant clang of iron. He was alone, his light lost. A sudden strange, awful silence closed down around him, a silence alive with suggestion of unseen, unknown dangers. He stood for a moment, then sank down upon the floor wearily.

———

Cashier Randall stood beside the ponderous door of the vault, watch in hand. It was two minutes of ten o'clock. At precisely ten the time lock on the massive steel structure, built into the solid masonry of the bank, would bring the mechanism into position for the combination to work. Already the various clerks and tellers were at their posts; books and money were in the vault. At length there came a whir and a sharp click in the heavy door, and the cashier whirled the combination. A few minutes later he pulled open the outer door with a perceptible effort, then turned his attention to the combination lock on the second door. This yielded more readily; but there was still another door, the third to be unlocked. Altogether the task of opening the huge vault required something like six minutes.

Finally Cashier Randall threw open the light third door, then touched an electric button to his right. Instantly the gloom of the structure was dispelled by a flood of light, and he started back in amazement. Almost at his feet, on the floor of the vault, was the huddled figure of a man. Dead? Or unconscious? Certainly there was no movement to indicate life, and the cashier stepped backward into the office with blanched face.

Others came crowding round and saw, and startled glances were exchanged.

"You, Carroll and Young, lift him out, please," requested the cashier quietly. "Don't make any noise about it. Take him to my office."

The order was obeyed in silence. Then Cashier Randall in person went into the vault and ran hurriedly through the piles of money which lay there. He came out at last and spoke to one of the paying tellers.

"The money is all right," he said, with a relieved expression in his face. "Have it all counted carefully, please, and report to me."

He retired into his private office and closed the door behind him. Carroll and Young stood staring down curiously at the man who now lay stretched full length on the couch. They looked at the cashier inquiringly.

"I think it's a matter for the police," continued the cashier after a moment and he picked up the receiver of the telephone.

"But how—how did he get in the vault?" stammered Carroll.

"I don't know. Hello! Police headquarters, please."

"Anything missing, sir?" inquired Young.

"Not so far as we know," was the reply. "Don't make any excitement about it, please. He is breathing yet, isn't he?"

"Yes," answered Carroll. "He doesn't seem to be hurt—just unconscious."

"Lack of air," said the cashier. "He must have been in there all night. It's enough to kill him. Hello! I want to speak to the chief of detectives. Mr. Mallory, yes. This is the Grandison National Bank, Mr. Mallory. Can you come down at once, please, and investigate a matter of great importance?"

Fifteen minutes later Detective Mallory walked into the cashier's private office. Instantly his eyes fell upon the recumbent figure on the couch, and there came with the glimpse a strange, startled expression.

"Well, for—" he blurted. "Where did you get hold of him?"

"I found him in the vault just now when I opened it," was the reply. "Do you know him?"

"Know him?" bellowed Detective Mallory. "Know him? Why it's Professor Van Dusen, a distinguished scientist. He's the fellow they call The Thinking Machine sometimes." He paused incredulously. "Have you sent for a doctor? Well, send for one quick!"

With the tender care of a mother for her child the detective hovered about the couch whereon The Thinking Machine lay, having first opened the window, and pausing now and then to swear roundly at the physician's delay in arriving. And at last the doctor came. Quick restoratives brought the scientist to consciousness within a few minutes.

"Ah, Mr. Mallory!" he remarked weakly. "Please have the doors locked, and put somebody you can trust on guard. Don't let anyone out. I'll explain in a minute or so."

The detective rushed out of the room, returning a moment later. He found The Thinking Machine talking to the cashier.

"Have you a man named Cranston employed here in the bank?"

"Yes," replied the cashier.

"Arrest him, Mr. Mallory," directed The Thinking Machine. "Doctor, just the least bit of nitroglycerin, please, in my left arm, here. And, also, Mr. Mallory, arrest any particular chum of this man Cranston; also a young man, almost a boy, possibly employed here— probably a relative or closely connected with Cranston's chum. That will do, doctor. Thanks! Anything stolen?"

The detective glanced inquiringly at the cashier.

"No," replied that official.

The Thinking Machine dropped back on the couch, closed his eyes, and lay silent for a moment.

"Pretty bad pulse, doctor," he remarked at last. "Charge your hypodermic again. What bank is this, Mr. Mallory?"

"Grandison National," the detective informed him. "What happened to you? How did it come you were in the vault?"

"It was awful, Mr. Mallory—awful, believe me!" was the reply. "I'll tell you about it after a while. Meanwhile be sure to get Cranston and——"

And he fainted.

———

Twenty-four hours' rest in his own home, under the watchful eye of a physician, restored The Thinking Machine to a physical condition almost normal. But the whys and wherefores of his mysterious presence in the vault of the bank were still matters of eager speculation, but speculation only, to both the police and the bank officials. His last words, before being removed to his own apartments, had been a warning against the further use of the vault; but no explanation accompanied it.

Meanwhile Detective Mallory and his men rounded up three prisoners—Harry Cranston, a middle-aged and long trusted employee of the bank; David Ellis Burge, a young mechanical engineer with whom Cranston had been upon terms of great intimacy for many months; and Richard Folsom, a stalwart young nephew of Burge's, himself a student of mechanical engineering. They were held upon charges born in the fertile mind of Detective Mallory, carefully isolated from one another and from the outside.

The Thinking Machine told his story in detail, incident by incident, from the moment of the telephone call until the trap door closed behind him and he found himself in the vault of a bank. His listeners, Detective Mallory, President Hall, and Cashier Randall of the Grandison National, and Hutchinson Hatch, reporter, absorbed it in utter amazement.

"Certainly it was the most elusive problem that has ever come under my observation," declared the diminutive man of science. "It was so elusive, so compelling, that I indiscreetly placed my life in danger twice, and I didn't know definitely what it all meant until I knew I was in the vault. No man may know that slow suffocation, that hideous gasping for breath as minute after minute went by, unless he has felt it. And, gentlemen, if I had been killed, one of the most valuable minds in the sciences would have been lost. It would have been nothing less than a catastrophe." He paused and settled back into that position which was so familiar to at least two of his hearers.

"When I got the telephone call," he resumed after a moment, "it told me several things beyond the obvious. The logic of it all—and logic, gentlemen, is incontrovertible—was that some man was in danger, in danger even as he talked to me, that he had tried to reach me, seeking help, that the first interruption on the wire came because perhaps he was being choked, and that the second came—the shot which wrecked the instrument—as a desperate expedient to prevent further conversation. The scene was quite clear in my mind.

"The wire was dead then. Central didn't know the number. There was no way to get that number save by the tedious process of testing the wires in the exchange, and that might have taken days. It took only two hours or so, fortunately; but I got the number at last from which I was called; that is, I got a wire which was inexplicably dead, and assumed the rest. The number of that wire was forty-one-seventeen. The records showed the street and number of the house where it came from. Therefore I went there. Before I went I took the precaution of calling up police headquarters to see if any report of a murder or attempted murder or anything unusual had come in. Nothing had come in. This fact in itself was elucidating, because vaguely it indicated that I had been called, rather than the police, because—well, perhaps because it was not desirable for the police to know.

"Well, as I explained, I searched the house; and by the way, Mr. Mallory, I don't know if you know the advantages of always holding your dark lantern as far away from your body as possible when going into dangerous places; because if there is danger, a shot, say, the natural impulse of the person who shoots is to aim at the light. Incidentally this precaution saved my life in the cellar, when I feigned death. But I'm going a little ahead of myself.

"I found telephone number forty-one-seventeen, and there was a heavy coat of dust on the receiver. Obviously it had not been recently used. The line was dead, it is true, but the instrument was in perfect condition. There was no sign of a bullet mark anywhere round or near it. If the bullet that was fired had killed the man who had been using the line, it would not have deadened the wire; therefore instantly I saw that the line had been tapped somewhere; that this instrument had been cut off from it, and the instrument which was demolished was the one on the branch wire.

"I knew this, and was going to the window to see if the wire led up or down, when I heard someone approaching. I first supposed that the person, whoever it was, was in the room with me, the steps were so distinct; but when I flashed the light, intending at least to see him, I knew he was above me. One loses the sense of direction of sound, particularly in the dark; and it is an incontestable fact that footsteps, or any sound above, can be heard more clearly than the same sound below. Therefore I knew that someone was in the room above me. For what purpose? Possibly to disconnect the branch wire on the telephone line.

"I waited until the person, whoever it was, came down and went his way; then I found the wire, and saw where the connection had been made on it. Then I went straight down to the subcellar. There I saw this Folsom lying on the ground, bound. He was not gagged; yet he didn't answer my questions; obviously because he knew if he did he would place himself in danger. The shot was fired at me, or rather at my light, and I went through the farce which ultimately placed me in a coal bin. Then I began to get a definite idea of things from the conversation, when Cranston's name was mentioned several times.

"Folsom persisted in an outspoken declaration to reveal everything he knew, including the story of my murder. He insisted until he placed himself in grave danger, and then, under cover of utter darkness, I extended one hand and pinched him twice on the ankle. He knew then that I was not dead, that I had heard, and did the very thing I wanted him to do—begged for his life. It was a bit of justifiable duplicity. I knew if he was the man his every act so far had indicated that he would humbug Cranston and the other man into letting him go, or at least not committing another murder. Subsequent developments showed that this conjecture was correct.

"From the coal bin I went back to the subcellar, knowing positively now that there would be no one there. Those men were frightened when they left me, and men run from fright. What they would do with young Folsom I didn't know. There, with my electric light, I found the branch telephone. The transmitter box had been ruined by a shot, as I imagined. So, thus far at least, the logic of the affair was taking me some place.

"And then I followed that tunnel through the subway into another tunnel. I should not have ventured into that second tunnel had I not been fairly confident that no one else was there. In that I was mistaken. I don't know now, but I imagine that young Folsom was temporarily being held prisoner there, and that possibly Cranston was on guard. Anyway, there was a fight, and the trap door was open—the trap door into the vault. And I don't know yet whether Folsom and Cranston, if they were there, even knew I was at hand. Certainly the trap door, once closed behind me, was not opened again. And you know the rest of it." Again there was a pause, and the scientist twiddled his fingers idly.

"Now it all comes down to this," he concluded at last. "Cranston dragged Burge into the affair—Burge is a mechanical engineer, and a good one was needed to do this work—they rented the house, and went to work. It took weeks, perhaps months, to do it all. Folsom in some way learned of it, and he is an honest man. He took a desperate means of getting the information into my hands, instead of the hands of the police. Why the telephone was in the house I don't know— perhaps it was already there, perhaps they had it put in. Anyway, of your prisoners, Mr. Mallory, this young Folsom is guilty only of an attempt to shield his uncle, Burge, while Cranston is the ringleader, and Burge the man who achieved the immense task of getting under the vault of the bank.

"This vault has a floor of cement, cut into small squares. The trap door is in that floor, and so perfectly concealed in the lines of the squares that it is invisible unless submitted to a close scrutiny, just as the doors in the tiled walls of the subway were invisible to a casual observer. They overcame tremendous difficulties, these two men, in cutting through the immense foundation of the vault, even the steel itself, but remember that they worked at night for weeks and weeks, and were making no mistakes. They did not actually rob the bank because, I imagine, they were awaiting the deposit there of some immense sum. Is that correct, Mr. Hall?"

President Hall started suddenly. "Yes, in a week or so we were expecting a shipment of gold from Europe—nearly three million dollars," he explained. "Think of it!"

Detective Mallory whistled. "Phew! What a haul it would have been!"

"Now, Mr. Mallory, either of these three men, if properly approached, will confess the whole thing substantially as I have told it," remarked The Thinking Machine. "But I would advise that Folsom be allowed to go. He is really a very decent sort of young man."

When they had all gone except Hatch, the eminent man of science went over and laid one hand upon the reporter's shoulder and squinted straight into his eyes for a moment. "You know, Mr. Hatch," he said, and there was a strange note in the irritable voice, "my first fear, when the telephone call came, was that it was you. You must be careful—very careful, always."

HARLAN ELLISON is the author of numerous short stories, scripts, essays, and reviews. He has written or edited more than seventy-five books including *Slippage* and *Angry Candy*. His awards include the Silver Pen from P.E.N., eight-and-a-half Hugos, three Nebulas, six Bram Stokers, two World Fantasy awards, two Edgar Allan Poe awards from the Mystery Writers of America, and four Writers Guild of America awards for Most Outstanding Teleplay. Among the anthologies he has edited, *Dangerous Visions* is the most celebrated. He lives in California with his wife, Susan.

A NOTE ON THE TYPE

The principal text of this Modern Library edition
was set in a digitized version of Janson, a typeface that
dates from about 1690 and was cut by Nicholas Kis,
a Hungarian working in Amsterdam. The original matrices have
survived and are held by the Stempel foundry in Germany.
Hermann Zapf redesigned some of the weights and sizes for
Stempel, basing his revisions on the original design.

MODERN LIBRARY IS ONLINE AT
WWW.MODERNLIBRARY.COM

MODERN LIBRARY ONLINE IS YOUR GUIDE
TO CLASSIC LITERATURE ON THE WEB

THE MODERN LIBRARY E-NEWSLETTER

Our free e-mail newsletter is sent to subscribers, and features sample chapters, interviews with and essays by our authors, upcoming books, special promotions, announcements, and news.

To subscribe to the Modern Library e-newsletter, send a blank e-mail to: sub_modernlibrary@info.randomhouse.com or visit www.modernlibrary.com

THE MODERN LIBRARY WEBSITE

Check out the Modern Library website at
www.modernlibrary.com for:

- The Modern Library e-newsletter
- A list of our current and upcoming titles and series
- Reading Group Guides and exclusive author spotlights
- Special features with information on the classics and other paperback series
- Excerpts from new releases and other titles
- A list of our e-books and information on where to buy them
- The Modern Library Editorial Board's 100 Best Novels and 100 Best Nonfiction Books of the Twentieth Century written in the English language
- News and announcements

Questions? E-mail us at modernlibrary@randomhouse.com
For questions about examination or desk copies, please visit
the Random House Academic Resources site at
www.randomhouse.com/academic